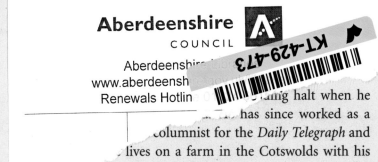

...ing halt when he ... has since worked as a ...columnist for the *Daily Telegraph* and ... lives on a farm in the Cotswolds with his ...ughter. His autobiography, *Crossing the Line*, and his first novel, *Citizen*, were widely acclaimed.

Also by Charlie Brooks

Citizen

CHARLIE BROOKS

Switch

blue door

Blue Door
An imprint of HarperCollins*Publishers*
77–85 Fulham Palace Road,
Hammersmith, London W6 8JB

www.harpercollins.co.uk

A paperback original 2012
2

A catalogue record for this book is
available from the British Library

ISBN: 978-0-00-743112-0

Set in Minion by Palimpsest Book Production Limited,
Falkirk, Stirlingshire

Printed and bound in Great Britain by
Clays Ltd, St Ives plc

MIX
Paper from
responsible sources
FSC™ C007454

To Rebekah – the best wife in the world – who inspires me with her sense of decency, her clarity of thought and her integrity.

PROLOGUE

Moscow

Max Ward knew something was up. Things often weren't as they seemed at the British Embassy on Smolenskaya Naberezhnaya, but that particular afternoon Max's antennae were twitching more than usual.

For a moment his attention switched from his immediate superior, Colin Corbett, to Pallesson, who was crossing the main atrium. Max watched through the heavy glass partition as Pallesson, the department's golden boy, gave some unfortunate underling a sharp dressing-down, then continued on his way with a quick glance at his watch. Max was now so far beneath Pallesson's sphere of operation that he didn't even warrant a greeting when they passed one another in the corridor. Their relationship had been poisoned long ago. It was unfortunate that they were now posted in the same city, but Max hadn't let Pallesson faze him in the past and he refused to let the bastard do so now.

Max pulled his focus back to Colin Corbett, the source of his current unease. Corbett was an efficient section chief and a pretty good communicator. A team player and as straightforward as they came, but something was radiating off him now that was arousing Max's instincts.

Considering he was the wrong side of forty, Corbett was in good shape. Mainly due to his obsession with tennis. Which was why no one ever questioned his exit from the office in his tennis gear every other afternoon. But something was different about him this Thursday and it had Max puzzled.

Max feigned interest in his terminal as he watched Corbett shuffle his papers. He had on his usual dark-blue tracksuit and the usual dark-blue bag lay on the floor with three racket handles sticking out of it. Corbett got up to go to the water machine. It was then that the first tangible evidence supporting Max's unease struck him. Corbett was wearing hiking boots, not tennis shoes.

When Corbett finally left the office, it was a full half-hour later than normal. Max decided to follow him. This was a man of regular habits behaving out of character. Of course, Max had nothing to go on. It was just a hunch. Besides, it would make a refreshing change from yet another afternoon spent trawling through endless chatter, looking for patterns that 12.5 million euros' worth of software couldn't see.

In a nondescript office car-pool Skoda, Max pulled out on to the Smolenskaya Naberezhnaya, which ran alongside the Moskva River. In the thick traffic, it was relatively easy for Max to follow him without being spotted. As they approached Park Pobedy it was at an absolute standstill. Corbett's car was a couple of hundred metres ahead of his, but neither of them were going anywhere.

Max believed Corbett to be a good man and an honest one. But something was most definitely up.

Max allowed his mind to drift back to the day's seemingly intractable problem. Seven offshore accounts. Numerous holding and shell companies. Millions flowing through and then suddenly disappearing around the same time every year. Always the second two weeks of March.

Then it hit him. Time zones. Specifically, that small window every year when London and New York are only four hours apart. A disconnect that invariably led to missed conference calls with Langley and red faces at Vauxhall. An anomaly that allowed the final issuing bank to hide its annual transfer outside its creaking accounting software. In his line of work it was so often about what happened in the gaps.

The traffic was moving again. Corbett continued out of the city, heading west by southwest, taking first Mozhayskoye Shosse, then Minskoye Shosse.

Corbett checked his tracking device. He was ten kilometres behind his target, which was about right, total gridlock notwithstanding.

After 120 kilometres the tracker finally left the major artery and turned off on to a smaller road. Corbett followed ten minutes later, unaware that Max was shadowing him. Five kilometres further on, Corbett's target quit the main road and went into the forest down a dirt track. After a couple of kilometres the track split into two. His target had come to a halt a further 500 metres along the left-hand fork. He went off to the right, drove for a couple of hundred metres, then pulled over into the trees.

Max had eased back, giving Corbett a little more space now that he was more exposed, but he could see the dust cloud thrown up by Corbett's car floating above the right-hand track. Max decided he'd driven as far as he dared. He reversed his car off the track into a clump of low-hanging trees and set off on foot.

After five minutes he found Corbett's car badly hidden in the trees. Careless, he thought. He tried the door handle. It opened obligingly. Very careless. Can't be too much to worry

3

about. Perhaps Max was making a complete fool of himself? Maybe Corbett never played tennis. Maybe his was a different game. Naughty old Corbett. It's always the quiet ones. Not that he wanted to expose him in any way. After all, it had been Corbett who'd stuck his neck out for Max after Saudi Arabia.

Max noticed the passenger glove compartment was hanging open. A large telescopic sight lay within. The kind that could find a target half a mile away. Well, if you're having a bit of fun, I might as well do the same, Max smirked. He'd get an access-all-areas view of Corbett on the job. Max grabbed the scope and headed up the hill to his left through the trees. Wherever Corbett had ended up, Max was more likely to be able to watch him from the high ground.

As Max approached the top of the hill, he heard a plane coming in low towards him from his right-hand side. It was either landing or crashing . . . but on what? Max scrambled to the brow of the hill, cursed that he was dressed for his desk, not for shimmying around rocks and scrub. He peered over. What he saw dispelled his flippant mindset.

A sea plane had landed on a narrow lake and was now taxiing across the water to a small dacha on the far bank. There was nothing pretty or enchanting about it. It was just a rectangular concrete box by the side of a lake with a stone terrace and a wooden jetty.

Max lay on his stomach and increased the scope's magnification as far as it would go. Then he centred on the three individuals standing on the terrace. Max gave a start as Pallesson's face came into focus. That was clearly who Corbett was tailing.

Max shifted his body in a vain attempt to get comfortable. He focused on the other two figures. Unmistakably Russian. One appeared to be almost disabled as he moved across the terrace. The other was shaven-headed. But there was something strange about his scalp.

Why was Pallesson with them? And where had Corbett got to?

Max trained the scope back on to Pallesson, who pulled out a cigarette case and offered one of the Russians a smoke. That told Max all he needed to know about Pallesson's relationship with them.

Max squinted as the sun emerged from behind a cloud, and instinctively covered the scope's lens with his hand. Corbett clearly hadn't been quite as fast. As Max squashed his body even lower to the ground he could see the shaven-headed Russian pointing towards a spot directly beneath his position while speaking into a radio set. Max quickly scanned his side of the lake.

Corbett had secreted himself into a duck-shooting hide. Crafty, but not lucky. Max looked back towards the dacha.

Before he could think of a way to warn Corbett, Max saw two men converging on the hide. Where the hell had they come from? What could he do about it? He didn't even have a gun and there was absolutely nothing to be gained from giving away his own position.

Max watched helplessly as Corbett was dragged out of the hide. A launch roared up to the shore. With two machine pistols now trained on him, Corbett was bundled into the craft, which then set off back across the lake.

Pallesson took a long draw on his cigarette. The granite-faced Russian mafia chief Sergei Kroshtov limped towards him. His hip had been shattered years ago by a truck trying to run him over. Pallesson tried to look unruffled.

'I thought you said this place was secure?' he said disdainfully.

'It is,' replied Kroshtov coldly. 'Whoever that is won't be leaving here.'

Kroshtov looked over towards Oleg and inclined his head in the direction of the dacha.

'Get my hunting rifle.'

Pallesson's eyes followed Oleg into the dacha. The proud, circular scar around his scalp gave the impression that someone had once tried to remove the top of his head. The lumpy scar looked like two pieces of leather, crudely sewn together.

Barry Nuttall unclipped his seat belt and pushed open the passenger door of the sea plane. He did a bit of piloting himself, but when he was on a drugs run he liked to have someone else 'at the wheel'.

He had his own airstrip on the Essex coast. They'd stayed low until they were away from the coastline to keep off English radar screens. It was a long way to come to pick up a hundred kilos of heroin, but a few routes had been shut down recently and supplies were tight.

He'd been going over the maths again during the flight. By the time the gear hit the streets, his investors would turn the two million euros he'd brought with him into twenty million. And he would take the cream off the top.

The Essex boy told his pilot to open the hold, straightened his Burberry cap and jumped down into the launch.

A few seconds later, the pilot passed down two black cases to the heavies in the craft. 'Don't drop those, for Christ's sake,' Barry joked. 'It really would have to go to the laundry then!'

Barry sat down on the centre bench and the launch sped towards the dacha.

'This is all very sociable,' Barry said drily to Pallesson as he placed the two cases on a folding wooden table. He nodded his head towards Kroshtov.

'How's it going, mate?' Barry asked Kroshtov with an air of casual indifference.

Kroshtov nodded.

'Who's our friend?' Barry asked Pallesson as he glanced

towards the hooded Corbett. Oleg was binding his hands behind his back twenty metres from them.

'Nothing for you to worry about,' Pallesson assured him.

'I wouldn't count on it,' Corbett said in a muffled, but perfectly audible voice. Oleg punched him in the side of the head. Hard enough to knock him over.

'So, going according to plan?' Barry queried.

'Everything's fine,' Pallesson confirmed. Kroshtov barked some orders towards the door of the dacha. A bottle of vodka appeared in an ice bucket with three tumblers. Kroshtov filled them half-full and handed one each to Pallesson and Barry Nuttall. He raised his glass to them and took a large swig.

'*Budem zdorovy!*' Kroshtov toasted.

'Let's stay healthy,' Pallesson chimed, translating for this Essex-boy partner.

'So . . . who is this?' Kroshtov asked Pallesson, pointing at Corbett as he banged his vodka glass on the table hard enough to make it quite clear that he expected a straight answer.

Pallesson would have liked to have been able to lie. It didn't look good, getting followed to a drop by one of his own. But it wouldn't be hard for the Russian to discover who Corbett was. Dead or alive.

'He's one of ours,' Pallesson admitted. 'He must have followed me.'

'Why are you here? Who sent you?' Kroshtov asked the hooded Corbett, who was still lying sprawled on the terrace.

'Pallesson asked me to cover his back.'

'He's full of shit. Oleg can dispose of him,' said Pallesson.

Kroshtov took orders from no one. He picked up his hunting rifle, made sure there was a shell in the breach and handed it to Pallesson.

'Your problem. You solve it. Take him down to the jetty.'

Kroshtov clearly welcomed an opportunity to demonstrate

that he was in command. Barry Nuttall knocked back the rest of his vodka as he watched Oleg frogmarch Corbett out on to the jetty. He wondered how Pallesson could be so sure their gatecrasher was working alone. The last thing they needed was MI6 crawling all over them. He admired the man's balls, though, even if he did dress like a Hampstead queer.

Max laid completely still behind the rocks he was using as cover. He knew there was every chance they'd be scouring the hillside, looking for any sign of movement. If he didn't attract attention, they'd probably miss him. Unless they had heat-seeking equipment.

Small, sharp stones were sticking into his elbows, and the undergrowth was clawing at him through his thin trousers. He tried to push all discomfort from his mind. The slightest movement would expose him.

This situation really was an utter shambles. That was the problem with instinct. The fact that your instincts had proved right counted for nothing if you didn't have the ability to deal with the scenario facing you. Max challenged whatever was stabbing his thigh to hurt even more. It focused his mind.

One of the Russians led Corbett halfway along the jetty and left him there. Max could see Pallesson was following closely behind with the rifle. It was pretty clear what was going to happen next.

'You bastard,' Max muttered under his breath.

It crossed his mind that he could create a diversion to buy Corbett time. But putting himself at such risk went against his training. His heart was telling him to do one thing; his head another.

He assumed that Corbett would be talking to Pallesson through the hood. Whatever he said made no difference. Without warning, Pallesson raised the rifle to his shoulder.

Max saw Corbett's head explode before he heard the shot

echo off the other side of the lake. The body slumped on to the jetty.

Pallesson walked back up to the dacha and handed the rifle to Kroshtov.

'Good thinking, getting him on to the jetty. Very messy,' he said coolly. 'Now, let's get this show on the road, shall we?'

Kroshtov issued some more orders. A man emerged from the dacha with a small metal case, followed by another carrying kilo bricks of heroin wrapped in heavy black plastic.

Pallesson had felt fear many times in his life; not least when his father used to come into his bedroom to beat him with his belt for not being asleep. But he had learnt to mask his fear by focusing on a particular spot on the carpet. He'd never let his father see that he was afraid.

As he walked over to the table and opened the metal case his hands were shaking. By placing his body in the way, he made sure Kroshtov couldn't see his fingers fumbling with the catches. He'd killed before, of course. Not that anyone had ever pointed the finger at him when his brother died. It had been accepted as a tragic accident. Two young boys ragging in a pool. The elder hit his head and drowned. After that the beatings stopped.

He tore himself back to the present and opened the metal case. Inside gleamed the Fabergé egg that he'd lodged with Kroshtov as collateral. A show of good faith that he and Barry Nuttall were good for the two million euros. Once the deal was completed, he would resume ownership of the treasure.

Pallesson was momentarily transfixed by the forbidden treasure. It had been made in 1894 and on the top of the egg was the image of Nicholas II, encircled by rose-cut diamonds. It was covered by translucent, dark-red enamel patterned with diamonds and was lined with off-white velvet. Sadly the 'surprise' inside the egg had long gone.

Until recently, it had been stored in a vault under the Hermitage Museum in St Petersburg. But its presence had now been erased from the records.

Pallesson took the egg out of its box and held it in front of him. He wanted to see it glint in the sunlight.

'Two million euros?' Pallesson confirmed with Barry.

Barry Nuttall nodded and opened his cases. He fondly ran his hand over the two million euros, giving them a paternal parting pat. Then he walked over to the bricks of 'gear' and picked one of them up.

'A hundred kilos?' he checked. Kroshtov nodded.

'Well, if it's okay with you, I'll get this lot loaded up and be on my way back to Blighty. *Budem zdorovy*, as they say in Essex.'

Pallesson snapped the Fabergé egg's metal case shut and turned to Kroshtov.

'Looks like we're done. Nice doing business with you, Sergei.'

Max lay on his back and focused on the clouds. He'd just witnessed his nemesis blow off the head of his colleague in front of a bunch of Russians of whom he knew nothing. He had no idea what had been going on outside the dacha. He didn't even know whether either Pallesson or Corbett were on official business. His instincts told him Pallesson was working for himself. And that he'd just murdered a British agent.

Max had known for too long that Pallesson was an evil son of a bitch. It was time to stop him. Time to get revenge. But he also knew that Pallesson was a master of compromise and blackmail. If he reported what he'd witnessed to someone under Pallesson's spell, it would be he who would be destroyed, not Pallesson.

He wasn't sure he could even risk confiding in Tryon, the man who'd recruited him into 'the Office'.

1

Monaco

Max Ward had to get out of bed when room service arrived with their breakfast. Gemma was pretending to be asleep. He slipped a ten-euro note into the waiter's hand and asked him to park the trolley by the window.

Max wanted to have breakfast with Gemma, so he poured her some coffee, added the exact amount of hot milk that she expected and took it through to the bedroom.

She was lying with her back to him, welded to the sheets in semi-slumber.

'Coffee?' he asked, sitting on the bed. She made an appreciative noise and rolled on to her back, keeping her eyes shut. Max slid his clenched hand under the sheet and found her knee. Then he started to stroke the inside of her thigh with the back of his fingers. She pulled the pillow over her face. Max opened his hand and rubbed an ice cube up her thigh.

'Oh no, you don't,' she said as her head jolted up from under the pillow.

'Breakfast then?'

While Gemma headed for the bathroom, Max sat down at the small table and gazed across the harbour. A wooden water

11

taxi struggled from one side to the other, dwarfed by the super yachts.

Gemma barely bothered to do up her dressing gown as she ambled towards him. Max thought about grabbing her and taking her back to bed, but his boiled eggs were getting cold. And they'd cut his toast soldiers half an inch wide, exactly as he liked them.

As she sat down, Gemma looked out of the window. Two women were power-walking down the Parcours Princesse Grace – followed discreetly by a bored minder. She wondered when they'd last had sex with their husbands.

Max leant over and kissed her. Then he set about his eggs.

'Why did they do *that*?' Max wondered aloud as he returned his attention to the window. 'Why did they cover this place in higher and higher concrete boxes? Jesus, you'd be pissed off if they'd trashed your view with that monstrosity, wouldn't you?' he asked, pointing at a recent erection that had blocked the sea view – any view, in fact – from the equally offensive apartment blocks behind it.

'Greed,' suggested Gemma.

'No one lives in them anyway,' Max said as he decapitated one of his eggs. 'They're tax bolt-holes. As long as you get your cleaner to run the taps every day and turn on the lights, they can't prove you're not living here.'

'Fine, I suppose, as long as you don't have to live in this ghastly place.'

'It's not that bad. And of course you have to pay someone to drive your car around too. But it's cheap living here, compared to paying tax anywhere else.'

'Could you live here?'

'Well, if you came to visit me every weekend, I might think about it.'

12

'Really? Where would you put your other girlfriends at the weekend then?'

'I'd send them back to Saint-Tropez, of course,' Max replied without missing a beat.

He looked around the room. Everything was so perfect. The orchids proudly erect in their pot, the imposing gilded mirror frame that perfectly matched the candle holders and standard lamps. Even the rails holding the thick, white curtains were coordinated. And yet everything wasn't perfect. It never was in Gemma's life.

'I get frightened sometimes, staying in places like this,' she said pensively. 'It reminds me, in a weird way, of what it's like to have nothing. Look at those little pots of jam. We're just going to send them back, even though we've paid for them. I didn't have any fucking jam when I was a kid.'

Max stood up, put his arms around her and kissed the top of her head. She was haunted. He wished he could do something about that. But she'd chosen someone else.

As they stepped into the lift, Max pressed the first-floor button for the spa and the ground floor for himself. He held the leather document holder loosely in one hand, deliberately keeping his eyes off it.

'Aren't you a bit overdressed for a massage?' he asked flippantly.

'Very funny. Actually, I've ordered a male masseuse who's going to strip me naked, cover me in chocolate and lick it off. It's a hotel speciality. Then I'm going shopping. What time will you be back?'

'Oh, I'd say about three o'clock. Then we can explore together.'

As the lift ground to a halt, Max kissed Gemma's neck under her long auburn hair.

'Stop it,' she said, taking a step away, but giving in to a wide smile. 'Or I'll drag you back upstairs. And then you'll be late for your mysterious meeting. Go on, tell me. What's in your holder?'

'You know I can't. Or I'd have to kill you with my bare hands.' With that he gave her neck a small bite.

'Call me to say where you want to meet.'

She waved as she exited down the corridor.

Max watched Gemma walk away. He wondered whether she swung her arse in that rolling manner for him. She still took his breath away. Her long flowing hair falling down her back, her dress clinging to her body just enough to be tantalizingly sexy, and best of all those exquisite calf muscles.

She was such a confused soul. Spoilt and self-centred on the one hand, and yet generous and insecure on the other.

He wondered why she half turned and took her sunglasses off in that mock-coquettish manner. Maybe she wanted to be sure that he was still watching her.

Max marvelled at the main reception of the Hôtel de Paris as he walked across the multicoloured marble floor. It was twelve o'clock in London, according to one of the clocks above the concierge's desk.

They built things beautifully in the eighteen hundreds. The high ceiling, the aged mirrors lining the walls and the glass atrium that flooded the whole area with natural light.

He looked at the old ladies sitting on the delicate Louis XV chairs and wondered what they did all day. They made him think about his mother. Was she sitting around in some hotel in Spain? Maybe she'd moved on? After all, she wouldn't have bothered to let him know. As usual, he cast her from his thoughts as quickly as she'd invaded them.

Max stopped in front of the wooden revolving door to let a woman in an apron come past. She was carrying a huge bunch of red and yellow roses, all perfectly coming into flower. Some guy must have been caught swimming outside the ropes, he thought to himself.

As he waited, he admired the magnificent bronze of Louis XIV on horseback, waving his sword around with an air of imperious egotism. The French had probably been all right, Max mused, until they had a revolution and became ridiculous socialists. Since then, they'd been nothing but trouble.

Max nodded to the doorman, bid him '*bonjour*' and stepped into the revolving door. It was a beautiful February day in the Casino Square, but the fresh, cold air made him reach for his coat buttons. He was a bit early and he knew he only had a couple of hundred metres to walk.

He had time to nip into the casino. Just to have a look around. No harm in that, although he knew he'd win if he had a crack. No one would know. It could pay for dinner. But a sign at the foot of the steps said: *Ouvert tous les jours à partir de 14 h.* Maybe that was a good thing.

Max's mind flashed back to his last 'gambling' dressing-down on the Embankment in London from his then immediate superior Colin Corbett.

Max had been leaning on the black railings watching the seagulls, opposite Vauxhall Cross.

'Do you have any idea why we're having this conversation here, and not in that building?' Corbett had asked, pointing across the river.

Max felt like saying, 'The weather?' but thought better of it.

'Well, I'll tell you why. We're here because I have to decide whether we let you go, or stay with you. And I'll be honest with you. Your file doesn't make particularly good reading. So I didn't want this conversation on the record. For your sake, Ward.'

15

Corbett was referring to the incident in Saudi Arabia that had led to Max being sent back to London in disgrace.

'My file?'

'Your file. History's repeating itself, isn't it?'

'No. What are you talking about?'

A squat Filipino woman walking a Yorkshire terrier had shuffled slowly past them. Corbett had instinctively shut up until she was out of earshot.

'Thrown out of Eton for gambling. Thrown out of Saudi for gambling. Any pattern revealing itself there?'

'I was trying to make some contacts.'

'We're not idiots, Ward. Don't think we don't know what happened. You let some card game compromise your work. And we had to bail you out of there.'

'I told you, I was trying to make a few contacts.'

'No. You weren't. You got sucked in like a mug. Because you have a weakness. Just like your father . . .'

'That isn't fair. He was a bookmaker.'

'He shot himself, Ward. Because he lost all his money.'

'That's cheap. Very cheap,' Max had said, watching the seagulls float on the air above the Thames. He hadn't known whether to smack Corbett in the face or just walk away. A seagull had perched on the railings a couple of feet away from them.

'They have a knowing look, don't you think?' Max had asked, buying time to compose himself.

'Fuck the seagull. Do you actually want this job? According to Nash, not that much.'

Max had paused, as if making up his mind. In truth, he was trying to control his anger.

'My father made a big sacrifice to send me to Eton. I wish he hadn't, because it killed him, one way or another.' Max's voice had wavered. 'So of course I want this job. Otherwise it was all for nothing. This bloody job is all I have to show for his sacrifice.'

Corbett's face had betrayed his relief. It was exactly what he'd needed to hear. Passion. And maybe the beginnings of regret. If he was to justify hanging on to him, he needed to believe that was what Max was feeling.

'You're going to have a couple of very boring years riding a desk. Step inside a casino and all bets are off.'

Max turned away from the casino and crossed the road to admire the fountain. Not just any fountain, either. Anish Kapoor's Sky Mirror.

His mind flickered to the dacha outside Moscow. Corbett being shot in cold blood. If nothing else, this mission could at least destroy Pallesson.

Wrestling his thoughts back to the present, Max admired the way the mirror reflected both the sky and the casino. As he watched his own reflection, he noticed someone standing on the steps behind him. When he turned around, the guy walked off towards the harbour. He didn't look back.

Max loved the adrenalin of being out in the field; loved the feeling of being on his toes. Being alert. Ready to react to anything. All the more so because it was such a rare occurrence these days, though he was certain nothing would happen in Monte Carlo. Or at least nothing he couldn't cope with.

He walked around to the other side of the square. There was a policeman standing in the middle of the road doing nothing, as far as Max could see. Nice work if you can get it. The policeman took a long look at him, as if he'd read his thoughts.

Max glanced at the clientele of the Café de Paris as they sipped their coffees. A man on his own with a newspaper open on the table seemed to be looking at him. Or was he looking at the leather document holder?

Finally, Max left the square and headed downhill towards his destination. He stopped just around the corner by the Zegg & Cerlati watch shop to see if anyone was following him. The watches were mesmerizing: Zenith, Jaeger-LeCoultre, Breitling, Franck Muller, Patek Philippe. They were all stunning. But one particular watch by Vacheron Constantin caught his eye. The 1907 Chronomètre Royal was a watch that Max had always thought was perfectly him. It looked classic, unembellished, but distinguished. He loved the eleven Arabic numerals in black enamel and the burgundy-red twelve, all set against a white face inside rose-gold casing. And definitely a brown strap, not black. Max looked at the price. Thirty-five thousand euros. That was about right.

After a while, Max realized that he was being scrutinized by a woman inside the shop. She beckoned for him to enter. He still had time to kill, so he went inside.

Gemma arrived at the end of the long, empty white marble tunnel. Instead of turning left into the hotel spa, she turned right, out into the street, and set off down the hill towards the harbour. She pulled up the hood of her coat, but resisted the urge to look back towards the hotel. Max would be long gone by now.

After fifty metres she walked past the Théâtre Princesse Grace. At the bottom of the hill she took the first steps on her left towards the water, then doubled back on herself along the seafront. All the big fuck-off yachts were moored next to each other along the harbour wall. Gemma was familiar with a few of them. There were a couple belonging to the Formula 1 crowd, a medium-size vessel from an oligarch's ever-growing fleet, plus the flagship of a minor Saudi prince, which she'd been aboard more than once.

Gemma walked past *Clementine*, *Paloma* and *Lady Nag Nag* – a joke, the cost of which didn't make it any funnier. The yachts were registered in Georgetown, the Cayman Islands, Monaco and Douglas, though the one she was heading for was registered in Montenegro.

Two crew members in immaculate white shirts and blue shorts were waiting for her at the end of the walkway. Gemma knew the form. She handed her shoes to one of them before she boarded. A third member of staff offered her a hot hand towel. Not for her own comfort, she suspected, but more in deference to her host's OCD.

He was waiting for her beyond a large set of double glass doors. It was a bit too cool for sitting around on deck.

'Gemma.' Alessandro Marchant beamed gushingly. 'Great to see you. Like the refurb? My new designer helped me.'

Gemma was relieved to see there were crew everywhere. At least he wouldn't be able to try it on, as he had done when her husband Casper and she had been staying with him in Corsica.

The 'refurb' had obviously cost a fortune, and had clearly been done by someone who'd had a taste bypass. They'd had one idea in their mind and stuck with it. Gold.

'My chef is cooking lobster for lunch.'

My this, my that . . . He hadn't changed.

Gemma was disgusted by her husband's craven submission to Alessandro Marchant and, even worse, the creepy Pallesson. So dark and vile was Pallesson that no one even applied a first name to him. And when he said jump, Casper leapt.

After they first got married, when she'd challenged Casper about it, he got very agitated and ranted that he would have no hedge fund, and she would be living in a council house, if it wasn't for Pallesson and Marchant. Now the whole subject had become off limits.

When she drank too much, she invariably brought the subject up. And threw in the likelihood that any money Casper was handling for them would almost certainly be bent. If he'd had too much – which increasingly seemed to be the case – he became abusive. Their marriage was falling apart. It was hardly surprising that she needed Max.

'Champagne?' Marchant asked expansively.

'Coffee.' It was a statement, not a question. She had to toe the line with Alessandro, but only up to a point.

'So what else brings you down here, Gemma?' Alessandro asked as he lay back on a sofa that had been made all but uninhabitable by a plague of cushions. He knew there would be a cover for her bringing him the memory stick.

'I'm here with a girlfriend. We're looking at an interior design job. It's going to be amazing.' At least, that was what she'd told Casper.

'You should use my girl,' Alessandro interrupted. 'She did all this.'

'Yes,' Gemma replied, with the minimal amount of appreciation. 'Probably not quite what we're looking for though.'

'You must both come and have dinner tonight.'

Gemma's stomach tightened. Monaco was too small for her layers of deceit.

'We can't, sadly. Hooked up with our client, I'm afraid. Obviously not allowed to say who. Oh, before I forget, your memory stick. Casper said he'd kill me if I lost it.'

2

Max thanked the sweet girl who had tried every gambit in the book to sell him the Vacheron Constantin and stepped gingerly back out on to the pavement. The two guys digging up the road stopped and looked at him. He told himself not to be paranoid and walked another fifty metres down the street. He could feel the cold flushing his cheeks.

He was glad the Restaurant Rampoldi was right there. The Sass Café would have been his choice, but it was closed at this time of year. And Rampoldi was very cosy. There were only a couple of other diners inside, so he had no problem getting the table right at the back of the restaurant. The owner, who looked like he'd had an eventful life, showed him over to it.

Max liked the simplicity of the place. The starched white tablecloths; the black-and-white cartoon prints of fat, jolly waiters. The unashamed stuffiness.

He quickly flicked to the red wines when the sommelier brought the wine list. And he was impressed. They had two of his favourites.

The 1997 Solaia made by the Antinori family was, in Max's opinion, the finest wine to come out of Tuscany for a long

21

time. He was amazed they had it. The production had been small and it was hard to find outside Italy. At eight hundred euros a bottle it was expensive, but rightly so. Yet how could he ignore the Château Lafite Rothschild 1990? Such an understated wine. He loved the clever combination of delicate and yet powerful and intense flavours. They also had the 1982 and 1986 vintages, but they were, as far as Max was concerned, for ignorant tourists. Any idiot could buy the most expensive wine on the list. So he went with the Solaia.

Under normal circumstances, such wine would have caused ructions had it appeared on his expenses. But he'd been told to look after his guest, so look after him he would.

Max knew Jacques Bardin would be getting on a bit, so when an old boy, probably in his seventies, with thin eyes above a beaky nose, wire-framed glasses and a long, scruffy tweed coat walked in, he was sure it was his man.

Jacques hesitated a moment to talk to the jovial maître d' by the door. He declined the offer to take his coat, then headed over towards the table. He was much frailer than Max had imagined.

'*Monsieur Bardin?*' Max smiled formally as he stood up to greet his guest. Jacques simply bowed his head in acknowledgement and sat down.

'A little red?' Max asked, trying to put his guest at ease.

'Thank you,' Jacques said, again nodding his head. He took a sip as soon as the waiter had poured, and smiled. The waiter showed him the bottle, but he didn't comment on the wine or the year, which surprised Max.

'*Très bon,*' was all he said.

There was a slight silence, which Max filled awkwardly.

'Hope it wasn't too much bother to get here?'

Jacques pursed his lips. He never told anyone where he lived.

'It was no trouble.' He helped himself to some bread. Clearly, this put an end to the subject.

Max took the hint. Jacques was not a conversationalist – or, if he were, not with strangers.

'Tryon is sorry he couldn't join us. He was most intrigued by your communiqué.'

Jacques took another sip of his wine and contemplated the young Englishman in front of him.

'Tell me a little of this Tryon, please?'

Max now occupied himself with his wine glass to buy himself some time. 'Well, obviously, I can't say too much. But he is my immediate boss. Though he's based in London, he keeps an eye on what's going on around the world. He is the overview, let's say. Out of interest, how did you come to contact him?'

Jacques thought about this question for a moment, as if it were a trap, and was silent. Max didn't fill in the silence. He wanted to draw the old man out. Eventually, Jacques answered.

'I have a friend in French Intelligence – through my work. When this problem got out of hand, he gave me Tryon's number.'

'And that is why I am here. To sort out this problem. But I need you to explain it all to me.'

The prospect clearly did not appeal to Jacques. He sipped his wine, tore off a piece of bread and then drank some more wine.

'I was a forger,' he finally volunteered.

'Unusual profession,' Max interjected.

'I was brought up to it. It was all I knew. When I was a child, I swept the floor of a great man's studio. He was a genius. And he took me under his wing. Han Van Meegeren. You have heard of him?' Max nodded.

'Everyone said he hated people. And passed on nothing. But he taught me everything.'

'How many paintings have you forged?'

'Hundreds,' Jacques answered matter-of-factly.

'So how does that work? How do you pass them off?'

Again Jacques paused and thought about his answer.

'Can you help us?'

'Yes. But only if you tell us everything. We're not the police. We don't care how many paintings you have forged.'

Jacques seemed to accept this.

'The forger has to deceive the so-called experts who pretend to know everything. I think Van Meegeren was more interested in fooling them than making money. I just did it because I was fortunate to be chosen by him. You pick an artist and create a work that he might have painted. So Van Meegeren created an entire period of Vermeers and managed to fool the idiots that they had discovered a whole lost period. During the war he fooled Göring into thinking that he was buying great masterpieces. And then the idiots threw him into prison for collaborating with the Nazis.'

Max kept nodding. He knew about Van Meegeren. It was Jacques he wanted to know about.

'So how did you pass off your forgeries?'

'By creating provenance. It is one thing to create a new painting. It is another to place it. So I would forge invoices, letters, magazine articles, pages from auction catalogues – anything that would place the painting in the past. You would be surprised by some of the people who have helped me. If you own a large château, and you can't afford to put a new roof on it, what could be easier? Go to some Parisian expert and tell him you've discovered a great work in your loft. Just pretend it must have been in the family for generations and no one realized.'

The memory seemed to cheer Jacques up. A philosophical smile spread across his face and he took another sip of wine.

'How come you got into copying paintings for Pallesson? It doesn't sound like you needed the money.'

The smile left Jacques's face as quickly as it had appeared.

'There is no art to copying paintings. No creativity. Any idiot can do it.'

'Why do it then?'

'Pallesson. He's a clever bastard. He caught me.'

'How?'

'He bought a Jan van Goyen that I created. Usual subjects – boats, windmills . . . The painting was perfect. But I made a mistake with the provenance. I forged a magazine article that referred to the picture, amongst others. Only for some reason the magazine wasn't published the month I chose. Pallesson checked it out, which was bad luck, and then traced the picture back to me.'

'What did he do about it?'

'He said I had to copy some paintings for him. All Dutch masters.'

'Which you did?'

'I had no choice. He said bad things would happen to my family if I didn't.'

Max nodded. That was Pallesson all over. First you find a way of compromising someone. Then you blackmail them.

Max smiled. 'As I'm sure Tryon has told you, art forgery or copying are not really our business. So why have you come to us? And why now? Why not before?'

Jacques tore another piece from the roll in front of him. He ate it slowly, considering what to say next. While he was thinking, the maître d' sidled up to their table and asked if they were ready to order. Jacques had the menu open in front of him. Max was pretty sure he hadn't looked at it; or the label on the wine bottle, for that matter. Which was strange for a Frenchman.

Jacques asked the maître d' about the specials and went for

the carré d'agneau. Max chose the eggs florentine followed by oysters. He had no truck with the bollocks that oysters didn't go with Solaia. While the maître d' refilled their glasses, Max casually took the Vacheron Constantin brochure out of his top pocket and pushed it across the table.

'These are beautiful, don't you think?'

A look of concern spread across Jacques's face. He didn't reply.

Max had figured out that Jacques's near vision had deteriorated.

'Jacques, why don't you tell me what the problem is, exactly?' Max asked bluntly.

The confidence and control that Jacques had up until this point been trying to exude rapidly evaporated. He suddenly looked vulnerable. He drank some wine and paused. Max waited.

'It's my daughter, Sophie,' he said at last. 'She is a very talented artist. And recognized, unlike me. She has a great future. She has work hanging in Paris, London, Milan, Amsterdam . . .'

'So what does she have to do with Pallesson?'

'I should have told Pallesson that my sight was gone. Finished. But I was too frightened of the consequences. Sophie helped me. I didn't want her to be involved, but she saw that I was struggling and how distressed I was. And then he tricked me. He worked out that she had helped me. Now he is blackmailing both of us. He says he will finish her career. That is why I come to you now. Can you protect her?'

Jacques's shoulders were stooped as he stared at the table-cloth. Max felt sick for him. His mind cast back to Pallesson trying to compromise him at Eton. And blowing Corbett's head off. He had to destroy him before his evil spread any further.

Max stretched his hand across the table and placed it on the old man's wrist. But compassion wasn't the foremost emotion churning in Max's stomach.

'Jacques, when did you send him the copy?'

'A week ago,' the old man replied. Which meant that Pallesson could make the switch any time.

'You've come to the right people,' Max said. 'We'll trap him. We'll finish him.'

He was going to nail the bastard, if they weren't already too late.

'So how long will it take Sophie to make a second copy of *The Peasants in Winter*? We're against the clock,' Max asked.

The waiter had cleared the table and served them with coffee. Now they were talking specifics, Jacques seemed much happier.

'Five days. It shouldn't take her longer than that. She has the work in her head. After all, it was only a few weeks ago that she made the first copy. It's ironic, really.'

'Why?'

'Well, Pieter Brueghel the Younger was a great painter. Certainly better than his brother, Jan, in my opinion. But he did sometimes copy the work of his father. There's no doubt in my mind that this is the case with *The Peasants in Winter*. He wasn't quite as subtle as Pieter the Elder, which makes Sophie's work a little easier. But it didn't stop him being a great artist. And it didn't stop him getting the recognition he deserved.'

Max picked up the undertone and switched the conversation back to Bruegel the Elder, who happened to be one of the few artists Max knew anything about.

'Was their father one of the greats?'

'Certainly.' Jacques nodded, taking another sip of his wine. 'He painted some great art. *The Massacre of the Innocents* is my favourite. Such movement, such detail. His style at its best, if you ask me. He could paint timeless landscapes, but at the same time he filled them with real people going about their lives.'

Max could feel Jacques coming alive. Energy was suddenly emanating from the tired old man.

'What about *The Bird Trap*?'

Jacques hesitated and pursed his lips.

'I'm impressed. You know your art?'

Max smiled bashfully and shook his head. 'Only a little, I'm afraid. And *The Bird Trap* is pretty much all I know about Bruegel the Elder.'

'Well, that is a good start. The winter landscape, *c'est magnifique*. The shades of colour are truly incredible. The figures on the ice are exquisite. The painting is so alive. But . . .' Jacques said, pointing his finger at Max, 'Bruegel's students made any number of copies of *The Bird Trap*. They were commercial. And yet history has not condemned him,' he said indignantly.

Max looked at the old man. He'd got himself into a mess. Just as Max's father had, and ultimately it had finished him off. Irrespective of what Jacques had been up to, Max was coming to his rescue.

'The canvas you asked for,' Max said, pulling his thoughts back to the present while he lifted a painting from the leather holder under the table.

'Is it the right age?'

'Apparently. No idea who the artist is, but it's 1600s. Don't suppose he'd have been too happy if he'd known when he painted it that you were going to strip his paint off one day.'

Jacques shrugged his shoulders and turned it over to look at the back of the canvas. He seemed satisfied.

'And the pigments?'

'Exactly as you requested.'

Max met Gemma in the American Bar at the Hôtel de Paris. Gemma had arrived back first and taken the small table in the corner looking out on to Casino Square.

28

'Shall we go to the casino this evening?' Max asked as he drew up a chair. He was feeling elated. Revenge was going to be sweet.

'And gamble?'

'Well, *you* could. Maybe a little blackjack? Stick on twelve if the dealer has sixteen or less.'

'You and your risk-assessing brain, Max. Always calculating the odds.' In fact, she was working out what chance there was of running into Marchant with him.

'Disappointing, this bar, don't you think? Very plain. No imagination. No feel to it. How was your meeting? Productive?'

'Yes. I think so. Drink?'

'Bit early for me. I'll have a cup of tea, please.'

Max caught the eye of a waiter who was busily doing nothing.

'*Monsieur, vous avez du Earl Grey? Et je voudrai également un grand whisky s'il vous plaît, Du Grouse, et une petite bouteille d'eau gazeuse.*'

'You're quite sexy when you speak French,' Gemma said from behind her newspaper.

'I'd be even sexier if I could write it properly.'

This was a sore point for Max, Gemma knew, but she didn't feel like hearing yet again how Pallesson had trashed him going to university. She put her hand on his thigh and rubbed it.

'Tell me about your meeting.'

'Well, anything I tell you would have to be erased from your mind. As for my mind, it's currently contemplating something else,' he whispered, reciprocating rather more daringly with his own hand.

'Are you sure you had lunch with an old man? You seem to be—'

'How was your massage?' he interrupted.

'Intimate. Very intimate. Anyway, I thought we were going to explore?'

But Max was having none of it.

'We could go upstairs and explore,' he said, downing his Scotch.

Gemma again made the mistake of walking out of the bathroom without tying her dressing gown. She may have got away with it that morning, but not now.

Max pushed aside her long hair and kissed the back of her neck. He felt a familiar response as her body shivered. Though he'd learnt most of his foreplay tips from the sex column in *GQ* magazine, over the years Gemma had taught him how to turn her on. Today, though, Max was in a rush. He was bursting.

As he pulled her closer to him, she could feel him rubbing against her La Perla-clad bottom.

Max had bought her the underwear a week before, after they'd shared a few glasses of champagne at the Harrods caviar bar. He'd tried not to show his shock when the shop assistant asked him for the best part of three hundred pounds in return for the small swatch of black lace. Now, as he pulled off her dressing gown, he could see it was money well spent.

'Someone's come back horny,' Gemma whispered. 'Who did you meet, again?'

His response was muffled as he carried on kissing and nibbling at her neck. His left hand reached round and unclipped her bra. She stopped asking questions and knelt on the bed in front of him.

Max just wanted to lose himself in an old-fashioned quickie.

'My God. Something's woken you up.' Gemma was totally in his grip. Max was squeezing her bum as hard as he could. He was feeling uncontrollably selfish.

'That wasn't very gentlemanly,' Gemma teased as Max collapsed on the bed next to her. 'You don't deserve it, but there's a present for you under your pillow,' she whispered into his ear. 'Now that you've finished.'

He ran his hand underneath the crisp linen pillowcase and felt a small box. He flipped it open and found himself looking at the Vacheron Constantin watch. He was now wide awake.

'Gemma! How did you know? This is . . .'

'Do you like it?'

'Like it?' He kissed her on the nose. 'I love it. But how . . .?'

'Oh, a little bird told me. Rather a sexy little bird, actually. If you hadn't flirted so much with her, she might not have remembered.'

'You shouldn't have. You spoil me.'

Gemma stroked Max's arm and put her head on his shoulder, looking away from him.

'I wish you had swept me up and given me security, Max,' Gemma said, surprising Max with such sudden intensity.

Having been given such an expensive gift, Max felt guilty as his brain rapidly calculated what giving Gemma security would cost. And then wondered if Casper would find the watch on Gemma's credit-card bill. Probably not. It would get lost amongst everything else.

'You wish I were Casper?'

'No, of course not. But you do understand why I married him, don't you?'

'Yes. Yes, I do,' Max said as he looked at the watch.

'You know I love Casper. In a way. We should probably have had children. That was my fault. I wasn't sure at the time and it's probably too late now. In more ways than one. But I can't bear the thought of having nothing again, Max. Does that make me a bitch? Being here with you?'

'No. Of course it doesn't. If you don't hurt Casper, how could it?'

Gemma didn't really register his answer. Her mind was doing what it always did when the present was threatened by the past: desperately trying to rationalize the status quo.

'Max, you wouldn't marry me even if I wanted you to. If I left Casper. Would you?'

'I'm not the marrying type, Gemma. The stay-at-home reliable husband . . .'

'Not all women are like your mother,' Gemma interrupted. 'You don't have to run away from all of us.'

Gemma had no idea how cruel her remark was. Max had never told her how or why his father died. So he couldn't be angry with her now. He stood up from the bed and poured himself a large glass of Scotch.

'Enough of this,' he said lightly. 'I want to take you out wearing my beautiful watch. At least if I run away from you tonight, I'll be able to time myself.'

3

Paul Wielart was a man of strict routine. Six days a week he arrived at his offices near the flower market at seven o'clock sharp. The bells of the local clock tower could have been timed to him turning the key in the door.

To the unknowing eye, his offices reflected the image of a dour accountant. It was well ordered, old fashioned and immaculately clean. You could straighten your tie in the reflection of the brass plate outside the front door. The black-and-white-squared marble floor gleamed in the hallway; as did the internal glass windows, which gave the offices a semi-open-plan feel.

Wielart's private office, however, was a lair shut away behind a heavy oak door. With the exception of his long-serving battleaxe of an assistant, none of the staff ever set foot in there. And not many of the firm's clients were permitted to grace the stiff brown leather chairs or the nineteenth-century velvet-upholstered chaise longue.

Wielart was a small, unimposing man. He wore a suit and tie every day of his life and a black homburg whenever he set foot outdoors. In his early twenties, he had married a cousin, who was glad to have a prosperous husband and knew her place. They had one daughter, Josebe, who'd never done anything wrong, but hadn't done much right either.

Having inherited the company from his father, together with a steady stream of respectable but mundane clients, Wielart quickly learnt that there were people who would pay extremely good money to have their accounts 'organized' and certified by a respectable accountancy firm.

Wielart bought his clients businesses on whose balance sheets cash could appear. Hotels, clubs and restaurants were initially his stock in trade. And then Wielart was introduced to Jorgan Stam.

Stam dealt in pretty well anything that was illegal. He'd started by trafficking prostitutes from Eastern Europe and then got into 'hard' drugs. The casino that he now owned – the Dice Club – had a rigged roulette table and only catered for losers. Any half-serious player was thrown out. Whatever Stam touched threw off cash.

It hadn't taken Stam long to persuade Wielart that it would be in both their interests to team up. Wielart would keep the façade of his accountancy business going but devote his skill and energy to legitimizing Stam's money trail. A fifty-fifty partnership, which Stam assumed would bind them inextricably together.

Wielart added a whole layer of supply companies to their operation. One of them, a vegetable retail business, turned over in excess of a million euros per annum. And yet it never so much as handled a sprig of broccoli.

The hotels and restaurants that bought these fictitious vegetables marked them up three hundred per cent, as the taxman expected, and sold them on to their customers – the vast majority of whom happened to be cash buyers.

The profits that all of these businesses made appeared to be legitimate. As did the money the vegetable farms made at the end of the chain. And their profits were constantly expanding.

There was some tax to be paid, but the bulk of the proceeds Wielart converted into more land or fresh businesses before the taxman got his hands on any liquid profits. And all the while he maintained the image of the dour accountant.

Wielart was the epitome of the respectable husband, though he cared little about his wife or daughter. He spent as little time at home as possible, and the rest of his hours behind his desk. His wife was plain, dull, excelled at nothing and appealed to few. Josebe took after her.

However, Francisca Deetman – Josebe's only visible friend – was everything that Wielart's daughter wasn't. A brilliant linguist, the best violinist in the school, as well as their most athletic hockey player, Francisca was traffic-stoppingly beautiful and rode like an angel on horseback. Her long blonde hair cascaded over her shoulders and her deep blue eyes paralysed men in the rare moments when she overcame her natural shyness and looked them in the eye.

Wielart wasn't interested in women, *per se*. But the sixteen-year-old Francisca stirred something in him. And he started to make sure he was at home when Francisca was coming over.

She didn't say much to him, but whenever he asked her about her father's shipping company, she not only knew exactly what was going on, but could articulate it with the precision of a financial journalist. As she got to know him, she began to look him in the eye when she spoke to him. It stirred a feeling deep inside him that he knew was wrong, though he soon became a slave to it.

Francisca came on Wielart family holidays over the next two years. She played and read and sang with Josebe. In fact, they were utterly inseparable.

By the time Francisca was eighteen, Wielart was totally infatuated with her. He couldn't be in the same room as her without darting a glance at her from behind his thick, round glasses whenever he thought no one would notice. She now had the body of a woman, not a girl, and he longed to see it, to touch it, to smell it. Occasionally, feigning innocence, he would walk into Josebe's room at an inopportune moment in the hope of catching a glance of Francisca in a state of semi-undress. But he never had any success.

Wielart's long-held aversion to swimming – his father had fervently believed that professionals must never risk being seen by their clients in anything other than a suit and tie – had robbed him of any chance to see Francisca in a bathing costume. All he could do was lust after her with growing desperation, while concealing his obsession with mounting self-loathing.

Pallesson made the short journey from The Hague to Amsterdam by train. Having deliberately left an hour's slack in his schedule, he headed southeast across the Centraal Station concourse rather than taking a more direct route to his assignation through the Magna Plaza.

As he walked past the magnificent spires of St Nicolaaskerk, Pallesson didn't have a religious thought in his mind. Far from it. In fact, the anticipation of the little treat he was about to give himself was making his armpits wet. He could feel the beads of sweat dripping down his ribcage.

A cold smile creased his face as he turned down the Oudezijds Achterburgwal. He looked approvingly at the swans gliding with menace along the canal – patrolling territory that stretched deep into the red-light district.

Pallesson hesitated as he walked past the first row of girls displaying themselves in the window, beckoning to him with their fingers. They beckoned to everyone. They had to. The only way they made any money was if they could earn more than the cost of the window they hired by the hour.

The top end of the red-light district offered the cheapest girls. They catered for a diverse range of tastes. Pallesson loved the illusion the windows gave that they were locked in cells. Animals in cages.

Like most bullies, he wasn't naturally brave. So it took him a few metres to slow his walk until he finally stopped by the window of a small brunette desperately trying to entice him. He laughed at her. She took no notice and kept beckoning to him. And he kept laughing. He was safe. What was she going to do about it?

After a few seconds, he moved further down the street, buoyed up by his entertainment. He felt empowerment coursing through his veins. His next target was an Asian girl. She was pretty, smiley and had a great body. Pallesson stood in front of her window with his arms crossed. A dark frown crossed his face, as if something was concerning him. He fixed the girl with his cold, grey eyes, and shook his head. The girl kept smiling and opened her door ajar to encourage him.

'Fifty euros for good time,' she said. 'Fifty euros.'

He gestured with his hand to dismiss her – though it wasn't as if she was going anywhere – and moved on.

A hundred metres further along the pavement Pallesson turned down a narrow side street. An observant tourist would have noticed that all of the windows in the alley either had a whip hanging inside the window, or a small card proclaiming S&M. Pallesson checked his watch. He had forty-five minutes.

The curtains of the first two windows were shut. He wasn't bothered. He'd used them both over the last few months. He wanted to try the last girl on the left. He'd noticed her before. She was large, strong-looking and, with any luck, German.

He was nearly shaking with excitement as he approached her window. The curtain was open. She was sitting on a high stool, talking to someone on her mobile phone. He caught her eye, expectantly. Unlike the other girls, she didn't rush to open her door or beckon to him. She just carried on with her conversation and made him stand in the narrow alley like a prick. He felt demeaned. He was now desperate to have her.

She knew what she was doing. This little jerk wasn't going anywhere. And she could see by the way he was dressed that she could up her charges. In her own time she opened the door and gestured with her head for him to enter. He stepped into her narrow window without saying a word. She drew the curtains behind him.

He left half an hour later, but without the shifty look that most of the punters had when they stepped quickly back on to the street and walked one way or the other, trying to blend into the general crowd. He liked being in control, not skulking about.

He checked his watch again. He had ten minutes to get to the jetty in the Oude Turfmarkt. He walked briskly along the canal past the magnificent houses that border the red-light district, making a mental note of the one he would like to live in. He then cut through the university campus, which brought him out opposite the Hotel de l'Europe. As he walked down the street he could hear the clock tower across the canal by the flower market chiming noon. He was bang on time. As he always was.

The old merchant's boat waiting to pick him up was tied to the jetty used by the tourist boats.

'Good morning,' he said to one of the thickset lumps of muscle standing on the jetty.

The man barely registered his presence.

'Let's go,' Pallesson said, unfazed.

The small boat had one cabin with a long narrow table and bench seats either side. One of the thugs shut the double doors behind him without so much as a word. He was now trapped in his own glass-sided cell, looking out on to the canal as the boat pulled away from the jetty.

Wevers van Ossen was the proprietor of the old merchant's boat. He was also a vicious psychopath. And leader of the Kalverstraat gang, which was notorious for its brutality. For over a decade he'd been running a ruthless protection racket in Amsterdam.

His authority, however, was now being challenged by Eastern European gangs who were prepared to stand their ground. And one Dutchman – Jorgan Stam. The level of violence employed by Stam's men was escalating fast. The balance of power was being tested.

So van Ossen had made a strategic decision. He was diversifying into drugs. It was simple for him. There were any number of desperate 'mules' prepared to take the risk of bringing heroin to Amsterdam by boat or land. All he had to do was warehouse and redistribute it. At no risk, given his position in Amsterdam. He'd 'protected' the docks for years. And Pallesson was the conduit and fixer for his first deal into England.

The two minders on van Ossen's boat could have been twins, with their shaven heads and wide noses. Both were reckless killers. They'd left behind their birth names when they walked out the back door of the garrison at Doorn, Utrecht, and assumed the new identities that van Ossen had created for them: Fransen and Piek.

As members of the Dutch Maritime Special Operations Forces (MARSOF), they had come through the most brutal of training regimes in every extreme terrain possible; and thrived on it.

During their tour of duty at Camp Smitty near As Samawah in Southern Iraq, they had fought in conjunction with AH-64 attack helicopters, clearing out subversives. They had put their lives on the line for the Coalition forces and their British commander. And they had bailed out wounded British troops, pinned down by sniper fire. Their heroics had gone well beyond the call of duty, and because of this the British had covered up for them.

Fransen and Piek had gone off-piste while on patrol in a village called al-Khidr. They had told their Dutch compatriots to turn a blind eye and cover their backs while they cleared up a small matter.

The small matter was a meeting of six civilians in a house on the edge of the village. Six civilians who, their informants had told them, were collaborating with those still loyal to the Republican Guard.

Fransen and Piek wanted to send a message to the other villagers. A message that reminded them they should work with the Coalition forces, not the insurgents, if they valued their lives.

The six men, who were all unarmed, didn't have time to react. They were shot dead with the Glock 17 sidearms that the Dutchmen were carrying. But that in itself would not have been a strong enough deterrent to the other villagers, desensitized as they were by the ravages of war. So Fransen and Piek cut off their victims' heads and lined them up outside the house.

There was no concrete evidence that the two Dutchmen were the perpetrators of this crime. The British commander had two options: either to bust them and put them through the military's disciplinary system, or to lose them fast. He chose the latter option. Within twenty-four hours the pair of them had been secreted back to Doorn garrison. It was their good fortune that the al-Khidr atrocity would be wiped from the record. As indeed would they.

Doorn's sergeant major had long been van Ossen's recruitment officer. The arrangement suited the military as much as it did van Ossen. He took embarrassing situations off their hands, and in return got the hardest recruits on the block. Van Ossen would be a hard man to usurp as long as this was the case. A fact that was not wasted on Pallesson.

Pallesson watched a large tourist boat passing them in the opposite direction. It was packed full of stereotypical sightseers. Some of them gawped at him as they glided past. He ignored them.

They passed the big, ugly Stadhuis-Muziektheater, built on the old Jewish quarter, then turned left by the Hermitage museum. Pallesson had no idea where they were going. Finally, they doubled back into a smaller canal and pulled over by some houseboats.

Van Ossen stepped aboard one of them, aided by another sour-looking bodyguard, and climbed down into the glass-sided cabin.

'Good to see you again, Mr Pallesson. I hope you don't mind a little ride on the canal. Do you like my boat? It was originally owned by a merchant, who used it to entertain his clients. Sadly, we had a little disagreement and he forfeited the boat. We don't have time for entertainment right now. Maybe one day.'

'That would be nice.'

'So, are you still in? You have the painting for me?' van Ossen asked bluntly.

'Everything is in order, I can assure you.' Pallesson was ruffled, but he kept his voice even. 'I'll have the painting next week. As agreed.'

'I want to bring the deal forward. End of this week.'

Pallesson had dealt with van Ossen's kind before. They liked to push people around. Partly to show they could, but also to protect themselves by changing locations, times. The only option was to stand up to them.

'That isn't possible,' Pallesson said calmly. 'Barry Nuttall won't have the money by then. And I personally guaranteed that *The Peasants in Winter* would be our bond. It can't be extracted until next week – I can't hand it over until then – that was our agreement.'

'So how do I know you're good for the deal?'

Van Ossen was irritated. And reluctant to sit on the drugs a day longer than he had to.

'Our deal is agreed. Barry Nuttall will bring over two million euros in used notes.'

'Are you sure?'

'I've done five deals as his partner – Russia and Turkey – never a problem. He's a pro.'

Van Ossen was renowned for his explosive temper. He was not someone you wanted to cross, a fact that many unfortunate associates had reflected upon as they were sinking to the bottom of a pitch-black canal. In spite of the cashmere overcoat and dark-blue suit, it was obvious which side of the tracks van Ossen came from.

'He better be,' van Ossen said with as much malice as he could muster.

Most people would have been unnerved by an irritated van Ossen. Not Pallesson. Faced with danger and threat, he had learnt to draw strength from the dark forces that he believed watched over him.

So a drug-running Dutchman didn't bother him. He was quickly back on the front foot.

'You know who I've dealt with in the past. Never a problem. And I think you'll find I'll be useful across several areas of your supply chain. Especially with the UK borders tightening up,' Pallesson said, holding his composure. 'We'll be ready next week. And then the beautiful Brueghel will be yours to treasure for a few days.'

* * *

Max breezed straight off the plane from Nice and strolled into the British Embassy in The Hague as if he owned the place. It was a surprisingly drab set-up. Three months earlier, when he'd first arrived from Moscow, Max had been expecting something much grander.

The semi-open-plan layout emphasized the seniority of some of its occupants. The ambassador had a large glass-fronted office with a secluded back room. Anyone else who merited private space got their own square glass box, which offered a degree of seclusion. Unfortunately, when Max had arrived, no 'executive' office had been available. So he'd had to muck in with the foot soldiers and take a desk in the open-plan area. This suited Max, as it gave him the chance to interact with the staff. It also secretly pleased Pallesson, underlining the chasm of importance that he believed had opened up between the two of them.

Max always paused at the front desk to talk to Arthur, who'd worked at the embassy for over twenty years. Max knew Arthur liked to have a chat. It broke up the routine of sorting the mail and making sure the office ran smoothly. He was a fanatical Queens Park Rangers fan, which gave Max the opportunity to take the piss out of him most weeks during the football season.

'See the game on Saturday? You lot were terrible.' Max had never watched so much as one kick of a QPR game, but Arthur seemed oblivious to the fact.

'Don't tell me,' Arthur would always reply, shaking his head.

Arthur had a son he was very proud of. Young Arthur was currently on manoeuvres in Germany. Max never forgot to ask after him.

Max had a very distinct view on office life. It wasn't about the number of hours that you spent rubbing your brow and

43

sending emails. It was about solving whatever was put in front of you as efficiently as possible – and then having a bit of fun.

The open-plan office afforded Max the perfect opportunity to work on Pallesson's attitude towards him. It suited Max perfectly that Pallesson should think of him as ineffective and a bit of a joke. And there was no better way to act the fool than playing office cricket.

Max had enlisted the aid of an unlikely recruit to perpetuate this sham. His immediate boss, Graham Smith, had played cricket for Chelmsford in his youth. Smith liked to be different. He liked to feel he was 'on it' and outside the box; young for his age, trendy and a bit of a rebel against the normal order. So he could be persuaded to bowl at Max as long as he was confident that the ambassador was nowhere near the building. He got used to Max's challenges arriving via email.

From: Max Ward
To: Graham Smith
Subject: Centenary Test, Lords 1980
DK Lillee bowling to DI Gower. Desperate run chase for England, but Gower still up for having a go at Lillee, who is throwing everything at it.
Play resumes at 5 p.m. sharp.

Smith knew Max would be standing at the end of the passage, bat in hand, at precisely five o'clock. He had to knock over the waste-paper basket behind Max with his tennis ball, or get tonked around the office.

His first ball that afternoon was short and Max pulled it to square leg. The tennis ball flew through Pallesson's open door and crashed into some photographs on his windowsill. It startled the hell out of him.

'Did that carry?' Max asked Pallesson as he retrieved the ball.

44

Pallesson could barely mask his contempt.

'For God's sake, can't you grow up?' Pallesson spat. 'You just don't get it, do you? You think everything's a bloody game. You're not the school hero any more, Ward. Maybe you should think about that. Maybe you should think about why you're going bloody nowhere.'

'So I can put that down as a six then?' Max replied nonchalantly as he wandered back to his crease. He resisted the temptation to throw a 'It's not going to kill anyone, you know' line, at the murdering little creep. If he was going to play Pallesson, he had to be smarter and more disciplined than his quarry. And he had to play to win.

The thought of Pallesson relentlessly climbing the diplomatic ladder terrified Max. The higher he got, the more disastrous the consequences would be. Max knew that Pallesson's loyalties lay with himself. He would betray his country in a heartbeat. He had to be stopped.

Gower's innings came to an abrupt end when the ambassador made an unscheduled entrance. Smith managed to lose the tennis ball and look industrious, but Max was still tapping down the carpet with his bat when they came face to face.

'Oh, you're in today, are you?' the ambassador asked. He had an air of superiority about him and enjoyed being a hard arse. Most of the staff were intimidated by him, but Max thought he was a pompous, pen-pushing prick.

'Ah, Ambassador. Good to see you.' Max smiled.

The ambassador didn't smile back. He was on the verge of asking Max why he was holding a cricket bat, but he knew he'd be on the receiving end of something flippant.

'How's Mrs Ambassador? All well? You must both come to dinner one night,' Max suggested. He didn't get a reply.

When Max got back to his desk, a harassed-looking Data Dave was waiting for him holding a USB key. Everyone called him Data Dave; indeed Human Resources were probably the only ones who knew his surname.

'We need this translated yesterday. It's the last twenty minutes of an arms deal. Sadly, that's all the tech boys could recover. There's Belgian, Dutch and Afrikaans in there. Should be a doddle for you, Ward.'

Max shook his head with mock resignation.

'And if you can work out where the arms are coming from, then that would be great too. There's nothing flashing on any of their standard routes.'

Max took the key and waved goodbye to the next two hours of his life.

Max was about to head off for the evening when a text message arrived on his phone. He wasn't going to look at it right away, but something told him it might be in his interest.

U fancy a drink tonight? it said anonymously. That's a bit strange, Max thought. But he was intrigued.

Well, give me a clue, he replied.

Arthur gave me your number. I'm sucking my pen, was the instant reply.

Max smiled as he looked up from his phone and glanced around the office. In the far corner, a very pretty, if slightly overweight, brunette was sucking her pen.

Well? she texted as Max hesitated.

Where did you have in mind? Max replied, even though he wasn't sure this was a particularly good idea.

Anywhere with a cold bottle of champagne.

Max and Louise ended up drinking two bottles of champagne in the bar of the Hotel de l'Europe. There had been a frisson of expectancy about their conversation.

Finally, Louise said, 'Shall we go now?'

'Where did you have in mind?' Max replied noncommittally.

'Your bed, of course,' Louise said, dropping her hand on to Max's thigh.

Max drained his champagne glass to buy time.

'Louise, that would be very nice, but I'm very unreliable. Here today, gone tomorrow. Very unreliable.'

Louise gave him a broad smile. 'Don't panic, Max. I don't want to go out with you. I have a perfectly nice boyfriend in England, as a matter of fact. So don't take this personally. Ever heard of a one-night stand?'

Max suddenly admired Louise. Direct, uncomplicated and thoroughly honest. And no games. He'd been up front with her, and she with him. Perfect.

'Louise,' Max said seriously, looking into her eyes, 'why aren't there more women like you?'

By happy coincidence, Louise had the next day off. Max made her a cup of tea, but she showed no interest in leaping out of bed.

'I have to get to the airport. London today. What's your plan?'

'My plan is to lie in your bed until I can think of something else I'd rather be doing. Why don't you get back in for ten minutes?' she suggested, pulling at his arm.

'Can't think of anything nicer, but I'll get shot if I'm late. So to speak.'

'Max,' Louise said, 'can we do that again?'

Max kissed her on the bridge of her nose.

'Well, you'd better check with your boyfriend first, don't you think?' he suggested, with an air-kiss on his way out the door.

'You're good,' she shouted after him, and rolled over to go back to sleep.

4

Max was used to curious looks when he was stuck in slow traffic. Most people had never seen a DMC-12 before.

John DeLorean had manufactured the light sports cars in Northern Ireland in the early eighties. The gull-wing doors and stainless-steel panels of the DMC-12, combined with a chassis designed by Colin Chapman at Lotus made the car totally unique. And as the company had gone bust fairly quickly, not many of the cars were now driving around London.

One of the punters who used to bet with Max's dad had given him the keys when he couldn't settle his account. Which was a slightly double-edged sword. On the one hand, the car was worth a few bob. On the other, Houston, Texas, was the only place you could get spare parts for it after an American company bought up the wreckage of the company. But the car had memories for Max and he wouldn't drive anything else until the day the spare parts stopped arriving.

As he sat in the West London gridlock, Max's mind drifted back to his first meeting with Tryon in a dimly lit vodka bar under the Leninsky Prospekt in Moscow. Tryon, the elusive overlord who had no title, but seemingly no superiors either.

After Max had witnessed Corbett's execution, he'd thought long and hard about his course of action. In the end he'd gambled on Tryon being the right superior to inform. Because if he'd chosen the wrong man – one potentially compromised by Pallesson – he would place himself in dire danger. But it had been Keate who had introduced the two of them, so he felt safe knowing that he was dealing with a friend of his old tutor.

Tryon hadn't said much. He'd acknowledged that he'd received an anonymous allegation that Pallesson had murdered Corbett. He'd refused to divulge why he was certain it came from Max. Having listened to the whole story with an impassive face, the old hand had simply stood up and left.

Until Max's orders had come through to move from Moscow to The Hague, he'd wondered whether Tryon had been running Pallesson from the very beginning, and still was. But if that were the case, surely he wouldn't still be alive?

The reason given for Max's addition to the Netherlands team – that they needed someone who could unravel local chatter across six different languages; chatter that centred on Dutch drug cartels that appeared to be doing business with Saudi-backed terrorists – seemed plausible. Whether Pallesson, who had made the same move six months before Max, had bought the story, he couldn't be sure.

As a bus carved him up, Max's mind went back to the school library at Eton. The vast dome-shaped room lined with learned books and populated by nerds who spoke in whispers. Max avoided the place like the plague.

He remembered the exact table where Pallesson had arranged to meet him. It was right in the centre of the building and very visible. He'd been baffled at the time as to why the slimy toerag wanted to see him, though his surprise quickly evaporated when Pallesson laid out the full financial record of Max's gambling syndicate on the table in front of him.

'Where did you get that?' he'd asked, without looking at him.

'You know I can't reveal my sources,' Pallesson had replied smarmily.

Needless to say, Max had wanted to thump the smug seventeen-year-old. He knew what Pallesson's angle was. Blackmail, plain and simple. But Pallesson had been wise to a hot-headed reaction – hence meeting him in a public place where any lack of decorum wouldn't be tolerated.

'I have copies, just in case you have anything rash in mind,' Pallesson said quietly.

Max had felt disgusted by Pallesson's cold, grey eyes, his slightly greasy black hair and his immaculate appearance. His tails, waistcoat and stiff white collar always looked brand new. Unlike his fellow pupils, whose uniforms were always frayed around the edges.

'I'm going to be your partner,' Pallesson had told him.

'No, you're fucking not, *Roderick*,' Max had replied.

Pallesson had imperceptibly winced at the sound of his Christian name, but hid it quickly. No one used his first name, and that was how he liked it.

'Look, we could make a great team. And I'm not just talking about now. We have a great future. Max. You and I can go as far as we like.'

'You and I are going fucking nowhere,' Max had replied, loud enough to attract the attention of one of the library wardens.

Max suddenly realized he was gripping the steering wheel like a maniac. Stop it, he told himself. Relax. Stay focused. After all these years, maybe this was his chance to nail Pallesson.

Yet again, Max went through the few details Tryon had told him when they'd met a week earlier in Amsterdam – ticking off each fact as he scrutinized it for subtext and gloss; anything that would give him even the smallest insight.

Pallesson, it transpired, was blackmailing a French forger,

Jacques Bardin, who had contacted Tryon through the French security services. No one had asked how or why. So, nothing out of character there, as far as Max was concerned.

The forger was alleging that he had copied *The Peasants in Winter* for Pallesson. After a few enquiries, the painting had been traced to the British Embassy in The Hague. On loan from the Dutch Government. The only possible conclusion, Max told himself as he edged forwards in the traffic, was that Pallesson was going to steal the original and substitute the copy he'd had made.

When Tryon had first outlined the art theft, Max was very happy. After all, they got Al Capone for tax evasion. Serious theft would end Pallesson's career. Although Max knew that was only scratching at the surface.

He parked in a wide, nondescript Chiswick back street. The pavement was like a skating rink. As he buttoned his thick black Russian overcoat, he wondered why they didn't just chuck some grit on it. He tried walking down the road, but it was no better.

At the end of the street there was a narrow alley leading down to the river. An officious-looking sign informed the public they had no right of way after six in the evening. Max checked his watch. It was four. He was going to be late. The alley ran between two large houses whose owners clearly didn't like the public wandering about, either. A CCTV camera with a red light glowing was trained on his route. Max wasn't overjoyed at being filmed, but he had nothing to fear, he told himself. And at least the path was dry.

Max timed how long it took him to walk halfway down the alley: two minutes and thirty seconds.

Where the alleyway met the river, Max had no option but to turn left, as he'd been told to. To the right was a metal fence with spikes and a STRICTLY PRIVATE sign glaring at him. Max cursed again. The river was lapping across the path.

When he'd turned the corner on to the towpath, Max stopped and checked his watch. The Thames was in full spate, bursting at its banks. It looked cold and hostile. Not a boat in sight. No one would survive a minute in there. He wondered where his body would be found. Maybe it never would.

He checked his watch again. One minute and fifteen seconds had passed. He felt suddenly exhilarated as he poked his head around the corner. But the alley was empty.

Trying to stick to dry land, he made his way along the footpath, but it was futile. By the time he'd gone fifty feet to the edge of the boathouse slipway, his feet were sodden.

Max paused and looked up the concrete slope. The boathouse was Art Deco simplicity. The whitewashed walls were cracked. And the big green metal shutters had seen better days. The place looked locked-up and sullen.

He imagined the frenzy of Boat Race day. The bleak concrete slope teeming with cameras and a macho Oxford crew carrying their boat down to the water. The boathouse bursting with last-minute nerves. All a far cry from this cold, damp, deserted winter evening.

Max was feeling increasingly on edge. It wasn't an evening for hanging about. His feet were already freezing. He gingerly walked up the slipway to the left of the boathouse and looked for the door. When he reached it, he could see that it was ajar. Tryon's bicycle was propped up against the wall. That was a good sign. The old hand had showed.

Max stepped tentatively inside. There wasn't much light coming in through the high windows. A mass of fragile-looking boats were stacked on metal shelves. He walked stealthily between them towards the back of the boathouse. As he'd been told.

He thought about shouting a friendly 'hello', but decided against it. It really wasn't the right way to announce your arrival at a clandestine meeting. Although he was a bit out of practice on that front. These days he spent more time poking around for a scrap of phonetically transcribed Flemish.

Max smelt the unmistakable aroma of pipe tobacco. Again, he was relieved. Not that he had any need to be. He was on home turf this time, after all.

'You're late, Ward,' barked a voice from behind a stack of boats.

'And wet,' replied Max with a deliberate lack of subservience. There was no point in producing an excuse, because there never was one. Never had been, in fact.

'What the hell were you doing at the bottom of the alley?'

'Just checking. How did . . .?'

'CCTV. There's only one way into this place when it's locked up. And I like to see who's dropping by.'

Tryon was sitting on an old wooden folding chair. He was digging away at his pipe with a look of focused intensity.

'Anyone follow you?'

'No. Couldn't we have met in Amsterdam again? Would have been a lot drier.' He looked down at his feet to reinforce the point.

'Very funny. The op's now live, and one never runs an off-books op from inside the theatre.' Tryon finally looked up from his pipe. 'So how did you get on in Monaco?'

Max looked around for something to sit on. There was a workbench just to Tryon's right. It was the bench of a very tidy craftsman, Max noted. He picked up a tin of varnish and sniffed it.

'Didn't know they still used this stuff.'

'They don't. Must be for an old boat. All carbon fibre now. How did it go?'

'Pretty good,' he replied airily. He studied Tryon for a moment. He was thin and gaunt, but on closer inspection as hard as nails. Still sporting the same scruffy brown raincoat and battered green trilby he had worn a week before. The same rustic tie and heavy cotton shirt. But today he looked tired, something employees of the Racket spent years cultivating the ability to hide.

'Jacques seemed happy with the canvas I took him. And Cornelissen's had sent the paint they asked for. All good.'

'Gemma enjoy herself?' Tryon asked flippantly, as if to pass the time while he fiddled with his pipe again.

'I think so. No hassle in her jet. Nice hotel.'

'Ask much? About what you were up to?'

'Not really. Told her I had a wee mission. Chance to get my feet out from under the desk. She didn't seem that interested.'

'Did she mention anything she might have been up to herself?'

'No. Up to what? Forget about her. Look, we're dealing with a bloody traitor. A murderer. And I have to walk into an office every day and pretend he's a valued colleague. It's pretty pathetic that all we're going to do is nail him for some sort of art theft.'

'It goes a bit deeper than that – quite a lot deeper, in fact.' Tryon lit his pipe. 'While you were having lunch with Jacques in Monaco, do you know who Gemma was meeting?'

Max could literally feel his blood defying gravity and flowing to his head. 'What are you talking about? She didn't meet anyone.'

'I know people down there, Ward. It's how Jacques found me in the first place. Through them,' Tryon said evenly. 'Gemma met someone behind your back. Someone we're really not sure about.'

'She probably just ran into them. She knows people everywhere.'

'She ran into him on his yacht in the harbour.'

Max had learnt to appreciate the old hand's desert-dry wit, though not so much when he was the intended target.

'She did say she was going down to the harbour for a walk. Who did she meet?' asked Max, conceding defeat.

'Alessandro Marchant.'

'Rich?'

'Rich! Either Marchant has psychic powers that enable him to see how currencies and stock are going to move – or he's one of the biggest financial insider dealers in the world. And guess who he deals through?'

'Go on.'

'Casper Rankin. Whose wife you happen to be sleeping with. We've been intercepting their emails, and listening to their phone conversations. But we can't nail them. They're careful how they pass information around.'

'Are you suggesting . . .?'

'I'm not suggesting anything, Ward.'

'Look,' Max said intensely, 'if I can't trust Gemma, I can't trust anyone. Not even you. Gemma is—'

'I know,' Tryon interrupted. 'You told me. It's just that I'm not entirely sure whether I sign up to your version.'

Tryon had made it plain that he suspected Max might have been targeted by Gemma. Which amused Max no end – or at least it had until now – as it couldn't have been further from the truth.

Max had first clocked Gemma at the opening of some dull art exhibition at a gallery in St James's. He'd then persuaded a mate of his, who also happened to know her husband, to have her to stay in the country for the weekend. Thankfully, her husband had been away.

It was a typical, wild Gloucestershire weekend party. Everyone drank far too much and a few people ended up doing things they shouldn't. Max remembered flirting with her and having no idea whether she was responding to him. One minute she seemed to be fascinated by him – the next, totally oblivious. Max had followed her upstairs to bed. By the time he knocked on her door, she was wearing the skimpiest of nighties. She'd let him in, and then resisted – to start with. But then she'd cracked. Once she had, Max remembered being taken aback by her urgency. She'd literally ripped the buttons off his shirt. His back had scratch marks for days.

'Well, if we're lucky, this relationship of yours could be very useful to us. Or you're being set up. Because guess who Casper Rankin's best mucker was at Cambridge?'

'Go on.'

'Surprise, surprise. Your old pal, Pallesson. Gemma tell you that?'

'This is all a bit tenuous. She might not know.'

'So she hasn't told you.'

'No. How do you—'

'You can be certain that Casper Rankin has laundered the proceeds of Pallesson's Russian enterprises. By now the money's probably found its way to Montenegro. Rankin has been investing in property down there. He seems to have second sight as to what the Montenegrin government is about to do. Gemma mention anything about that?'

Max didn't answer. He pushed himself off the workbench and landed on both feet. They were numb now.

'She has no idea what her husband does. And less interest. They've drifted apart. He works and works. Never in the same place for that long. She goes where she likes. Does up rich people's houses for them.'

'Pallesson is up to a lot more than art theft,' Tryon interrupted, as if he suddenly wasn't interested in Gemma any more.

'I'm not fucking stupid, Tryon. 'Of course he is.'

'We have a mole inside the operation of a nasty piece of work called Wevers van Ossen, based in Amsterdam. He's into trafficking, prostitution, protection.'

'What do we care?'

'We didn't – until now. He's moving into drugs in a pretty spectacular way.'

'So?'

'The source of his drugs is using the proceeds to fund operations in Somalia, which we care about a lot. More to the point, guess who's lined up with van Ossen to move the gear over here.'

'Our old friend?'

'Exactly. He's brought his unpleasant habits with him from Moscow. And you're going to nail him. All on your own.'

'Why all on my own?'

Tryon didn't reply. He appeared to be studying the boats, and his pipe had gone out again.

'By the way, how was Jacques?'

'His sight's gone,' Max replied, happy to let his question hang. 'Had to get his daughter to help him copy paintings for Pallesson. The cunning little shit worked that out – that's how he blackmailed both of them.' Max walked over to one of the larger boats and stroked its sleek side.

'This is probably my favourite place in the world,' Tryon said, watching him. 'I still row a couple of times a week. There's no better feeling than being on the water in an eight. Going full tilt. I rowed in the Boat Race one year, you know.'

'Oxford?'

Tryon nodded.

'Did you win?'

Tryon nodded again.

'Of course you did. This would hardly be the best place in the world if you lost, would it? I never went near the river at

Eton. Apart from crossing it to get to Windsor Racecourse.' He swung round to face Tryon. 'So why on my own?'

Tryon paused as if he was confirming in his own mind what the plan should be. After a few seconds spent hunched over his pipe, he had clearly decided.

'He'll use this painting to get into a drug deal – as he did in Moscow. You saw him holding something by the lake where he liquidated Corbett. He'll be using the painting as collateral to cut himself into the deal with van Ossen. Same pattern. But we need to know where this deal is taking place. We'll have to hide a tracking device on the second copy of the painting.'

'How do we bust him?'

'How do *you* bust him, you mean. We can't rely on the Dutch police – they're riddled with informants – but there is one officer we can work with.' Tryon set himself to relighting his pipe. 'This has got to be completely out-of-house on our side. Who knows who Pallesson has got to? Just you. Go and see Pete Carr. Get a tracking device from him.'

'Who's our mole? Why are you only telling me all this now?'

'Grow up, Ward – you know how these things work.'

He handed Max a worn business card. Max read it a couple of times then handed it back to Tryon.

'He's not that secure, by the way. Chequered past. Don't tell him anything. But we've got to take this outside the Office and he's our best option at this stage. Then get down to Gassin. Fast. Did Jacques give you his address?'

'No.'

'Doesn't matter. I'll email directions to the drop box. No satnav please. Get a flight back down there tonight. Commercial. Without your girlfriend. We've only got one shot at this. If you don't steal that painting in the embassy before Pallesson, we're cold.'

Max had one more question. 'What happens if I get caught? Could be a bit embarrassing, to say the least.'

'You won't. But if you do, I didn't make contact and we've never discussed this.' He took several short puffs on his pipe and looked Max straight in the eye. 'I've never even heard of *The Peasants in Winter*. Or in any other season, for that matter.'

Wevers van Ossen treasured his Sunday mornings. At eight thirty every week he bundled his eight-year-old daughter, Anneka, into the back of their four-by-four and strapped her in securely.

The drive to the stables where Anneka's pony was kept only took ten minutes. And those minutes were packed with talk about which jumps Anneka was going to take on.

Van Ossen loved watching Anneka ride. But he was less keen on the jumping aspect of it.

'Perhaps you should concentrate on your flatwork,' van Ossen suggested. He'd even learnt the lingo they used at the stables. Anneka knew flatwork meant trotting and steady cantering – which wasn't to her liking as much as jumping.

'Mustang likes jumping, Daddy,' Anneka objected. She knew she'd get her way. She always did.

Mustang was probably the most expensive pony ever sold in Holland. It hadn't helped that Anneka had told the world that she was in love with Mustang before van Ossen could do the deal. He'd had to break all his principles to buy it. If it hadn't been for Anneka he would have wiped the smirk off the stable owner's face and walked away. Instead he gritted his teeth and wrote out the cheque.

Van Ossen pulled a couple of sugar lumps out of his pocket for Mustang, and placed them on the palm of his hand. He'd have liked to strike a deal: My daughter's safety guaranteed, or no more sugar. (It was a bit late to couch the deal in more severe terms: Mustang was already a gelding.) Since there was no hope of the pony understanding the deal, he settled for a straight gift and a friendly pat on the neck.

As usual, van Ossen inspected Anneka's tack thoroughly. He trusted no one with her safety. Reins, cheekpieces, girth, neck strap – each item was subjected to scrutiny. Then he went over her equipment, making sure her crash helmet was done up properly and her body protector zipped up.

For the next hour, Anneka did what she bloody well liked. Her instructor would have loved to grind some discipline into her. But he knew that wouldn't be wise with Mr van Ossen leaning against the rail. The plastic safety rail that he'd bought to replace the old wooden fence that encircled the school.

Occasionally, van Ossen took his BlackBerry out of his pocket and surreptitiously went through a few emails. Anneka was alert to lapses of attention on his part and taking a call would inevitably spark a tantrum, so the constant calls coming in from Piek that morning irritated him. His man knew that he never took calls of a Sunday morning, so why did he keep ringing? There had to be a reason. In the end, van Ossen cracked and answered his phone.

'We have a problem, boss. The new guy. He was seen in the wrong company last night. We've got him at the warehouse.'

Before van Ossen could reply, Anneka – having seen her father's lack of concentration – furiously gunned Mustang at some poles that were far too big for him. The pony very sensibly jinked at the last moment and ducked out to the right. Anneka, however, failed to anticipate Mustang's jink and flew out of the saddle. She hit the poles as she flew through the air, and then landed on the deck like a rag doll.

Van Ossen vaulted over the plastic rails and ran, heart in his mouth, to Anneka. Her instructor was already leaning over her. She was winded, and struggling for breath. The instructor was trying to loosen her body protector, but van Ossen pushed him out of the way.

'Idiot! Why did you let that happen?' van Ossen raged as he fell to his knees. His hands were shaking as he fumbled with her zip. 'What have you done to her?'

The instructor was speechless with terror. Van Ossen's eyes were bulging out of his crimson face.

'If anything has happened to her . . .'

Anneka started gasping for air and groaning. The instructor could see she was fine, but he didn't dare do or say anything.

'That was your fault,' Anneka finally said as she got her breath back. 'If you'd been watching properly, it wouldn't have happened.'

'I'm so sorry, my baby. I'm so sorry.'

Van Ossen picked up Anneka and cradled her in his arms. Mustang had been caught by the instructor, but van Ossen didn't once glance towards them. He carried Anneka towards the car. She could have perfectly easily walked, but she was enjoying being the priority.

No sooner had van Ossen dropped Anneka at home than he was on his way out again. Anneka promptly burst into tears – her mother's sympathy wasn't anything like as satisfactory as her father's – and only calmed down when van Ossen promised he'd be back within the hour.

When he got to the warehouse, he was still steaming. How close had Anneka come to cracking her head on the wooden poles? Would the crash helmet have saved her? Why had the instructor left the jump in place? Van Ossen felt sick as he mulled over the near miss.

The 'new man' had worked for van Ossen for three months. He wasn't one of the back-door army recruits but a drop-out from the police academy. Right now, he was a mess. His arms and legs were secured to the metal chair he was sitting on by leather straps. His face was swollen from the beating Piek and Fransen had enjoyed handing out.

'Who was he with?' van Ossen asked, expecting the answer to be the police.

'He was in the Dice Club. We watched him with them for a couple of hours.'

For the second time that morning, van Ossen could feel the blood pumping to the back of his head. Anger raged inside him. How had he been taken in?

'Who put you into us?' he asked the terrified traitor. 'Those Dice scum?'

'No one, boss. I was trying to get some information from them.'

That was when van Ossen snapped. This episode had nearly claimed his daughter's life. And someone was going to pay.

'I HAVEN'T GOT TIME FOR THIS. I SHOULD BE WITH MY DAUGHTER. NOT HERE WASTING MY TIME.'

His eyes scanned the room for the metal bolt cutters, his preferred instrument of torture.

The traitor tried to broker a deal. 'I can infiltrate them for you,' he desperately babbled.

One glance at the boss's face and Fransen knew what was coming next. He grabbed the traitor's hand and pulled the thumb out as far as it would go. Van Ossen rammed the blades of the bolt cutter either side of the man's thumb, and slammed them shut with a vengeance.

The ex-police cadet screamed his head off as his thumb was crushed. The bolt cutters failed to cut cleanly, so the severed thumb hung by a thread of skin. Blood spurted across Fransen's face, and then gushed on to the floor. Then the traitor passed out.

'I haven't got time for this,' van Ossen said impatiently. 'Finish it off. Bring him round and cut his fingers off one by one. Let him bleed to death. Then dump him somewhere his friends will find him. Every finger,' van Ossen screamed over his shoulder as he left the warehouse.

Anneka was playing in the garden when he got home. She'd built herself a jumping course using her mother's best cushions. And she was now pretending to jump them on Mustang. The whole lot would have to go to the dry cleaners tomorrow.

'First prize,' announced Wevers van Ossen, striding on to the lawn, 'is a big tub of ice cream.' And he presented Anneka with the chocolate ice cream that he'd bought on the way home.

'What about Mustang?' Anneka demanded. Before he could be chastised again, Wevers dashed back into the kitchen to get some sugar lumps.

Her fall had rattled him. He was going to have to do something about that instructor.

5

Farnborough, Hants
Pete Carr worked out of a discreet industrial unit in Farnborough.
The board listing the companies at the end of the road was full
of electronic and aviation small businesses. But there was a
blank next to Unit 46.

Max knocked and waited. A square of glass set in the door
looked on to a narrow staircase. The place appeared to be
empty. After a couple of minutes, a pair of feet descended the
stairs. The door was unlocked and opened.

'Carr?' said Max.

'Pete, please. Sorry about the delay,' Carr said jovially. 'Only
me here this morning. Stuck on the phone. The boys are
working on a tricky one. Someone's nanny's been a bit naughty.
They're out wiring up the kids' schoolbags.'

Pete Carr didn't mind what sort of business he took on as
long as it paid. He sailed close to the wind. Broke the law,
provided the client made it worth his while. Sometimes it was
surprising who was prepared to sub-contract out illegal jobs.
Governments, lawyers, even the police.

Max smiled. He liked him immediately. Carr was someone
who clearly loved his job.

'Come on through, mate. Coffee? Tea?'

'Tea would be great, Pete. Thanks.'

Max followed him through to the back room. Got him talking.

'Had a close shave yesterday,' said Pete as he made the tea. 'I was bugging a finance director's computer – commissioned by his CEO. Wasn't sure what he was up to. Anyway, bugger me, the bloke walks into his office as I'm halfway through the job.'

'Trouble?'

'Nah. Told him I was working on the IT system. So you're one of Tryon's spooks?'

'Tryon? Never heard of him.'

'Very good.' Pete laughed. 'I'll tell him you said that.'

Max looked around the workshop. It was in stark contrast to the empty appearance of the front of the unit. The place was heaving with stuff.

'How much is this kit worth?'

Pete did a comedy blow through his teeth.

'Probably cost you four hundred grand at today's prices. I've added to it as I've gone from task to task. Reason I get so many jobs is because I have everything here.' Pete pointed around the room. 'Bugging stuff, scanning gear, jammers, mikes, cameras . . . This jammer's worth a few quid,' he said, picking up a small box.

'What would you use that for?'

'I take it on the train. When some twat starts wah-wah-wah-ing it, I jam his phone.' Pete grinned. 'Doing loads of cars at the moment. The thieves have worked out where the manufacturers put the tracking devices, so they have them off and ship the cars over to Qatar before you can blink. They won't find ours though. Only trouble is, most of the time it takes two trips. Nobody's making bumpers out of metal these days, so we have to go round the night before and glue a metal plate inside the bumper. Then we fix the tracking device the next day with magnets. You see, the tracker has got to be able to see the sky.'

Pete would have chatted all day. He liked people. But he could see Max was ticking. 'What can I do you for then, mate?'

'How small a tracker have you got, Pete?'

'What for? A human?'

'A painting.'

'A painting. Hmm. That isn't so easy.'

'And it needs to be hidden.'

'Frame?'

'No,' Max said, shaking his head. 'We don't have access to the frame. Only the canvas and the wooden stretcher.'

'You might be in luck. Got the very latest miniature tracker in, a couple of weeks back.' Pete delved into a drawer, pulled out a few cardboard boxes and then held up something the size of a very thin box of matches.

'How about this?'

Max nodded. He was pretty confident they'd be able to hide it.

'That should be okay.'

'Power, though. That's the problem with trackers. They need power. How often do you need to contact it?'

'What do you mean?'

'Well, if you want a constant signal, the battery will run out very quickly. But if we programme it to give off a signal, say, once every five minutes, the battery will last much longer.'

'Once every hour is more than enough.'

'How about geo-fencing it?'

'What?'

'I can get it to tell you when it's leaving a certain location.'

66

Max thought about that, but it sounded too complicated. 'Once an hour, Pete, that's all I need.'

'Okay. We can turn it off, anyway. Which is not a bad idea. It saves the battery and makes it harder to detect. We'll follow the tracker on the Internet. Through a server based in France. Don't worry, it will have its own account. No one else can see the information.'

'Can you follow it for me?'

'Sure. No problem.'

Nothing was a problem for Pete. Drilling into hotel bedroom walls to place listening probes, installing keyboard loggers into computers, or scanning rooms for listening devices. It all came easy to Pete, as long as he was paid.

Eton

It felt weird, driving under the archway into College Yard. The place hadn't changed much since it was built in the 1400s. Max appreciated it more now than he had done when he'd walked there every day for the best part of four years.

He pictured himself rushing under the arch in his tails and scholar's cape. Terrified of being late for a lesson and placed on Tardy Book. Max Ward: one small insignificant dot in Eton's history. A sometime scholar who'd completely wasted the opportunity to really make something of himself.

He looked at the immaculate lawn – showing the effects of winter now, but he remembered how regimentally striped it always was in the summer. Boys, of course, weren't allowed to walk on it. He was tempted to saunter across it and see if anyone shouted at him.

You can leave Eton, Max mused, but Eton never leaves you: the ethos, the discipline, the respect, the fear of failure – even when you know you've already failed. Ten years on, and he still woke up with issues swirling around his head.

It was the physical aspects of school that he treasured. The smell of the cloisters outside the head master's study. The organ bellowing out bass tones that reverberated through your ribcage. The vast expanse of playing fields sloping down to the Thames. The rowers thrashing up the river. And the mud being ground into your face while you played the Wall Game.

Strange, Max thought, that the situation he was now in was so closely linked to Eton. If it hadn't been for the school, he wouldn't have joined the Office. He wouldn't have been sent to Saudi – and later to Moscow. And he wouldn't be in The Hague now.

Pallesson cast a shadow over everything, but the endgame was fast approaching and only one of them was going to come out of this in one piece.

Max checked his watch. He was quarter of an hour early, and he knew that if anything annoyed M. J. Keate more than a boy being late, it was a boy that was early.

Max wondered if the other beaks at Eton realised what a dark horse Keate was. On the surface, a slightly bumbling tutor. But underneath, a covert, active spy. Max knew that Keate was always economical as to the extent of his work with Tryon. But he assumed it was more than he let on.

He walked round the corner, past the school office into the cloister below Upper School. To a passing tourist, the notice-boards stuck on the stone pillars were random information. To Max, the team sheets posted on them had meant the difference between exhilaration and utter depression. He remembered the day he'd walked up to see who else had been picked to play in the first eleven football team, assuming that he was a certainty. But his name hadn't been on the sheet. Max felt sick even thinking about it now. He walked on through School Yard, past the Founder's statue into the inner cloister. The last time he'd been here was when he was expelled.

In four years, he'd never taken in the spirit and tranquillity of this quadrangle. Jutting out from the walls were memorials to fallen Old Boys in both wars, dedicated by their mothers and sisters.

For Valour, one large slab of marble read. King Edward VII was quoted: *In their lives . . . they maintained the traditions that have made Eton renowned.*

The last Old Etonian, of many, to be awarded the VC caught Max's eye.

1982 VC Lt Col H Jones Parachute Regiment

'Colonel H – Falkland Islands,' Max said out loud. He could remember being captivated by this charismatic soldier who led from the front and died in front of his men. Then he realized that time was running away from him and he was going to be late.

The gate at the foot of Keate's garden path still made a nasty squeak. Max remembered suggesting that a bit of oil would do the trick. 'It's the noisy gate that gets the oil,' Keate had chuckled to himself. 'But still, don't you dare. How else am I to know when someone's coming?'

As Max walked up the path he knew Keate would be watching from the big Georgian study window. He didn't look up though. If he waved, his old tutor wouldn't wave back. And then he'd feel like a small, insecure boy. Or that was how he'd always felt in the past – at least, until he'd learnt not to look up.

Max knew the door wouldn't be locked. It never was. He pushed it open and walked into the familiar hallway, which was clad with oak panels. How often had he stood in here, waiting for Keate to finish tutoring other boys? A hundred times probably, but only one day really stuck in his memory.

He remembered being taken aback when Keate had apologized for keeping him waiting. It was so out of character; the old boy never did that. And there'd been a sudden awkwardness about him.

'It's about your father, Ward,' Keate had mumbled. 'Not good news, I'm afraid.' Then Keate had paused, as if he couldn't get the words out. The delay only lasted for a second, but it felt to Max like an eternity. He remembered being frozen to his chair. Paralysed by whatever it was that Keate couldn't say. 'I'm afraid he's dead. Terrible shock. Dreadful.'

Max hadn't taken much else in at the time. Keate had spared him the details.

Trying to shake off the memory, he paused to look at the frieze on the wall opposite Keate's study. He hadn't seen it before.

'Interesting, isn't it?' Keate said over his shoulder. 'Some jacques took the oak panelling down to get at the pipes and found it underneath. Dates back to the sixteen hundreds. English Heritage went mad – told us we can't smoke near it. Come on in.'

Max followed his tutor into a large, bright study.

'Help yourself, old lad,' Keate said breezily, as if they'd already talked at length that day. Max was used to his dismissive familiarity. He'd always been like that. Never one to make a fuss about a departure or a return. Even if they were divided by years. It was probably his way of dealing with being so close to his protégés one minute, and seeing them gone the next.

Keate beckoned towards his drinks cupboard in the corner of the room. For the first time, Max really took in the magnificence of the piece. The arched scallop frieze, the carved shell and Vitruvian scroll, the big heavy doors.

'Beautiful cupboard, Keate,' he remarked.

'What's the matter with you? Been there for years. My aunt Mary gave it to me, bless her. George II. Mahogany. Hopefully she'll leave me her flat in Sloane Avenue, too. Cranmer Court. Rather nice block. Amazing old girl. Still does *The Times* crossword every day and rants about split infinitives. But there you go. I'm rambling. Are you in love? Old boys always come and see me when they're in love. God knows why.'

Max wasn't really listening to him. He stood with his back to Keate, studying the painting hanging behind the desk. The old man had always been blasé about it, as if embarrassed that he knew so much about the Flemish and Dutch masters. This 'very poor example' of Jan Asselijn's work, he would say dismissively, was all he could afford.

But like all the great tutors, Keate had instilled his pupils with an everlasting interest in the subject that was his passion. Max remembered him taking a few of them to Windsor Castle to study Hendrick Avercamp's paintings. Pallesson had been forensically attentive and ingratiatingly unctuous on that visit. As ever, he had to appear the most interested and enlightened.

'Well, I might be,' Max mumbled. 'But that isn't why I've come to see you.'

Max still had his back to Keate while he poured himself a weak glass of Islay whisky and water. It was at Eton that he'd been introduced to the peaty taste, drinking with a boy in his house whose father owned one of the distilleries on the island.

Keate watched him, remembering the boy he had once been. When his father's accountants sifted through the wreckage after his death, they had found the coffers were empty. Keate, loath to see natural talent go to waste, had been prepared to make up the shortfall. But Max got himself kicked out. Keate had felt disappointed rather than let down. Nevertheless it had created a hiatus in their relationship.

Max sat down and faced his old tutor as he fiddled with some papers on his cluttered desk.

'Why did the Office take me on, Keate?'

Keate took his glasses off and looked up at Max. 'Why? Probably because no one else would have had you. You weren't exactly flavour of the month on your departure from this establishment.'

'That isn't an answer, and you know it,' Max replied impassively.

Keate couldn't follow his drift. Why the sudden desire to go over old ground? He assumed his former student wasn't looking for affirmation that he was a brilliant linguist – the best he had ever come across – or that he possessed an equally remarkable talent for lateral thought. Those were the skills he had used to sell Max Ward to Tryon, and they were hardly a secret.

But those weren't the talents that had made him beseech Tryon to take Max on. Keate had an almost religious belief in the Instructions of Amenemopa, the great Egyptian leader. And in all his years he had never come across a boy in whom he had such faith to promote Maat – a world of truth and order. In Max, Keate saw the silent man: calm and self-effacing, knowledgeable, thoughtful and temperate. He saw someone who could make a difference.

The great irony – although Keate often wondered if it hadn't been more than a coincidence – was that an incarnation of Isfet had come along at exactly the same time. Isfet being the tendency of men towards evil, injustice, discord and chaos. Pallesson, Keate had come to realize, was one of its princes.

'What's this all about, Max?'

'Can I trust Tryon?' Max asked bluntly, feeling no need to qualify his question.

Keate stood up from behind his desk and wandered towards a table crammed with lead toy soldiers. Their red-and-blue Napoleonic tunics were intricately painted. He picked one up, studied it carefully, then put it down again.

'Can you trust Tryon?' Keate repeated. 'Well, I suppose that depends on whether you can trust me. And that in turn depends on whether you are helping or hindering.' He paused to fiddle with his glasses and reflect. 'I asked Tryon to see you were hired because I knew you had a talent that would be of use. A rare talent, if channelled in the right direction. More importantly, I felt that the Office would force you to develop the one thing you lacked: patience.'

Keate paused again and looked out of the window. Max followed his gaze. A couple of boys meandered out of the college entrance bouncing a football between them. Max recognized their long, woollen socks. The association football colours. For a second he felt jealous. Jealous of the expectation that he'd always felt before any game.

'You were different. You were also a risk. I asked them to take you much younger than they normally would have done. I told Tryon you might fall between the cracks if they waited. That was why they parked you in Oman. To see if you would learn. I couldn't explain that at the time; it would have upset the delicate flow of the process. But obviously they were pleased, otherwise you wouldn't have been moved to Moscow.'

Max still said nothing. He'd come to listen. He took a long sip of his Scotch and water.

'In your game, life is rarely simple. To fight for good, sometimes you have to collaborate with undesirable people to get the end result. Although I don't know any details, there may be times when you won't understand the big picture. But what you must have is faith. You should have faith in Tryon, Max. Make friends with the just and righteous man whose actions you have observed. Remember Ani, Max?'

Max nodded and put his glass on the small table next to his right arm. 'Well, Keate, I hope you're right,' he said hesitantly.

*   *   *

The dining room was small, compared to the generous space of Keate's study. The housekeeper had cooked them a fish pie, peas and cabbage. Neither of them said anything until they'd helped themselves and sat down. Max was the first to speak.

'Wherever I go, I run into Pallesson. He arrived in Moscow, quite the little star from Cambridge. And he was very successful. Too successful. Did you recommend Pallesson as well?'

Keate finished his mouthful of fish pie. 'It's a complicated system. It's not as simple as that.'

'Bollocks. Did you underwrite him or not?'

Keate carried on eating his lunch. Max said nothing. He wanted an answer. For nearly five minutes neither of them said a word. Keate finished his fish pie, then ate the last pea on his plate. Finally he put down his knife and fork and gave Max a long look. Max didn't meet his eye.

'I was compromised,' Keate said.

'What do you mean, you were compromised? Compromised by whom? How?'

Keate really didn't want to answer. He had never discussed the matter with anyone, had never intended to. He subtly shifted the conversation back on to Max. 'Is it wise to be in conflict with Pallesson? You know how dangerous, how destructive he is. Keep your distance from those with hate in their hearts.'

'Ankh-Sheshonk,' Max observed.

'Well, there's nothing wrong with your memory.'

Max wanted to tell Keate what he knew. That Pallesson, one of his recommendations, had executed Corbett in cold blood. But he knew that would be crossing the line.

'What do you mean by "compromised", Keate?' Max persisted.

Keate removed his glasses and rubbed his eyes, not for one moment diverting his gaze from the dark-brown polished table. 'He drugged me. He came round to see me one evening about some essay. I remember feeling very strange drinking my sherry as I went through it with him. I remember feeling dizzy. Then nothing. When I woke, I was on the floor . . .' Keate's voice tapered off. 'I'm not gay, Max. Never have been. In fact, I've never been interested in sex at all. That's the way I am. But that little bastard threatened to disgrace and humiliate me. Ruin my life. Yes, to answer your question, I pulled strings to get him into St John's. Then when he graduated I had Tryon pull strings to get him hired by the Office. It's as if he had the whole thing mapped out from the very beginning.'

Max was stunned into momentary silence. He was horrified. Horrified that it had happened, and horrified that he had dragged it out of Keate in such an inconsiderate manner.

'Keate, it isn't your fault.' Max hated himself. He realized that he'd stumbled on something much worse than he ever could have guessed.

'Yes, it is. I didn't stand up to him. You did. He didn't screw *you* over. You threw it all away rather than be under his thumb for evermore. But I didn't. I couldn't.' Anger was now boiling inside the usually unflappable tutor.

'There's something else I need to know, Keate,' Max said quietly. 'Could he have compromised Tryon?'

6

Max felt slightly morose. The contrast between flying in Gemma's jet to Nice a couple of days before and making the same journey crammed into a commercial plane on his own wasn't doing much for his spirits.

He buckled his seat belt and established squatting rights on the armrest with his elbow. How they got away with calling such tiny seats 'club class', he had no idea. He shut his eyes to avoid any contact with the girl sitting next to him. He hadn't even noticed whether she was pretty or not.

It wasn't long before his nemesis crept into his thoughts. Vivid images of Pallesson were haunting him: laying out his evidence on a drug op before his station chief in Moscow, smugness personified; and worse still, the memory of him obliterating Corbett's head. Then the possibility that he had got Corbett killed by stumbling in on the party.

'Bastard,' Max said, not quite under his breath. He opened his eyes and glanced at the girl to his left, who was regarding him with a slightly perplexed look on her face. She was reading one of those crap magazines that girls of her age always read on planes.

As it turned out, Max thought she was cute. He didn't generally find girls with short hair sexy. It made them look too boyish, in his book. What would Gemma say if he ran off with this girl, he wondered? Would she be happy for him? Or would she be furious? Of course he couldn't be with anyone who read that rubbish. What would they talk about?

'How can you read that crap?' he asked, glancing towards the girl.

'Probably because I'm the editor,' she replied caustically.

'Dinner tonight?' he asked, on the basis that it was better to make a bad impression than none at all.

'I'd rather starve to death,' she replied, without looking up from her magazine.

Max shut his eyes. And kept them shut.

Max turned off the road to Saint-Tropez and pointed the Mercedes Sport up the hill towards Gassin. He'd memorized the route and deleted the email from the anonymous account, just as Tryon had instructed. The road to the village was a succession of tight switchback bends. Max gave the car its head and let it rip past a few other drivers before breaking late into the next turn. He loved the growl of the car's engine and the smoothness of its steering.

He was a child behind the wheel.

Max took the west road in front of the caserne de pompiers out of Gassin. After half a mile he saw the steep lane to the left. Tryon had described it perfectly. He eased the car carefully down the slope, waiting for the front to scrape on the stones. After a hundred metres he came to some solid-looking wooden gates. He pressed the intercom button.

''Allo,' said a soft, French voice.

'Sophie?'

'*Oui.*'

Max switched to English, effortlessly feigning the hesitation and embarrassment of a tourist – a skill at which he excelled in at least twenty different languages. A skill, because in truth Max spoke every one of them perfectly.

'Sophie? It's Max. I met your father two days ago.'

'What are you doing here?'

'Well, if you'd let me in, I can explain. We need to change something.'

Sophie was extremely reluctant, and insisted that she get her father.

Once he'd finally talked his way in, Max threw his jacket over his shoulder and walked casually down the wide steps to the front door of the old French *mas*. The garden was waiting for spring to arrive, but he could imagine how beautiful the lavender bushes either side of the steps would be.

The heavy wooden doors at the bottom opened slowly. But it was Jacques, not Sophie, who stood between them.

'Slight change of plan,' Max said breezily. 'Nothing to worry about.'

'No one told us,' Jacques replied grumpily.

'Best not to talk about this sort of thing on the telephone, don't you think?' Max was civil, but firm. His body language made it quite clear to Jacques that there was no room for negotiation.

'Well, the painting is not finished.'

'No. I didn't suppose it would be. But at least I'll be here when it is. In the meantime, we have another small issue. This tracker . . .' Max fished the small device out of his pocket and laid it on the palm of his left hand. 'We have to hide it somehow.'

Before Jacques could give his opinion on the possibility of doing so, Sophie arrived in the hall. Max assumed she was Sophie, anyway. His stomach tightened as he looked at her a little too deliberately. She had extraordinary dark-green eyes and soft olive skin that he immediately wanted to touch. Her glistening, silky brown hair fell off her shoulders. Her beauty radiated from her like an aura.

Sophie was not impressed. She launched into an agitated exchange with her father in mumbled French. Max looked at them blankly, understanding every word. Finally she turned on him.

'What are you doing here? You are not supposed to come here. You were meant to meet my father in Monte Carlo.'

Max was impressed with her perfect English. He tried to think of some charming, witty reply. But all thought failed him.

'Sorry about that. Slight change of plan. If we're to help you, I need to leave with the painting as soon as possible.'

'So you just invited yourself?'

'Not quite. I was told to come here straight away. We are fighting the same enemy, by the way.' Sophie didn't reply. 'And in case you've forgotten, I seem to remember you are the ones with the problem, not me.'

Max guessed she'd been painting when he arrived. She was wearing baggy jeans with paint on them, a blue T-shirt, and not much else as far as he could see. She turned on her heel and left Jacques and Max alone.

'Probably not a good moment to tell her about the tracker,' Max remarked.

'No,' agreed Jacques. 'Perhaps a glass of wine?'

As he led the way through the lounge, Jacques knocked into a large terracotta pot, which stood at one end of a long sofa. He shook his head, swearing under his breath, and rubbed his leg gingerly. The old man's sight was obviously becoming a problem even in his own home.

Max wondered how his father would have aged. He just couldn't imagine him as an old man. He wondered if he would ever have given up taking risks and settled down to a quiet retirement.

'Jacques, do you ever gamble?'

'That is a strange question. Why do you ask?'

'Just wondering. My father loved it.'

'I used to go to the hippodrome at Cagnes-Sur-Mer. We used to bet on the trotting horses mainly. I'm sure it was fixed. I thought I'd backed the winner one day, and right before the line, it cantered! Placed last. But we did back a few winners too . . .'

After an hour or so, Jacques and Max went through to the studio. Sophie had in fact made good progress. She was a quick, instinctive painter. She'd settled back into working mode, which in her case had to be serene, or she couldn't paint. So it was a much less bad-tempered Sophie that Max now stood in front of.

'May I?' he asked, arching his neck in order to see the front of the canvas. She answered with a nod of her head.

'Amazing,' was all Max said when he saw her second copy of *The Peasants in Winter* taking shape. 'Truly amazing.'

Max had admired the original painting in the embassy at close quarters a couple of times. What he was now looking at appeared distinctly younger, but the detail was uncannily similar.

The scene depicted in the painting was dominated by figures skating on a frozen river. Some appeared to be playing ice hockey, others were huddled into groups. Dogs and small children were aimlessly amusing themselves on the bank of the river as a large cart bearing firewood made its way past them. In the background, the snow-covered steeple of the church stood tall amongst the houses.

Sophie had captured the actual cold of winter. And caught

the contrast of the bleak winter landscape interjected with cosy little snow-clad houses, puffing out smoke from their fires. In their winter pursuits the peasants seemed carefree; materially poor, but happy.

Most importantly for the job in hand, Sophie's style and technique were as if Brueghel had taught her himself. His deft brushstrokes and intricacies radiated off the canvas.

'Thank you,' she replied. 'It's easier the second time. But there's still a lot to do. I half heard what you said to my father. You have a tracking device?'

Max pulled it out of his pocket. She pursed her lips when she saw it.

'We should have dealt with this first,' she said almost desperately. 'If it has to go in the wooden canvas stretcher, we might damage the painting.'

'Sorry about that. Clearly, someone didn't think it through. Is it possible?'

Sophie arched her eyebrows and scrunched up her mouth as she regarded the canvas.

'No. Clearly someone *didn't* think it through.' She ran her hand along the stretcher. 'Is it possible? To a point. It would be better to cut out a piece of the main frame.'

'I don't doubt that. But the frame happens to be in the British Embassy in The Hague around the original. And we are here. So it will have to be hidden in the canvas stretcher.'

Sophie gave him a sarcastic look and was then silent for a while. Max shut up and tried to concentrate on the painting, not her. Which was difficult.

He went round to the back of the canvas and measured with his finger the thickness of the wood holding it taut. It was thick enough, if Sophie had the skill, the tools and the inclination to do it.

'I'll finish the painting first. Then we'll see,' she conceded.

Max stood looking at the painting and thinking.

'What?' Sophie asked. 'You're irritating me.'

He paused, and then spat it out.

'How will I know the difference between my copy and Pallesson's? And, for that matter, how will I know the original? Can you make a deliberate mistake that won't be obvious?'

She looked at him with pursed lips again.

'Of course.'

'So will you leave something out?'

'No. Someone will always notice something that isn't there but should be. They're much less likely to see something that is there that shouldn't be. Because they're not looking for it.'

'Psychologist as well as artist. And devious too. Very dangerous. So, Madame Freud, what did you add to Pallesson's copy?'

Sophie pointed to a group of children on the ice.

'He has a small dog in the middle of that group. It's a million to one shot that anyone would notice.'

'Does he know that?'

'Of course not. Why should he?'

'Just wondering. You might as well tell me what you're adding to mine, or we'll be here all day.'

Sophie pointed to a tree on the right of the picture. Max looked at the image of the original she was working from and the copy. He couldn't see the difference.

'Go on. Stop teasing me. Put me out of my misery.'

Sophie was delighted he couldn't see her change. It proved her point.

'Extra bird,' she said with satisfaction, pointing it out with her paintbrush.

Max drove down to Saint-Tropez for the afternoon to pass the time. After a moment's hesitation, Jacques declined to accompany him, claiming that he was tired. The town was very quiet at that time of the year. Max looked at a couple of galleries, but he soon got bored.

As he wandered into the harbour, his eyes alighted on the blue awnings of the Hotel Sube. The thought of the maritime bar on the first floor, overlooking the waterfront, proved an irresistible lure. He decided to stop by for a quick one.

The bar was even quieter than the rest of the town. An unmistakably French woman was feeding her poodle biscuits whilst she fussed with a pot of coffee. Which left the barman all to Max.

'Quiet?' Max asked after he ordered a lager. The barman nodded.

'Any lively boats?' The barman shook his head.

Max was about to give him up for a bad job and admire the view of the harbour instead, when the barman rallied.

'There's a lunatic in the Hotel Byblos. Russian. Walks like a cripple, but that doesn't stop the women. All over him.'

'No boat?'

'No. They've taken over half the hotel. Up all night in Les Caves. And asleep all day. Spending a fortune.'

Max's ears pricked up at the barman's 'walks like a cripple' description.

'Any idea who the Russian is?' he asked casually.

'He walks like someone had a go at removing his legs. Never goes anywhere without the freak by his side – now that is one scary bastard! Someone must have scalped him, left him with this big revolting scar. Revolting people. You should see the way Mr Big sits at a table with his mother, his children, his wife, his mistress and any other girl he's having at that moment. They're animals.'

Max wasn't taking in the domestic sexual arrangements. So Kroshtov and Oleg were in town. That seemed a bit too much of a coincidence. His mind flashed back to the concrete dacha in the woods outside Moscow. He'd managed to identify the mafia boss after the event, but he hadn't dared dig too deep or go anywhere near Kroshtov's operation for fear that Pallesson would learn of his interest. Why was Kroshtov here now? To meet up with Pallesson? Was he about to broker another deal with the Russians and the mystery man in the plane?

Having extracted everything he could from the barman and his beer glass, Max went for a walk. Hugging the coastline, he walked to Pampelonne beach. He barely saw a soul. The beach was deserted. He walked up the sand as far as Cinquante Cinq, which was firmly boarded up. He thought of the times he and Gemma had drifted on to the beach after a long lunch and been ferried back out on to a yacht to drink the rest of the afternoon away. It was probably the happiest he and Gemma had been. But only ghosts were on the beach now.

Sophie was sitting on the veranda when Max got back, drinking a large glass of white wine. She offered him some. He didn't particularly like white wine, but he didn't want to pass up the chance of talking to her.

'My father has gone out to play bridge with some friends. It's the only thing he'll leave the house for these days. To be honest, I was surprised he agreed to go to Monte Carlo to meet you. Thank God for bridge. They take it far too seriously.'

'Would those be the friends who know Tryon? The ones who followed me in Monaco?'

Sophie shrugged her shoulders and smiled. She obviously wasn't going to admit to anything of the sort. 'Do you play?'

'A little. But it's not my idea of how to relax after dinner. And you?'

'I was brought up with it. No choice. In the winter here we

sometimes play all afternoon. My mother was the best. She taught me when I was very young.'

'Including English?'

'Absolutely – while I was still very young.'

'Lucky you. My mother taught me nothing. Except . . .' He was silent for a moment. Then he summoned the brightest smile he could. 'Can I buy you dinner tonight? Anywhere you like. In the village here? Saint-Tropez?'

'I have so much to do, really.'

'You still have to eat. You need a break at some point. Go on.'

'Really, it is very kind of you but—'

'I'm not going to take no for an answer,' Max interrupted. 'I don't bite. Besides, we have a common enemy. He might be trying to bugger your life up, but he's already screwed up mine.'

A questioning look flashed across Sophie's face. Max had said exactly the right thing.

7

Gassin

The café in the square at Gassin was by no means a gastronomic utopia, but it was quiet and cosy. Max and Sophie walked up the steep drive, then followed the road into the square. There were no old men playing boules on the sand in the middle of the square, no tables and chairs on the pavements. Gassin in early spring was asleep.

Max ordered a bottle of Domaine Ott.

'The Bandol Ott, I'm pleased to see,' he said a little too smoothly. 'So much better than the Côtes de Provence, don't you think?'

'Don't give me that,' Sophie said. 'I've drunk both all my life. If I blindfolded you, you wouldn't know the difference.'

'Well, you're welcome to blindfold me.'

'Yeah, right.'

'That's not a very French expression. Where did you pick that up?'

'I'm not a very French girl. Tell me about Pallesson. How did he screw up your life?'

'It's a long, awful story.'

'Do you mind telling me?'

Max had never wanted to tell anyone. But she was different, somehow. Maybe he needed to tell her, to protect her? To make her realize what an evil bastard she'd got mixed up with.

'We were at school together. He was a manipulative creep. Always manoeuvring for influence. Like a power-crazy politician. His every move was either stitching someone up, or compromising them. So he could use them. Once he had something on whoever was his target, he'd blackmail them.'

'Did he blackmail you?'

'No. But he tried to. He discovered that I was running a gambling syndicate. Rather a successful one, too. My father was a bookmaker, so I'm good at that sort of thing. Pallesson wanted a cut. I stalled him for a bit, pretending to think about it, and then told him to go fuck himself. I went to the head master's office and busted myself.'

'Admitted everything?'

'I had to. Or he would have manipulated me. You should have seen the look on the head master's face. He practically tried to stop me telling him.'

'What happened?'

'I got kicked out,' Max replied in a slightly less euphoric voice. 'All those school fees wasted. No chance of going to university. The end of my world. Except that I wasn't compromised – unlike everyone else he had wrapped around his little finger.'

'Your family must have been furious.'

Max hesitated. Then he took the plunge.

'It gets worse. Much worse. He targeted my father.'

'How?'

'While I was stalling him, he opened an account with my father under a bogus name. He sucked my father in by losing like a mug punter, all the while gradually increasing his stakes. When the bets got too big, Dad should have laid off the risk;

but he thought his new client was such an idiot he stood all the bets. And then Pallesson hit him with the sucker punch and cleaned him out.'

'He bankrupted your father?'

'Worse. He killed him – as good as. My mother walked out as soon as the business folded, then Dad committed suicide.'

Sophie was horrified. She hadn't intended the conversation to go so deep.

'I'm so sorry. That's terrible. I didn't mean to . . .'

'He was a wonderful man. We used to have such fun in the betting shop together. Unfortunately he never really understood probability and risk.'

'I'm sorry . . .'

'It's okay. I don't really talk about it. But I wanted you to know what sort of person you're dealing with.'

'That's terrible.'

'Shit happens. Life goes on though. My tutor persuaded the Office to hire me.'

'The Office?' Sophie asked, relieved to move the conversation on.

'Sorry. The secret service. We call it "the Office". Obviously, we don't go around telling people we work for the service. I guess you already had some idea how I earn a crust.'

'You must have been very young.'

'They took me and buried me abroad while Pallesson marched on. He's a bastard, Sophie. The Devil incarnate. He drugged his housemaster and slept with him so that he could blackmail the guy. The housemaster had a mental breakdown. It's pretty disgusting really.'

'He sounds like a total sadist. Why didn't someone bust him?'

'I doubt there was anyone in a position to do so who wasn't compromised. Even our poor tutor. He couldn't bring himself to tell me exactly what Pallesson had done to him, but he was forced to use all of his influence to make sure the bastard got into Cambridge, and later the Office.'

Sophie could see that Max was becoming agitated.

'I don't blame you for being angry about it.'

'I'm sorry.'

'Don't be. You should be angry.' She made full eye contact with Max. He broke it first and looked down at the menu. He didn't want her to see any more emotion welling up inside him.

After the waiter had taken their order, Max grasped the nettle with Sophie.

'What, if you don't mind telling me, is your situation with Pallesson? How far has it gone?'

'Papa has copied six paintings for him. Always valuable works, obviously.'

'Why?'

'Pallesson rumbled a forgery Papa had done. Some mistake with the provenance. He blackmailed Papa to do the copying, but he was struggling with his eyesight. So I helped him. He didn't want me to get involved, but I couldn't sit back and watch him struggle.'

'And Pallesson fingered you, too.'

'Yes. He figured out that Papa's eyesight was gone. He tricked him somehow.'

'Not difficult. I'm amazed he can still play bridge.'

'Only just.'

'So how deep in are you?'

'*The Peasants in Winter* is the third copy I've helped with. But he's never going to stop. He knows he can wreck my career.'

Sophie took another swig of her wine and made eye contact with Max again.

'Please don't think badly of Papa. His family were incredibly poor. When Van Meegeren offered to take him under his wing, teach him everything, Papa had no other choice. He has done nothing that any other human being wouldn't have done in those circumstances.'

'We kill people, Sophie. I'm not going to judge your father. Did Pallesson ever come to Gassin – to your house?'

'Yes. Twice. He delivered the first painting Papa copied for him. An Avercamp. And he came back to collect them. Is that a problem?'

'Hopefully not,' Max replied, without much conviction.

Max thought about putting his arm around her on their way back from the restaurant. Then thought better of it.

'Tell me about your mother, Sophie,' Max asked as they walked out of the square.

She thought for a few seconds before answering.

'It was always just my mother and I, going off on our own to do things, even going away on holidays, while Papa spent hours in his studio. In the end she got sick of his detachment. Or maybe she was sick of always having to be there for me. I couldn't stop crying when she left. She said I'd live with her as soon as she sorted everything out, but she never did.'

'Where did she go?'

'Not far. Only a couple of villages away, in fact. I think that's why Papa never really went out after that. Unless he knew exactly where he was going and was sure he wouldn't see her. It was a kind of torture. I was aware she was close, but I didn't see her that often.'

'That's terrible. Why?'

'It was the man she ran off with. He had his own children and he didn't want me. My mother kept promising to sort it out. In the meantime, I looked after my father. Even though we hardly knew each other at that point.'

'How old were you?'

'Six.'

'A very old six-year-old.'

'And I suppose not a very happy one. Papa never prevented me having friends, but I knew he wasn't comfortable if I invited them over. So they soon stopped inviting me.'

'I don't know what would have been worse,' Max said. 'Having my mother round the corner with her lover, or her disappearing forever.'

'Her lover?'

'Well, she did the same thing as yours.'

'What?'

'Yup. She blamed her departure on the "shame" of dad losing all his money, but it was an excuse to run off with the only straight hairdresser in Warrington. I didn't realize it at the time – she was my mother, after all – but she was only content with my father as long as he was making loads of money and she could spend it. As soon as things went wrong for my dad, she was off. Went to Spain and never came back. At the time it felt like she'd abandoned me – which she had – but maybe that was better than what you went through.'

Sophie knew she should be feeling bad for Max. Yet he seemed quite philosophical about it. And she was relieved to be able to talk to someone who'd been through something similar.

'Oh, Max, who looked after you? Surely your mother came back for you?'

'She didn't even come back for Dad's funeral. I haven't seen her since the day she left. I'd like to think it was guilt that kept her away, but I don't know. Everything was always about her. Even me going to Eton was about her. God, I bet she bored

91

the pants off everyone at her coffee mornings, telling them about that.'

Sophie pushed the code into the gate security system, and the gates swung open in a ghostly silence.

'She was a snob? Your mother.'

'Of the worst kind. And the irony – the real irony . . .'

Max had to pause. He wasn't going to let tears roll out of his eyes.

'The friends I had at Eton were so kind to me. Half-term, school holidays. One of them always had me to stay. But she loved them for all the wrong reasons.'

Sophie could see that talking about his mother was upsetting Max. She changed the subject.

'Gassin, as you can see, is very quiet – apart from the tourists, who don't count. My life was with my mother. And then my father.'

'What about schoolfriends?'

Sophie shook her head.

'My father said my mother could teach me better than any school. Then, when she went, he said that all I needed to know was how to paint, and he'd teach me.'

'So you never had friends of your own age?'

'Not really,' Sophie said, as if embarrassed and ashamed.

When they reached the front door, Sophie had to fiddle around inside her bag for the keys. She could feel Max standing close to her. A little too close. She'd heard the emotion in his voice while he'd been talking about his father. And she was suddenly nervous he'd get 'emotional' with her. But to her relief he didn't 'jump on her' as she put the keys in the locks.

'Sorry about this,' she apologized as she undid the third lock. 'Papa is so security conscious.'

'This place still isn't secure, Sophie. We need to talk to your father tomorrow. It isn't safe for you both to stay here for the next few weeks. Until we've brought down Pallesson.'

'We'll never get Papa to move.'

'We have to.'

Sophie knew she had to make her excuses and get off to bed. She didn't want to sit up all night talking. And she certainly didn't want to give the impression that she was up for anything else.

'Thank you for dinner,' she said quickly.

'Nightcap?'

'Not for me. Please, help yourself. I have an early start.'

Sophie leant forward and gave him a sisterly peck on the cheek. He made no effort to turn it into anything else.

Max wandered over to Jacques's drinks tray and poured himself a rejected man's measure of whisky and sunk into the most comfortable-looking chair in the room. A wry smile spread across his face.

'Rome wasn't built in a day,' he toasted to himself, and took a glug of the Scotch.

Sophie slid the bolt across her bedroom door and told herself that she'd done the right thing as she slid into bed naked. And then she couldn't sleep.

She thought about the half-truth that she'd told Max, about not really having any friends of her own age, and forgave herself.

It had been a painful episode. When she was eighteen she'd fallen madly in love with a boy from Saint-Tropez who worked on the yachts. He'd seemed very glamorous. Much more sophisticated than her. But she'd thought he was in love with her, too.

By the end of the summer he was pressurizing her. He wanted to sleep with her. She hadn't been ready. She kept telling him that they had the rest of their lives to do that. He kept telling her that she'd do it if she really loved him. And then they'd split up.

Less than two weeks later, he'd found someone else who would sleep with him. Sophie's best friend.

She put the past out of her mind and let it run away with thoughts of Max. But she was being ridiculous. He was a secret agent. He probably had a woman in every country. And yet, now that she was in the safety of her bedroom, she rather wished he had shown some physical interest in her.

Max poured himself the other half. He wondered where Gemma was. Probably at the charity opening of some ludicrous new restaurant, swirling around with her vacuous girlfriends looking expensively glamorous.

And then he thought about Sophie, again. He needed to be careful. Distractions were dangerous in his business.

8

Gassin

Max rose early the next morning. Sophie was nowhere to be seen inside the house. He went up the steps outside the front door and walked through the lavender bushes to her studio. He gave a gentle tap on the door and pushed it open. The canvas wasn't on its easel. Sophie was leaning over a workbench. *The Peasants in Winter* was suspended in mid-air by four clamps.

'I could kill you,' she said without looking up. 'It's a nightmare cutting the wood away without smudging the paint. Luckily I have these clamps. Anyway, I think this should do it.'

Sophie had cut a hole big enough to put the tracker and its battery inside. She'd used a tiny rotary blade that could make very precise incisions.

'Where did you get that?' Max asked.

'It's for carving. Happy?'

'Very.'

'Sure?'

'Yes. Sure. But won't it be obvious where you've cut the wood?'

Sophie gave him a withering look and carried on with her work.

'Won't they X-ray the painting?' Sophie asked without looking up.

'Don't know, to be honest. If they do, they'll see the tracker. There's too much I don't know, in fact.' After a few minutes, Max couldn't wait any longer. 'Is . . . is the painting finished?' he asked, aware that he was treading on eggshells.

'Yes. Don't worry. You'll be away soon. All I have to do now is paint over the wood and put it in the oven. I put the last layer of varnish on this morning.'

'The last thing I want to do is leave, actually. But—'

'You'll be away this afternoon,' she cut in.

Max was picking up on something in Sophie's attitude, but he couldn't put his finger on it. Maybe she was just pissed off about the tracker.

Eventually, Sophie turned the canvas over and put it on an easel.

'*Voilà*,' she announced. It was perfect.

'You're a genius. I don't know how you've done that so quickly.'

It was a rhetorical question, but she seemed keen to tell him.

'You have to start with a canvas of the right age. That's the first thing they test. The canvas you gave my father was circa 1600. Don't suppose whoever painted it would thank you. It was rather good, as it happens.'

'How did you get the paint off?'

'It flakes off quite easily. Don't ever believe a movie that shows someone folding or rolling up a painting. It would be a disaster.' She shuddered at the thought. 'Then you have to use the right pigments. We were short of a few, that's why we asked you to bring some to your first meeting with Papa from Cornelissen.'

'What an amazing shop that is. Like going back a hundred years. There were some very strange-looking customers in there.'

'They're called artists. They go there because Cornelissen's have the old pigments: Alizarine Carmine, Phthalo Green, Raw Sienna, Yellow Ochre, Antwerp Blue.'

'And they keep the paint in rows of big glass jars.'

'Pigments, Max. But there is one colour that is most important to fool the experts. Which you can't get at Cornelissen's, by the way. It's a yellow paint that used to be made in India from the urine of cows fed only on mangoes. This paint was banned in the 1700s. So any picture containing that paint is presumed by fools to pre-date that time. Papa still has his own supply. A farmer near Avignon has one cow he only feeds on mangoes.' A little smile crept across her face. 'If you asked for it in Cornelissen's they'd probably have you arrested.'

Knowing that it might prove important further down the line, Max was trying to concentrate on what Sophie was saying. It wasn't easy. Her T-shirt was very loose around the tops of her arms. But every time he moved imperceptibly to a more illicit angle she seemed to move too.

'Will you paint a picture of your own for me?'

'No. You're not listening. I'm trying to teach you,' she said dismissively.

Max couldn't tell whether she was being cold or professional.

'We have to be careful about the ageing process,' she continued. 'The smell, for instance. Old paintings don't smell, new ones do. So we use poppyseed oil rather than linseed oil. For the ageing, we add formaldehyde to the paint. And for a Brueghel finish I add some larch turpentine.'

'Very devious.'

'And old paint is very hard. Fortunately, Van Meegeren taught Papa a way of dealing with that. We add Bakelite.'

'Of course. Just what Mr Bakelite had in mind when he was in his laboratory.'

Max was trying to thaw Sophie. But she was oblivious.

'I'm still worried.'

'About what?'

'The smell. Normally I would wrap a painting in muslin and bury it in earth for a week. That's the best way to draw the smell out. The poppyseed will help, but it's still a risk. There will be a very faint smell for a while if someone is looking for it.'

'Well, it's a risk we'll have to take. How do you make it crack?'

'The bottom layer of varnish is oil based, and the top layer is water based. They dry at different speeds.'

'Amazing,' Max said, pulling his concentration together and beginning to enjoy his lesson. Even if he was still trying to catch a glance inside her T-shirt.

'Now it's ready for the oven. It needs to bake with some acid chemicals in the oven to age it. You'll be away by five.'

Max spent the rest of the day kicking his heels around Saint-Tropez. He tried to get Jacques to go with him, but he wasn't budging.

Out of guilt, he made an effort to get hold of Gemma, but she wasn't answering her mobile. Probably still asleep. Which was a relief. Because there was only one person inside Max's head: Sophie. He kept replaying the night before. At one point she'd put her hand on his arm when they were walking down from the square. She wouldn't do that if she didn't like him, would she? Yet that had been it. She'd shown no other sign of attraction at all. And it seemed strange that such a sexy girl appeared to have no man around. Maybe men weren't her thing?

He rang the consulate in Nice to check that Tryon had fixed things.

'I'm not sure whether I'll be with you this evening or tomorrow morning,' he told his contact.

'We close at five,' the contact replied uncompromisingly.

'Of course you do, you're French.' A small smile creased his face.

Max turned into the plant nursery on the road back up to Gassin. He wanted to buy a present for Sophie. Ever since his first visit to the South of France, he'd always longed to buy one of the old olive trees that all the nurseries seem to have for sale. The trees at this place were particularly gnarled, old and magnificent. All about eighteen feet high and three or four feet around the trunk.

'How much?' he asked a bloke with a wheelbarrow.

'They're very expensive,' the man replied, with a ridiculous Gallic shrug of his shoulders. 'Over one hundred years old,' he added in deliberate English.

'I'm sure they are. Even though you probably got an EU grant to scrub them out in the first place. How much?'

'Five thousand. That's my best price.'

No, it isn't, Max thought.

'I'm not a tourist. I'm a landscape gardener. How much for two?

'Nine thousand,' the Frenchman replied, holding up nine fingers. Max didn't look like a landscape gardener as far as he was concerned.

'Eight thousand.'

The Frenchman threw his arms around in despair and looked disgusted.

'Fine. Forget it. There are about fifty other places between here and Marseille where I can get them. Good day,' Max said as he walked off towards his car waving his hand.

The Frenchman cracked before Max had walked ten paces. He wasn't letting eight thousand euros walk out of his nursery.

What he didn't know was that he was going to have to deliver them to Gassin straight away.

Sophie reacted quite badly at first. She gave the distinct impression of being put upon. Max assured her he'd paid for them to be planted as soon as she liked, but she still appeared somewhat discombobulated.

'It is too much. Too generous, Max,' she said resentfully, sitting on the veranda, shaking her head. 'You can't give me such an expensive present.'

Max wasn't enjoying her rejection.

'You could paint that picture for me. I'd like a self-portrait, please.'

'I don't think so. Anyway, you're in a big rush.'

'Hmmm. Annoyingly, the consulate in Nice closed at five. Doesn't open again till ten tomorrow morning. I could make an early start.'

'What does the consulate have to do with anything?' she asked.

'I can't walk through Customs at Nice – or Amsterdam, for that matter – carrying *The Peasants in Winter*,' he told her. 'It's different in a private jet. You can walk through those terminals with pretty much what you like. So I'm going to post it to myself at the British Embassy in The Hague using the diplomatic bag.'

'Won't someone open it before you get there?'

'Absolutely not. Protocol.'

'Isn't the painting too big to go in a diplomatic bag?'

It was now Max's chance to lecture Sophie. He took the opportunity to make a lot of eye contact.

'It doesn't work like that. The Russians once put an entire lorry in their bag. It's a figure of speech.'

'So who invented it?'

'The Vienna Convention on Diplomatic Relations – 1961, I believe. Although something very similar existed around the time of the French Revolution.'

'Surely countries breach the code, don't they? Have a quick look to see what's inside?'

'It's a big deal if they do. We suspected the Libyans of trying to smuggle out the gun that shot PC Yvonne Fletcher from their embassy in St James's Square in London. So we X-rayed their bag when no one was watching – strictly against the rules, of course.'

'And?'

'It was in there. Nothing we could do about it though. We would have been in more bother than them.'

'That's outrageous!'

'Tell that to the Libyans.'

Sophie seemed engaged enough by the black bag. But she showed no interest in holding Max's eye contact.

Jacques, who had been sitting quietly in the corner of the room, perked up.

'At least you could offer him a drink,' he suggested, rebuking his daughter. Jacques, it seemed, was rather enjoying Max's company. 'I think he might enjoy a bottle of red I have.'

The old man got up from his chair and shuffled towards the drinks tray. Sophie and Max said nothing. Max smiled. Sophie didn't. As Jacques manoeuvred himself past the sofa, he caught his thigh on the large terracotta pot.

'*Merde! Pas encore!*' he tutted, though he wasn't about to let his obvious pain darken the mood. 'Maybe a few olives would be nice,' he observed.

Sophie got the hint and retreated to the kitchen. Jacques delved into the cupboard below the drinks tray.

'Can I help?' Max asked.

Jacques waved him away.

'I know where it is.'

Max walked over to the terracotta pot, tilted it to one side and rotated it so that it moved six inches further from the sofa. It was bloody heavy and a few of the leaves from whatever plant it contained fell on the floor. Max picked them up and cast them on to the soil in the pot.

'*Voilà*,' Jacques said, holding up the bottle. In his hands was a 1988 Château Haut-Brion.

'Papa!' Sophie said, reprimanding him as she arrived with the olives.

'That is too generous, Jacques,' Max concurred.

Jacques turned to look at both of them.

'I have never had anything more important to thank someone for. Besides, I'm going to drink a third of it.'

Sophie was about to suggest some other wine. Why should they waste their best bottle on this man? Then the position of the terracotta pot caught her eye. She wasn't an artist for nothing. She noticed detail, and the order of things. In any case, she could see the circle outlining where the pot had been standing moments before.

'Papa,' she continued. 'Shouldn't we decant that and let it breathe for a minute?'

Max took a good sniff of Jacques's wine, when Sophie finally poured it. And made the appropriate noises. Then he could no longer resist asking Jacques about the painting on the wall above the drinks tray.

'Permit me to ask you a question?'

'Please do.'

'When we had lunch in Monte Carlo, you explained to me that you didn't copy paintings, you forged them.'

'Indeed.'

'And yet, even I know that the painting hanging above the drinks tray is a copy – I must say, a rather brilliant copy – of

102

one of Picasso's greatest works. In fact, I'm pretty sure it's hanging in the Louvre as we speak.'

A look of doubt spread across Sophie's face as she turned to look at her father. But he didn't look concerned. Far from it. In fact, he looked rather pleased as he took a sip of his drink.

'You are very observant. But you make one false assumption. Why do you think that is a copy?' Jacques asked, looking up at the picture for the first time.

'It's a real Picasso?' Max asked incredulously. Jacques smiled.

'I wish it was. We would be very rich if that was the case.'

'Papa,' Sophie said, 'are you sure . . .?'

'Max is our friend, my dear. We will have no secrets from him by the time we are finished. We have to trust him.'

'Of course. I give you my word.'

Jacques wanted to tell this Englishman his secret. It was gut instinct.

'Do you remember where that great painting was found?' Jacques asked. Max cast his mind back. As it happened, he remembered very well where he'd been when the news of the discovery had broken. Eating breakfast in the Grand Hall at Laidlaw Castle.

'Search the cellars,' Lord Todd had told his son and Max. 'If some bloody Frenchman can find a Picasso in his cellar, why shouldn't we? If you find anything worthwhile, I'll split it with you.'

Max had spent all morning convinced he was going to get rich. But by lunchtime cricket had held more appeal.

'Am I right in thinking it was found in a cellar somewhere?' Max asked.

'Indeed. You are well informed. It was found in the cellar of a hotel near St Paul de Vence. The very hotel where Picasso often stayed.'

'Why would anyone hang a Picasso in a cellar?'

'Again, you are mistaken in your assumption. It was not hanging. It was being stored in an old sealed casement.' Jacques gave Max a knowing smile.

'You are joking,' Max said, a large smile beaming from his face. He looked at Sophie and started laughing.

'The hotel belonged to an old friend of mine. His family had owned it for generations, but "the roof needed fixing", and he was a bit short,' Jacques continued, enjoying his role as storyteller. 'I created a letter on old paper supposedly from Picasso to one of his ancestors, offering the painting by way of thanks for his stay that summer. Then my friend "discovered" the painting and the letter in his cellar. It took us six months to find a casement of the right age – in Bordeaux, of all places,' Jacques said rather proudly.

'Unbelievable,' Max muttered. 'And now it's hanging in the Louvre.' Jacques nodded. Then it dawned on Max: Jacques hadn't answered his original question.

'So why this copy on your wall?'

'It is no copy, my friend. It was, let us say, my first attempt. I quite liked it, so I decided to keep it. The painting in the Louvre may appear identical. But not to me.'

Sophie stood up and poured Max some more wine.

'You can see why we don't welcome visitors. I keep telling Papa we should put it somewhere no one will see it. It has no value, but it could expose him. Nevertheless he insists that's where it's staying.'

'Indeed it is,' Jacques said. 'Of course, the bastard who owned the hotel never gave me my share. But what could I do?'

'Talking of staying,' Max said, looking at Sophie. 'I hope you're not?'

'Papa, Max says we must get out of the house for a few weeks. It isn't safe here until *he* is exposed.'

Jacques made a few discordant noises.

'I'm not letting that bastard drive me out of my home.'

'It won't be for long, Papa.'

'No. I'm going nowhere. You should go, Sophie – to Paris, or London. But no one will bother with an old man like me. They wouldn't find me down here anyway.'

Sophie walked over to her father's chair and put her hand on his shoulder.

'Papa, just to keep me happy, please come away with me. I couldn't bear it, thinking of you here on your own.'

'You know my mind, Sophie. I am safe here. And armed. I have my pistol.'

Max thought about joining in, but he could see they were getting nowhere. Hopefully, Pallesson would have too much going on to bother with them. Hopefully.

9

The Hague

The embassy was in turmoil when Max returned the next afternoon. The builders had finally arrived to refurbish the building and Arthur had decided to make the worst of the disruption.

'How's Arthur?' Max enquired. He was fond of Arthur. Knowing that most of the embassy staff came and went without so much as a good morning, he always made an effort. Besides, he enjoyed their banter.

'I'd be all right if I had a new knee,' he grimaced, reaching under the desk for a package. 'This arrived in the bag for you this morning, Max. From France. It's quite light. Papers I should think.' The carbon fibre protection around the painting had been designed to be strong and light.

'Good man,' Max said, grabbing it a bit too quickly. 'I see the builders have started.'

Arthur nodded ruefully.

'They always make such a mess. And we've had to take on extra staff this week.'

'Extra staff?' Max enquired as casually as he could.

'Increased security. I've got another boy on with me. Young

Dutch lad called Gus. He doesn't look the sharpest, if you ask me, but he'll do as a pair of legs. Knees are playing me up and the lifts are on the blink.'

'Why increased security?'

'Because we've had to disable half the alarm systems. Something to do with the rewiring. There are no alarms up in the offices at all right now, so don't leave the crown jewels lying around.'

'No. I won't do that,' Max replied, while thinking: You clever bastard, Pallesson. He didn't like the sound of the new lad prowling around.

'So, Gus – the new lad – does nights, does he, Arthur?'

'That's right. Starts at six. Does half an hour with me, then works through.'

'Excellent. Anything else going on? Is the old man playing up?'

Arthur loved a gossip and nothing went on that he didn't know about. Max always referred to the ambassador as 'the old man' during his 'Arthur briefings'.

The old retainer looked around the reception area conspiratorially before he answered.

'Still going to visit his lady friend on Thursdays,' Arthur said, raising his eyebrows towards the ceiling.

'Mrs Ambassador know about this little arrangement?'

'Well, she can't talk. Goes back to London more often than the Zeebrugge ferry.'

Max feigned interest as Arthur outlined the suspicions of the embassy support staff network, but the ambassador's wife's affairs were of no interest to him. After humouring Arthur for a couple of minutes, he finally cut to the chase.

'What about Pallesson? What does he get up to?'

Arthur pulled a disapproving face.

'I shouldn't say. But it isn't right. I mean, I'm as open-minded as anyone, but it makes you think.'

Max nodded encouragement.

'German woman at the moment.'

'Nothing wrong with that, is there?'

Arthur shook his head discreetly.

'Still, it isn't right, is it? What they get up to. Whips, chains and God knows what. How do they get into it in the first place? That's what I'd like to know.'

Max sympathized with Arthur and extracted the address from him before he headed for the stairs.

Upstairs, half the offices had been emptied and shrouded in dustsheets. The other half were accommodating the refugees, with desks crammed in wherever there was space.

Smith, emboldened by the general chaos, threw his tennis ball at eye-level straight towards Max as he threaded his way through the mayhem. Max had both hands holding the picture. His instinct was to raise them – and the picture – to protect his face. The tennis ball thumped into the padded envelope and Smith roared with laughter.

'Derek Randall would have caught that, mate. Catches win matches.'

Max forced a grin as he swore under his breath. For the time being there was nothing he could do but casually prop the envelope up on the floor behind his temporary desk.

Max spent the next couple of hours shuffling paper and making himself look busy. He was desperate to check that the painting wasn't damaged, but that would have to wait until everyone else had left. He daydreamed of Sophie, painting naked in her studio. Him creeping up behind her and kissing her neck. Feeling her pushing her weight back against him. She made passionate love to him for a few minutes . . . Then a nagging doubt invaded his head. Did she even go for men? And that spoilt everything, so he had to start all over again. But it wasn't as good second time round. The passion had gone. He couldn't persuade himself that her heart was in it. And that doubt came back.

From his desk he could see straight through the glass wall into the ambassador's meeting room. The long mahogany table was ready for a briefing session the next day. The square blotting-paper pads were immaculately laid out; the French matching mahogany chairs lined up like soldiers on parade. And on the far wall, Max could see *The Peasants in Winter*, in pride of place above the disused fireplace. He was itching to wander over and check the painting. Had Pallesson beaten him to it? After all, he'd had Jacques's first copy for about ten days. If that were the case, the whole plan was a non-starter.

Max then thought about Sophie again. Maybe she just didn't fancy him? Which was good, he persuaded himself, because she had become a distraction, and the quicker he dealt with that, the better.

At five forty-five, the last person left the office – as far as Max could see. He had a quarter of an hour before the new Dutch security guard came on duty; it was as good as guaranteed that Arthur, with his gammy knee, wouldn't climb the stairs before then.

Max was all set. He cleared some space on his cluttered desk, took the paper knife and heavy-duty tape out of his top drawer and carefully began to cut open the padded envelope. For one very irrational moment, his mind flashed to his mother making them peel the Sellotape back on Christmas presents so they could use the wrapping paper again. He had no idea what he was going to do if the picture was damaged.

His phone started vibrating. He looked at the screen and, to his horror, saw he had just received a text message from 'one-night stand' Louise. But everyone had left, hadn't they? He looked across to her desk. It was empty. Still, he couldn't risk it. He put the package down and opened the message.

What u doin 2nite? Fancy the 2nd half?

Max could feel his heart pounding. A cold sweat formed on his forehead.

Where are you? he texted back.

He got an instant reply: Tucked away nr lifts.

'Fuck.' That was why he hadn't seen her. Tryon would not have been impressed.

Snowed under tonight afraid. Manic, Max replied.

Can wait. No rush. Playing solitaire on PC.

'Fuck,' Max said out loud again. Could he switch the paintings while she was growing ever more impatient just around the corner? No bloody way. She might come round to see him. He daren't risk it. And he could hardly tell her to stay at her desk until he was ready. Or could he? Maybe he could tell her he was going to be on a top-secret call? His phone vibrated again with another message.

Bored now . . . thinking bout wot we could get up to.

Max had to make a decision. He either had to wing it with her around the corner or get rid of her. The next message made his mind up.

Shall I come sit on ur lap?

Meet you bar Hotel Europe in 10. You leave now. Can't be seen leaving together again, Max replied.

He waited what seemed like minutes. Then she replied:

OK . . . don't be long. x x

Max checked his watch. It was five to six. The Dutchman was clocking on in five minutes. Max grabbed his paper knife, the tape, the padded envelope and the roll of brown wrapping paper on his desk. He pulled open the glass door of the ambassador's meeting room and laid the padded envelope on the table over the blotting pads. Quickly, he slit open the top end and pulled the carbon-fibre-wrapped canvas out. He needed to prise open the packaging enough to slip the canvas out, but not damage it to the point that he couldn't re-use it. Exactly as his mother would have done. But the paper knife wasn't sharp enough.

Max cursed again, under his breath this time.

He tried again. It wasn't going to work. All he managed to do was stab his finger. Beginning to panic, Max ran back into the office. There had to be something else. A Stanley knife. A penknife. Anything. He looked wildly at the desks crammed in everywhere. Then, in the corner of one of the emptied offices, he saw a builder's toolbox. He hurried over and opened it. Nothing but spanners on the top layer. He pulled apart the drawers to get into the main box. All he could see was sandpaper. He swept the sandpaper to one side. Underneath was a chisel.

He was running out of time. Tryon's answer to 'What happens if I get caught?' started echoing around Max's head. He would be on his own.

The chisel made quick, neat work of the carbon fibre. Max slid the canvas out of the packaging and gave it a nervous glance. If it was damaged, he was fucked. But the painting was in immaculate condition.

Holding the copy and the chisel, Max crossed the room to where *The Peasants in Winter* was hanging, between two other paintings. He'd nearly forgotten about his earlier worry. Had Pallesson beaten him to the switch? His pulse racing, Max located the group of children on the ice. He prepared himself to see a dog with the children. Which would mean he was too late. There was no dog. He exhaled with relief. It was the original. He'd beaten Pallesson to it.

Max carefully lifted the genuine painting off the wall. As

he freed it from its hook, a cobweb floated into the air. Would it occur to Pallesson that there were no cobwebs when he effected his switch? Surely not. He couldn't be *that* obsessive, could he?

Placing the painting on the floor face down, exactly as Sophie had shown him, he pushed back the catches that were holding the canvas in place, then turned the frame over and pushed on the corners of the canvas. It didn't move. He pushed it a bit harder. Still it didn't move. Max picked up the sharp end of the chisel and bashed the corner of the canvas with the chisel handle. It gave. He gave the diametrically opposite corner a whack and the canvas fell on to the carpet.

As he turned the frame over, Max couldn't stop himself glancing into the office. He knew he was dead in the water if the young Dutch guard appeared. He couldn't even rely on the noise of an approaching lift to warn him.

He pushed the copy into the frame. Again he had to use the handle of the chisel to force it in. Clicking the catches back, he stood up with the painting clasped between both hands. He was now right in the sight line of the door. Feeling like a man who was about to get shot in the back, Max reached up towards the hook on the wall. Agonizing moments passed while he struggled to guide the wire of the frame on to the hook, expecting to be interrupted by a shout from the guard.

Max stepped back and made sure Sophie's work was hanging straight on the wall. His eyes focused on the extra bird in the right-hand tree. And before his brain could tell his body to get on with it, she swam into his thoughts again. He stood motionless, losing valuable seconds, which he didn't have, picturing her.

Somewhere outside the building a clock struck six. Telling himself to focus, Max raced back to the table with the original canvas and slid it into the carbon-fibre packaging, then put the wrapped canvas into the padded envelope. That was when he heard the guard behind him.

'Mr Ward?'

Max spun around. The guard was standing in the entrance of the meeting room. What had he seen? Max's heart was in his mouth.

'Yes?'

'I couldn't see you. Arthur said you were up here. Everything all right?'

'Well, not really,' Max said quickly. 'It's a bloody mess in that office. Clobber all over my desk. I'm trying to wrap these charts up. There's nowhere to lay them flat. Can you give me a hand?'

Max laid the padded envelope on the wrapping paper, and folded the paper over.

'Put your finger on there a minute, would you?' he asked. The guard complied. Max tore off the tape as quick as he could. A couple of minutes later the package was thoroughly wrapped.

'Thank you very much.' Max smiled. 'You arrived just at the right moment. Sorry, I didn't catch your name?'

'Gus,' the guard replied.

Max looked over Gus's shoulder. The chisel was lying on the floor by the disused fire. Fuck. If Gus looked that way, he couldn't fail to see it. Max clumsily knocked the tape on to the floor towards the door as he picked up the package. Gus instinctively turned towards the door and bent down to pick it up.

'Thank you, Gus. I'll be out of here in five minutes,' Max said as he ushered him out through the door.

Max addressed the package to Tryon in London, waited until he'd heard Gus walk down the stairs, then cleared up the chisel and the builder's toolbox. All he had to do now was get it out of the embassy. Which was as straightforward as getting the copy in.

Max found Arthur in the main reception preparing to head home.

'Goodnight, Arthur,' he said in his normal friendly tone. 'Oh, and Arthur, could you take this package down to the post room? It must go in the bag to London tonight.'

'No problem, Mr Max,' Arthur replied. 'I'll see to it on my way out.'

'Thank you, Arthur. By the way – you're going down this season.'

Arthur chuckled. Pity we haven't got more like him, Max thought as he watched the old man set off for the post room.

Max stepped out into the street and allowed himself a small smile. Then he remembered his little problem. Sleeping with Louise twice in one week was way too familiar, but he had to ensure that she didn't become an operational liability.

Amsterdam, six months earlier
The last person Wielart had expected to see in his office first thing one Saturday morning was Francisca. She looked flustered. Not her usual demure self at all. He sat her down on one of his luxurious leather armchairs and enjoyed being able to stare at her without worrying about anyone else watching him. Her usual glow of innocence and calm was absent. In its place, her soft, creamy smooth skin wore a mask of anguish.

'What is the matter, my dear?' Wielart asked her softly.

'My father,' she said, holding her face. 'He's in terrible trouble.'

'What sort of trouble?'

Wielart pulled out his crisp white linen handkerchief from his pocket – clean every day – and revelled in being able to put his arm on her shoulder and brush her hand as he handed it to her. He didn't return to his desk. Instead he perched on the side of the sturdy armchair and left his hand resting on her shoulder. Francisca didn't notice it.

'He's in desperate trouble. He says we might lose Deetman Shipping if the taxman has his way.'

Francisca's floodgates now opened and Wielart stroked her shoulder a little more firmly as he continued to comfort her.

The girl was right. From the vague outline of what she told Wielart, her father was in trouble. But if Wielart acted fast enough, he could probably avert the problem. After comforting Francisca for a further half-hour, Wielart told her that, in order to help, he would need to see all of the documentation.

'From now on, it is better no one knows you are coming to see me. There is a side door to this office that has no closed-circuit cameras on it – it is totally secret. From now on you must only ever come via that door.'

Francisca nodded willingly.

'Can you bring me all of the papers tomorrow?'

'Yes,' she nodded. 'They're all at home. My mother has taken my father away for the weekend. He's broken. He could barely leave the house.'

'I will see you at eleven o'clock tomorrow morning. On the dot.'

Francisca nodded like a compliant schoolchild.

'I'm sure there is something we can do. I have contacts.'

For the first time, Francisca smiled and her facial expression returned to something like normal. But her smile was nowhere near as gleeful as Wielart's once he'd shown her out of the side door.

10

In his own mind, Roderick Pallesson was a rare and gifted creature. Subtle and culturally aware enough to be a great judge of fine art. But at the same time so strong, powerful and pragmatic that he could cut his way through the pathetic madding crowd who got in his way.

He'd been born with a strong belief that he would achieve great power. And that belief had survived, despite his father's constant efforts to demean and patronize him. For he had learnt as a young boy that he possessed extraordinary powers. This understanding had crystallized in the school playground, where he discovered that, if he focused hard enough on another child, he could 'make' them have an accident. Simply by willing it.

That 'actual' ability had diminished as he grew older, but his sense of being shielded by dark forces – and the confidence that gave him – remained as strong as ever.

Pallesson lived on Van Ostadestraat in a large house, which had once been an artist's studio. He'd chosen it for the light.

It tilted at an alarming angle, due to subsidence, like every other house in the street. But it was perfectly anonymous, and spacious without being conspicuous.

Pallesson had a methodical mind that had channelled his love of art. And the way he collected it.

He had five paintings in his special collection. Five original masterpieces: his girls. They were arranged in his front sitting room, where the light was best. Every day he stood before his girls to admire them. They would soon be joined by a sixth, whose place on the wall had remained vacant: *The Peasants in Winter*.

A room at the back of his house, where the light was moderate, housed the remainder of his collection. That was where his two big mistakes hung: his sluts.

The Jan van Goyen had been an expensive purchase. He'd fallen in love with it as soon as he'd seen it. But he should have examined its provenance more carefully before he bought it, not afterwards.

There had been a significant silver lining to that cloud, however. It had led him to Jacques. Indeed, so thick a silver lining was it, that Pallesson had often considered hanging Jacques's van Goyen forgery with his girls. But he just couldn't bring himself to do it.

The other slut was his first and only mistake with Jacques. He'd been so gullible; he'd made assumptions that he would never make again.

It had seemed such a good plan. During his Eton days, thinking it would be useful to have someone inside the Royal Household, Pallesson had forged a 'friendship' with the assistant curator at Windsor Castle. All it had taken was a degree of sexually inappropriate behaviour with a minor – as Pallesson was at the time – and the man was on the hook. A reminder of these old indiscretions was sufficient to persuade the curator to let Pallesson borrow one of the Hendrick Avercamps from the collection. Jacques would then make a copy, which would be returned in place of the original. Even if the curator had doubts about the painting when it was returned, there was no danger of him kicking up a fuss. Not when he faced disgrace and a possible prison sentence if certain photos came to light.

To start with, everything went according to plan. There had, however, been a sting in the tail. When Pallesson went to pick up the Avercamp and its copy from Gassin, Jacques was adamant that the original painting from Windsor Castle was no such thing. It was a copy; an impostor. Pallesson was disgusted.

From that moment onwards he changed his modus operandi. There were too many paintings around Europe on the walls of the aristocracy that were fake. In future, he would ensure that the paintings he intended to steal were originals. He would obtain confirmation from a reputable restorer before substituting Jacques's copy.

It had taken Pallesson quite some time to identify which member of the Rijksmuseum's staff he should target. They had to be senior enough to gain him the illicit access that he and Jacques needed. And they had to be actively involved in the restoration and cleaning work that went on at the museum. But above all, they had to have committed a sufficiently heinous crime in their past to make them vulnerable to Pallesson. As ever, by digging deep enough, Pallesson and his guiding light found the necessary skeleton in the right man's cupboard.

Once that individual had been compromised, there was no shortage of paintings for Jacques to copy. And even if an owner did detect any subtle differences in their painting on its return, they put it down to the restoration work carried out by the museum.

Although every one of his girls had had to work for their place in his collection – by providing collateral for various drug deals – before they 'retired', Pallesson had been faithful to the ethos of his collecting. Loyalty to the succession of talent passed down from master to master.

The first painting Jacques copied had been a Rembrandt;

one of his many self-portraits. A duke from the north of England had sent it to the Rijksmuseum to be cleaned. He had been delighted with the cleaning carried out by the museum. The switch would only ever come to light if one of the duke's successors went broke and tried to sell it.

The next addition to his troupe was by a pupil of Rembrandt, Carel Fabritius. Fabritius was, in Pallesson's opinion, the greatest painter of them all. Brilliant and inventive. His work was rare, though, courtesy of his premature death in an explosion at the Delft municipal arsenal. The opportunity to acquire one of his works of art had been extreme good fortune. But Pallesson understood how to will that.

The final link of this particular chain was, by a long way, the most outrageous. Yet to Pallesson it was so obvious.

Fabritius's influence had been extremely important on the development of the Delft school of genre painters. And the finest graduate of that establishment had been none other than Johannes Vermeer. If Jacques couldn't copy a Vermeer, after his training with Van Meegeren, who the hell could? This audacious switch had made Pallesson feel like a genuine patron, a seventeenth-century grandee, commissioning a great work.

The problem was that there were only about thirty Vermeer paintings in existence. But one was all that they needed. The painting depicted a rather wistful-looking woman looking out of a window, perhaps waiting for a gentleman visitor. It was a classic Vermeer, and had been a treasured heirloom of the elderly Frenchwoman's family for generations.

It was the trusted advisor from the Rijksmuseum who first suggested to her that she should have it cleaned. And how right he had been, she thought, when she saw the result. The painting looked so much fresher.

Jacques had almost lost his nerve on that one, but Pallesson had calmed his compromised, terrified pawn and assured him that the elderly owner would be long gone before the substitution was ever discovered.

Pallesson's other line was slightly dysfunctional, in as much as he'd had to collect them out of sequence. The gap on the wall was for the beginning of this particular chain. For a Pieter Brueghel the Younger.

While Pallesson conceded that Brueghel wasn't quite in Fabritius's league, he had great empathy with Pieter Brueghel the Younger. He imagined the son, overshadowed and humiliated by his famous father, just as he had been. Pieter the Elder telling his son that he would never amount to anything. Patronizing his son in the same way that Pallesson had been demeaned by his father.

The opportunity to steal *The Peasants in Winter* from the British Embassy had been an exit from his new strategy, but he was one hundred per cent certain of its provenance. The prospect of her triumphant arrival after the van Ossen deal was electrifying Pallesson.

Beneath the gap hung a David Vinckboons. Vinckboons excited Pallesson because he was the conduit between Brueghel and Hendrick Avercamp. Vinckboons, Pallesson had decided, must have worked alongside Brueghel the Younger and given him moral support.

Vinckboons had been Avercamp's master in Amsterdam. His original work hanging in Pallesson's collection was along the lines of a classic Brueghel winter scene.

The final 'girl' was by Arent 'Cabel' Arentsz, and again it was a winter scene on ice. But Pallesson didn't mind the repetition of this theme. Far from it, he was preserving and holding together the legacy of the great Flemish and Dutch painters. And as preservation was so important, his girls had to be light on their feet. Ready to move at the shortest of notices.

Every one of them could be clicked out of her cumbersome

gilt frame in a matter of moments. And in the backyard – which Pallesson thought rather resembled a Vermeer scene – he had a van on standby. It was filled with the sort of tat that one would find on a market stall: poor attempts of landscape scenes, crude portraits and worthless prints. Perfect cover for original masterpieces being smuggled across international borders. No Customs officer was going to pick his way through that rubbish and discover the treasures secreted amongst them.

After Pallesson had completed his daily inspection, pausing briefly to greet his sole Fabergé egg, which didn't excite him that much, he admired himself in the gilded mirror in the hall.

'Perfect,' he said to himself as he tilted his immaculate brown trilby just so.

Pallesson stepped out into Van Ostadestraat, checked his watch and set off on the short walk to Sarphatipark.

Iain Jenkins had worked at the heart of the government's listening organ, GCHQ, outside Cheltenham, his entire career. He was loyal to his country and his heart was in the right place. And while he felt a degree of frustration sitting behind a desk all year, he also knew that fieldwork was not for him. But, by offering a little extra assistance to the boys on the front line, he felt that he made a difference.

He was waiting nervously in the park for Pallesson. Although his wife adored their short breaks to Amsterdam, devouring the museums from dawn to dusk, he enjoyed them a little less. The authorities were unlikely to see things his way if he got caught passing on classified information.

Pallesson arrived at the edge of the park and quickly scanned the area. A large willow hung gracefully over a pond. Ducks were scrabbling around beneath, busily filtering any errant weeds that happened to float past. Two lovers had parked their bikes up against a tree and were now wrapped around each other on the grass, oblivious to the entire world.

A young mother pushed her pram past Jenkins, who was sitting on a bench under a tree, trying his best to look casual. He was also trying his hardest not to stare at the young couple. It had been a long time since he and Mrs Jenkins had behaved like that up on Cleeve Hill, overlooking Cheltenham.

'Iain,' Pallesson said brightly, drawing the name out with apparent affection as he approached. 'How are you? Not too cold?'

'No, very good, thank you. It's lovely for this time of year.'

'Indeed it is. Hotel all right? Mrs Jenkins beavering around the museums, I trust?'

'Oh yes,' Jenkins said, smiling awkwardly.

'And your mother, Iain. Is she well?' Pallesson asked, softening his voice at the end of the sentence.

'Yes, good, thank you.' Jenkins always felt overawed by Pallesson.

'How's her bungalow?'

'Fine. Yes. Very fine.'

'Good. It's marvellous when friends can support each other. And you are a great support, Iain. For those of us in the field to know there are people watching our backs at home so we can fight for our country. It means a lot.'

'I do worry sometimes whether I should pass on . . . you know . . . information.'

'Iain, let me make this absolutely clear. It's crucial. A lot of the senior men are out of touch. They simply don't understand how we have to operate in the field nowadays. They don't understand that we have to break the rules here and there. You understand that. As do I. But they don't. One of those old boys nearly got me bloody killed in Moscow because he didn't understand that. By giving us the odd heads-up, you are saving lives in the field, Iain. You are the unsung hero. And it's the least we can do, to help out with your mother. Now, something's obviously on the bubble in London.'

'Yes. It's funny you should mention the old boys. One of them was running an internal check on you. Tryon. And he's been stirring them up about you. At the highest level. He's been questioning your methods. Paper only. No data trail. He even suggested they put someone on you to keep an eye—'

'Have they done that?' Pallesson interrupted, his annoyance momentarily getting the better of him.

'No. Not according to the records. His request was turned down. It would appear he had no evidence.'

Pallesson took a breath and smiled benignly.

'Amazing, isn't it? An old boy totally out of touch – hasn't been to Russia for decades, I would imagine – while I've been out there, dodging the mafia's bullets. And *he's* casting aspersions on *me.*'

'Disgusting,' Jenkins concurred, suddenly feeling better about himself and his trip to Amsterdam.

'Iain, these men were heroes in their day and we must nurture them. But once their judgement goes they're dangerous. Thank God there are men like you to keep an eye open.'

Jenkins blushed. What a man Pallesson is, he thought. A bloody hero – and forgiving too.

Pallesson made a bit more small talk, then checked his watch.

'Must keep moving, Iain. You know how it is. And don't forget: guys like you *are* the service. Take good care of yourself,' Pallesson said, making it sound as though he really cared about Jenkins as he shook his hand warmly before striding off out of the park.

Jenkins had an extra spring in his step as he made his way back to the Hotel Renaissance, where he wasn't paying the bill.

Pallesson took out his phone as soon as he was out of sight. He dialled a number in England that answered after one ring.

'Tryon needs to be dealt with. Fast. No evidence, no body. Just make him disappear.'

11

Max could feel a surge of excitement racing through him as he wandered across the Museumplein towards the Rijksmuseum. But he was also irritated with himself.

Sophie's message had appeared right out of the blue – 'Coming to Amsterdam to see how they've hung some of my work. Will you be around?' She'd said nothing about it when he was in Gassin.

He'd considered telling her he wasn't in town. He was, after all, in the thick of some serious business. He knew only too well that Pallesson would kill anyone who got in his way. This was not the time to let himself be distracted. Yet here he was, acting like a sailor lured by the sirens. He was potentially heading for a shipwreck, but he couldn't help himself.

Max was blind to the magnificent Gothic structure in front of him and only had a passing interest in the works of art inside it. Sophie was waiting for him at the top of the steps. Max noticed she was standing exactly under the middle of the arch. She certainly knew how to attract the eye, even if she was unconscious of just how much.

Max gently placed his hands on her hips as he kissed her

hello. He felt her breasts pressing against his chest. Did she know she was doing that, or was it accidental?

He backed away as they locked eyes. She seemed pleased to see him, he thought. Pleased because she was a stranger in a foreign place, or pleased because she wanted to see him? He couldn't tell.

He tried to stop his mind undressing her, but it was impossible. Her jeans, blue jersey and grey scarf were hardly an attempt to look sexy, but Max couldn't drag his eyes off her.

'Well, here I am. Surprise, surprise,' she said, giving Max a smile he couldn't really interpret.

'You look wonderful.'

Sophie gave an awkward laugh.

'So. How amazing – you have some work in the exhibition here. Incredible. You never said.'

She shrugged her shoulders bashfully. 'I wanted to thank you. For my trees. And for helping us. I thought I might as well come and see how the pictures look in the museum.'

Max thought her body language was very stiff. Not the girl he'd had dinner with in Gassin at all. So that was it? She'd come to Amsterdam to thank him. His daydreams of the two of them passionately making love were being incinerated fast.

'Your father? Has he come too?'

Sophie shook her head.

'I tried desperately to get him to come. He strung me along, the old fox. He said he would, and then at the last minute dug his toes in. Literally, when the taxi arrived. I begged him.'

'Sophie, this could go off at any time.'

She looked disquieted, and then changed the subject.

'Would you like to look at my paintings? You might as well see what you're trying to protect?'

I might as well get on with my bloody job, Max thought.

125

But she was here now, so he might as well try again to impress on her just how dangerous Pallesson was. She needed to take her father off and lie low for a while.

'I have the tickets,' Sophie said, moving on and holding them up as if she was a lottery winner. 'Let's go.'

Max followed her towards the queue. He thought of the time he'd tried to persuade Gemma to look round the Van Gogh Museum. She'd taken one look at the line of people, asked why they didn't have VIP tickets and told him to forget it.

'They have so many amazing artists in this exhibition, Max,' Sophie enthused. 'I can't believe I got into it. I didn't think they'd like my style.'

It suddenly occurred to Max that he had no idea what her style actually was. Presumably it wasn't Brueghelesque. He couldn't exactly ask once they were standing in front of her pictures, and he knew he wouldn't have a clue which were hers anyway.

'So who's your inspiration, Sophie?' Max asked as they made their way down a long corridor lined with marble statues, most of them naked.

'Well, my father, I suppose.'

Fat lot of good to me that is, Max thought.

'Yes. Of course,' he replied, unashamedly letting his eyes linger on one of the heroine statues.

'Anyone else?'

'I suppose I always wanted to paint like Mary Cassatt. She's amazing – I wish I could paint with her conviction.'

'Well, we all need heroes to aspire to,' Max replied, thinking: Who the hell is Mary Cassatt when she's at home? He couldn't ask if there was anyone else.

Mary Cassatt had been Sophie's inspiration all her life. But she knew there was no way Max would have heard of the American-born Impressionist. No chance he would ever have

126

seen or understood her amazing depiction of intimacy between mother and daughter.

Then Max tried again.

'And your favourite painting? Am I being a bore, asking too many questions?'

'Not at all.' She smiled, turning to look at him. But the smile gave away nothing.

'*Dance at the Moulin de la Galette*, is my all-time favourite,' she said.

Max smiled and nodded.

'Ah yes,' he said, wearing his very best poker face.

'The joy on their faces is something I don't think I have ever felt,' she continued. 'But Renoir must have experienced such happiness to have been able to paint that.'

Renoir. What a relief. Even Max knew he was an Impressionist. He even thought he might know the painting Sophie was talking about, but he wasn't going to push his luck.

Sophie's paintings were hanging together in the far corner of the room housing the exhibition.

'This is it,' she said as she waved generally around the room. 'I'm in here somewhere.' She knew exactly where she was hanging, but she didn't want to feel like some child presenting her homework for appreciation.

'Help yourself,' she said. 'I won't be a minute.' And then she wandered off.

When Sophie returned ten minutes later, she could see Max was standing in front of her work. She took a deep breath and walked up behind him.

'Well?' she asked.

He didn't say anything.

'Do you like any of them? You've been there,' she said, pointing to the largest of the three paintings. It was the square in Gassin. Max thought it was quite good. There was definitely a sense of the tranquillity of the place.

'It's perfect,' he said rather detachedly. As was the smaller painting on the left of Saint-Tropez harbour, which was a riot of colour. But it was the painting on the right that had Max spellbound.

'This is quite extraordinary,' he said quietly, without turning to look at her.

'Most people prefer the Gassin scene. It's meant to be my best picture.'

'But it isn't,' Max said firmly. 'Not by a long way.'

The painting that had him transfixed was of a small girl with a woman in a hay field. The girl was looking back over her shoulder. The woman, whose face you couldn't see, was leading her by the hand.

'Why do you like that one?' Sophie asked.

Max pursed his lips and thought.

'Lots of reasons. To start with, it's brilliantly painted. I can feel the grass swaying in the wind. There's so much movement.'

Sophie was completely taken aback by Max's critique. The whole point of setting the scene in a hay field had been to get that sense of movement. She was almost certain he didn't have the first clue about Impressionism. So maybe he wasn't so dumb after all?

'That's good,' she said. 'I was trying to create that.'

'The light is awesome too. I can almost feel the shadows dancing around. You must have painted it in the evening.'

Sophie was now very impressed. She only ever painted original work outside at twilight. It made her a very unproductive artist.

'Correct. My God, you are an art expert after all.'

'Sadly not. In fact, I know nothing about art or Impressionism, I'm afraid.'

'Maybe you know more than you realize.'

'I doubt it. But I do know that neither the light nor the movement are what makes this extraordinary.'

'Really?'

'Really. This is a very unhappy painting, isn't it?'

Max turned and looked Sophie straight in the eye. She said nothing, but her eyes became slightly watery. He couldn't stop himself. He put an arm around her, and to his surprise, she leant into him. Her hair smelt delicious as he stood holding her.

After a few seconds she surreptitiously wiped her eyes and stepped away from him.

'You are that little girl, I assume?'

'Yes,' she said guardedly.

'With your mother?'

'Yes.'

'You look so sad—'

'Yes,' she interrupted.

'Are you looking at your father?'

'Jesus, Max. Did I tell you about this painting in Gassin when I was drunk?'

'You never were drunk.'

'Are you sure?'

'Positive. Why wouldn't your father go with you?'

Sophie paused and involuntarily wiped her eyes.

'I don't know. He never would. He'd never go anywhere with us. My mother and I used to go to the beach together. We used to walk up in the hills. But he would never come. We were never a family. And then my mother ran off. That is what she . . . I . . . am thinking.'

Max now had a strange feeling in his stomach. A feeling of horror that this little girl should have been so unhappy. And still was. He wanted to sort that out. But what was he thinking? He'd never made anyone happy in his life. That wasn't what he did. Or what he could do. Max Ward was not a healer of broken hearts, and he knew that. And anyway, he had Gemma. But he couldn't let Gemma pollute his feelings for Sophie.

As if on autopilot, Max took hold of Sophie's hand and looked her straight in the eye.

'You were right.'

'What?'

'You were right to make me come and look at what I'm protecting. And I should have told you not to come to Amsterdam when you rang. You have to leave straight away. You're too close to Pallesson here. We need to make sure your father's safe too. In case something goes wrong.'

Leaving Amsterdam was now the last thing on Sophie's mind. When she'd arrived at the entrance to the Rijksmuseum she'd suddenly felt threatened. What was she doing, throwing herself at a virtual stranger? But when Max had started to talk about her paintings, she'd relaxed. And cast her mind back to their conversations in Gassin. Max was no predator, she assured herself.

The food in the Brasserie Keyzer was distinctly Dutch, but it had a good atmosphere, and Max liked the bar staff. Sophie ordered shrimp croquettes, which were edible, and mashed potato, which wasn't. It didn't take her long to demolish a bottle of Sancerre. And Max wasn't far behind her with his St-Émilion Grand Cru – the only halfway decent red they had.

'It might get nasty around here if Pallesson or whoever he's dealing with finds the tracking device.'

'I'm staying the night, whatever you say.'

'Okay. But you must promise me you'll go in the morning.'

'You want to get rid of me, Max, don't you?'

'Yeah right,' he said ironically. 'But—'

'Do you have a girlfriend?'

Such an abrupt question hit Max like a bolt out of the blue. He wanted to lie. He didn't want to scare her away. He wouldn't be able to explain it properly now. How could he tell her that he loved Gemma, but he wasn't in love with her? He had never felt for her what he was beginning to feel for Sophie.

'Tell me the truth, Max. Please.'

Max rubbed his temple with his left hand and screwed up his face.

'It isn't that straightforward. I see someone when it suits both of us. She's married, but I'll sort it out. Please don't run away.'

Sophie took his hand and stroked it. Then she followed the lines on the palm of his hand.

'Strong, honest and loyal. That's what your palm says. Thank you for telling me the truth.'

'I haven't been here long,' Max said as he approached the front door of his flat. 'And I hope I won't be here for much longer, either.'

It wasn't the first time in his life that Max had excused the lack of grandeur of where he lived. Whenever he'd taken a mate home from Eton to Warrington he'd always been aware that their butler probably lived in a bigger house. Not that his mother didn't try pretentiously to make a silk purse out of a sow's ear. But it had never fazed him. He took people for what they were and he expected them to do the same.

'I don't care, Max. As long as you've got something to drink – and a bed.' Sophie squeezed Max a little tighter around the waist as he turned the key in the lock.

'Well, as it happens, you might be in luck. I have some very good vodka, which I got out of the kitchen door of the Kremlin. Nothing like the vodka you buy in the shops. My bed, however . . .'

'You don't have a bed?'

131

Max shook his head in mock sadness and turned to face Sophie. He stroked her long silky hair down the back of her head and then stooped to kiss her neck.

The flat was at least warm, which partially made up for its blandness. The furniture was typical of rented flats. If it hadn't come from Ikea, it certainly looked as if it did.

'How long have you been here, Max?

'A few weeks. If I end up staying in Amsterdam for any amount of time, I'll move to a more interesting area. But I can't see it.'

Sophie ran her hand across Max's shoulder as he pulled the bottle of vodka out of the freezer.

'Hell will freeze over before this stuff. I hear they shoot barmen in Siberia if it freezes – means they've been watering it down.'

Sophie wasn't listening. She was pulling Max round to face her, leaning into him as he turned. Then she kissed him gently – at first. Max had never felt such a soft mouth. He looked into her eyes and felt himself shudder as she worked her tongue around his mouth. For the next few minutes, Max pinned her to the kitchen sink. Until finally Sophie pulled away.

'Time for a drink, don't you think?'

Sophie perched on the sideboard by the sink, letting her legs dangle in the air. She raised her small frosted glass to Max, clinked his glass and took a sip.

'Wow. My God, that's rocket fuel!'

'Hits the back of the throat, doesn't it?'

'And the lungs. I can feel it going down. It tastes so . . .'

Max wanted to taste it in her mouth. He leant forward and kissed her again with a mouth full of vodka. And gently let it trickle into her mouth.'

'Tell me about your friends at Eton, Max. Didn't Prince William go there?'

Max laughed.

'Well, my friends at Eton were very rich, and taught me lots of bad habits. I was quite useful to them, because most of them liked gambling, and I was better at picking winners than them. They didn't understand risk and value, and I did.'

'Were you happy with these people?'

'Yes, I was. After all, we were all brought up on estates. Theirs were in the shires, and mine was owned by the council.' Sophie didn't get the joke. Max didn't bother to explain.

'And their sisters?' Sophie asked.

Max hoped there was a hint of jealousy in her question.

'None of them were my type. There were a few who might have fancied playing with me. But I'm not a fish to be reeled in and tossed overboard.'

'Hmm. I know what the English are like.'

'Really. What are they like?' Max asked with faux interest.

'They get drunk, and fight, and then have sex with each other.'

'Is that right? And the French?'

Sophie knew he was making fun of her.

'We drink for the taste, and then eat.'

'And then . . .?'

'Then we marry.'

'Disappointing. Care to taste another glass of vodka?'

'Why not? Then we can fight.'

'Excellent,' Max said, filling her glass. 'Step by step.'

'I bet you had fun. Did you play polo with the royal family?'

Max decided not to let the facts ruin a good story.

'Yes. A little bit.' On the same pitch a couple of hours later would have been more like it. 'We used to go down to Goodwood and race cars,' he added quickly. 'Now that I could do. There's nothing quite like belting flat out down a straight and seeing how late you dare break. I used to love screaming past the boys into a bend and braking after them. It's all about how much you enjoy frightening yourself. And I seemed to enjoy it more than the others.'

'Why does that not surprise me? Do you have any hobbies that don't involve trying to kill yourself?'

'Well, I can hold my own at snooker if it's going to hurt enough losing. The trick is to be slightly less drunk than your opponent. And then there's Frieda. I was the Gloucestershire Frieda champion one year.'

'Frieda. What is Frieda?'

'Competitive and nasty game. Good for working off dinner. Very bad for your hips, which get bruised on the corners of the snooker table. You have to keep the red ball moving by throwing one white ball against it. Only from one end of the table or the other, of course. Always causes fearful rows. And then there's Naked Frieda, but I don't think I'll go into that,' Max smirked provocatively. Sophie punched him on the chest.

'You see,' she complained.

Max didn't want to talk about himself. He wanted to know more about Sophie.

'I loved your paintings,' he said. 'They're fantastic. So full of life. So literal. You're an amazing talent. You must do what your father didn't.'

Sophie looked pensively at the floor. Max was worried that he may have overstepped the mark – criticizing her dad.

'You're right about Papa,' she said after a few moments. 'I think he regrets not being himself. Expressing his own style. Rather than fooling others and then getting trapped into that. I feel sad when I think about it.'

'He's played a dangerous game, Sophie.'

'But life is dangerous, isn't it? Don't tell me your life has been straightforward.'

Max poured both of them another glass of vodka and put the bottle back in the freezer.

'I've been the architect of most of my problems,' Max replied, and took a gulp. 'But you won't be impressed. There were no bullets flying past me. No heroism. It was all pretty . . .'

'Boring?'

'No. Far from boring – and that was the trouble. Pretty seedy, I suppose.'

Now it was Max's turn to look at the floor. Sophie could feel her face beginning to glow from the vodka. And it was making her feel rather elated.

'Go on.'

'Well, I didn't think it was a problem, to start with. Gambling. Because I was very good at it. Much better than my father. In fact, whenever I won, I felt like I was just getting back what was his. Then I had a bit of bother in Saudi Arabia. But you don't want me to bore you with that.'

'Oh yes, I do.'

'Really?'

'Really.'

'Okay. Stop me when you're about to die of boredom.'

'I'm all ears.'

'Well, it was my first posting from the Office. And it reflected my unqualified status. I was drafted, undercover, into the British Trade Office at al-Khobar in Saudi Arabia. On the face of it, I was there to help develop and strengthen trade ties between Britain and the locals. In reality, I was there to gather intelligence and monitor the behaviour of anti-regime extremists.'

'Sneaky.'

'Of course. We don't wear badges. For the most part I was confined to the diplomatic compound after nightfall. There wasn't anywhere else to go, anyway. Or so I thought for the first few months. Then I got wind of an illegal card school in the basement of an international hotel not that far from the compound.'

'An ill wind?'

'Very good. You're better at English than . . . the English. Anyway, I felt it was my business to stray from the mainstream diplomatic community. To swim outside the ropes a bit and find out what was really cooking amongst the natives. And it seemed logical that the dodgy folk pitching up for an illicit card game would be able to furnish me with information that I'd never get to hear if I played too straight a bat. So I had a clear conscience about getting involved in a few card games. I was also fairly confident that I could supplement my meagre wages, which certainly weren't going to keep me in the comforts I'd adopted from my alma mater.'

'Good to hear you have a conscience.'

Max smiled, but he ignored her.

'The gambling den was a depressing, bare-walled room with one light bulb hanging from the ceiling. It smelt of cigarettes, sweat and fear. There were no windows and only one stairwell leading back up to ground level. There was no escape.'

'From what?'

'The smell, the people, the place. I certainly wouldn't have chosen to hang out with the other members of the card school for their personalities and social graces. Every time I sat at that table it felt like I was in the Wild West surrounded by gold prospectors. There was something desperate about them. They were all on the wrong side of middle age, and they'd gone there out of circumstance, not choice. Most of them talked a big game about the future. None of them mentioned the past.'

'How depressing.'

'They were. Lost, most of them. They drank heavily. Copious amounts of Scotch, in particular. If you were going to get busted for illegal gambling, you might as well get done for drinking while you were at it. I drank plenty, too. They'd probably have thrown me out of the game if I hadn't. I didn't drink quite as much as the others, though.'

'But you were so young.'

Max's mind was now back in Saudi Arabia. He barely heard Sophie.

'They varied the games, but Tuesday night was blackjack. I was better at it than the other punters, and better at it than the house liked. I drove them mad, sticking on twelve when the dealer had sixteen or less. And I consistently walked away with their money. It all seemed so easy until one night they fixed the shoe. I should have figured it out, but I was too cocky and too bloody naïve.'

'Surely not?'

'When I got there, the game had already started. That should have raised an alarm bell. They were usually drinking and exchanging their jaundiced, cynical views when I arrived. But not that night.

'There was one spare seat left at the table. Between the American who pretended he worked for an oil company, but was clearly CIA, and the overweight CEO of a construction company who hated Arabs nearly as much as he hated Jews. He didn't get the joke when I asked him if he'd ever considered being a diplomat.'

'In Palestine?'

'I fared well enough to start with, but after half an hour I got up to pour myself a large Scotch, and the dealer must have switched the shoe while my back was turned. All the other players would have seen it happen, but they didn't care. The house had cut them in on the deal.

'The house knew exactly what my strategy would be. So they'd arranged the cards to beat me two out of three times; letting me win enough to stay oblivious to the sting. The CIA man and the fat constructor played their parts with gusto.

Cursing their losses and gloating over their winning hands. After an hour, I was cleaned out; but by this point I'd convinced myself I was smarter than my opponents. And that my luck would change. So I asked the Saudi who ran the joint if I could have a line of credit. Which was my second mistake that night.'

'Max, you nutter!'

'If I hadn't been so certain, I might have noticed that none of the other players had missed a hand. When they'd stood up for a drink the game had always waited for them. I then took a bath over the next hour.'

'You madman. How did you pay?'

'As I left, I was reminded that the debt would be due, in full, within six days. I had no idea how I was going to settle up. And as it turned out, I couldn't.'

'I knew I wasn't going to be popular when I turned up a week later with a quarter of it. But I was one of them, I thought. They'd cut me some slack. I was wrong.'

'Oh, Max.'

'The CIA man and the constructor wouldn't make eye contact with me once I came clean that I didn't have the money. The Saudi had clearly second-guessed this scenario and had his debt collectors waiting close by. They took me into an alley around the back of the hotel and kicked the shit out of me. But they weren't stupid enough to leave me covered in blood near their patch. I was bundled into the boot of a car and driven off.'

'Oh my God. You are joking?'

'Oh no. I was still conscious in the darkness of the car boot. My ribs screaming. Breathing was agony. I didn't care where I was going, because dying through lack of oxygen was going to be my fate if I couldn't find some way to breathe through the pain. The car journey ended very quickly. I was pulled out – sending more pain through my ribcage – and dumped on the side of the road.'

'Bastards.'

'"Get the money!" they shouted at me, then they drove off.'

Max fell silent, reliving the events of that night in his mind.

Time disintegrated into a blur as he lay by the side of the road, intermittently passing out from the pain of his ribs. It felt as though every last one of them had been smashed to pieces. Then at some point during the night two policemen arrived.

They shouted questions at him, becoming increasingly agitated when he failed to answer. Max could barely breathe, let alone talk. Their response was to hit him on the legs with a baton.

'Embassy,' Max had kept whispering. 'Embassy.'

They finally went through his pockets, found his ID and called an ambulance. The last thing Max could remember that night was someone putting an oxygen mask over his face.

Barnaby Nash had been the first person Max saw when he came round. Nash was working for the cultural attaché in Riyadh. But he didn't know much about culture.

'Barnaby Nash,' he'd said formally, ignoring the empty seat by the bed. 'Cultural attaché's office. How are you feeling?'

Not that Nash cared in the slightest. In fact, he was positively hostile. Why should he have to go around cleaning up after whichever young idiot the Office cared to send out to his patch? No. Concerned, he wasn't.

'Sore,' Max had replied gingerly. He could feel his ribs throbbing under the sheets; talking was bad news.

'So?' asked Nash, cutting straight to the chase.

'So what?' Max had replied.

'So what happened?'

'What does it look like happened?'

Nash didn't care for smart arses.

'Ward, we work for the same people. So don't give me any bullshit. What the fuck happened?'

Max had had no idea who the prick standing at the end of his bed was, but he sure as hell wasn't going to tell him anything.

'What happened was I got jumped by a few locals as I was walking along the road.'

'Bollocks! That doesn't happen here. And if you had been, you wouldn't be here to tell the tale. Someone would have been eating your testicles for breakfast. So I'll ask you again: what happened?'

Max's ribs had not been up for conversation.

'Piss off, Nash,' he'd said, as firmly as he could, and shut his eyes.

For a moment, Max involuntarily shut his eyes; but then he felt Sophie's soft hand on his cheek.

'It was no big deal. I should have known better. They stitched me up and I got sent back to London, which was a bit of a relief, quite frankly. But it was in London that the real problem started.'

Max drained his glass. Sophie still said nothing. She could tell he was struggling, but she wanted to keep quiet – to let him talk.

'To start with, it was just for the craic. Before I went to work in the morning, I'd study three or four sporting events that day. Racing, football, tennis, whatever. And I'd programme my account on a betting exchange to back the horses or players if they were a longer price than they should have been. Or lay them if they were a shorter price.'

'Lay?'

'Sorry. Lay means take a bet on them. Like being the bookmaker.'

'Okay. Go on.'

'I was cautious – to start with. I put a limit on how much risk I would let my account take on any one outcome. But the fun was being at work all day – where I couldn't look for a second at what was going on – and then the adrenalin rush of getting home, opening my account and seeing what had happened.'

'Max! Did you lose a lot?'

'No. Quite the opposite, in fact. I won steadily. Too steadily. It killed the anticipation. There was no fear or excitement when I got home. So I changed things.'

'You were winning and you changed things?'

'Yup. By then I'd accumulated a fair bit of capital in my account. So I stopped putting a limit on how much I could lose. That reignited the tension. I'd be sitting at my boring desk, listening to foreign telephone exchanges, supposedly trying to identify terrorists, while all the time I was wondering what was going on with my account. By then it was more like twenty events every day.'

'And you lost everything? Just like your father.'

'Well, no. I didn't. I kept winning. But it was taking over my life. And then I crossed the line.' Max slipped off the sideboard and got the bottle out of the deep freeze.

'You crossed the line?'

'I was spending a lot of time listening in to conversations between government officials in small countries, and I was hearing stuff that had an impact on world currency markets.'

Sophie pulled a rather alarmed face.

'Well, sometimes terrorism is state-sponsored, so we have to listen to more than you would expect. It's the job . . .'

'But obtaining financially sensitive information isn't, surely?'

'No. It isn't. I was wrong to do it. That was when I realized I was out of control. I stopped, Sophie. And I promise you, I'd never do it again.'

'How did you stop?'

'I went to visit my father's urn at the crematorium. It was amongst a bunch of people I'd never heard of. It looked so anonymous, so lost. And I decided then I didn't want to end up like that. When I get buried, I want to know my family will come and join me one day.'

'Did you make a lot of money?' Sophie asked mischievously, deliberately lightening the mood.

'I did.'

'What did you do with it? Give it to charity?'

'On my wages? Don't be ridiculous. I bought the most expensive burgundies I could find and laid them down at the châteaux. They should be ready to drink in about eight years.'

Max wondered if Sophie would disapprove. But she was, after all, Jacques's daughter, and black rabbits don't breed white rabbits.

'Excellent. I guess that makes us both criminals,' she said with a naughty smile. She was indeed her father's daughter. 'What was your best currency deal?'

'I'm not sure . . .'

'Go on. Tell me.'

'Well, there was a small country in Africa we were listening in on. We thought they might be behind a terrorist attack. So we listened to their governmental switchboard. And I couldn't believe my luck. I found myself listening to whoever was meant to have some control of their finances – although control would have been the wrong word – being told by his department that their foreign currency reserves had plummeted.'

Sophie was riveted by Max's confession. She poured them both another glass.

'The only way out of their looming balance-of-payments crisis was to devalue their currency,' Max continued. 'I can't tell you how hard it was to stay at work for the rest of the day.

Anyway, as soon as I got home I bet against their currency big time. I know it was wrong.'

The more Max told her, the more fascinated she was. He was totally unlike anyone she'd ever met before. He was solid, strong and true. And yet he was naughty. He was a risk-taker and he wasn't straight down the line. He was, in fact, quite like her father in some ways.

'Did anyone you work with know about your gambling?'

Max thought immediately of Colin Corbett. The man who had bailed him out after Saudi Arabia. The man he'd then watched being executed in Russia. He knew he shouldn't tell Sophie what had happened at the dacha outside Moscow. But she was involved with Pallesson now. And the guilt he felt over Corbett had been eating away at him. So he told her everything.

'That is why you have to get out of Amsterdam,' Max said finally. 'That is how dangerous he is. I wonder every day if I shouldn't have done something to try and save Corbett. That was what my heart was telling me to do. Create a diversion. Anything. But my head stopped me. They train your heart out of you, Sophie. And I let him die.'

Max slid down from the sideboard and put his hands around Sophie's waist. She slipped her arms around his neck and he lifted her up and pulled her towards him.

'Shall we skip the English fighting tonight? Bed or very comfortable Moroccan rug?'

Sophie was too busy thinking about other things to register the incongruousness of such a luxurious rug amongst all the other cheap furniture.

'Rug, I think,' she whispered into Max's ear.

'Good choice. I'd hate to think of you hiding yourself under any sheets.'

12

Max kissed the back of Sophie's neck as she sat at his kitchen table drinking tea with no milk.

'That was the nicest shower I've ever had,' she said as she leant back to press against his mouth.

'Sorry about the milk situation. Wasn't expecting visitors.'

'Just as well. Your fridge hasn't got any shelves. I've never met anyone with an empty, shelf-less fridge.'

'I hope you've never met anyone who had a shower with you like that either?'

'Max,' she said with a scornful look on her face. 'Gentlemen don't ask such questions!'

'Sorry.'

'Of course I haven't, by the way. Anyway, you need a housekeeper.'

'I know. This place is a dump. I'm never here. I haven't spent one evening in this place.'

That wasn't strictly true, but Max was subconsciously rewriting history. He just prayed she wouldn't ask him if Gemma had ever been there. He really didn't think he could lie to her. But Sophie was too smart to ask that.

* * *

Max didn't do airport goodbyes, but he needed to know that Sophie was safely on her flight to Nice before he flew to London. And he was worried about Gassin. He also needed to buy two new pay-as-you-go phones. One for him, one for her.

'Don't talk to anyone on your normal phones. When we talk, it must be on these two phones. Keep the conversations short and don't use any word that might alert listening devices. Like my name. Sophie, you must persuade Jacques to move. Please. At least until this has all blown over.'

'He won't go anywhere. Papa's a stubborn old man.'

'This isn't the time to be digging your heels in. These people could do anything. And if they think you've double-crossed them, they'll kill you. You have to get out of Gassin.'

Sophie gave a shrug of her shoulders, then planted one last kiss on Max's lips before walking up to passport control. She gave him a small wave after her passport had been examined, and then she was gone.

Max watched her disappear, his heart in turmoil. He'd dropped his guard. If Pallesson knew they were emotionally attached, he'd try to use her as a bargaining chip. Max knew he shouldn't have gone there, but he hadn't wanted to stop either. He was smitten. Life was not going to work out unless he turned Pallesson over. His mission had gone from a job to something much more personal.

He'd also trashed the order of his life, and that needed addressing. Max pulled out his phone and dialled Gemma's mobile number as he walked towards the British Airways desk.

Gemma had made Casper his usual breakfast, though she wondered why she bothered.

'Fancy going out to dinner tonight?' Casper asked. It was normally the one conversation he could have with Gemma that didn't end in an argument.

'Where?'

'Why don't you choose?'

'Because you never like the places that I do.'

'Rubbish.'

'You don't like Zuma.'

'You know I can't hear a word anyone says in there. And I can't stand all those spivs who crowd around the bar. They still think it's the trendiest place in London.'

'I suppose you want to go to Scott's and mingle with all the other city wankers?'

'I like the food at Scott's. And I like Sean, the doorman.'

'Well go on holiday with him then.'

'How about Dinner?'

'I don't like snail porridge.'

'You've never eaten it. And he does snail porridge at The Fat Duck, not Dinner. Even A. A. Gill raves about the food at Dinner. It's good old-fashioned English grub.'

'Okay. We'll go to Dinner. But I'm not eating snail porridge.'

Casper retreated behind his newspaper. God, she was so bloody ungrateful. He ignored her for the next five minutes.

'I'm thinking of going to Amsterdam tomorrow,' Gemma said for the third time in as many minutes.

'That's good,' he muttered from behind his paper.

'There's an important interior design exhibition on.'

'Great.'

He really didn't care, Gemma thought.

'I'll probably have oral sex with my yoga teacher today. She's very cute,' Gemma said neutrally.

'What?' Casper pulled down his paper.

'Just checking you were listening. What did I say before that?'

'I've got to rush – late already.' Casper stood up and put his jacket on.

'When are you seeing your therapist?'

'He says you need to come and see him too.'

'Yeah, I bet he does. Then he can charge double.'

As he closed the front door, she breathed a sigh of relief and turned her thoughts to Max. Thank God for Max. She would have gone insane without him.

She'd tried to call him a couple of times the night before, but he hadn't answered. Nothing unusual in that. It happened quite often. But she'd felt lonely and isolated and she'd desperately wanted to speak to him.

Then, as if on cue, an 'Unknown Number' rang on the phone – which she knew would be him. A big smile spread across her face.

'Hello,' she said brightly.

'Gemma,' Max replied.

'What's the matter?'

'Nothing. Why do you say that?'

'Your voice. It sounded like something's wrong.'

Max immediately felt on the spot. This wasn't how he wanted to tell Gemma about Sophie.

'Oh, no. Nothing out of the usual. You know, work.'

Neither of them said anything for a moment.

'Well?'

'Well, what?' Max asked.

'Well, what about me? When are you going to make time for me?'

Max was familiar with Gemma's demands.

'I'm going to be in London today. Something's come up. Usual place?'

'Something's come up? Oh, how very convenient. I'd be so grateful if you could fit me in too.'

'Gemma, come on . . .'

'What time?' she asked sulkily.

'Six.'

Max rang off. He knew there was no point chatting to her when she was in that mood.

Gemma poured herself some more coffee. Max had sounded stressed. But then he had that sort of job, she reasoned. Anyway, at least she would be able to spend the evening with him. She'd tell Casper she didn't feel like dinner after all. He'd go to his club. He always did.

Maybe her and Max could go to a film and cuddle up in the back row and behave like teenagers? Or go to a trendy bar in the Fulham Road where none of her friends would be, and get drunk?

Max made a call from the payphone in the departure lounge.

'Jacques?'

'Yes.'

'Jacques, Sophie is on her way back to Gassin,' Max said, deliberately not using his own name. 'But you both have to lie low somewhere else for a while. This whole thing might go off, and our friend will send in the heavy brigade if he thinks he's been double-crossed.'

'This is my home. This is where I will stay.'

'Jacques, please . . .'

'I have my father's pistol. It stopped plenty of Germans in the war. It will be waiting for anyone who invades my home.'

'Jacques. For Sophie's sake . . .'

The phone went dead.

Max walked up St James's with a heavy heart. He was dreading his meeting with Gemma. She'd given him so much, and now he was dumping her. He decided to duck into White's for a stiffener.

'Can I help you, sir?' a rather cocky hall porter asked from his glass-windowed cubicle. Which was code for: I don't recognize you, are you a member?

Max had been a member for ten years, but he'd been abroad for most of that time. In fact, if he worked out the cost of his subscriptions, every drink in the place had cost him about five hundred pounds.

'I don't think so,' Max replied blankly, and walked on through the entrance hall, past a load of umbrellas hanging on their hooks, to the bar. The porter would have to figure out for himself whether he was or wasn't a member. Max wasn't volunteering his name like a naughty schoolboy.

'Evening, sir,' the barman greeted him, standing virtually to attention in his short, immaculate white jacket. 'What can I get you, sir?'

'Vodka martini, please.'

Max glanced around the empty bar. It was reassuringly old. When you were standing at that bar, you were definitely in your club.

'On account, sir?' the barman asked.

'Yes, please. Max Ward.' Sensing that the barman was far too polite to ask his name, Max put him out of his misery.

He wandered past the grandfather clock into the large sitting room. At the far end a rather portly figure was spreadeagled over the billiards table, playing on his own. If it hadn't been for his bright red braces, his trousers would have given up the unequal struggle as he reached for his shot. He heard Max approaching as he missed it and looked up from the table.

'Well, well, well. Look what the cat's brought in – Max Ward.'

Max half recognized the flushed red face, but he couldn't put a name to it.

'Johnny Jameson. Remember me?'

'Johnny. Yes of course. Lovely to see you.'

Johnny Jameson had put on about six stone since Max had

last seen him at Eton. He also looked like he'd soused himself in gin.

'Max, you look just the same.'

'You too, Johnny,' Max said with every ounce of sincerity that he could dredge up.

'So where you been hiding?'

'Abroad mostly. Working for the Foreign Office.'

'Really. Meet any of those spooks? Rather fancy having a go at that sort of thing myself. Somewhere behind enemy lines. Keeping an ear to the ground. Know what I mean?'

'Yes. Think it would suit you, Johnny. So what are you up to at the moment?'

Johnny made a strange noise with his lips as he pondered this question.

'Been through a bit of a rough patch, actually. Wife left me.'

'Sorry to hear that.'

'Usual thing.'

'Usual thing?'

'You know. Had a bad run on the horses. You were pretty hot at that, weren't you? Ever hear anything these days?'

'No. Bit out of touch really.'

Johnny Jameson then got into his stride and regurgitated a few people they'd been at school with. All of them seemed to have done rather well, or had a spot of bad luck. Johnny appeared to take heart from the latter group.

'Anyway, must be getting on. Good to see you,' Max said after five minutes, now desperate to escape.

'Yes. Good to catch up. Watch how you go. Oh, and let me know if anything comes up at the Foreign Office, would you?'

'Yes, of course,' Max said cheerily as he retreated towards the reading room.

'Well, that was a bit of luck,' Johnny Jameson said to himself as he lined up the next ball.

Max had a quick read of the evening paper as he finished his Martini, and then looked at his watch. He was tempted to have another, but he was already late. He looked out of the window at the traffic backed up in St James's. It was solid.

It was only a thirty-second walk from White's to the Ritz. Gemma was already at their normal table in the corner of the Rivoli Bar, her back to the wall. Max had been unsure of meeting there when they'd started their affair, but Gemma had pointed out that no one would be stupid enough to take their mistress to the Ritz for a drink.

Max ushered his way past the head waiter, who was ritually humiliating some customer who'd taken the liberty of not wearing a tie.

'Sorry I'm late. Some idiot who's too rich, too stupid and too green has decided to dig up all the roads. Why don't they just leave it alone?'

Gemma clearly wasn't in the mood to discuss roadworks in London. She smiled thinly and bent forward to kiss him.

Under normal circumstances, the old-fashioned streak in Max loved the Lalique figures set into the walls and the polished wooden panels. But he was oblivious to them today.

'I think I'll have a gin and tonic for a change, please,' he said to the waiter, who was trying to give him a cocktail list. 'And another vodka martini with an olive, please, for madam.'

'Gordons or Bombay, sir?'

'Bombay please.'

'Any particular vodka?'

'Yes. U'Luvka, please.'

'Very good, sir.'

Max's heart sank as he looked at Gemma sitting demurely across the table. There were two moods of Gemma. The confident, selfish, swashbuckling, devil-may-care Gemma who holds no fear. He was comfortable with that Gemma. She could look after herself; wherever he was, whatever he was doing. Then there was her alter ego: a lost, defenceless, moribund little girl. She didn't appear very often. But she was sitting in front of him right now. He could read all the signs.

'You sounded tense on the phone, darling. What's the matter?' she asked as she reached out and put her hand on his. 'I felt worried last night when I couldn't get hold of you.'

Max was desperate for his gin and tonic.

'Things are a bit difficult. Delicate operation. Anyway, you know not to worry about me.'

The waiter arrived at Max's shoulder with their drinks on a silver tray, which bought him a few seconds as the waiter unhurriedly placed them on the stiff white cotton glass mats.

'How are you apart from that?'

'I'm desperately unhappy, Max,' Gemma said, blinking as she looked at him. He suddenly felt sick. Gemma looked shattered. She drained her glass and fixed Max with intense eyes.

'I want to tell Casper.'

'What? No, Gemma, that's madness.'

'I don't think he'll care. Really, he won't.'

'No. You, can't. Not now . . .'

'Why would he care? I can't even remember the last time we had sex.' Gemma emphasized the 's' and said it far louder than she needed to. A couple of tables away, two businessmen in slightly shabby pinstripe suits couldn't stop themselves staring.

'Gemma, we're in a bloody bar. There's no need to shout.'

As Max looked around them, the waiter expertly caught his glance and was at his side in an instant.

'Thank you. The same again, please,' said Max.

'Certainly, sir.'

Max had played out several versions of this conversation on the plane. None of them had gone like this. It was one thing to end a relationship with a tough, swashbuckling, thick-skinned mistress, but quite another to take a vulnerable, miserable girl who'd supported him through thick and thin and snap her like a twig. He just couldn't do it.

'Please, Gemma. We're not ready for this. Besides, things could get messy my end. I really can't cope with any distractions. Please. Let's wait.'

Their conversation went round and round. Max tried to spit it out, but it was too awful. He felt like a vet looking down at a defenceless family dog that had been sent for destruction because no one loved it any more. There was no way he could do it.

She didn't get a romantic film or a drink in the Fulham Road, either. In fact, she was back home before Casper, and in the spare room pretending to be asleep when he got in – much to his relief.

13

The Hague

Max was the last to arrive at the weekly briefing session. He'd been delayed talking to Arthur at the front desk.

'Thirty seconds early,' Max said half jokingly, half defensively as he pulled out a chair.

Graham Smith was at the head of the table. Max noticed that he was wearing a buttoned-down-collar shirt and loafers. Good old Smith, still young at heart. What a joy to work for him rather than the stiff-shirted pillock who took over from poor Corbett in Moscow.

It was Smith's meeting to chair. He was fiddling with his phone in his lap and didn't seem to be in any hurry to kick off.

Max glanced over towards *The Peasants in Winter*, but it was impossible to tell whether his copy was still on the wall or whether Pallesson had substituted his own. And he couldn't risk Pallesson picking up on any further interest.

Max was sitting immediately to Smith's right and, to his surprise, Louise was beside him. Surprise, because she didn't normally take notes at these meetings. She was writing something on her pad and didn't look up at Max, which he welcomed.

Pallesson was directly opposite. He was leaning back in his chair with a supercilious smirk across his face. Max didn't give him the satisfaction of appearing to notice him, even though there were only five people in the room. His mind flashed to the dacha outside Moscow. He pictured Pallesson raising the rifle towards Corbett's head. If he was going to destroy Pallesson, he had to be cleverer than him.

Max took a deep breath and put all thoughts of Moscow from his mind, occupying himself with the present.

The fifth person in the meeting was Data Dave, their digital analyst. Max liked Dave. He had no ego, and always helped out, however late it meant he had to stay. But he really didn't seem cool enough to be a Dave. Whenever Max caught a glimpse of him across the office, he was always rubbing his eyes with a pained expression on his face. He looked pale and his hair was always a tad greasy. He should have been given a bookworm's name such as Cornelius.

'Morning all,' Smith said genially. 'Louise has kindly volunteered to sit in for Sally today, who's off sick. Thank you, Louise.' Louise smiled in the direction of Smith, but caught Max's eye as she did so. Volunteered, Max reflected, for a meeting at which he was always present. Was she stalking him? He looked away from Smith towards Data Dave, in case his face gave anything away. It was unlikely Dave would ever pick up on anything remotely human.

'Pallesson is going to brief us on progress with Jorgan Stam this morning,' Smith continued. 'So fire away,' he said, looking at Pallesson and gesturing towards the whiteboard against the wall.

Pallesson picked up his notes and stood with an unnecessary amount of ceremony, given those present in the room. God, you're a prick, Max mused. So bloody vain, you can't help showing off even when there isn't anyone to show off to.

'Jorgan Stam,' Pallesson said, in a staccato voice that he clearly thought conveyed gravitas. He peeled a photo, supposedly of Stam, from the top of his notes and fixed it to the left-hand side of the whiteboard with a round, coloured magnet. The individual in the picture had thin, sandy, swept-back hair and a stubbly moustache.

'Stam has been involved in pretty well everything over the years. Cinemas to start with, until one got burnt down. Then high-end girls, which he still controls. And coffee houses, of course. He hangs out at the Dice club, off Oudezijds Achterburgwal. The hoods he employs unimaginatively call themselves "the Dice Gang".'

'Stam sticks up two fingers to everyone. Heroin from Afghanistan is his latest move. So nothing that would worry us, if it wasn't for the network he's part of.'

Max noticed Louise's left hand dropping down on to her thigh. She was wearing an innocuous enough patterned skirt. Innocuous enough, that was, until she pulled it across her thigh. It had a large split down the middle, which happily opened to reveal suspenders.

He knew Pallesson and Data Dave wouldn't be able to see, because of the table. He glanced across at Smith, whose eyes were glued to the whiteboard. Max guessed that he was blocking Smith's sight line to Louise's thigh, anyway. But one thing was not in doubt. If she wasn't stalking him, she was doing the next closest thing.

'There's a bit of a mystery about his number two, if he even exists,' Pallesson said. 'No one knows who he is. He seems to sit in the background, away from the front line. But the name Wielart has been mentioned. Paul Wielart.'

Max shifted in his seat, imperceptibly shifting his eyeline away from Louise.

'If he does exist,' Pallesson continued, 'he makes this lot

difficult to read. It seems strange that a thug like Stam would have a shadow.'

Louise made a brief note.

Max was regretting Louise. She'd been too close to home. He'd have to sort it out. He focused on the photo of Stam.

Pallesson stuck up five more photos, linked them all with lines and looked very pleased with himself as he briefed those present on the details of each individual.

'Now we come to the bit that interests us. My source in Stam's operation has put us on to how they're tied up with the Taliban and al-Qaeda.'

'Which one is your source?' Smith asked, focusing on the board. Pallesson smiled patronizingly, even though Smith was his section chief.

'Come on, Graham. I've got to keep that tight. I gave my word. Just me. No one else on our side . . .'

'But you're talking about *us*, Pallesson. Not the whole goddamn service. Just us. Sitting in this room,' Smith replied fairly robustly.

'I gave my word,' Pallesson replied, equally forcefully. 'Tight is how it is, and tight is how it's going to stay. We're nearly there.'

Smith knew Pallesson was acting within his operational rights. But he wasn't particularly happy about it.

'It's hardly in the spirit of a small team, though, is it? It's not as if what you tell us is going to crash around Vauxhall, be put on a disk and left on a train, for God's sake.'

'Graham, please let me do this my way. It will work.'

Pallesson now had Max's full attention. He'd heard that last line before, in Moscow. Word for word. But it hadn't led them anywhere near Kroshtov or his operation. And Max knew why.

'Those who sail with a lie will find no berth, and their boat will not tie up in a port,' proclaimed Pallesson, smugness oozing from every cell.

Indeed, Max thought, that's *exactly* what will happen if I have anything to do with it.

'You're the man,' Max said unctuously, leaning forward slightly in his chair. Pallesson was throwing up a diversion, as he had done in Moscow. This was all an elaborate ruse to set everyone looking in the wrong direction. Max needed to look as though he was falling for it.

'The Taliban, as you know, process opium into heroin, which is then shipped to Amsterdam via various routes and in different guises. But the Taliban don't receive any payment from Jorgan Stam,' Pallesson continued, getting into his stride.

Max wanted to chuck in a flippant remark along the lines of 'that's very generous of them', but instead he nodded earnestly.

'So how do they get paid?' Smith asked.

Pallesson raised the palm of his hand towards Smith to silence him. Smith bit his tongue and waited for an explanation.

'Two ways,' Pallesson said smugly. 'The first is beautifully simple. There's a very generous cash supporter of an Amsterdam-based charity called Aid Somalia. Millions of euros find their way into this charity; then it gets moved to Somalia – where, of course, it doesn't aid Somalis at all. It funds al-Qaeda training camps. The second way is through a bank account in the Dutch Antilles. It's paid into a German bank through various offshore companies.'

'Is this all tracked?' Max asked, throwing the question as much towards Data Dave as Pallesson. Dave said nothing but nodded his head.

'Oh yes,' Pallesson said triumphantly. 'All tracked. The account Stam's operation uses in the Dutch Antilles is fed with freshly laundered proceeds from the heroin that they sell around Europe. Quite a lot of it ends up in London, needless to say.'

'Who owns the bank account in Germany?' Max asked, still giving the impression that his concentration was locked on.

'A Saudi called Khalif Ashmal. In fact, he has German nationality. He processes the money through his German company, runs it through various subsidiary companies and subcontractors until it arrives at its destination. It's a labyrinth.'

Data Dave nodded his head theatrically, confirming that he had trawled through the money trail.

'What's the destination?' Smith asked in a slightly irked tone. He didn't appreciate Pallesson's cliff-hanging style.

'We're pretty sure it's going to a network of al-Qaeda cells around Europe. Probably the UK, Spain and Turkey. But we're still in the dark here. It makes sense. It completes the circle, because al-Qaeda then supplies the Taliban with weapons in Afghanistan. And that answers your question, Graham. That's how the Taliban get paid.'

Pallesson let silence settle over the room. Dave nodded slowly. Louise scribbled shorthand on to her pad. Pallesson sat down in his chair. Graham Smith scratched his head. And Max was quickly trying to think of something to say that would give the impression he'd taken the bait.

'Good work,' Max said. 'First class. But where do we go from here? Intercept a shipment? That won't achieve much. We need to identify the cells—'

'If I may interrupt,' Pallesson said with a satisfied smile, 'I am confident that my man can get us the information we need—'

'Why would he do that?' It was now Smith's turn to interrupt. 'What is he? A bloody charity? Why is he giving us this stuff?'

'He has his reasons,' Pallesson said firmly. 'If he can step away from the wreckage of Stam's gang before we strike – and he will – he'll be well placed in the future—'

'To keep the supply line open?' Max said instinctively.

'Yes, Ward. To bring in drugs. Not our problem. Unless I'm mistaken, it's *our* job to stop innocent civilians being blown up. Not to nanny their private lives.'

Max kicked himself for sounding like a dissenting voice and looked across at Smith. It was his call, not Max's.

'How long?' asked Smith.

'A couple of weeks.' Pallesson was very sure of himself.

Max bit his lip. There were some blatantly obvious questions to ask. How would a member of Stam's 'Dice Gang' be able to find out where the money ended up after Ashmal had washed it? That was ridiculous. And the assumption that al-Qaeda supplied the Taliban with weapons by way of payment for the heroin that came through Amsterdam could be a huge guess and nothing more. Max wanted to see the data that tracked the money into and out of the German bank account. But now was not the moment.

Anyway, this was all clearly irrelevant. Whatever Pallesson was planning with *The Peasants in Winter* would be far removed from any criminal activities involving Stam, which tallied with the steer from Tryon that Pallesson was planning something with van Ossen, Stam's rival. That was Pallesson's game – distract everyone from what he was really doing.

'Okay,' Smith said, tapping the table with his hand. 'Keep me posted. I want to know everything and anything as it comes in. Got me?' he asked Pallesson, looking him right in the eye.

'Without delay,' Pallesson confirmed. He didn't appreciate being given orders so bluntly, especially not by an idiot like Smith, but, for the time being, he would put up with it.

Max's mind had already drifted to his main concern. How was he casually going to look at *The Peasants in Winter*? It was hanging on the wall to Max's right with two other paintings either side of it. It would be odd if he stayed behind at the end of the meeting, but he couldn't just jump up and walk over to it.

Even though he knew it would make life harder down the line, Max could only think of one line of attack. As Louise stood up, he rose from his chair at the same moment and got his body between her and the door.

'Do you like art, Louise?' he asked casually whilst subtly pushing her towards the pictures.

'I do, as a matter of fact,' she replied and was happily shepherded towards them.

Max focused first on an oil painting of Venice. The plaque on it said Antoine Bouvard.

'Bouvard,' he said, as if it struck a resonance with him. 'Amazing light, don't you think?'

'Amazing orgasm is actually what I'm thinking,' Louise replied softly with a happy smile on her face.

'Shut up. Concentrate,' Max said urgently to a now confused Louise.

Max moved a couple of metres to his right. As he did so, he felt a presence behind them.

'Brueghel,' Max said. But he wasn't looking at the plaque on the frame. He was looking for the dog that should have miraculously appeared among the skating children. The dog that Sophie had added to Pallesson's copy. And it was there. Max couldn't stop a smile creasing his face. Pallesson had taken the bait.

'But which one?' Pallesson asked from behind him. Max's smile disappeared. His heart missed a beat.

'Sorry?' Max said, as casually as he could.

'Which one? Elder or Younger?'

Max breathed a sigh of relief.

'Elder, I would imagine.'

'Wrong,' Pallesson said triumphantly, looking at Louise. 'I suggest you ask someone who knows what they're talking about to tell you about art, my dear,' Pallesson said as he walked off.

'I know *exactly* what I want to learn from him, creep,' she said under her breath with a lascivious look.

Max cleared his throat.

'Louise, we need to have a chat.'

14

London

Max was the first off the early London flight the next morning. He made straight for his De Lorean, in a corner of the short-term car park, retrieved his keys from the magnetic box attached to the chassis by the exhaust manifold and opened the boot manually. The remote unlocking system had been removed so that it couldn't activate a bomb.

Inside the boot was a large mirror on the end of a pole. He'd parked in the corner to avoid agitating the natives as he checked for explosives.

Once he'd looked under the car, he opened the bonnet and used the mirror to check the engine was clean. If anything went wrong with this operation, Pallesson and whoever he was in cahoots with would think nothing of a little collateral damage if it dispensed with a direct threat. And it struck Max as the perfect place to booby-trap a vehicle; plenty of cover and no one asking any questions about someone milling around a car with a bag.

As soon as he came out of the tunnel leaving Heathrow, Max called Sophie.

'Hello,' she answered without saying her name, as Max had told her to.

'Are you okay?'

'We're fine.'

'Where are you?'

'Still at home. Can I say that on this phone?'

Sophie wasn't enjoying covertness. She'd already worked out it was very impersonal.

'The bird has taken the bait,' Max continued. 'They could find the tracker any time. You must get out of the house for a bit. Just in case this goes tits-up.'

'Nice expression,' she replied in a slightly injured, offended voice.

'You have to move your father. Don't tell me where.'

'He won't go,' she replied grumpily. 'He's a stubborn—'

'Make him. We should have organized this for you. I don't know why it wasn't done.'

'Papa says he has a gun. I'm not even sure if he knows how to use it, but he won't leave.'

'Look, I have to go. I'll speak to you later.' Max ended the call. They'd spoken for long enough.

Max knew that Sophie would feel pissed off and rejected after their call. Maybe even a bit violated. He'd been through this before, and it never worked well.

He decided to break the rules and send her a text. But as he sent his message – **Xxxx** – an incoming message arrived. All it said was **Piss off Max**.

Mindful of the risk that a text message trail could link him to Sophie, putting her in danger if the wrong person got hold of his phone, he immediately deleted it.

He felt a pang of guilt, knowing how pissed off she was with him. Half of him wanted to ring her and tell her how much he loved her. The other half wanted to give himself a good kicking for letting her distract him mid-operation. But he knew he'd fallen for Sophie so badly that there was nothing he could do about it.

If he hadn't been wrestling with those thoughts, he would have remembered to text her back reminding her to delete their messages.

As Max turned on to the M4 towards London, he thought about Tryon. Why hadn't he covered Sophie and Jacques's safety? He must have known they would be vulnerable if the operation went wrong. And why had he insisted on the tracking device at such a late stage? Sophie had done an unbelievable job in hiding it, but it would have been a very clumsy undertaking if she hadn't managed to get hold of the right tools. He had more than a few questions for Tryon when he got to the boathouse.

Max parked a couple of streets away and walked around to the alley. He looked at the height of the walls on either side. If they came at him from both ends, he'd have nowhere to escape to. He'd never get over the walls in time. The CCTV cameras would be interesting for the police trying to solve his murder; but not much help to him while he was fighting for his life.

Halfway down the alley, Max questioned why he was using this route again. Only because Tryon had told him to, he figured. He needed to raise his game. He wasn't sharp. He was sleep-walking around.

Max resisted looking behind him, and no one appeared in front. He felt a slight wave of relief when he got to the river-end of the alley. That would be the last time he approached the boathouse that way.

He checked his watch and timed one minute and fifteen seconds. Then he carefully stole a glance down the alley. It was empty. He continued along the towpath, which was now dry. It wasn't high tide today. Max wondered if that would ever be important. Not if he was going to use a different approach next time. Whatever his instructions.

As Max walked up the concrete slipway towards the side of the boathouse he noticed one of the big doors, through which the boats were brought down to the river, had been slid back a fraction. There was probably a good reason why it was open, he reasoned. Perhaps to get a draught through the building to help dry the boats off. But there were also several good reasons why it wouldn't be left open if no one was around. And the whole point of meeting in the boathouse at this hour was because there was never anyone around. Max was ready for anything now, although a Glock would have come in handy.

Tryon's bike was leaning up against the wall as usual. Max wondered how much earlier than him Tryon arrived for their meetings, because he knew *he* wasn't late today. A fraction early, in fact.

Max caught a slight whiff of Tryon's tobacco as he walked between the boats towards the back of the boathouse. He waited for Tryon to chastise him for being early . . . or late . . . or on time, but there was silence. Max stooped down to look under the boats, back towards the workbench where he'd sat during their last meeting. No sign of Tryon. Max's antennae were picking up some bad signals. He could feel the hair standing up on his arms and legs.

Stealthily he worked his way down towards the big doors. He could just see the Thames through the narrow gap. Max pushed against the doors and took a couple of steps down the slipway, but there was nothing on the ground between the boathouse and the river.

A cold sweat bubbled up on Max's forehead. Resisting the temptation to shout out Tryon's name, he carefully made his way back through the boathouse to check whether the old hand – or his body – was there. Or anyone else's for that matter. But the place was empty.

Max's instinct was to get out of there fast, but that, he

reflected, was what any hostile presence would expect. They'd had the option to attack him inside the boathouse and they hadn't taken it.

If they'd thrown Tryon into the river, a man his age would have no chance of survival. Max pictured the desperate image of Tryon drowning as the river swept his body away.

He knew one thing: it wouldn't be smart to return to his car. Maybe they planned to follow him. Maybe Pallesson had already worked out he'd been done up like a kipper and wanted the original picture. But how would he have linked the picture to Tryon? And him, if they hadn't got to Jacques and Sophie?

Max spotted a small motor launch, the kind used by rowing coaches to bellow instructions at their crews. It was on a light-framed trailer, which he could easily guide down the slope into the river.

Someone is going to be very pissed off, he thought, as he submerged the boat and let the trailer sink to the bottom of the river. Max watched the bank for any unusual movement as he set off upstream. The water looked dark, bitterly cold and in a hurry to get to the sea.

Hoping for a miracle, he dialled Tryon's mobile, but wasn't surprised when it cut off unanswered. He suddenly felt very exposed out in the middle of the river. And in very real danger without Tryon as his head cover.

Max spent the next five minutes analysing his position as he hugged the far bank of the river to maintain some cover. There were two people who might be able to help him: Pete Carr and Keate.

Max pulled his 'Sophie' phone out of his pocket and sent her another message. Things happening. Get your father out.

Max then rang Pete Carr on his usual phone while he waited for Teddington Lock to fill up.

'How are you, mate?' Pete asked cheerily.

'Good, thanks. Bit damp where I am, but apart from that, I can't complain. And you?'

'Good, mate. Nothing that a million quid wouldn't sort out.'

'Well, I'm sure a man of your resources won't have too much trouble laying your hands on that. Can you get on to that French satellite and see where our tracker has got to? She's on the move.'

'Hang on. I'll have a look for you now. Give me thirty seconds . . .'

Max checked the faces around the lock yet again. They all seemed to be busy with whatever they were doing and completely disinterested in him. He would go upstream for a few locks. Hopefully anyone after him would guess wrongly that he'd gone east towards Docklands.

'Right, mate,' Pete's voice reported. 'She's sitting still in Amsterdam. There's been no movement for over a day.'

'By the way, Pete, have you spoken to Tryon today?'

'Not for a few days, actually. Why?'

'Just wondering. I was meant to meet him today and he didn't turn up.'

'Shouldn't worry about that, mate. That's Tryon for you. They seek him here, they seek him there. And the rest of the time they haven't got a bloody clue *where* he is. Probably how he stays alive.' Pete laughed. 'There's one thing you can be sure of with Tryon: it's never straightforward with him. Smoke and mirrors, mate, smoke and mirrors.'

'Well, maybe.'

It was hard to read Pete Carr. Max weighed up in his mind whether he was just a bit casual, or being evasive. Was he in cahoots with Tryon, and holding something back? After all, it was Tryon who had directed him to Carr. Had Tryon been compromised by Pallesson? He needed to press Keate on that again. If he had been, the whole *Peasants in Winter* operation

168

had been concocted to set Max up. And he'd get a good stretch for stealing a work of art from the British Embassy. The only thing that Max was certain of was that there was no one else in the Office he could turn to. Tryon had made sure of that.

As Max pulled away from the lock his phone started vibrating. Gemma was calling. He really didn't want to talk to her at that moment. But he knew, given her state in the Ritz, that she would keep ringing. He'd have to deal with it.

'You all right?'

'I'm fine, Max. Obviously I want to ask you where you are, but that isn't allowed, is it?'

'No. Definitely not. More not than usual, in fact.'

'I'm planning on coming over to Amsterdam.'

That was not what Max wanted to hear. Not on any front.

'Gemma, I can't say anything. I'm fully operational. I'll ring you when I can. 'Bye.'

Max suspected the ''Bye' must have sounded very flat. Dreadful, in fact. But he had more important things to worry about. For all he knew, someone was about to take him out.

By the time Max made it to Molesey Lock, he'd seen the ghosts of a handful of assassins along the towpath. It would be too easy for them to find him on the river.

He chucked the rope up and managed to lasso it around one of the solid metal moorings way above his head. The water poured into the lock from upstream, drowning out the sound of anything else. No one would hear a gunshot. Max thought he might as well be wearing a bullesye on his back.

As soon as the boat rose high enough, he pulled himself up on to the side of the lock. He could see a way out at the far end. Without looking right or left, Max strode towards it. He heard a shout behind him. There was a gate about twenty metres away. Max legged it, swerving as he ran.

A large figure appeared in the gateway. Max hit him with a straight-arm smack on the solar plexus. The giant was immediately poleaxed. Two bags of shopping that he'd been carrying back to his barge went flying as he lay moaning on the floor. Max shook his wrist and kept going down the lane. He didn't have time to stop or think. The man on the lock platform probably wasn't trying to kill him; he wouldn't have shouted if he had been. But he probably knew he'd stolen the launch. At the bottom of the lane, Max saw a sign to Hampton Court railway station. It wasn't ideal, but it would have to do.

Max lurked outside the station as he waited for a train heading back towards London. His heart had stopped heaving and his head was clearing. What were his options? There were only two scenarios he could get his head around. Either Tryon was dead. Or he was hanging him out to dry.

15

Amsterdam, six months earlier
Wielart had been at his desk for an hour when Francisca knocked on his side door at exactly eleven o'clock. The bells were chiming as he smiled at her and closed the door behind her. He knew no one could see her entering. And he had a clear vision of his two objectives, and the order in which he would achieve them.

Francisca started by outlining the problems in detail, as far as she knew them, from what her father had said when he'd broken down in front of her and her mother. Then Wielart got her to copy each document as he read it and absorbed the contents.

After two hours, Wielart stopped reading and told Francisca to leave the photocopier.

'I can help,' he said slowly and unhappily. 'But it will be at considerable risk to myself.'

Francisca didn't know how to react. She was both relieved and uncertain.

'We'll do anything for you,' she said, desperation in her voice.

'Will your father?'

'Yes, yes. He'll do anything.'

'Very well. You are sure of that?'

171

Francisca nodded. The stress had made her face look more interesting, he thought. He wanted her, but he'd have to wait until he'd secured his first objective.

After a pause, Wielart continued: 'The only way this situation can be saved is if Deetman Shipping is amalgamated into one of my companies. That way I can alter the figures, call in a few favours and cover up what your father has been up to. As I said, it will involve a substantial risk for me.'

'Would my father lose his company?'

'Francisca, at the moment your father is facing the prospect of losing everything and going to prison. If I help, he'll still own half of his company and he won't go to prison.'

The penny dropped straight away. Francisca got it. But there was nothing she could do about it. She would have to persuade her father this was the only way out.

'I will draw up an agreement for your father. If he accepts, I can get to work right away and make this disappear. He can still run the company, but I will be his partner. Life will be good for him, again, Francisca, and he'll have you to thank.'

Francisca really didn't know how to feel as she listened to this. Her white knight, the father of her best friend, was using this situation to steal half her father's life's work from them. And there was nothing she could do about it.

'In addition, Francisca, you and your family will never breathe a word of my involvement and help to your family. You have never been to my office. Does anyone know you have come to see me?'

'No,' Francisca replied truthfully, wanting to be sick when he used the word *help*.

'Do you understand that? It is for your own sake.'

She nodded again. She wanted to kill him.

Wielart set to work immediately drawing up a simple contract that would give him control of fifty-one per cent of

Deetman Shipping. Fifty-one per cent that Jorgan Stam would never know about.

'Bring this back signed by your father at seven o'clock tomorrow evening – not before – and I will save him and his company. And to avoid confusion, please bring his passport so I can check the signature against it. Formality.'

'But how will he know that he can trust you?'

'I'd hardly want to own half a company that was about to be shut down by the taxman, would I?' Wielart replied with a certain amount of impatience.

Clutching the documents in her hand, Francisca let herself out of the side door. Her father would have to accept the deal. But she knew Wielart was helping himself, not them. And she vowed that she would get even.

One of Pallesson's phones vibrated as he walked along the quiet canal. There were only three people who currently had that number for him. Shifting the light suitcase to his other hand, he pulled the phone from his pocket and looked at the text message from his man in London. Job done was all it said. That was all it needed to say. Pallesson let a satisfied smile spread across his face. He deleted the message and snapped his phone shut. He wouldn't be getting any more attention from Tryon.

If Jenkins's information had been correct, he'd wiped out the threat in one easy stroke. And if for some reason the threat had spread wider, there was no evidence trail back to him. No harm done. It had been a prudent step to take. Keep on top of the detail and cut off any weeds as soon as they appear.

It didn't bother Pallesson that he was rendezvousing with van Ossen at an unfamiliar address. He expected to be kept on the move. While there had to be an element of trust, the fact that he was obliged to lend van Ossen the Brueghel as collateral showed it wasn't in abundance. That was normal. It did mean, however, that van Ossen had the upper hand.

Pallesson checked the door number he'd been given. It was down a fairly narrow street that didn't have much light at eight in the evening. As he approached the door, he saw a gold plaque on the wall. He knew enough Dutch to know that *Dierenkliniek* meant 'Veterinary Surgery'.

Fransen and Piek appeared from the shadows behind him. They were still wearing the same dark jackets and black polo-neck shirts.

'Good evening,' Pallesson said.

Neither of them replied. Piek pushed past Pallesson and opened the door.

'Remind me to buy the two of you some new clothes before we next meet,' Pallesson said to Fransen. He got no response.

The inside of the surgery smelt clinical. Even though the last operation – a repair on a gunshot wound to a human patient – had been carried out three weeks before.

Pallesson followed van Ossen's men along a corridor festooned with leaflets and posters of happy-looking animals. The door at the end of the passage opened to reveal a high-tech operating room.

'Ah. So you're a veterinary surgeon,' Pallesson commented sarcastically to Piek. 'I'll bring my cat round. It needs neutering.'

Piek ignored him and took up position by the door, his back to the wall. Fransen did likewise at the other end of the room. It was evident that no one would be leaving until their boss gave the nod.

Van Ossen was standing at one end of an observation table. Two men in their early sixties stood beside him. Pallesson glanced around the immaculately tidy room. The only clutter was a tray of scalpels on a trolley.

'*Goedenavond,*' van Ossen said formally, as if he was meeting a client of the surgery. 'No problems, I trust?'

'No problems at my end,' Pallesson confirmed confidently. 'Yours?'

Van Ossen hadn't taken to Pallesson, and he certainly wasn't going to answer insolent questions.

'So. The Brueghel. Let us see.' Van Ossen beckoned Pallesson to place the suitcase on the observation table. No sooner had Pallesson opened the catches, than the taller of the two other men pulled his glasses out of his top pocket and stepped forward to examine the painting. Pallesson sensed an air of academia about the man. He was slightly unkempt, in an old-fashioned sort of way. His corduroy jacket was long overdue at the cleaners and he needed a haircut, but he exuded the confidence of an expert. Van Ossen gave no introduction.

The expert made a bit of a palaver of putting his glasses on then got to work, stooping over the painting. First, he stood it up vertically and examined the back of the canvas and stretching frame. This seemed to satisfy him, if his appreciative nods were anything to go by.

'It's come straight out of the embassy, as I told you. Unless your government has loaned our ambassador a pup, you're wasting your – and my – time,' Pallesson said, now unable to stop himself from sounding defensive.

'He will be the judge of that,' van Ossen replied, watching every facial expression of his man, who had now stepped back and was having a general look over the front of the canvas.

Pallesson, meanwhile, glanced around the room. In the corner was a substantial structure. Unmistakably an X-ray machine, with its manoeuvrable boom hanging over a large trolley with padded sides. The second man, Pallesson assumed, was probably a vet. A totally corrupt vet.

Pallesson reminded himself he had nothing to worry about.

He knew it was authentic. He had removed it himself. Perhaps this twerp poking around the painting might try to justify his no doubt significant fee by disputing which Brueghel had painted it. That, Pallesson would argue, was semantics. It was still a Brueghel and more than valuable enough to guarantee that Barry Nuttall was committed to his side of the deal.

The expert studied the canvas for about three minutes. He didn't seem to find anything untoward, as far as Pallesson could see.

'Satisfied?' Pallesson asked the expert impatiently. The expert ignored him and walked over to the tray on which the scalpels were lying. Van Ossen's men tensed slightly, looking towards their boss for instructions. Van Ossen gave an almost imperceptible shake of his head: no action required.

Scalpel in hand, the expert started gently to scratch at a dark cloud at the top right corner of the painting.

'What the hell do you think you're doing?' Pallesson asked, stepping forward to stop him. Like lightning, Piek was standing between them.

'You can't start messing around with that painting. Do you have any idea . . .?'

The expert raised his hand to acknowledge Pallesson's complaints and put down the scalpel. Then he did something very strange, which Pallesson had not been expecting. He leant forward, put his nose to the canvas where he'd been scraping, and started to sniff the picture.

Finally, he turned to van Ossen.

'This is hardly the best place to perform such delicate investigations, though the light is good.' He took a step back and tilted his head to one side. Obviously, his verdict was on the way. 'The painting is most impressive—'

'Of course it bloody is,' Pallesson interrupted.

'But it's a fake. A very recent fake.'

'What the fuck are you talking about?'

Fransen took a couple of steps towards Pallesson. Both of van Ossen's men were now on full alert.

'There are many smells here,' the expert continued, addressing van Ossen. He wrinkled his nose for dramatic effect, triumphant in his discovery. 'Modern smells. *Clinical* smells. But even so, I can still determine a faint whiff of paint where I have roughed up the surface of the canvas. And trust me; if it were painted in the seventeenth century, I would not be able to smell any paint at all. It's truly magnificent, but it's not the genuine article.'

'It must be. This isn't possible.' Pallesson could hardly force the words out quickly enough.

'Shut up,' van Ossen barked, as he indicated with a flick of his head to his heavies. They grabbed Pallesson by both arms and forcibly rammed him into a modern, metal chair.

'X-ray it,' van Ossen said to the second man, who had been tinkering with the machine in the background.

'For Christ's sake, I took it out of the embassy myself,' Pallesson continued. 'He must be wrong. What makes you think he's so bloody clever?'

'He,' van Ossen said deliberately, 'is the greatest expert on the Brueghel family in Holland. If he says it's a fake, it's a fake.'

The vet laid the painting exactly where it needed to be and disappeared behind a screen. The machine gave a couple of clanking noises then the vet called to van Ossen, who joined him behind the screen, followed by the art expert.

The wait felt like an eternity to Pallesson. How, he kept asking himself, could the painting not be the real thing? He couldn't have put the original back in the frame by mistake. He quickly scanned his memory of the switch. No. There was no way he had fucked up.

The vet appeared first from behind the screen, carrying the

X-ray. Pallesson craned his neck, but from where he was sitting he couldn't see the film. The expert picked up the painting and carried it back to the treatment table where he laid it on its front. Then, to Pallesson's horror, he picked up the scalpel and started digging into the wood of the canvas stretcher. Pallesson could feel sweat dripping down the inside of his armpits. This was going horribly wrong.

Without warning, van Ossen slapped Pallesson with a full-blooded swipe that made his neck recoil. Piek smirked. He was going to have some fun.

'What are you playing at?' van Ossen demanded.

'Nothing. Nothing. I stole it from the embassy last night. Last night, for God's sake.'

Van Ossen turned back to the expert, who had now finished extracting the tracking device that Sophie had hidden so delicately. He handed it to van Ossen.

'That will be all, gentlemen,' van Ossen said to the two professional men. 'Thank you for your time.'

They didn't need telling twice. Neither of them knew what would happen next and neither of them wanted to know. Offering out-of-hours advice on works of art was one thing. Being an accomplice to murder was another. They were gone in a second.

'So, you thought you could set me up, did you?' van Ossen asked in a calm voice.

'Why would I do that? I *want* to do this deal with you. I'm the one who introduced you to Nuttall, for Christ's sake!' Pallesson replied, slightly emboldened by van Ossen's calm approach.

'THEN WHAT THE HELL IS THIS?' van Ossen shrieked, grabbing Pallesson by the throat. Pallesson could feel the gangster's fingers grip his windpipe. He was being choked to death. His whole body tensed as excruciating pain radiated outward from his neck. His bladder emptied as he gasped for his last breath. But van Ossen hadn't finished with him. When Pallesson was within seconds of losing consciousness, the gang boss relaxed his grip.

Van Ossen picked up the scalpel and turned it over in his fingers.

'Do you know what Piek is going to do to you with this?'

Pallesson tried to say something, but his larynx was in shock. He shook his head.

'He's going to neuter *you*, instead of your cat. Much nicer for your feline friend, don't you think?'

Pallesson swallowed a few times. He was desperately racking his brains. What had gone wrong? Who had tripped him up? He finally found his voice.

'The forger. He must have stitched me up,' he said with a half-broken voice.

Pallesson was desperately trying to work out what had happened.

What had Jenkins said to him in the park?

Tryon. He's been stirring them up about you.

Had Jacques contacted Tryon? Thank God he'd had Tryon taken out. He certainly wasn't telling van Ossen about him.

'What forger?'

'The forger who copied the painting,' he said, his voice petering out.

'For Christ's sake, give him some water,' van Ossen barked.

Pallesson gulped the water down. And prepared to tell as many lies as it took to save himself.

'I couldn't just take the painting without substituting a copy,' he continued. 'So I kept smuggling the forger into the embassy to copy it. He must have made two copies and taken the original himself.'

If van Ossen had analysed the bollocks that Pallesson was

talking, he would have seen that it was an unlikely story. But his mind was focused on the tracker, not the painting.

'So whose tracker is this?'

'Must be the forger's.'

Van Ossen weighed that up. He couldn't think of a reason why a forger would want to track a copy.

'Why?'

'He's mad. I'll get you the original tomorrow.'

'How do I know you weren't trying to set me up? Track me to the handover with this painting?'

Van Ossen was still focusing on the threat of the tracking device. And overlooking the unlikely scenario that the forger himself would have the original.

'I'm not that clumsy – my record speaks for itself. I'll get the original. And I'll wipe out the forger. He's double-crossed us.'

'You,' van Ossen corrected. 'He's double-crossed you. If I call off the deal, I don't need the picture – and I don't need to be dealing with you.'

He was bluffing. He needed to shift the drugs ASAP.

'I can get you the original painting. We're good for the deal. And plenty more.'

Van Ossen hesitated. And Pallesson knew the bastard had blinked.

'No one knows about this at MI6?'

'God, no. No one,' Pallesson said desperately.

Van Ossen's instincts were to kill Pallesson there and then. He picked up the scalpel, blade facing upwards, and moved it towards the Englishman's face. Pallesson flinched, but both heavies grabbed his hair, pulling it tight as they did so.

With a practised precision, van Ossen slid the scalpel inside the right nostril of Pallesson's nose, so that he could feel its blunt edge pressed against the bone.

'You're a lucky man,' he said as he pulled the scalpel out of Pallesson's nostril, making a deep cut as he did so. Blood burst on to Pallesson's shirt.

'Get him a towel,' van Ossen ordered. Pallesson clutched his face as soon as his arms were released.

'You're getting a second chance. You better not fuck it up.'

16

Pallesson had to move fast. He needed to know exactly whom Jacques had spoken to and what he'd told them. Under normal circumstances, it was a job for the man who'd dealt with Tryon. But he wasn't answering his phone. And Pallesson didn't have time to wait. He needed someone in Gassin fast.

Then a thought came to him. Sergei Kroshtov was a regular out-of-season visitor to Saint-Tropez. He liked it there when everything was a bit quiet. Holed up in the Hotel Byblos.

Kroshtov owed him a small favour. And they'd been planning a deal together. He was sure his old friend would help him out.

His instincts had proved correct. Kroshtov was in residence there, and he'd been happy to dispatch Oleg, whom he said was getting grumpy with boredom, to lend a hand for a few days. He would be in Gassin within the hour.

Pallesson tried to gauge the extent of the damage brought about by Jacques's treachery. From what Jenkins had told him, he could assume that Tryon had been contacted by Jacques. But who else might know? Because unless Tryon had switched the painting himself – and that was highly unlikely given his stature in the Office – someone else in the embassy had to be involved.

Oleg would squeeze the pips out of Jacques before silencing him permanently. Sophie, on the other hand, might be of more lasting use. There was no point in rubbing her out at this stage.

Max's immediate instinct was to return to Amsterdam and seek out Tryon's contact at the Dienst Nationale Recherche; he'd specifically referred to one officer amongst the informant-ridden Dutch police force who could be trusted.

He called Pete Carr from a public payphone.

'Pete. Max here. Where's she at?'

'Hang on a minute, mate. I'll just have a wee look.'

'Pete, have you heard from Tryon?' Max added as casually as possible while Pete tapped some keys.

'No, mate. Any reason why I should have done?'

That was a strange question to ask, Max thought.

'Not really.'

'I wouldn't worry about that. He'll pop up somewhere.'

'But there's a live op running and he's gone AWOL. It doesn't make sense. Why would he bail on his own operation? He hasn't answered calls or emails for over twenty-four hours.'

'That doesn't sound like him,' Carr said flippantly. 'What can I do to help? Billable by the hour, obviously.'

'I need to know his contact in the Dutch police. And I need to know now.'

'I'll have a look, but Tryon's cloud data is all encrypted. Even I can't access it. Designed it so I couldn't. Didn't even put in a back door. Maybe I take too much pride in my work, but when someone asks for maximum-strength security, that's what I give them.'

'There must be another way . . .'

'I could do a blinking-cursor start. Use probability algorithms to determine the asset most likely to be Tryon's contact. Luckily, the Dutch National Police computer has as many holes as a leaky dyke; though identifying the man himself with any level of certainty won't be easy. So it'll cost you time-and-a-half.'

'Whatever it takes. Clock's ticking. What about the tracker?'

'Here we go. She's still in Amsterdam. Moved across the city a bit, but not too far. Need to know the street?'

'Not right now. First, I need some help on the ground. I need Tryon's contact.'

Sophie woke up early and felt a sense of relief that the night had passed and nothing bad had happened. She opened her shutters and looked out at the sun rising on the other side of the valley. There was no way anyone could get in through the windows, which all had ornate, wrought-iron metal bars across them. And the heavy wooden doors had big, solid bolts. Nevertheless, Max had told them to get out and she trusted him. She couldn't spend another night terrified of every noise outside.

Halfway down the stairs she smelt the coffee that her father had on the go in the kitchen. It told her he was all right.

'You see,' he said accusingly as she walked into the kitchen. 'You'd need an army to get in here.'

Sophie noticed, however, that he had placed his pistol on the kitchen table.

'I couldn't sleep. He told us to leave, so he must have a reason, *non*?'

'His kind are paid to worry. No one has anything to gain by coming here. Except to make us work.'

Sophie sat at the kitchen table and tore a piece off a stale baguette.

'We need fresh bread,' Jacques pointed out, as if everything were entirely normal.

Sophie poured hot milk into her coffee.

184

'Look, we can't just sit here like prisoners. Let's go along the coast. We could go to Porquerolles for a few days. It needn't be for long.'

The old man went to the fridge to get some butter.

'What makes you think you'll be safe there?' he asked with his back to her.

'Because no one will know we're there,' she said exasperatedly.

'The only place I'm going to is the village to get some bread,' he said defiantly.

As he spoke, a small white Citroën van pulled up in a lay-by half a mile below their gate. Oleg got out, a woollen beanie covering his distinctive scalp scar, and disappeared into the olive grove.

Jacques wandered down the hill past the fire station with his baguettes. Sophie could get on with her painting and leave him in peace.

He punched the security code into their gate security system, waited for it to open, and walked on down the twisting, steep drive. The shrubs and bushes around the house were partly why Jacques felt safe and secluded in their little farmhouse. No one had ever given them any bother there.

Oleg slipped through the gate twenty metres behind Jacques as the gates closed.

Jacques cut one of the baguettes into two, sliced each half down the middle and clumsily spread butter inside. He folded cold meat into his and cheese into Sophie's. Then he poured them each a cup of coffee. And loaded the whole lot on to a tray to take out to Sophie's studio.

Outside the kitchen window, Oleg smelt the coffee and waited.

When Jacques got to Sophie's studio door, he shouted out.

But the door wasn't locked. It wasn't even shut. She told him to come in. Jacques pushed the door open with his shoulder, and stepped into the studio. She obviously wasn't that worried about their safety, Jacques thought to himself.

'So much for your security,' he grumbled.

Oleg had stealthily followed Jacques from the house to the studio door. He stepped into the room behind the old man. Jacques was oblivious of Oleg's presence, but he saw the horror etched across Sophie's face. Oleg grabbed him from behind. His grip was strong enough to crush the frail bones. The tray crashed to the floor.

'Don't make a move, or I'll hurt him very badly,' Oleg said calmly.

Jacques was struggling and cursing, but he was never going to escape. Oleg held him with one hand, took a strap out of his pocket and started to bind the old man's arms. He kept one eye on Sophie. She was sitting mute and motionless behind her canvas.

Oleg had orders to kill Jacques, but not before he'd questioned him. As soon as he'd immobilized him with a few more straps, he advanced on Sophie, who hadn't moved a muscle. But as soon as Oleg stepped away from her father, she raised the pistol above the canvas. Her eyes looked terrified, her hands were shaking. She pulled the trigger.

The kick of the pistol threw her aim way over Oleg's head. The bullet embedded itself in the wall behind him. The Russian charged her. In a panic she loosed off another shot. It whistled past Oleg's knee – straight into Papa. Blood exploded from his chest as he was thrown backwards.

Sophie had blown her chance. Oleg threw himself at her before she could get another shot off and grabbed her wrist. He practically broke it taking the pistol off her and then knocked her out with a belt to her temple for good measure.

Oleg cursed as he turned the old man over. He was lying in a pool of dark-red blood. He was stone dead. Whatever information he might have had was gone.

La Mole airfield was barely five minutes from Gassin. The plane was waiting for Oleg and his cargo. The wooden box that held the unconscious Sophie wouldn't get a second look from the airport staff. They were well squared up by the Russian boys, who regularly used La Mole to supply Saint-Tropez with its marching powder. Oleg would be delivering her two hours later to a small airstrip outside Amsterdam.

The feedback Pallesson had received from the Russian was enlightening. Only three text messages on her phone. And one name – Max. That told him exactly what he needed to know.

Casper Rankin found a quiet table in the corner of the White Hart in Shepherd's Market and ordered a large gin and tonic. He tried to read his paper, but he couldn't concentrate. He'd been spooked by Pallesson's text message: Make sure you are on your own in half an hour. Non negotiable.

It had to be a problem with the Montenegro deal; and that put the wind up Casper. Pallesson had always assured him that they had total government protection out there – that there would never be any questions regarding where their money came from – which was just as well. Because a novice would be able to see that the provenance of Pallesson and Alessandro Marchant's money wouldn't stand up to much scrutiny by any financial authority. And as the fund manager moving the money around, he would be the one to take the bullet.

The Montenegro deal was beautifully simple. A couple of government ministers tipped them off as to where the big centrally funded infrastructure projects would take place; then they either bought up the land ahead of the game and sold it on to the government, or they acquired adjacent land that was then hugely uplifted in value. And cut the ministers in.

Nonetheless, Casper had always had concerns about Montenegro blowing up in their faces. If the political climate changed, so would their protection. And there was no guarantee that an unfriendly regime wouldn't confiscate their assets – or worse. It all hung on the influence Pallesson wielded.

Casper's phone vibrated exactly thirty minutes after the text message.

'Morning,' Casper said, trying to sound normal.

'You've got a problem,' Pallesson replied.

The bluntness of his voice surprised Casper. Normally, Pallesson coated his greetings with sugar, however blunt the message he was about to deliver might be. Casper hesitated.

'Or at least you did, until I sorted it out for you.'

'Sorry?' What are you talking about?'

'Someone came into the Office to shop you for money-laundering. Luckily they were pointed in my direction. They've been eliminated. But the problem hasn't quite been cleared up.'

Casper went white. He couldn't believe what he'd just heard. He stood up from his table and walked outside into Shepherd's Market.

'You are joking, aren't you?' Casper asked, knowing that he wasn't.

'No joke,' Pallesson said. 'And you need to act fast.'

'What?'

'Casper, wake up. Unless you want to go down for money-laundering and murder, you have work to do.'

'What do you mean, murder? Are you fucking mad?'

'Oh no,' Pallesson replied. 'If you don't get on with the clean-up, when they find your whistle-blowing friend's corpse, they'll be coming after you.'

Casper had slipped into the role of bent fund manager fairly readily. But being implicated in a murder was way outside his comfort zone.

'You're off your head. What do you mean, clean-up?'

Casper was now pacing around in a tight circle. Anyone watching him would have known he wasn't enjoying his call.

'What I mean is we have to make sure that anyone who might harbour bad thoughts about you, and your transactions, doesn't blow the whistle on you. You don't want that, do you? Banged up for the next ten years.'

'Who, for Christ's sake? Who is on to us?'

'On to you. Not me. No one can trace a penny back to me. It's you I'm looking after.'

Casper could feel the rug being pulled from under his feet. He was being isolated. Any minute now the fraud squad would be storming his office.

'What is going on?' he said desperately.

Pallesson paused, for the briefest of moments. It felt like an eternity to Casper.

'Max Ward is trying to bring you down,' Pallesson said sympathetically.

Casper was stunned.

'Who?' he asked too loudly. A couple of suits having a cigarette break ten metres away looked at him. 'I've never heard of him. Why would he want to bring me down?'

'Casper, I don't know how to tell you this,' Pallesson replied. 'He's one of ours. And he's been having an affair with your wife for a long time.'

Casper felt his stomach curl up in knots. Gemma, having an affair with someone he didn't know?

'What?'

'I'm afraid so.'

'Are you sure?'

'Positive.' Pallesson was getting bored now.

'How are you so sure?'

'I'm a bloody spy, for Christ's sake. As a matter of fact, so is he. Not a very good one, but good enough to screw your wife without getting caught by you.'

'How dare—'

'We haven't got time for this. He's going to nail you.'

Casper was now as good as punched senseless. He stared down at the cobbled ground, nauseous, feeling sick to his stomach.

'What are we going to do?' he asked, as if on autopilot. He knew Pallesson would call the shots.

'Simple,' Pallesson replied. 'You're going to tell your wife you need her to deliver some information to Alessandro Marchant. He's staying at a castle near Amsterdam.'

'She's going there anyway,' Casper said limply. 'To an interior design fair.'

'Good. Perfect.' Interior design fair, my arse, Pallesson thought on the other end of the phone. More like shagging Max Ward fair. But he spared Casper his thoughts.

'What does that have to do with Max Ward?'

'She'll meet him there. He's based in Amsterdam.'

'Meet him there?'

'Yes. It's about an hour from the city. They'll hook up. It's just far enough out of Amsterdam for them to spend the night there.'

'What?'

'Don't worry. We won't let that happen. We'll be persuading him to back off you. And your wife.'

'How?'

'Relax. I told you, he's one of ours. We're hardly going to rough up one of our own, are we?'

Casper thought about that. It made sense. But the idea of sending his wife to spend a night with her lover didn't.

'I'm not sending Gemma off to be with him.'

'You won't be. We'll be there,' Pallesson said irritably. And then, in a flash, his temper boiled. 'Casper, you'll do as we fucking well say. Or shall I just take you down to the police station now?'

Casper was rocked by this explosion. He'd crossed Pallesson before. And the result had been memorably unpleasant. He knew he had no option.

'Okay,' he said quickly. 'What do I do?'

'You're going to go home now. You're not going to tell Gemma you know about Max. You're going to ask her very nicely, but very firmly, to help you out by taking some information to Alessandro that can't be sent any other way. If she's going to Amsterdam anyway, that shouldn't be a problem.'

'What shall I give her?'

'A courier will drop a package off at your home this evening. In it will be a vacuum-packed memory stick. Tell her not to open it.'

'What's on it?'

'It doesn't bloody well matter. She just has to deliver it. The rest will work itself out.'

17

Barry Nuttall never panicked. But by anyone's standards, he'd had a catastrophic morning.

For five years, Nuttall had leased an old farmyard about ten miles from Felixstowe. The buildings were no longer any use for agriculture; they were too small and disjointed. But they were secure and in the middle of nowhere.

Nuttall paid the retired farmer in cash, which suited the old boy very well. He'd given the Inland Revenue plenty over the years; so the taxman wasn't having any of the rent. And the farmer didn't care what Nuttall did with the buildings, as long as he looked after the gutters and put back any slates that came off. Which Nuttall did without fail.

Nuttall had explained that the buildings were used to store products, but it had all sounded very complicated to a man in his eighties who thought his Nokia phone was cutting-edge technology. If the farmer, or anyone else poking about, had been foolish enough to get into any of the sheds, all they would have found were a couple of hundred empty cartons of Azerbaijani laundry detergent. And then one of the

German shepherds locked in the sheds would have savaged them.

Nuttall's 'distribution centre', and the four lieutenants who ran it for him, had served a network of drug dealers in the southeast very efficiently for the last five years. The drugs went out as fast as they came in, and there was never a great deal of stock hanging about. Nevertheless, Nuttall kept himself one step removed from the action. His job was to ensure the supply line into the farm didn't dry up. It was down to his boys to take care of the distribution. It was safer that way.

'So what the fuck happened?' Nuttall asked Jermaine, the black kid in standard-issue designer trainers, who was now sitting in the passenger seat of his car.

'They hit us about six o'clock this evening. Hundreds of 'em, man.'

'Hundreds?'

'Hard to say, man. I counted about six cars and vans.'

'And where the hell were you?'

'I was well lucky, man. I'd been doing a drop, and saw all the blue lights from the road on me way back.'

I'll bet you did, Nuttall thought. The police had nicked his entire team, apart from this kid. He'd been out on a drop. Convenient. Very convenient. Nuttall knew that once the police had cottoned on to the farm, they'd have watched it for weeks. No one would have slipped the net that easily. And even if he had, Nuttall didn't fancy the cops' chances of getting their hands on Jermaine. Alive.

'You'll have to keep out of the way for a bit. I've got a bloke who'll look after you.'

'Thanks, man. Appreciate it. What about the others?'

'They're fucked. Someone must have grassed on them.'

Nuttall's face gave nothing away. His three-day stubble and Burberry baseball cap were like a mask. He picked up his prepaid phone and rang Vince.

Vince wasn't a real farmer. But he kept some pigs, and he did all of the little jobs that Nuttall had progressed from. And Jermaine was about to become one of them.

'I'll be with you in twenty minutes,' Nuttall said economically. 'Got something I need you to deal with.' Vince knew the form. If Barry needed something doing, he did it.

Nuttall's problems now ran much deeper than a police bust. The only stock he held was whatever was in the distribution pipeline. When that was exhausted, he wouldn't be able to deliver. And that, he knew, was commercial suicide. Others would soon move in; the business he'd worked hard to set up would disappear overnight. He was also going to have to make a lot of phone calls to some very unhappy investors.

Generally speaking, when Barry brought a shipment of drugs in, he would get funding from about twenty investors from around the country. On average, each of those investors would have broken their slice of the action up amongst at least ten others. Which meant around two hundred people were going to be out of pocket. And that meant aggro on a major scale.

Nuttall dialled Pallesson's number. He was now reliant on the Amsterdam deal going through smoothly and quickly to keep his supply lines open.

'Everything okay?' he asked abruptly, when Pallesson answered.

'Pretty well,' Pallesson replied.

'What the fuck does that mean?'

'Nothing, nothing. Everything's under control,' Pallesson lied.

'It better fucking had be. All you've got to do is give him that poxy picture. You done that?'

Pallesson was now squirming on the end of the phone. There was an unpredictable autistic side to Nuttall that unnerved him. Tough, ruthless gangsters he could cope with, because logic usually applied in the end. Psychos were another matter.

He wasn't going to admit to Nuttall that he'd been outwitted; and he certainly wasn't going to flag up any problems with the Office for fear the Essex man would duck out. Of course, he had no idea how desperate Nuttall was for this shipment.

'I don't want any problems with this deal, Pallesson. Have you got that?'

'There won't be, there won't be. It's all under control. Van Ossen's happy.'

'He better be. Because if he isn't, we all know where your mother's nursing home is, don't we? Just round the corner from Hemel Hempstead. And it won't be Interflora visiting her if you fuck this up,' Nuttall said calmly.

Pallesson didn't reply. There was no point having a conversation like that with a psychotic lunatic.

'I'm surrounded by fucking idiots,' Nuttall said to Jermaine as they approached Vince's smallholding. 'Thank fucking God for you, Jermaine. The only one who had the brains not to get caught.'

'I'm the man.' Jermaine nodded. 'You can count on me.'

'I will, Jermaine, I will. We'll have some more gear by the end of next week.'

'Where that coming from, man?'

'Holland, mate. Holland.' And, Nuttall thought, there are now two people in this car who know that. And that's one too many.

Vince stood six feet four in his blue overalls and black gum boots. His shoulder-length black greasy hair hadn't been washed in years. He suited Nuttall, who knew Vince would never be launching a takeover bid. He was happy just feeling important. Being involved. Nuttall needed more men like Vince. Men who knew their place and were happy with their lot.

The shed doors were open when Nuttall arrived. He drove straight in, and Vince shut the doors behind him. Even if Jermaine had realized how much shit he was in, there would have been very little he could do about it, unless he was carrying – which he wasn't. But he was cool. After all, he was the man.

Jermaine never saw what hit him as Vince walked up behind him. But it knocked him out cold. When he came round half an hour later, his hands were bound behind his back by a chain, which was suspending him from a steel girder. His shoulders felt as if they were about to dislocate. And Nuttall was standing in front of him, smiling.

'Who did you tell, Jermaine?' Nuttall asked once Jermaine had regained most of his senses.

'No one, man. No one.' Jermaine was in agony. His body was paralysed by fear, his eyes bulging with terror.

Nuttall loved the detachment he now felt. In control, but taking the overview. He would've liked to sit down, but there was nowhere clean. So he took his chamois leather gloves off and lit a fag. He never smoked with his gloves on. Spoilt the leather.

'One last chance, son, or Vince is going to barbecue you. Who . . . did . . . you . . . tell?'

Jermaine pleaded innocence to start with and sobbed as Vince taunted him with the blowtorch. Vince liked to take things nice and steady to start with. That way, Barry got what he wanted to know before the victim started passing out. In Jermaine's case, he sung like a canary as soon as the flame seared his right knee. He'd snitched on Nuttall to the Filth. How much pain he felt while his toes were being flambéed was hard to say. By the time his testicles were torched, he was way beyond feeling anything.

Once Vince had finished, he unchained Jermaine and laid him on the floor. Thirty seconds later came a sharp crack that would have been heard by anyone within a hundred metres of the building. The bolt from the humane killer that Vince used to slaughter his pigs passed cleanly through Jermaine's skull just behind his ear. Barry stood well back. He didn't need blood spatter all over his coat.

'Nice bit of tea for the pigs,' Vince said to Nuttall as he heaved him into the pen and opened the gate.

18

London

Casper watched the children running and shouting inside the running track at the old Duke of York's barracks site as he walked home in a daze.

He turned left off the King's Road into Chelsea Square. He'd always loved that square; and he'd worked bloody hard to buy a house there.

Casper got a first at Cambridge after a good deal of sweat. And on the back of that, he could have secured a job with any of the big banks and made a shedload of money. He could have advised his clients to take one position and then traded against it as well as the rest of them. Had he done so, by now he would probably have had two houses in Chelsea Square and no one on his case.

Instead, Pallesson had 'persuaded' him that founding a private wealth investment fund was a better idea. And the truth of the matter was that he was in no position to disagree. Because although Casper had worked hard at uni, he'd also enjoyed himself a bit too much.

From the time they first met, Pallesson always seemed to have a lot of money at his disposal. While Casper had none.

So the free ride that Pallesson had given him – 'Because you're like a blood brother to me' – seemed natural. Whenever Pallesson organized a night out for 'his inner circle', it was full on. They drank Mouton Rothschild because Pallesson adored 'Philippine', the owner of the château. And the coke, which was washed down with the claret, had to come from one dealer; Pallesson saw to it that no junk was cut in.

One of these nights out had proved to be the game changer for Casper. Pallesson had been drinking whisky and doing lines long before two girls had arrived from London. And he'd been in a very aggressive mood. For a while they were all messing about, and the girls had handcuffed Casper to a metal bed 'for a laugh'. But when the 'fun' started, it had been Casper, and not the girls, who'd got Pallesson's attention.

Over the next few months, Pallesson became even more generous towards Casper.

'We're the chosen ones, Casper,' Pallesson drawled one night. 'Stick with me, and you'll end up being very rich. Betray me, and I'll snap you like a twig.'

While Casper spent his holidays desperately trying to catch up with work, Pallesson took off to travel abroad. He never seemed to have a problem with tutors or his degree. He just sailed through everything.

When they left Cambridge, Casper was left in no doubt that his career path would be chosen and facilitated by Pallesson. He moved straight into a palatial office off St James's with an instant list of clients, introduced by Pallesson, such as Alessandro Marchant. Men with money to invest – and relocate.

Pallesson's support had made Casper very rich. And for years things had run smoothly. But now, his life was in a crisis. He'd been sucked into something completely out of his control, and he had to find a way out of it. If that meant putting his wife in harm's way, then so be it. Not that he was unduly bothered by her infidelity. What concerned him more was how much she'd told her MI6 lover. It was the threat to his security, rather than his pride, that was bothering him as he turned the key in his front door.

Gemma was upstairs packing. She was relieved that Casper called up to her from their sitting room on the second floor instead of coming upstairs. Otherwise he would have caught her red-handed – the underwear she had laid out was a bit of a giveaway.

'Gemma, would you come down please,' Casper called up the stairwell.

When she appeared, Casper was standing rather formally by the fake fireplace. He didn't bother with any niceties.

'I need you to do something for me. There's some data that has to go to Alessandro Marchant. He's near Amsterdam. It's highly classified – I can't email it or send it by courier. I need you to take it.'

'But I'm—' she started to reply.

'It's important, Gemma. I need you to do this.'

'But, Casper—'

'You're heading that way anyhow.'

'Casper, I really—'

His tone of voice changed then. No longer requesting but ordering.

'Just do it, Gemma. No bloody questions. You're going tomorrow.'

Gemma had no idea why Casper was turning on her. He couldn't suspect anything about Max, surely?

'He'll meet you at Castle Vleuylen tomorrow evening. It's about an hour from Amsterdam. Why don't you stay there? It's meant to be fantastic. They can fix you up with a driver to take you to the trade fair.'

Gemma didn't like the sound of that. It would mess up her plan to spend the night with Max.

'Marchant will call in for the memory stick. He has to fly out tomorrow night.'

That information eased Gemma's concerns. In fact, the whole thing sounded perfect, now she came to think of it. It would be nice to spend a couple of nights with Max somewhere different. The restaurants were no great shakes in Amsterdam. And if Max had to work, it wouldn't be far for him to drive in to the office.

'Of course, Casper. I can do that,' Gemma said. As she said it, she was surprised to see a look of relief on his face. She'd taken data to quite a few places for Casper. But in the past it had always been proposed as a jaunt for her. This time there had been an edge in the way Casper had asked her. She was relieved that it fitted in with her plans, because she sensed he wouldn't have taken no for an answer.

Max was worried about Sophie. He kept ringing her number. And it kept switching to voicemail. He had no other way of getting hold of her, and he couldn't just do nothing. His instincts told him he needed to act.

So he Googled 'sapeurs-pompiers Gassin' and quickly found their telephone number. On the third ring, the phone was answered.

Max gave the address of Jacques and Sophie's farmhouse – all of one minute away from the fire station – and told them he was a neighbour and that someone was drowning in their swimming pool. Then he slammed the phone down before they could ask any questions. He would ring them again in an hour and try to discover whether they found anyone at the house.

Max was remembering how it had felt, kissing Sophie's neck and feeling her naked body pressing against him, when his phone rang. It was Gemma.

He was reluctant to answer. But he knew he couldn't hide from Gemma. He had to be honest with her.

'Hello, darling,' he said, wiping all thoughts of Sophie out of his mind.

'Max, please tell me you're not operational. I can't stand talking to "operational Max".'

In theory, Max was operational and could have used that, but he didn't. Gemma, after all, had been the closest person in the world to him. He would always treat her with the respect she deserved. If life had worked out differently, they could have been husband and wife.

'On standby,' he said cheerfully, 'but not actually dodging Russians or bullets right now.'

'Well, that's a relief,' she replied, as if she'd been told her dentist could fit her in at short notice. 'I'm coming to Amsterdam tomorrow, Max. Please tell me you're there.'

'Yes, Gemma, I'm here. What brings you to Amsterdam all of a sudden?'

'To see you. We are lovers, in case you'd forgotten.'

'But you hate Amsterdam. You always want to meet me somewhere else.'

'Well, how about a compromise? You meet me at the airport and we'll stay the night at Castle Vleuylen. It's not that far from Amsterdam.'

Max knew that was a bad idea. A romantic tryst at a grand castle was not where his head was. A frank talk to each other was.

He reminded himself of the words of Merikare: 'Show respect for the lives of those who are frank.' Gemma was nothing if not frank.

'Darling, I might need to be on hand in the city. It would be better if we were here.'

'But it's only an hour away. Isn't that close enough?'

'It might not be.'

Gemma paused and took a deep breath.

'Max. I have to stay the night at Castle Vleuylen. Casper has asked me – well, commanded me, more like – to deliver something to Alessandro Marchant, a business contact of Casper's. I don't know what time he'll be there to pick it up.'

'Well, that will look cosy. Us bumping into him.'

'He's not staying there. He won't see us.'

Max barely heard her. His mind had leapt ahead. Tryon had talked about Casper, Marchant and Pallesson being linked to each other. Why was Marchant in Holland now? And why was Casper sending Gemma to see him? Were they in on Pallesson's drug deal? Was it a trap?

Having a quiet poke around Castle Vleuylen, however, suddenly seemed like quite a good idea. It had to be relevant to what Pallesson was up to.

'Okay, darling,' Max said breezily. 'When does your plane get in?'

Max rang Pete Carr as soon as he put the phone down on Gemma.

'Pete, where is she now?'

Pete got the lack of pleasantries.

'Hang on a minute. I'll have a look.'

Thirty seconds later, Max heard Pete whistle.

'Bloody hell. She isn't hanging about. She's off, all right.'

'Where?'

'All I can tell you is she's heading East-East-South. If we have another look in a couple of minutes, I can tell you at what speed. Just need to plot two points over a known period of—'

'I know, Pete,' Max interrupted.

Hmm. Bit stressed today, Pete thought. It's going off.

Seventy miles an hour was Pete's guestimate of the speed the tracker was moving at.

'Rather slow for a car carrying a stolen work of art, wouldn't you say?' Max asked. And he was asking the right man. Pete had monitored hundreds of devices.

'Yes. More likely to be a van or a lorry, I would say.'

'Can you let me know if it goes over any borders, Pete? No news from Tryon, I take it?'

'None at all, mate. But I've got that other stuff for you. How shall I send it to you?'

Max gave Pete a new, untraceable email address and thanked him.

19

Amsterdam, six months earlier

Francisca knocked on the side door of Wielart's office at seven o'clock precisely. She was surprised by his appearance. He had no tie or jacket. Only a shirt. She'd never seen him dressed like that before – not even on holidays.

'Come in, my dear,' Wielart said as he opened the door, his eager eyes searching for the brown envelope into which he'd placed the contract.

He caught her aroma as she brushed past him into the office. It had frustrated him so often in the past. But that was about to change.

'How is your father? Relieved?'

Francisca noticed Wielart locking the door and putting the key in his pocket. He hadn't done that yesterday when she'd come in via the same entrance.

'He's very upset,' she replied, not qualifying exactly what part of this crisis was upsetting him.

Wielart noticed the black bags under her eyes, which had appeared since her first visit to his office. But it did not detract from her beauty. Or her perfect, lissom body.

'Does he want me to help him?'

She wanted to tell him what she thought of his definition of help, but she knew her words would be pointless.

'Yes, he does,' she answered, unbuttoning her cloak and pulling the brown envelope out. Wielart beckoned with his head for her to bring it to him.

Wielart checked that each page had been initialled and that the signature appeared to be valid against the passport.

'Excellent,' he smiled. 'Now we're partners, we must have a drink together.'

'I have to be going,' Francisca said.

Wielart's body stiffened as he walked towards the fridge where he had a bottle of champagne open.

'I haven't signed the contract yet,' he said coldly, without turning to face her. 'Until I do, your father is going to prison.'

Francisca didn't reply. Instead, she sat meekly in one of the leather armchairs and waited for Wielart to hand her the crystal glass filled with fizzing champagne.

'Cheers,' he said, looking her in the eye. 'You are now a woman of business, not a girl. Which means you have to keep your word.'

'How do you mean?'

'It's simple, Francisca. You told me you'd do anything to save your father. But what you're going to do for me is not much of a price.'

'I don't know what you're talking about,' Francisca replied, becoming alarmed. What was this weird little man getting at?

'Do you want me to sign that contract or not?' he barked aggressively.

'Yes . . . yes, of course I want you to.'

'Then stop behaving like a child. You're a woman, Francisca, and you know what I want.'

Until that moment, Francisca hadn't. But she did now. She

was repulsed, and her body language showed it. Wielart went back to his desk and picked up the contract. Then he held it in front of her face.

'Do you want me to rip this up, or are you going to do as I tell you?'

She couldn't speak. She hadn't expected anything like this.

'Well?' he shouted.

'Don't rip it up,' she said, as tears started to roll down her cheeks.

Wielart grabbed her arm and pulled her across the room towards the chaise longue. She could feel the burn on her wrist; but apart from that, she was frozen with horror.

'Take off your clothes,' he ordered. She didn't move. She just sobbed.

'Take them off. I won't tell you again. And shut up.' He slapped her across the face in fury.

Francisca descended into an awakened coma. She was unconscious, in the real sense of the word, but able to physically function. She started to undo the buttons down the front of her dress.

Wielart helped it off her shoulders, and it fell to the floor, leaving her standing in only her shoes, her bra and knickers. Wielart slowly removed them without any help or hindrance from Francisca. Then he pushed her gently backwards until she was lying on the chaise longue.

It wasn't how Wielart had planned it. He'd pictured Francisca being an enthusiastic lover, unzipping his trousers and pulling him on to her. But it mattered not. She was now naked in front of him, ready for him to do whatever he wanted. Totally in his power.

Her body was even more gorgeous than he'd imagined. Her breasts had burst out of her bra, bigger and firmer than he'd dreamt of. He bit her nipples with an animal ferocity.

'I can't, I can't,' Francisca pleaded. 'I've never been with a man. Please stop. Please.'

The only doubt that had crept into Wielart's fantasy was her possible reaction to his penis, which had been deformed by a botched circumcision. But if she'd never been with another man, she would have nothing to compare him with. This was a huge relief to Wielart. He undid the buckle around his waist, and pulled his trousers down.

The whole attack took less than quarter of an hour. Francisca was aware of the violation happening to her, but she felt unable to do anything about it. Her brain was in denial.

When he'd finished, Wielart started shouting at her. She was a selfish little slut who had known all along what she was doing, he told her.

However much she blocked out of her memory, she would never forget his final words as he pushed her out of the side door.

'I can send your father to prison any time I like. And if you ever betray or disobey me, that is what I will do.'

Ruud Dekker had been inquisitive by nature when he was a child. And he'd had an obsession with his mother's underwear. When he was sixteen, she'd caught him going through her drawers. The scar of her hysterical reaction had never healed.

As a rising security officer at Amsterdam Airport Schiphol, he now had the power to riffle though any baggage that took his fancy. On the whole, he was very principled. But occasionally, if a particular suitcase caught his eye – one that looked like it might belong to a female – he allowed himself a look. Always through the X-ray machine first; and then, if his superiors weren't about, the odd rummage if it looked promising.

Ruud also worked with some interesting 'outside' agencies.

He was particularly useful to them, because he didn't mind facilitating operations that might not have the correct paperwork in place. He subscribed to bending the rules if that's what it took to get results. And he felt empowered by his association with these people who worked quietly behind the scenes. Who knew, one day he might join their ranks. So any favours he did them felt like an insurance policy for the future.

The request he'd received that morning from one of his invisible associates was, however, unusual. A Mrs Gemma Rankin would be on the first London flight, he'd been told. He was to establish whether she left the airport with Max Ward (photo attached), who would not be a passenger.

Ruud decided that if a job was worth doing, it was worth doing properly. Since Mrs Rankin was that important, any information gleaned from her luggage might earn him a few points with his associates.

It was easy for Ruud to identify Gemma's suitcase as it came into the terminal. He removed it from the rest of the luggage and took it over to the X-ray machine.

A wry smile crept across his face as he examined the contents. Ruud could recognize toys at a glance. 'She's on a mission,' he muttered to himself as he unzipped the case for a closer inspection.

Ruud had watched her queuing at passport control. She'd looked stiff, cold and unobtainably sexy. Underneath that cool exterior, she was obviously as hot as mustard, judging by the underwear that Ruud was now sifting through. He got very turned on as his fingers brushed her lace knickers. But his fantasies were brought to a rude halt by the X-ray operator, who was being too attentive. Ruud secreted a pair of blue knickers into his pocket and shut the case.

The CCTV system was quite capable of tracking Gemma through the airport. But Ruud wanted to get closer to her. He wanted to smell her. And he could drift as close to her as he liked and remain invisible.

Max was waiting at the coffee bar. Tryon's words were echoing around his head:

'Gemma met someone behind your back. Someone we're really not sure about.'

'If I can't trust Gemma, I can't trust anyone,' he had told Tryon. And he was still clinging on to that. But there was a nagging doubt in the back of his mind. It was too convenient that Gemma was meeting Marchant an hour from Amsterdam just as the operation was about to go off.

Max had prearranged with Gemma that they wouldn't acknowledge each other in the airport terminal. Max had checked the car park, and found an area no CCTV cameras appeared to cover. As agreed, he had written down that exact spot and left the note at the passenger information desk. Gemma knew he would be watching her as she queued for the message.

If Ruud had been watching his CCTV screens, he could have easily picked up Max at the coffee bar, even with his cap and glasses on. But Ruud was more interested in getting close enough to Gemma to breathe in her scent. So he took the opportunity to stand behind her in the queue.

Gemma became aware of someone invading her space. She turned round to find a security officer standing very close to her. He awkwardly stepped backwards and looked away from her.

Gemma thought nothing of it, but Max, watching from the coffee bar, sensed something odd about Ruud's body language. Enough to keep an eye on him when Gemma walked off towards the car park exit. Sure enough, the security officer followed her.

Max sent Gemma a text: Stand still for a minute and pretend to read your phone messages. Gemma duly stood still. Max watched Ruud peel away from Gemma, and observe her from a distance.

You're being followed, was Max's next message. **Get in a taxi and go to a hotel nearby. Will pick you up there. Check your tail.**

Ruud followed Gemma to the taxi rank and watched her leave alone. He then rang his associate and reported as much, congratulating himself on his covert operation.

Max finally met up with a slightly disgruntled Gemma a mile from the airport. After a warmish greeting – during which she felt she was embracing a business partner, not her lover – they hit the road.

'Well, that was romantic,' Gemma said sarcastically. 'Flowers and whisking a girl off her feet have clearly been replaced by information desks and budget hotels.'

'Very funny,' Max responded without taking his eyes from the road. 'You seem to have attracted some attention in the airport. Make a pass at the passport controller?'

'I was merely pointing out that you don't appear to be ecstatic that I'm here,' Gemma replied, injecting a hefty dose of hurt into her voice.

Max felt like pointing out that he wasn't ecstatic that she'd crossed the line. She was now inextricably linked to his operation. He also wanted to point out that she had lied to him in Monte Carlo. But that would have meant showing his hand, and he wasn't about to risk that until he'd discovered whose side she was on.

'I'm sorry,' he said softening his voice and stretching out his arm to rub her leg. 'But I was worried. You were being followed. What's going on?'

Gemma looked straight ahead.

'I don't know,' she said, with an air of resolve. 'I just don't know. Casper has asked me to take data abroad for him before. Usually to give to Alessandro Marchant. But this time it was different.'

Max tried to comfort her by rubbing her leg a bit harder, but she carried on staring out the windscreen instead of looking at him.

'What have they given you?'

Gemma delved in her handbag and pulled out the vacuum-packed memory stick.

'That's annoying,' Max said, glancing across at the small package. 'Unless we can find a vacuum-sealing machine at the castle, we can't very well check out the data. Did Casper mention Pallesson?'

'Pallesson? No. Why would he have mentioned him?'

Max hesitated. Was she fishing?

'I don't know, darling. Maybe we'll find out something at Castle Vleuylen?' Max had no doubt that there was more to this than Gemma simply delivering a memory stick to Marchant. It was all too conveniently close to Amsterdam.

After thirty-five minutes, they picked up signs to the castle. Max was silent. He was formulating his strategy.

'By the way, who booked our room? You or Casper?'

'There's a girl in Casper's office. She always makes my arrangements. Why?'

'Because this is probably a set-up,' Max said without any emotion. 'So we have two options. We run and I hide you until it's safe. Or we play along and outmanoeuvre them.'

'You're deluded, Max. You've been doing your job for too long. I told you: I'm delivering some data. I've done it before. It's as simple as that.'

Max shook his head.

'I don't think so. If that was the case, why were you being trailed through the airport?'

Gemma shrugged her shoulders.

'Anyway,' Max said. 'There's no harm in taking precautions.'

He pulled into a lay-by and told Gemma to sit in the back. Then he retrieved the Glock 19, which he had taped to the underside of the tailgate, and put on the chauffeur's cap, which was also in the boot.

'Come on,' Gemma laughed sceptically. 'This is ridiculous. You've lost the plot, Max.'

'Trust me. And when you check in, insist that you change your room.'

'But—'

'Make them give you a different room.'

'Max—'

'Just do it. Trust me, Gemma, and we'll be fine.'

Gemma rejected the room she was given by the receptionist.

'I've had that room before. It's simply ghastly. Get me another one . . . please,' she lied to the girl, who seemed resistant. She assured Gemma that it was their nicest suite, with a magnificent view across the lake.

'That is as maybe,' Gemma conceded, 'but I would like a different room, please.'

A smooth concierge appeared and took over from the receptionist.

'That will be no problem, madame,' he said with a laboured Italian accent. 'Welcome to Castle Vleuylen.'

The Italian picked up some keys from behind the desk. If Gemma had spotted the receptionist's expression, she would have noted a degree of bemusement.

'I will show you to another room, myself,' he said smoothly. The porter obediently followed them to the lift.

As they walked along the dark corridor on the third floor,

the Italian gestured at a door on the left, guarded by a suit of armour.

'Are you sure you wouldn't like to see the room we had prepared for you?'

'No, no. Please . . .' Gemma beckoned along the corridor.

Their new room was a few doors along on the right. It too had a suit of armour outside it. She was relieved that they had such a nice suite to put her in after she'd mucked them about.

She loved the massive four-poster bed draped in brown fur. She would soon melt Max, lying naked on it. The tapestries hanging from the walls, of grandees deer hunting on horseback, were magnificent. Most importantly, the marble bathroom was Olympic size. In fact, so blown away was she by the grandeur of the suite, she forgot to admire the view of the lake from the window.

Gemma didn't hang about. She started to run her bath and sent Max a text. Got new room. It's like private house. No numbers or room names. We are three doors along on right from lift. Third floor. Have left hair clip attached to suit of armour by door. Hurry up.

Max was pleased that the car park was busy. It would help him blend into the crowd. The castle was vast. The cylindrical towers on every corner gave the place a Germanic feel. Max wasn't a hundred per cent sure whether the size of the place was going to help or hinder him. The main thing was that whoever they were dealing with must believe Gemma was on her own.

From the car park he headed towards the spa entrance rather than the main reception. Once inside, he followed the signs to the main hotel, keeping an eye out for staff-only doors providing access to each floor. After a few false turns, he found a steep stone circular staircase to the upper floors.

20

Castle Vleuylen

Gemma didn't linger in the bath. She wanted to be sprawled across the fur when Max made it to the room. She left the door unlocked so that she wouldn't have to ruin the scene letting him in.

She'd wanted to wear her favourite blue knickers, but she seemed to have forgotten to pack them. So instead she put on a black lace bra and G-string, then lay back, sinking into the fur that cushioned her skin.

Max hadn't given their relationship any thought since Gemma had mentioned on the phone that Casper was sending her over to see Marchant. She had become a piece in the Pallesson jigsaw, and he was totally focused on that.

He found her hair clip and quietly knocked at the door. He couldn't hear any reply, so he tried the handle. The door gave a creak as he opened it.

Max knew he was in the right room, because he could see Gemma's suitcase on a bench. He couldn't see her, but he did hear her.

'Hello,' her voice said from the direction of the bed. 'I thought you'd never come.'

Max was taken aback when he got closer to the huge double bed. Sex had been the furthest thing from his mind. But he wouldn't have been human if the sight of Gemma, half buried in fur, seductively curled up with her naked bottom pointing towards him hadn't stirred something.

It felt as if a thousand thoughts were racing through his head, and all of them said throw her a towel and step away. He tried reminding himself why he'd thought going to the castle was a bad idea in the first place. He was meant to be telling Gemma gently about the future, not going to bed with her. But to turn her down now would be a crushing insult to Gemma, and he couldn't face the turmoil of that. Besides, she looked unbelievably sexy in her black lace G-string. Max became aware of a pulsating ache in his groin, which was being drawn to the bed like a magnate. Gemma crawled across the bed and went straight for his belt. She unbuckled it, and slid his zip down. Any chance that Max was going to behave honourably had gone up in smoke.

For the next hour, Pallesson and Oleg watched Gemma and Max thrashing around on the bed in the adjoining suite. They had two microphoned cameras hidden in the room. The one in the roof of the four-poster bed had been particularly revealing. When Gemma told Max what she wanted him to do to her, Oleg had nearly lost control of himself.

'Why don't we take the girl, too?' Oleg asked. Pallesson knew exactly what he had in mind for her. And the last thing he needed was the police finding the body of a raped Englishwoman.

'Don't complicate matters. We grab Ward and we get out of here.'

When Gemma's head finally collapsed on to the pillow, Max lay back equally shattered. Of one thing he was certain: she hadn't come here to set him up. But talking about their relationship now was definitely off the cards.

Max needed to monitor Marchant, and see who he was with before Gemma handed over the memory stick. There was still a chance that she was at risk. If Pallesson knew about them, he could use her.

Max also needed to talk to Pete Carr. The tracker must have reached its destination by this time. But he'd left the pay-as-you-go-phone, which was the safest way to talk to Pete unmonitored, in the car.

'Darling, I have to go down to the car to get a phone. Lock the door behind me. And even if you hear my voice, don't let me in unless I knock seven times.'

Pallesson had heard his chance.

'Let's go. We'll get him in the car park.'

Gemma refused to let Max go for a couple of moments, pulling him on top of her. That gave Pallesson and Oleg a fatal head start.

It was dark when Max stepped out of the spa exit. There was some discreet lighting along the path that led up to the car park, but no one was about. Max noticed a large white Transit van parked in the first bay of the car park. As he walked parallel to it, a stocky, thickset individual with a black woollen teapot hat stepped out of a shadow in front of him. Max knew then he was trouble, but the man didn't appear to be armed. He slid his right hand inside his coat to pull out his pistol, but as he did so he felt a searing pain in his arm. Pallesson had crept up behind Max and clubbed his arm with a baseball bat.

Max's arm recoiled in pain, dropping his pistol. Instinct told him the best way to escape whoever was attacking him from behind was to go forward. He lashed out with his foot and caught the first assailant right between the legs. The man doubled up in agony and surprise. But before Max could react again, he felt a spasm of pain in his right knee, as it gave way. His other assailant had belted him across the knee with his bat. As Max fell to the ground he felt the weight of someone jumping on top of him. And then he smelt the chloroform as a wad of cotton wool was held to his face. He struggled for a minute, not breathing. But he knew he was losing the battle. So, breathing as little as he could, Max let his body go limp.

Pallesson dragged Max into the back of the van and started tying him up while Oleg clutched his groin and moaned.

Once Max was secured, Pallesson told Oleg to go and collect their equipment. The cameras and mikes could be retrieved later, but they couldn't leave the monitor hanging around.

Before Oleg unplugged the monitor, he watched Gemma on the bed.

He thought about knocking on her door seven times and having some fun with her. But he knew that disobeying orders, even if they came via Pallesson, was a bad idea. So he reluctantly unplugged the equipment and headed off.

After half an hour of waiting for Max, Gemma got pissed off. He was obviously playing the spy around the hotel. So she sent him a text. After an hour she got concerned, and rang him. There was still no reply. She waited for him to ring her back or text her, but nothing.

A cold fear wrapped itself around her body. The fur was no longer making her feel warm. Something was wrong. She opened her briefcase, took out the memory stick and extracted it from its plastic wrapping with some scissors from her wash bag.

She then slid it into her Apple Mac and double clicked on the memory stick icon. It was blank.

'You little bastard,' Gemma said in disbelief, staring at the empty contents of the memory stick. As she said it, she dialled her husband's direct office line.

'Casper Rankin's office,' the efficient, clipped voice of his PA announced.

'Can I speak to Casper, please? It's Mrs Rankin.' The PA and Gemma had never made it to Christian name terms.

'Certainly, Mrs Rankin. I'll just put you through,' she replied with no warmth in her tone at all.

'Gemma,' Casper said, trying to make his voice sound normal.

'Cut the crap, Casper. What the fuck is going on?'

'Sorry?'

'Casper, don't muck about with me. The memory stick. It's blank.'

'What?'

'Don't bullshit me, Casper.'

'Look, these lines aren't secure, Gemma. Wait till you come home and I'll explain everything then.'

'Oh, no. I don't know what you're involved in, Casper, but I'm not coming home until I've found out.'

'Gemma, don't be stupid. You're out of your depth here. Come home.'

'Don't patronize me, Casper.'

Casper knew he had no option.

'If you want to see Max again, alive, you pack your bags, say nothing and come home.'

Gemma was stunned. He knew about Max. Yet he'd just referred to him as if it was no big deal.

'You don't know what you're involved in, Gemma,' Casper repeated. 'Just keep quiet, if you ever want to see him alive.'

Noises brought Max round. He'd managed to inhale very little of the chloroform. His hands and legs were bound up. He could feel nylon rope cutting into his wrists. Whether by chance or design, he'd been left lying in the recovery position and his mouth wasn't taped up. He thought about shouting out, but the first people alerted by his cries would be the ones who had put him there in the first place. There was nothing but darkness. But he could handle that.

Max could remember vividly the first time he'd been afraid of the dark. It was shortly after his tenth birthday, when he'd been given a new football. Wherever he went, the ball went with him. He could flick it on to his head, roll it down his back or balance it on his foot. He was the next Eric Cantona. Like a lot of other little boys in Warrington.

There were some boys, however, who were slightly older than Max and who resented him. He was a clever little bastard – too clever to be one of them. He stood out and that made him a target.

As he was constructing a set piece to win the FA Cup final, a group of boys called him over to the back of the communal sports field. They'd taken the metal cover off the entrance to the drainage gully, and were looking down into it. There was an eight-foot drop to the bottom, which was lined with a foot of mud and sludge.

'On the head, Max,' one of the boys shouted, as he approached. Max obligingly flicked his ball towards him. But instead of heading the ball, he caught it and tossed it into the drainage gully.

'That wasn't very nice,' one of the others said, in mock scorn. 'Come on, Max, I'll give you a hand to get it.'

Max knew it was a set-up. How stupid did they think he was? But he was going to have to go down into the gully to get his ball anyway, so he played along.

They dangled him down, head first, and lowered him into

the hole. Then, just as he was about to reach the ball, they let go of his ankles – and he fell into the sludge. It stank. And they laughed their heads off.

Max didn't really care – it was only mud – so he picked his ball up, and stretched a hand up for them to pull him out. But they had other ideas.

'Enjoy yourself,' one of them shouted, as they pulled the metal cover back across the entrance. The light disappeared, but their laughter didn't as they closed it off. Bar a couple of holes, which were designed to let workmen pull the covers off, he was in pitch-darkness. He could hear them jumping around on the cover, but he could see virtually nothing.

Don't shout out, he told himself. It will only give them satisfaction. Don't shout out. Just do nothing and they'll get bored. And let you out.

Max sat on his football and waited. For five minutes he could hear their muffled voices, getting slightly less animated. Then there was silence. The bastards were obviously going to leave him there for some time. And then come and pull him out when they felt like it. He was meant to be frightened. He was meant to be screaming and begging. Well, fuck them – he was going to be none of those things.

As they'd dangled him down, Max had seen the drainage tunnels that fed in and out of the manhole. One went towards the church; the other went back across the pitch. They were big enough for him to crawl along, but not big enough for him to turn around in. The only way to retrace his steps would be to crawl backwards.

Max decided to head for the church. Chances were, he'd come to another manhole quicker that way. Although it was pitch-dark, he pushed his ball along in front of him. It gave him something to focus on.

'This is fine,' he kept repeating. 'There's plenty of air. You're not going to die. And those bastards are going to get the fright of their lives.'

Crawling through the pipe was more uncomfortable than Max had anticipated. His knees soon got sore. He tried to pull himself along with his elbows, letting the ball move against the top of his head, but that was worse.

After half an hour he started to have doubts. His knees were now killing him. He thought about going back, and gave it a go. But it was a lot harder than going forwards. He was getting tired.

Max lay there for ten minutes to get some rest. He was now regretting his plan. Then he thought of how demeaning it would be to wait until he was rescued like a cowering wretch. And how much pleasure that would give them. So he kept going.

Minutes later, Max thought he saw a glint of light. As he moved towards it he had a feeling of space around him. He looked up and saw the most glorious sight he'd ever seen in his life: two small shafts of light coming through the holes of a metal cover.

Max had 'got lucky' twice. Not only had he chosen the right direction to crawl in – if he'd gone the other way, he may never have been seen again – but the entrance to the drainage system that he'd crawled to had metal attachments set into the concrete wall to climb up. The metal cover was temporary and with two hands pushed up relatively easily.

Max appeared, like a mole, in the graveyard of the church, observed by no one. He could now carry out the most satisfying part of his plan.

By climbing out of the graveyard into a farmer's field, Max could get home without anyone seeing him. He knew no one would be around when he got home. His dad would be in the shop taking bets, and his mother would be in Warrington doing whatever she did as mutton dressed like lamb.

He let himself in and got straight into the bath. It was the best bath he'd ever had in his life. He lay back and laughed out loud.

If anyone came to the door, he wasn't going to answer it. And when his parents got home, he was going to say nothing.

His tormentors were about to become the tormented. As far as Max was concerned, the search could commence.

Max was wrestling with Gemma's role in the whole business when the van moved off from the spa car park. What had they done to her? Maybe nothing. Maybe she had been used to lure him to the castle.

He decided to focus on keeping the time. It was a concentration exercise that he'd learnt at Eton after lights out. If he focused on the face of a large clock, he could visualize the second hand rotating. Max kept focused and counted. When the van stopped he was up to twenty minutes. As the back doors opened, he let his body go limp and pretended to be out cold.

Casper left his office in St James's and got a taxi home. He was dreading Gemma's return, but he knew he had to be at the house when she got back.

Even at the best of times, Gemma was prone to wild mood swings. She could go from a full-on tour de force to a crumpled, depressed wreck. Casper was expecting the former to step through the door that day. She would pose a problem, but he had to contain her somehow. If he didn't, he dreaded to think what Pallesson would do to both of them.

As soon as Casper entered their spacious Chelsea Square house, he called out in case Gemma had arrived early, or the housekeeper had stayed on later than usual. He was met by a reassuring silence.

He walked up the flight of stairs to the main reception room, and went straight to the table where they kept their drink. There was a huge array of bottles on the tray: brandy, Armagnac, sloe gin, tequila and a few malt whiskies. Casper went for the tequila.

He then looked at the bookshelf, as if making a decision as to which book he would read. He was, in fact, wrestling with the thought of getting a certain book down from the top shelf. After a brief pause, he pulled an ornate chair out from the Edwardian desk and gingerly stood on it to reach up to *The Long March*, which was jammed tightly between *Catch-22* and *The Big Sleep*.

Casper wasn't a habitual user of cocaine – although he had been in the past – but he kept a stash of it in the hollowed-out account of the Red Army's retreat. He couldn't remember which witty friend had given him the hiding place – but at least he wasn't likely to forget where he'd hidden his coke, and there was no danger of anyone else pulling that particular tome down from the top shelf for a quick read.

The wrap was folded within a scrap of shiny magazine paper. Casper opened it and poured a generous helping of the white powder on to the glass table in the middle of the room – and then added a little more for luck, before folding the paper up, putting it back into the cavity in the book, and replacing the book on the shelf. Then he took a credit card out of his wallet and chopped the coke into two fat lines, both a couple of inches long. He then trimmed a bit off the end of each line, and scraped them to one side with the credit card.

Casper rolled a twenty-pound note up and snorted one line up each nostril. He then dampened his index finger, dabbed it on the remainder of the coke, and rubbed it on to his top gum. He liked the numbing effect it had. Finally he dusted the table with the sleeve of his jacket to remove any incriminating evidence and then poured himself another shot of tequila. Which he threw back in one gulp.

Half an hour later, Gemma still hadn't arrived home. Casper had been fiddling and fussing around the house; generally whipping himself into a state of paranoia. He went down to the fridge to get himself a little treat. At the back of the top shelf was a kilo tin of beluga caviar. He prised the metal lid off and started eating it straight from the tin with a tablespoon, crunching the eggs in his mouth manically. He then got a vodka bottle out of the freezer, and had a shot of it to wash the caviar down.

Where could Gemma have got to? Had she done a bunk? Had she gone to the police? If she had, the shit would really hit the fan.

To start with, Gemma had been completely freaked out that Casper knew about her and Max – and had clearly sent her out to Holland, knowing she would meet up with him. How long had he known? And why had he said nothing before?

It didn't take long for her shock to turn to anger. Max had vanished, and as far as Gemma could tell, Casper was involved in his disappearance. If Max hadn't been in danger, he would have let her know. He wouldn't have just wandered off without so much as a word.

Gemma's instincts told her the best form of defence was attack. She would lie about her relationship with Max and threaten Casper with exposure if anything happened to him. She knew Casper couldn't handle her when she went off on one.

Casper was pouring himself a gin and tonic – going light on the tonic – when he heard Gemma coming through the front door. He'd been thinking of getting *The Long March* down again and having a top-up. But that would have to wait now.

He tried to relax and look calm as he heard her steps coming up the stairs.

'You'd better have a bloody good explanation,' Gemma said aggressively before she'd got to the last step, 'or God help you.'

Casper had guessed right. Full-on Gemma had arrived. He decided, like a salmon fisherman, to give her some line and let her run before he jerked the hook in her mouth.

'If anything happens to him, you and your revolting friends will swing. Pallesson is behind this, isn't he?'

'Drink?' Casper asked, unaware that he was licking his lips manically and sniffing.

'I'll help myself,' Gemma said, dismissively brushing past him.

'Your boyfriend is perfectly capable of looking after himself. He doesn't need you shouting your head off and making a fool of yourself.'

'He is NOT my boyfriend.'

'Oh really? Well, whatever he is, he doesn't need your help.'

'You listen to me—'

Casper had heard enough. He'd given his fish enough line. It was time to reel her in.

'No. You listen to me.'

'I'm—'

'SHUT UP!' Casper screamed at her. The ferocity of his voice and the madness in his eyes stopped her dead.

'You are not going to do or say anything. Do as you're told and you will be fine. Otherwise . . .' Casper's voice tailed off and they looked at each other in silence. But Casper could see that he hadn't knocked the fight out of her.

'You have a nice life, Gemma, and I don't bother you. We have lots of money because I do what I do. And I let you do as you want. We can stay like that. But if you cross me, you'll have nothing but the clothes you stand in.'

Gemma had been about to fight back, but Casper's last sentence literally sent a chill down her spine.

'Divorce?' Casper asked. 'It won't get you anywhere. Remember when you signed the deeds to transfer the house into a Montenegrin trust for tax reasons? That trust is in my name. You won't see a penny of it. My salary? It's nothing. So you'll get half of nothing. All of our profits are tucked away offshore. Your lawyer will never find them. You won't even have a car – it's leased.'

Casper licked his lips and rubbed his nose. Gemma was too rattled to pick up on it. He had hit her right where it hurt. Her mind was racing; imagining what it would be like to get to the cashpoint and find nothing would come out. This was her worst nightmare coming true. She had always lived with the fear that one day everything would be ripped away from her.

'What's happening, Casper?' she said in a weak, soft voice, avoiding eye contact with him. He knew then he had his fish safely in the landing net.

'Everything will be fine,' Casper said, with a conciliatory tone to his voice. 'But we have to stick together.'

21

Holland

Max had been through every stage of reaction to his torture. He'd screamed. He'd threatened. He'd tried to bribe his scarheaded tormentor. He'd sworn. But Oleg carried on asking the same question over and over.

'Where is the painting?'

'I am an officer of the British secret service,' he kept telling the Russian. 'They will find me. And they will find you.' But he didn't let on that he recognized him from the dacha outside Moscow.

He'd lost all sense of time and every joint of his body was screaming. The shackles around his wrists felt as if they were made of spikes. He couldn't support the weight of his arms any more. And every time he lost his balance the shackles dug into his skin. They were grating it raw.

In spite of his condition, Max could now sense a second person in the room, behind him.

Max knew it had to be Pallesson. But he also knew that his chances of getting out alive would not be improved if he identified Pallesson. In fact, the opposite was true, so he threw up a smokescreen.

'Who are you working for?' he mumbled over and over again.

Max reckoned he had not slept for about sixty hours – they had given him no opportunity. He was standing in the middle of a cold, damp cell strung to the ceiling. His soaking wet clothes were clinging to his shaking body. He was blinded by the flood-lights in front of him, though his eyes were screwed shut.

But time was not on Pallesson's side. And even if it had been, he knew they only had a few hours to get their answer. After that, Max would start hallucinating and talking random gibberish.

Max had long passed the point of needing sleep. His head felt like it was going to burst. The involuntary micro-blackouts were in no way repairing his brain. He was closer to meltdown than his captors realized.

'Where is it?' Oleg growled yet again.

Max kept his eyes clamped firmly shut. 'I don't know,' he whispered. 'It's nothing to do with me.'

Oleg looked at the ice floating on top of the bucket and smiled as he slowly poured the freezing water over his captive's head. Max's body was all but shut down and he was barely conscious of it.

'We're going to kill you if you don't tell us. Where is the fucking painting?'

Max wasn't going to last another few hours.

Pallesson's phone vibrated. He stepped far enough from where Max was being interrogated to take the call in private. Van Ossen wanted to know if they had found out where the painting was. And he spelled out the timeline to Pallesson.

It reminded him of a dressing-down he'd had as a small child when he'd demanded to look at a newspaper without saying please. The ferocity of the explosion that had erupted from his father had caused the small boy to lose control of his bladder. Pallesson had to focus on not letting the same thing happen now.

His time was running out. But he had one last trick up his sleeve.

Oleg bundled Sophie through the door into the cellar. She was gagged, blindfolded and clearly not very happy.

What Max really felt about Sophie was about to become apparent to Pallesson.

Pallesson gestured to Oleg to untie Sophie and lock her in the cell with Max.

As soon as Sophie felt her hands were free, she grappled with her blindfold and pulled it off. Pallesson saw the reaction in her eyes before she pulled the gag out of her mouth. But what would Max's be?

'Max! Oh my God,' she said, going straight to him and putting her arms around him to try to support him.

Despite everything he'd been through, Max realized that Sophie had walked straight into Pallesson's trap.

'You don't know me,' he said hopelessly.

Seconds later, Oleg came through the door and grabbed Sophie. She tried to evade him. He took great delight in slapping her across the face. The pain and shock of his blow stunned her. Oleg bent her arm behind her back to the point of breaking it. Max knew it was the end of the road. There was another rope-and-tackle system hanging from the ceiling in front of him. He wasn't going to watch them torturing Sophie.

'I know where the painting is,' he said.

Oleg hesitated, then turned to him.

'Where?'

'Max desperately needed to buy some time. Keate. Keate has it.'

Oleg left the room. To consult with Pallesson. Who was now confident that Max would try to save Sophie. But he'd already had Keate's house searched. And they'd found nothing. He told Oleg to push harder.

'The schoolmaster's house? We've looked there,' Oleg said aggressively when he went back into the cellar. And gave Max a slap around the face.

'It's there. You just didn't know where to look. I can show you. There will be clues you have to follow,' Max flannelled.

Oleg left the room again.

'Max . . .' Sophie said.

'I'm sorry, Sophie. I'm sorry,' Max whispered. There was little point in trying to keep up the pretence. Pallesson had obviously worked them out.

Oleg returned before they could say anything else; he grabbed Max by the hair and pulled his head back.

'Okay. Let's go and get it then. But if we don't find it, she'll pay.'

He locked the shackles around Sophie's wrist, attached them to the rope and wrenched them above her head. The shackles dug into her wrists and she gave out a sharp cry. He then systematically ripped her clothes off so that she was hanging from the ceiling naked.

'Let's go,' Oleg grunted. 'The quicker we get back, the quicker she gets down.'

22

Amsterdam

Oleg boarded the train at the start of a journey which would take them back to London. He chose the first group of four seats on the right in the carriage and signalled to Max to leave the window seat empty, as he did.

Max had noted from the station clock that it had taken them forty minutes to get from the cellar to the station. As the train pulled out, a stocky gentleman with a flamboyant scarf around his neck came to a halt next to them.

Philippe Levert's grandparents had fled from Continental Europe before the Second World War. But the Englishman was now making a tidy packet by trading there.

'Morning,' he said to Max, who ignored him.

'I said, good morning.'

Max looked out of the window and avoided eye contact.

'Anyone sitting there?' Philippe asked, pointing at the window seat next to Max.

'You can't sit there,' Oleg said in his thick Russian accent.

'I beg your pardon,' Levert replied, unfazed.

'Taken.'

'I know it's taken – by me. I think you will find I have reserved this seat.'

Max was beginning to enjoy the fix that Oleg was now in. Whoever this bloke was, he was clearly not moving for anyone.

'You can't sit there,' Oleg persisted.

'I think you're forgetting something,' the portly Englishman replied. 'This is my seat and I intend to stay here, thank you very much. Dear oh dear, what a carry on. Is he a friend of yours?' he now asked Max.

Max nodded.

'Well, I would have thought you could put some manners on him. I've never heard anything like it.'

'Sorry about that, er . . .' Max said, his sentence tailing off.

Philippe Levert was as English as they come. He'd made his money in the rag trade and commuted frequently to Amsterdam to buy stock. But he was not in the business of letting anyone push him around.

'You all right? You don't look too good,' Levert asked Max.

'Nothing a good night's sleep won't put right.'

'Oh. You've been on that stuff, have you? You look too old to be doing all that. Been on the toot with him?'

Max nodded his head contritely, but his mind was elsewhere. Sophie was incarcerated in some rank cellar, having God knows what done to her. He had to get her out of there as soon as possible. But who could help him. The Dutch police?

And then there was Gemma. Where was she? Dead? A prisoner? Or sitting in the Ritz having tea with one of her vacuous pals?

'The rag trade's my business. Philippe Levert's the name. You've probably heard of me.'

Levert produced a business card and pushed it towards him. Oleg looked suspiciously at them. He was totally out of his comfort zone. None of his training had taught him how to

233

deal with a situation like this – apart from just shooting everyone.

'Dear oh dear, you do look rough. How much of the bloody stuff did you smoke?'

'A fair bit,' Max conceded.

'Well, I'll give you the name of a drinking club I go to. Just a bit of fun, you know.'

Max thanked him and shut his eyes for a few minutes. He was knackered and desperately needed some sleep.

A couple of hours later the train shuddered and Max woke up with a start. His new friend Philippe Levert was fast asleep, wheezing a bit as he breathed. Max noticed his phone sticking out from under his newspaper.

Oleg had his eyes shut. But he wasn't asleep. He hadn't got much rest over the last twenty-four hours either. Max slid his hand along the table, and relieved Mr Levert of his phone.

Once he had the phone slid up his sleeve, Max cleared his throat loudly. Oleg opened his eyes . . .

'I'm going to be sick,' Max told him.

He looked unconcerned. So Max started to retch in Oleg's direction. Eighteen stone has never extricated itself from a train seat quicker.

Oleg followed Max to the toilet. Luckily there were a few people hanging around in the corridor, which prevented Oleg going in with him.

Max had been considering his plan of action before he'd nodded off. There was no one at the Office he could risk approaching. It was more likely that he'd get hung out to dry for stealing a painting from the embassy, than, with no evidence whatsoever, have his allegations against Pallesson taken seriously. Tryon had told him he was on his own if the plan went wrong. And that was when Tryon was still alive. Now he'd disappeared off the face of the earth, Max was definitely flying solo. There was only one way out of this. Tryon had been working with someone inside the Dutch police force. Someone who almost certainly had different motives and targets, but would at least be roughly on the same side. And the one person who might conceivably be able to find out the identity of the Dutch police officer Tryon had referred to was Pete Carr.

To Max's relief, Levert's telephone was older than the hills, so it had no locking facility. Max knew he wouldn't get away with ringing Pete Carr – Oleg would be listening at the door, and wouldn't think twice about forcing it open if he felt he needed to – but he could text him.

Fortunately, Max had a photographic memory for phone numbers.

He tapped the number in and started writing his message.

Pete Max here need to know who Tryon was working with in dutch police pls start digging.

There was a rap on the door.

'Let me in,' Oleg barked.

Max made some more retching noises and kept texting.

Urgent dont reply on this no will be in touch.

Max pressed send, and checked the message had gone. Then he slid the window open a fraction and pushed Philippe Levert's phone out of it. It shattered into little pieces on the rail track somewhere in Kent.

'Sorry about that,' Max said under his breath. 'Time you got a new one anyway.'

As Max opened the door, Oleg forced him back in and shut the door. Then he searched Max from head to toe.

'You took my phone, if you care to remember,' Max said. 'What are you searching me for?'

Oleg said nothing as he finished his search, and then unlocked the door and pushed Max out. A small boy was waiting outside the toilet with his mother.

'What have those men been doing, Mummy?' he asked as they filed past him. His mother didn't answer.

'Why were they in the loo together?' the boy persisted.

'Disgusting,' his mother muttered, deliberately loud enough for Oleg and Max to hear.

'It's a free world,' Max said, glancing over his shoulder.

'What does that mean, Mummy?' the small boy enquired of his mother, who was having second thoughts about her son using the facility.

Max was hoping that Levert would still be asleep when they got back to their seats. In fact, he hoped he stayed asleep until the train pulled into London. Because he assumed Levert wasn't the type to take the loss of his mobile phone quietly. He nearly got his wish. Levert woke up five minutes before the train pulled in.

To start with, he shuffled his papers, and looked out of the window.

'You look a bit better,' he said to Max. 'You won't be doing that again in a hurry, will you?'

Max shook his head compliantly.

'Four minutes late. No surprise there,' he said, hoping that by engaging Levert's attention he might distract him from thinking about his phone. But Oleg was glaring at him; and the message was quite clear.

Just as Max thought he was going to get away with it, Levert started rummaging in different pockets, and looking under his papers.

'Can't find my phone. Have you seen my phone?' he asked Max, panic beginning to spread across his face. Max shook his head.

'It must be here somewhere,' Levert said desperately.

'Maybe it's fallen on the floor?' Max suggested. The rest of the carriage was starting to get ready to alight. For any of them to begin looking under the table would cause chaos. Levert would have to wait until everyone had got off. But Max had stirred a suspicion in Oleg.

'What's the number? I'll ring it,' he said in his thick Russian, slyly looking at Max to see if he would make a move to get rid of it.

'Good idea,' Max chirped.

'Shut up.'

'There's no need for that,' Levert said.

'Don't worry about him,' Max said. 'Harrow education.'

'Dear oh dear. I've never heard the like of it. Young men these—'

'What's your number?' Oleg interrupted.

Levert could see it was in his interest to offer it up. Even if the level of brusqueness was quite unacceptable.

Max tilted his ear to the floor as Oleg punched in the number. Then shook his head solemnly as silence prevailed.

'Maybe it's on silent. I'd have a good look under there anyway,' Max suggested helpfully. 'Perhaps we could . . .' Max knew any offer of help would be rapidly countered by one of his travelling companions.

Oleg nodded his head towards the door, and Max obeyed.

'Sorry we can't stay to help. I'll give you a shout when I'm next in Amsterdam,' Max lied. What he couldn't say was: I'll get MI6 to send you the money for your new phone.

But if he survived, that was exactly what he would do.

Pallesson had all the information that he wanted from Sophie. She and her blind father had obviously betrayed him to Tryon, who had in turn recruited Max to thwart him.

She would have to be dispatched. But not just yet. She might still be a tradable commodity if things didn't go according to plan.

Once Max and Oleg had departed, he untied her and let her put on what was left of her shirt. She was in a state of shock. Terrified of her captors, traumatized by the memory of her father's chest being blown to pieces, and completely disorientated. She had no idea where she was.

When Pallesson came back into the room, she was sobbing in the corner. He picked her up. She didn't struggle. So he made the mistake of releasing his grip on her hair. She sank her teeth into his arm and bit as hard as she could. He yelped with pain and jerked his arm away, then belted her as hard as he could. She fell to the floor unconscious. Pallesson checked his arm: her teeth had penetrated the skin and left a vicious bite mark.

When Sophie regained consciousness, she was sitting in the corner again, on a mattress. Strapped around her waist was a padded belt. It was full of plastic explosive. There were wires coming out of the belt; they were connected to a device that was fixed to the wall a couple of metres from her.

'I'm going to explain this device to you,' Pallesson said, standing over her. 'Listen to what I tell you. For your own sake.'

Sophie said nothing. A stabbing pain was piercing her head.

'You have enough explosive around your waist to blow you to pieces. But that will only happen if the electric current from the battery is cut off. There are three ways that can happen. Understand so far?'

Sophie tried to focus, but her vision was blurred.

'If you stay still, you'll be fine. But if you take the belt off, you'll break the current and it will go off,' Pallesson continued. 'If you pull the wires out, or someone cuts them, it will also go off. So don't.'

Pallesson wasn't sure if he was getting through to her. Which didn't matter in the short term, because he hadn't activated the bomb. But once he had, if the mad bitch decided to blow herself up, she could take them with her.

'Those two wires go to a liquid mercury fuse, which is attached to the wall. If someone pulls it off the wall, the mercury will rock around in the ball-shaped glass, breaking the current that flows through it. And the bomb will go off.'

Sophie shut her eyes. He decided she hadn't taken in a word he'd said. He must have hit her too hard. The guard would have to go through it all again when she came round.

23

Oleg was a couple of strides behind Max as he approached
Keate's gate; out of range of any sudden, desperate lunge he
might be stupid enough to attempt.

'We've looked there,' Oleg had said before he'd slapped him
again in the cellar in Holland. Had they searched Keate's house
while Keate was there? If so, what had they done to him? Had
Pallesson accompanied whoever had done the search? Would
he have gone easy on the old boy? Of course not.

When Max pushed the gate, it opened without a sound. The
normal squeak had gone. Glancing casually in the direction of
the hinges, he thought he could see traces of oil.

He turned the handle of Keate's front door. Max had never
known it to be locked, but then he'd never visited when the
schoolmaster wasn't in residence. Only when they passed
through a deserted College Yard had Max realized that it was
now the school holidays.

The door opened when Max gave it a tentative shove. As he
stepped through the door, he apprehensively called out Keate's
name. There was no reply. Oleg shoved Max along the corridor
and shut the door behind them.

The door to Keate's study was open. It looked as if a bomb had gone off in there.

Max didn't like the way Oleg smiled.

'Where's the picture?' Oleg barked. 'If you don't find it, you'll live to watch us torture your girlfriend. We might even have some entertainment before we kill her – and you. No games. Where is the picture?'

Max glanced around the room again. The lead soldiers had been scattered on the floor and trampled. The sight enraged Max.

Keate's Jan Asselijn had been ripped from its gilt frame and it, too, lay on the floor.

Finding any sort of clue in there would be almost impossible amid such carnage – but Max was fairly certain that wasn't where to look, anyway.

'Fine bloody mess they made in here,' he said as he pushed past Oleg and walked towards the dining room. The pictures in the dining room had also been pulled out of their frames and chucked on the floor. Broken crockery was piled up in front of the big cupboard that they'd emptied.

This mess might not be found for weeks, Max thought. Keate would be God knows where and the housekeeper would have gone away for the holidays.

'Let's have a look outside,' Max suggested.

Keate's shed was tucked away at the bottom of the garden. Whoever Pallesson had sent to search the house had missed it. Oleg pushed in front of Max and entered the shed first. If he thought he was going to find the picture sitting on a shelf, however, he was disappointed.

Max's eye was immediately drawn to the workbench. On it there was a big adjustable spanner and a can of oil lying on its side. Only a very careless person would leave a can of oil leaking on its side – and while Keate was slightly shambolic, he wasn't careless. Keate must have oiled the hinges on the gate for a reason.

Oleg wasn't taking much notice of Max. He was too busy checking that the painting wasn't in the shed. So Max picked up the oilcan and turned it over in his hand. Scratched on the back of the can were two words. AUNT MARY.

Max mulled the words over. His immediate thought was the cocktail cupboard in the sitting room that had been a gift from Keate's aunt. But that was now in pieces. The painting obviously hadn't been hidden in there.

Hopefully she'll leave me her flat in Sloane Avenue, Keate had said. Max recalled thinking it unlikely that Keate would be happy living in Cranmer Court surrounded by old ladies.

He looked at the bicycle leaning against the door. Its tyres looked pretty hard. Hard enough to get him to Windsor Bridge and up the hill to Windsor Central railway station.

Max showed Oleg the oil can.

'Here's the clue. His aunt Mary was always clearing out the attic when she came to stay with him. It must be up there.'

As anticipated, Oleg took the bait and set off back towards the house. Max gave him twenty metres, then grabbed the bicycle and shot out of the shed towards the gate that opened into the lane behind the houses. There was a shout from behind him as Oleg turned from the back door and set off in pursuit.

Max fiddled with the catch on the gate; it seemed reluctant to open. Oleg was halfway to him. With a desperate tug that made the metal catch dig into the top of his ring finger, Max yanked the gate open. The grass inside the gate obstructed its progress, but he bulldozed his way through, leapt on to the bike and was off down the lane five seconds before Oleg got to him.

Max pedalled furiously past the entrance to School Yard

before swerving off the road to take the pedestrian walkway past College Chapel. He glanced over his shoulder, but there was no sign of Oleg. Rejoining the road, he went as fast as his legs could make a bike with no gears go. He was halfway down the High Street when he heard a car horn behind him. Oleg was in pursuit, but getting held up by the other traffic. Pushing himself harder, Max flew past Tom Brown Tailors and on towards the bridge. All the while the Russian was getting closer as he slewed through the traffic.

Oleg now had Max in his sights. His instructions were to kill him if he stepped out of line. He would drive straight over him and finish him off with a bullet in the head if need be. Pulling the balaclava down over his face, the Russian felt under his seat for his pistol.

As he neared Windsor Bridge, Max saw a bunch of Japanese tourists standing in the middle of it. They were hovering around the concrete bollards that stopped vehicles using the bridge. He aimed to the left of the group and shouted at the top of his voice.

Oleg was only ten metres behind Max now. If he'd known the bridge was closed to traffic, he would have taken a shot at him. But before he could react, Max had scattered the tourists like ducks being frightened off a pond. In the mayhem, Oleg slammed the brakes on, narrowly missing the hysterical, camera-wielding throng. He jumped out of the car to take a shot at Max, but the panicking tourists were in the way. Oleg ran after him, but Max had disappeared round the corner.

Max had two choices. He could either take a train to London from Windsor Riverside or go up the hill by the castle and catch a train from Windsor Central to Slough, changing for London Paddington. He decided that Windsor Riverside, being closest to the bridge, was too obvious. So he kept off the main road past the castle and made for Windsor Central.

Though he couldn't afford to hang around, Max was desperate to ring Carr. So he ducked into a phone shop at the top of Windsor High Street and bought a pay-as-you-go phone with a credit card which had been sewn into the top of his trousers.

He tried not to think about Sophie. There was a chance that Pallesson would take his escape out on her. But her only hope of getting out of that cellar was if Max could trade her for the painting. And he would be in no position to negotiate terms while Oleg was holding him prisoner.

Having made it to the station, Max boarded the train and kept his eyes on the only entrance to the platform, expecting Oleg to come hurtling into sight. Only when the whistle blew and the doors closed and the train began to pull out of Windsor Central did he finally relax.

Max dialled Pete Carr's number as the train rattled across the suspension bridge over the Thames. He looked out of the window at the river and had a very vivid flashback.

They'd done it dozens of times before; it was the easiest way to get to Windsor Racecourse, and as safe as houses. Or so they thought. All you had to do was hop over the wooden post-and-rails fence, scramble up the bank on to the railway line, and run across the single-track bridge when no trains were coming.

They normally waited for a train to pass before they climbed over the fence. That way they knew they had plenty of time before the next one came along. But that evening they were late for the first race. And they'd had a big tip for the second favourite. There was no time to sit on the fence.

Max said he'd go first and give the rather rotund Howard Minor a lead. He danced from sleeper to sleeper; it only took him thirty seconds to get to the end of the bridge. But as he got there, to his horror, he heard the unmistakable echo from the rails of a train approaching from Windsor.

He turned, expecting to see Howard Minor on his heels, but he wasn't even halfway across. He'd stopped and was messing around with one of his shoes.

'Go back,' Max had shouted.

'What?' Howard Minor replied. 'Be with you in a minute.'

A minute, however, wasn't going to work. There was unlikely to be room for Howard Minor and the train on the bridge.

Max made a split-second decision. He set off back along the bridge towards Howard Minor. When he got to him, he could see terror blazing out of Howard Minor's eyes. The train from Windsor was bearing down on them.

'Over the side,' Max said.

'I can't,' Howard Minor said. 'I can't—'

Max grabbed his mate by his tie and backed him up to the solid, waist-high metal girder. Then he got one arm behind Howard's knees, the other under one armpit and spun him over the side.

Howard Minor gave a blood-curdling wail as he rotated through the air into the River Thames.

Max leapt like a frog up on to the girder as the train thundered past. He felt the whoosh of air buffet him as the carriages flashed by. It was a close shave; Max took a deep breath and looked down into the river. Howard Minor was trying to drown himself.

'Fucking hell,' Max observed, throwing himself off the bridge. 'The bloody horse will definitely win now.'

As the train trundled along the red-brick viaduct – or Hundred-arch Bridge, as they'd called it at school – Carr's voicemail cut in.

'Annoyingly, I haven't answered,' Pete's voice said cheerfully.

Yes, it is bloody annoying, Max thought, and waited for what seemed like an eternity to leave his message.

'I'll keep calling, Pete,' Max said quickly, and hung up.

He had another six minutes till the train reached Slough. After that he'd be trading this empty carriage for the mainline train to London. Packed in like a battery chicken with city-bound commuters, it would be impossible for him to speak privately. So as the train passed Eton golf course, Max tried Pete's number again.

'Sorry, mate,' Pete said, finally answering. 'Had my head stuck inside a suitcase. Don't ask.' Max didn't. There was no time for banter.

'Any news on Tryon, Pete?'

Pete got the urgency in his voice.

'Nothing, mate. Not a squeak.'

'Doesn't sound good, does it?'

'Well, you never know. But it is strange.'

'There's too much I don't understand, Pete. The tracking device, for instance. How bloody obvious was it that they'd find that?'

'Well, I did mention that to Tryon, to be honest with you. But he didn't seem too concerned.'

'Exactly. And why not? Why the last-minute instruction to take it to France? Was he setting me up, Pete?'

'Look, mate, that isn't for me to say. But I can't see that he was. After all, you weren't trying to palm it off on anyone, were you?'

It was a fair point. And as Max thought about it, he realized exactly what Tryon had been playing at. It wasn't Max he was trying to set up by putting such an obvious device into the frame. It was Pallesson. Tryon didn't care about working with the Dutch police to bust a drug ring; he'd just gone all-in to get someone else to take out Pallesson.

But Tryon had given no thought to the consequences of his actions. He'd made no provision to ensure the safety of Jacques and Sophie until it blew over. And now Sophie was hanging from the ceiling of a cellar, and as for Jacques . . . Max didn't care to think what had happened to the old man.

Though he couldn't be sure he had all the pieces in the correct order, Max was struggling to come to any other conclusion.

'How about the Dutch police, Pete? Did you get anywhere there?'

'I've done due diligence, mate. Took a while. Went through the Dienst Nationale Recherche personnel records. Hacked Interpol – and that's not easy, believe you me – looked for cops with a particular aversion to drug dealers. Then cross-referenced that with cops who have worked with Interpol on multi-territory busts. Boiled those down by crossing with cops who have overlong disciplinary records for stepping out of line, being a bit of a maverick, but no hint of corruption – not even the kind crooked cops use to fit up the one honest guy. There's a detective who fits the bill: Aart de Vater. He's a loner, far as I can see. Been in some serious hot water over the years. Sort of guy Tryon would take a chance with.'

'What kind of hot water?'

'Well, mate, there was a bust-up a couple of years ago. Looks like de Vater caught up with a drugs gang. Only he didn't get any of them into court. He killed three of them. And that doesn't get you promotion. Although it probably should. Let's just say his record would suggest he doesn't always play things by the book.'

'Anyone else?

'A couple of others, but de Vater's your man.'

'Telephone number?'

'Christ, you don't ask for much, do you?'

'Pete, there's an innocent girl hanging from the ceiling of a cellar having God knows what done to her. And there's a load of heroin heading for England. So no, I'm not asking for much, as it happens.'

Pete knew stress when he heard it. He read de Vater's phone number out to Max and wished him good luck.

24

London

The connecting train from Slough was heaving. There was no way Max could talk to de Vater. So he stood in the buffet car and ate a stale all-day-breakfast muffin. But he really didn't care. He was starving.

There was twenty minutes to kill before the train got into Paddington. So he tried to make sense of what was going on.

Clearly it was of no importance to Tryon that he was blowing any chance of the Dutch police busting the drug deal. Eliminating Pallesson had been his only concern.

The safety of Jacques and Sophie had been overlooked; either by design or accident.

But none of that explained why Tryon had gone missing. Leaving Max with no one to work with from within the Office.

De Vater was now his only possible ally.

Max walked out of Paddington Station across Praed Street into London Street. He passed all the tacky shops selling crap to tourists and only dialled de Vater when he got to Sussex Gardens. Aart de Vater answered after two rings.

'Yee-s.'

'Mr de Vater?'

'Yee-s.'

'Can you speak?'

'It depends who wants to speak. What is your business, please?'

'I work with Tryon. British secret service. Or used to. He's disappeared – as you may know?'

'Hold on please.' The line went quiet. Max had no idea whether the cop was instructing someone to trace the call or finding somewhere more private so he could talk freely. It didn't matter.

'What is your name, please?'

'Max Ward.'

'Can you prove that?'

'Within reason, yes. If I was to tell you that I am trying to track down the original *Peasants in Winter*, would that help?'

There was silence again.

'I know a tracker was put in the copy. It hung me out to dry as much as it probably did you. And now I need your help.'

'What is your problem, Mr Ward?'

'My problem is that a girl is being tortured somewhere in Holland. The girl who copied the painting. My problem is that Pallesson will either try to kill or frame me. Probably kill me. And there is the small matter of a shipment of heroin heading towards England under your nose.'

'Under my nose? I hardly think so. If your Mr Tryon hadn't double-crossed me, none of this would have happened.'

'I've come to the same conclusion myself. Now I need your help, because no one else knows about this. You have to find the girl.'

'How?'

'All I can tell you is that she's being held in a cellar approximately twenty minutes from Castle Vleuylen and forty minutes from Amsterdam Centraal railway station.'

'That could be a lot of places, Mr Ward.'

'No, it couldn't. If you think about it, it could only be two places. Draw a circle around the castle twenty minutes away from it. Likewise forty minutes from the railway station. The circles will cross twice.'

'I'm perfectly aware of that. But it's not as simple as you make out.'

'Well, unless you happen to know where van Ossen tortures his victims, that's about all we've got to go on. It's a start.'

'Where is the picture, Mr Ward?' de Vater asked, changing tack.

'Probably in London. Obviously, I can't say on an open line. But I'm on the trail. I need to get it back to van Ossen – or Pallesson – to save the girl.'

'Are you seriously telling me you are about to give the painting to a drug dealer?'

'Yes, I am. A girl's life is at stake.'

'That painting is Dutch government property.'

'It's also the only chance you have to bust the drug deal,' Max said, trying to find a way through to de Vater.

'How do you figure that out?'

'No painting, no deal. And even if there is a deal, you won't know how or when. If the painting is handed back, you can follow it. It will lead you to the deal.'

'So you say. But I had a similar arrangement with Tryon; we were going to work together to trap Pallesson and bust a major criminal organization. Only it turned out Mr Tryon had his own agenda.'

'How do you know that?'

'From the start, Tryon was afraid that Pallesson would slip away during the drugs bust. Or not even be there. So he had that tracking device planted in an effort to get Pallesson killed. Which has screwed any chance I had of busting the deal.'

'I can get it back on track. Trust me: I want Pallesson alive. A bullet in the brain is too good for this bastard.'

Aart de Vater thought this over. It was a risk. He could demand the return of the painting, and take the credit for that. But finding stolen works of art wasn't what turned him on. A big drugs bust was much more his style.

'Okay, Mr Ward,' de Vater said after a moment. 'I'll get my pen out and start drawing circles. If we can locate her, we'll go in.'

'And if you can't?'

'If we can't, then I guess we have to hope she'll be released when you hand over the painting. Ring me when you're back in Amsterdam with it, Mr Ward.'

Max got a black cab from Paddington to Sloane Avenue. From his conversation with Keate he knew that 'hopefully she'll leave me her flat in Sloane Avenue'. But he had no idea which flat Aunt Mary lived in.

Cramner Court was a large development of flats off Sloane Avenue. When he got out of the cab, the snow was swirling around in a frenzy. Max turned up his collar and made his way along the pavement until he found a shop that looked as though it might sell suitcases. Extremely expensive ones, as it turned out. No matter, it would all help. Then he slipped into the newspaper shop on Sloane Avenue. He bought the largest box of chocolates they had and a copy of *The Lady* magazine. Braving the snow again, he made his way around the corner into Cramner Court, heading for the first entrance he could see under a brick archway. He was fairly confident the old girl wouldn't be out in this weather.

Albert Sharpe had been a day porter for two decades. If he hadn't been addicted to crosswords, he would have died of boredom. But Albert was of the same generation as most of the residents, and he was comfortable working there. Over the years his 'owners' hadn't changed much. They were all getting old gracefully together. The flats very rarely came on the market. A lot of them were owned by family trusts who handed them down to the next generation when they became available.

Albert was in particularly good humour that morning. The Christmas envelopes had started to roll in slightly earlier than usual. It was Albert's job to pool the contributions and dispense them among the porters. This year had all of the makings of a record year, and Albert took that personally.

His crossword was going rather well, too. Although twenty-three across was proving to be a bit of a stumbling block. *Pub quarrel in Cumbrian town [6]* was delaying his progress when Max emerged through the glass double doors.

'Good morning,' Max said through a broad, genial smile. 'I don't suppose you can help me . . .'

Albert was inclined to say he didn't suppose he could, not until he'd got twenty-three across, at any rate. But his job was to be on hand at all times for his 'owners' and their guests. This young man was clearly of their ilk. And judging by the box of chocolates and the suitable magazine that Albert's intuitive radar had already picked up, Max was an appropriate sort to be in the building.

Max put the chocolates and *The Lady* down on Albert's desk, just in case the old boy hadn't spotted them.

'Coming to stay, sir?' Albert asked.

'Just dropping by, actually. Brain like a sieve, though,' Max said vaguely. 'Come to see old Aunt Mary every year, and never can remember her flat number.'

'Mary, sir?'

'Yes. Mary Keate. Salt of the earth.'

'Indeed, sir.'

It was Albert's job to accept delivery of parcels, dry cleaning and generally direct any guests. He took pride in being able to sift the wheat from the chaff without constantly bothering his 'owners'. And time was of the essence. If he could get twenty-three across cracked, he would be on for his best time that year.

'Third floor, sir. Flat number three.'

'Yes, of course. I'm the third nephew. Think I'd be able to remember that, wouldn't you?' Max guffawed.

Albert knew better than to agree, as the slightly dippy young man headed for the lift.

Max gave Aunt Mary's doorbell a good, long push on the basis that she might be a bit on the deaf side. He had no idea what he was going to say to her. Or indeed, how he was going to get through the door. If she was as bright as a button, things weren't going to be too easy. But if she was getting on a bit – and being Keate's aunt she had to be pretty ancient – he ought to be able to case the joint without too many problems.

To his relief, a very frail-looking lady answered the door.

'Who are you?' she said bluntly.

'Max. Max Ward. I'm a pupil of your nephew, Mr Keate.' The words sounded odd to Max as they came out of his mouth. 'He asked me to drop in on you. Make sure you were okay in this weather.'

'Of course I am. If I need anything I ask him downstairs. Sitting around all day. Never does a thing, you know.'

'Really,' Max said rather limply.

'You're not coming to stay.'

'No, no,' Max said quickly. 'Just passing.'

'Good. Well, you'd better come in. What did you say your name was?'

'Max. Max Ward.'

The flat was exactly as Max had imagined it would be.

Slightly gloomy, faded wallpaper with frail furniture that looked as though it had been there for ever, and curtains that had been.

'Have you seen Mr Keate recently?' Max asked.

Aunt Mary smiled at him.

'What did you say your name was?'

'Max Ward.'

'Oh yes. So you did. Would you like tea?'

'Thank you. What a lovely room,' Max said, casting an eye around. There was no sign of the painting.

'No, it isn't. Shabby and old. Like me. But we get along all right. Tea?'

'Thank you.'

'He'll have this flat one day. I suppose he'll do it up,' Aunt Mary said as she shuffled into the small kitchen.

'Could I use your loo, please? Terrible weak bladder.'

'At your age? You wait 'til you're as old as me.'

'Yes. Not good,' Max said as he turned towards the corridor that led out of the sitting room. There were three doors leading off the dimly lit corridor. Max opened the first one. Aunt Mary's bedroom. The least likely place Keate would have put the painting. The next door was her bathroom. A non-starter, unless he'd put it in the airing cupboard, which was unlikely. But the last room looked more promising.

Aunt Mary clearly didn't have people to stay. There was junk piled up on her spare bed. Max knelt on the floor and looked under the bed. Right at the back he could see the very same packaging that he had posted from the embassy to Tryon.

Max pulled the painting out. There was no time to check it now. But he didn't need to. He just needed to sneak it out past Aunt Mary, who wouldn't miss it. She probably didn't even know she had it.

Aunt Mary was still waiting for the kettle to boil as Max

crept back along the corridor. He quickly opened his suitcase and slipped the painting into it. By the time Aunt Mary returned to the sitting room, he was sitting innocently looking at the faded pattern on her curtains of foxes being hunted by a pack of hounds.

Max swallowed his tea as fast as he could.

'Have you seen Mr Keate recently?' Max asked again.

'He's coming to see me, is he? Oh good.'

Max gave up – and looked at his watch.

'Oh dear, is that the time?' he said weakly. 'Must be off, I'm afraid.'

'Of course you must,' Aunt Mary said, with a hint of regret in her voice, Max thought. A sudden pang of guilt made him remember belatedly to hand over the chocolates and the magazine.

'Thank you, young man,' Aunt Mary said. 'And tell that nephew of mine to come by again soon. Well, I'll be seeing you. I hope you found whatever it was he said you'd come for.'

'When did he say that?'

'Well . . . I simply can't remember. Good day.'

Max blushed. He felt a right idiot as he waited for the slowest lift in England to arrive.

Amsterdam, two months earlier

For months Wielart had been left frustrated and unfulfilled by his sexual encounter with Francisca. Even though he'd helped her family out of a crisis, she'd been too ungrateful to welcome the chance of thanking him with a few simple, physical gestures. It was a rejection, and a humiliation, that he didn't wish to repeat. But that didn't mean to say that he couldn't use his new asset in a different way.

If Wielart was to have ultimate financial control of the

Amsterdam black market, he had to get rid of Jorgan Stam and find a way of liquidating their main rival, van Ossen. Which meant finding and manipulating van Ossen's Achilles heel.

Stam had successfully planted a man inside van Ossen's organization. The most revealing feedback that they'd received was van Ossen's slavish devotion to his daughter; and their Sunday visits to the riding school.

What could be more natural than a beautiful young girl hanging about a riding stable, totally unaware of the effect she had on middle-aged men in her tight jodhpurs, Wielart had concluded. Van Ossen would suspect nothing.

Wielart had felt Francisca's contempt blazing at him when he'd summoned her back to his office. Her appearance disappointed him. She was no longer the innocent apparition who he'd spent hours lusting over. She looked as if she'd gone to pieces. And indeed she had. Her eyes were now sunken and sullen. A pity, Wielart mused.

Francisca had fallen into getting wasted in the coffee houses since Wielart had raped her. Not surprisingly, she had also wiped the formerly inseparable teenage friendship with Josebe from her mind.

Josebe had been distraught about the distance Francisca had put between them; and sought the counsel of her parents. Wielart had put it down to Francisca having poor morals and advised his daughter to keep her distance.

After Wielart had reminded Francisca that she was an ungrateful bitch, he told her what she was going to do for him. Unless, of course, she wanted to renege on her promise to 'do anything' and keep her father out of jail.

She was now studying at a further education college in Amsterdam; but there would be nothing unusual in the daughter of such a successful businessman having a cool, modern apartment in the centre of Amsterdam. And that was exactly what Wielart was going to provide her with. In addition to the show horse, which she would have at her disposal at the same riding school that taught van Ossen's daughter. And she would be there every Sunday morning to ride it.

'Van Ossen is a very important man. If you care about your father, you will become his mistress for a while. Not long. Just until we have enough information to bring him down,' Wielart had instructed her.

Francisca had shown no emotion when Wielart set out his proposal. Her heart had frozen over. She already felt like a prostitute; and the more important she was to Wielart's dirty world, the sooner she could exact her revenge.

Wielart felt spurned when she put up no objection and nodded compliantly. Was he so disgusting that this little slut would happily satisfy van Ossen's sexual gratification and yet reject him? Bizarrely, Wielart found he now had a personal, as well as commercial, motive for destroying van Ossen.

It had taken van Ossen a nanosecond to clock Francisca gliding around the arena next to Anneka. Her blonde hair was flowing behind her shoulders under her silk riding hat. Her legs seemed moulded into her horse. No heterosexual man in the world would have missed her.

Francisca had put her horse back in the barn and hung around until Anneka finished tormenting her instructor. Van Ossen fell into the honey trap like a bear.

Francisca had flirted with him, and he had reciprocated. She told him she'd heard all about him, and he was flattered. She was the smart daughter of a successful businessman; why wouldn't she be attracted by his power and money?

When their affair started, van Ossen didn't question how she could have afforded such a magnificent and convenient apartment. Deetman Shipping was a big affair, after all.

Francisca made him talk about business too. But that too

seemed only natural. She had been brought up to know about such things. And he enjoyed showing off to her. The more he told her, the more physically charged she seemed to become. Francisca was a good actress. But she needed stronger and stronger dope to get her through the charade.

Van Ossen was smitten. After the Nuttall deal, he was seriously thinking of disappearing to some Caribbean Island with his billions; and Francisca.

25

London

Max smiled as he walked down Sloane Avenue. An old lady in her nineties had seen straight through him. And he was meant to be a secret agent. What he couldn't figure out was whether she was genuinely forgetful, or feigning vagueness in order to conceal Keate's movements. Max sent Keate a text message, although he didn't expect a reply.

He was still starving, and couldn't resist the Starbucks on his left before he jumped into a cab. Even though he had a stolen masterpiece under his arm. After all, who had ever had a work of art stolen from them in Starbucks?

Max only had to wait a couple of minutes to hail a black cab when he came out holding his venti latte with a triple shot.

'Heathrow, please,' he asked the driver as he collapsed into the seat.

'Certainly, sir,' the cabbie replied joyously. That would be him done for the day and off to the driving range.

Max had been postponing ringing Gemma. Because, what-ever the truth, he now had to treat her as an enemy at best, or a liability at worst. Hopefully not a damaged, injured liability. Either way, it was over. The job came first.

Casper had gone out to give Gemma some space. Before he left the house, when the coast was clear, he'd taken *The Long March* down from the shelf and slipped its contents into his pocket. He'd have a top-up in the lavatory at his club.

Gemma was lying in a deep bath, fermenting in Cowshed bath oil when her phone rang. It was a strange number. She didn't answer it. Then it rang again. She knew it would be Max.

'Hello,' she said rather awkwardly.

'Gemma, are you all right?' Max asked.

'Yes. I'm fine.'

'Are you on your own? Can you talk?'

'Yes.'

'You don't sound all right.'

'Well, I did get abandoned by someone in the middle of Holland.'

'Abandoned?'

'I suppose you went off on one of your capers?'

That's good, Max thought to himself. Get on the front foot – sound like the injured party. He wondered who'd taught her that.

'Now hang on a minute—'

'I didn't think you could talk when you were *operational*?'

'Give me a break, Gemma.'

'Where did you go? Off to shag that little French girl.'

Max was genuinely stunned by that. How did she know about Sophie? Did she know where they were holding her?'

'How do you know about Sophie?'

'So you're not denying it then?'

'Sophie has been kidnapped – maybe murdered. What do you know about it?'

Gemma's bitterness exploded inside her. What Casper had told her about Max and Sophie was obviously true – any hope that she'd harboured that Casper was merely 'poisoning the water' had gone up in smoke. And Max didn't care one little bit that she knew about Sophie. Her face was being rubbed in it.

'What do you know about Sophie, Gemma?'

'Sod off, Max,' Gemma said as she hung up on him.

26

Aart de Vater was feeling irritable. And the Englishman's plane was late. He wasn't even sure it was a good thing to be meeting him in the first place. One British agent had already stitched him up, so why was he about to trust another?

But there was more to de Vater's black mood than an irritating Brit. He was questioning whether there was any point his remaining in a job where none of his comrades trusted or appreciated him.

The senior command had made it clear that they considered him a loose cannon after three drug dealers had died from wounds inflicted by his weapon. As far as he was concerned, he should have been promoted and feted. Instead, he'd been warned, admonished and lectured about procedure.

Worse, however, was the attitude of rank-and-file cops towards him. They shunned de Vater because, unlike the rest of them, he wasn't prepared to take a bung and turn a blind eye. None of his fellow officers wanted to work with someone who got in their way of making a few quid.

Why did he bother? Why put his neck on the line when no one appreciated what he was doing? Sod it. He'd knock the job on the head, take Frits out of school for six months and go on a cruise. Maybe to the Far East? Marianne was always banging on about travelling. He'd do it. Then take up the job he'd been offered in Bahrain. Once he'd put this business to bed. Aart may have been hacked off, but he'd never walk away from a job half-cooked.

When Max finally walked out of the terminal, de Vater was relieved to see he was carrying a bag that looked capable of holding a painting.

As they were up against the clock, there'd been no time to come up with a safer way of getting the painting back into the country. The Dutch policeman was going to have to make a decision on the hoof. If he got the feeling that Max was going to double-cross him as Tryon had, he would drive him straight to the police station and arrest him for being in possession of stolen goods. He was already on his final warning, as far as working outside the rules of the force was concerned.

If, however, he felt that Max would genuinely work with him to entrap van Ossen and his men – whether they picked up Pallesson, or not – then he would take the punt.

However, de Vater still had one major reservation: he didn't like the idea of giving them the original *Peasants in Winter*.

'Good morning. Everything okay?' de Vater asked as Max slipped into the passenger seat of his Audi.

'Fine,' Max said. 'Only twenty minutes late. Any news on Sophie?'

'I'm working on it. I've had a few guys checking out your info. But we're talking about a huge area. It's like looking for a needle in a haystack.'

Max was frustrated. He knew Data Dave in the office could boil it down to a smaller area. But he couldn't risk involving him.

'How many men are on it?'

'I've got a problem with that. I'm having to keep this operation very tight. We've got a mole somewhere – there are only four men I can trust.'

'Four,' Max said with derision. 'Please tell me you're joking.'

'I only wish I was. But—'

'Did Tryon know that?'

'Yes. I told him the situation.'

'And you're surprised he went off on his own agenda? If you've got information leaking from your team, I can guarantee Pallesson will be the first to hear.'

'The painting?' de Vater asked, gesturing towards Max's case and changing the subject.

'Yes. Never looked better.'

Neither of them said another word until they got out of the airport and on to the motorway.

'Is it definitely the original?' de Vater asked.

'Definitely. Not that most people would notice if they had a cold.'

'A cold?'

'Yup. The only give-away that Sophie – the forger – was worried about was the smell. The paint on the original is so old, it's inert. But if you disturb the paint on either of the copies, they will give off a slight aroma. Even though she used materials to minimize this.'

De Vater was pleased with this information. He was getting a sense that the Englishman was being open with him. Unlike his predecessor, Tryon.

'By the way, I'm not happy, either,' Max said a couple of minutes further down the road. 'You think Tryon stitched you up – what about me? I'm the one who's liable to end up in prison for stealing a Dutch work of art. Not you. You don't even have to know about it.'

It was a fair point, de Vater conceded to himself, and for the first time he felt vaguely in control of the situation.

'Why do we have to give them the painting?' he asked, without looking at Max.

'Because the deal falls apart if Pallesson can't offer van Ossen the original painting as up-front security. If Pallesson doesn't deliver the painting, van Ossen will sell the drugs to someone else, and you are back to square one. At least if you let the painting run you'll know who's in the deal.'

'But that isn't why you want to give them the painting, is it?'

Max's reply would determine whether de Vater worked with him, or cuffed him. One ounce of bullshit, and he was through with the British secret service.

'That is partly true,' Max said. 'But as you already know, an innocent girl is hanging from a ceiling somewhere. She is a key witness. So unless you locate her, and we get her out, like now, swapping her for the painting sounds the best option.'

De Vater was happy with Max's answers. If the Englishman had stayed quiet, and seemingly accepted everything he'd just been told, he wouldn't have trusted him. His department was a mess. But Max's outraged reaction, and defence of Tryon, had been genuine.

'I want to control the swap,' de Vater said, knowing that he was now condoning handing back the picture.

'I recommend somewhere open,' Max replied, realizing there was no point arguing. 'We need to see what he's doing.'

'The Museumplein next to the Van Gogh Museum,' de Vater suggested.

'Can you secure all the exits?'

'No,' de Vater replied, shaking his head. 'I don't have enough men I can trust. Besides, what if Pallesson doesn't go for that?'

'I'll suggest another location first. He's bound to reject my first choice.'

'Just make sure he can't get away with Sophie.'

'We'll do our best.'

*   *   *

266

Eduart was beginning to feel better about life. He'd been living on the streets of Amsterdam for two months, drinking his way through the little money he could get his hands on during the day and smoking dope in the coffee houses at night. But he wasn't proud of some of the things that he'd done to get by.

Still, there was light at the end of the tunnel. His exasperated daughter had flown in from Canada to get him back on his feet. To give him one last chance. Eduart's brain was fairly addled now by the amount of grass he'd smoked, but that was all about to change.

Eduart had promised his daughter that he'd get treatment for his addictions once she'd fixed him up. Yet in spite of that undertaking, she'd resisted giving him any money, paying instead for his food and lodgings at the hostel.

Eduart had begged enough that morning from passers-by outside the Van Gogh Museum to buy a couple of cans of cider. He went to sit on a bench on the edge of the Museumplein to figure out how he could get some more. Two cans helped, but he felt lousy until he'd had six. After that he'd ease on to the Heineken for the rest of the day, if he could find the money.

At first, Eduart didn't take any notice of the man who sat on the other end of the bench. If you didn't look too good, and felt even worse, conversation with strangers was something to be avoided. But even though his senses had taken a pounding over the last few months, Eduart could feel that the stranger wanted to interact with him. So he turned his body away.

'Morning,' Max said, not trying to make eye contact. Eduart didn't reply.

'Cold enough,' Max persisted. Still nothing from Eduart.

'Fancy a can of cider?' Max asked. He'd been watching the tramp on the bench and had taken care to buy the same brand. He slid a can along the bench.

Eduart had been picked up like this before. The first time it had happened, he'd assumed he'd met a soul mate. Until they'd started beating him up.

However, the free can of cider now sitting next to him was too much of a temptation. He reached out for the can without looking at the stranger and pulled it towards him.

'Will you be in the Museumplein for an hour or so?' Max asked, as if he was passing the time of day.

'What's it to you?' Eduart replied, dropping his defence of silence.

'I wondered if you could do something for me. All you have to do is sit on a bench in the Museumplein for an hour and give someone this parcel.'

Eduart didn't like the sound of it. He'd been tricked before.

'I'll give you six cans of cider.' Still Eduart said nothing.

'Twelve – or I'll get someone else to do it.'

Eduart had never been a good negotiator. And he didn't like the idea of losing twelve cans of cider if all he had to do was sit on a bench. Which he'd be doing anyway.

'Twenty-four,' Eduart countered.

'Done. Half up front, half after the job.'

Max explained to Eduart what he had to do. It sounded too good to be true.

'What's in the parcel?' Eduart asked.

'Just a photo of a friend and me. He wants it back, but I don't want to see him. Too many memories,' Max said, looking at the floor. Eduart understood.

Max watched the tramp shuffle across the park towards the bench that he'd indicated to Pallesson he'd be on, dressed up as a tramp, in his last text message. He checked his watch. There was still an hour before the rendezvous. The tramp would be in position well before Pallesson arrived.

De Vater's men were scattered around the edges of the park. Max didn't know who they were, and as long as they kept on the move, they wouldn't stand out. It was too cold to be standing around aimlessly and not stand out.

Max was not concerned about the painting. The police would follow it. Sophie was his concern.

Would Pallesson have figured out that he could walk off with the painting – for the time being – even if he reneged on his side of the deal and didn't bring Sophie?

The corner window of the café Max had secreted himself in offered a perfect view of the Museumplein towards Honthorststraat on the other side of the park. Max had his back turned to the rest of the customers, who probably hadn't noticed he was watching the park through a small pair of binoculars. And what if they had? He was just another tourist admiring the amazing houses along the far side of the park.

Max was looking for a couple. Sophie and a minder. He wondered what Sophie's body language would be. Would she be able to walk unaided? Max checked his watch again. Ten minutes to go.

A few pedestrians beetled across the park on their way to work. Wrapped up against the cold. Streams of bicyclists criss-crossed the tarmac paths in their dozens. Amsterdam was, after all, the city of the bicycle.

Eduart cracked open his fifth can of cider, and wished more people could fall out with each other; then use him as their agent. Maybe there was something for the future in this? He'd suggest the idea to his daughter. She could set him up, find him a nice warm office somewhere to operate out of. He looked at the light padded parcel on the bench next to him and drank to the future.

Max only noticed the thickset man when he stopped about fifty metres behind Eduart. He assumed he must be one of de Vater's men.

269

Bloody idiot, he said to himself. What was he doing so close to the drop? Pallesson would see him a mile off. Max checked his watch again. One minute to go.

'Get that man out of there, he's too close,' Max hissed into his radio when de Vater answered.

'Out of where?'

'The park. By the bench.'

'I haven't got anyone by the bench.'

'Any sign of Sophie?'

'Negative. No one has entered the park that looks right.'

'Any unusual vehicles? Maintenance? Gardeners?'

'Negative,' de Vater replied.

At that moment the bells from a nearby church struck up. It was nine o'clock. Oleg walked directly towards Eduart. Like everyone else on the square he was wrapped up against the weather: black beanie, scarf around the lower part of his face. Max didn't recognize him from a distance.

Oleg pushed the muzzle of his pistol between the folds of his overcoat and squeezed the trigger. The only sound was an imperceptible thud. The bullet made a small hole as it passed through Eduart's coat and into his heart. He slumped forward slightly and dropped his can of cider. Eduart's last chance hadn't come quite soon enough.

Max watched perplexed as the bench was surrounded by passing cyclists, who'd appeared from different directions. About a dozen of them. The church bells chimed the ninth hour, and as quickly as they had appeared, the cyclists scattered as randomly.

De Vater watched the same scene with horror. Once the cyclists had dispersed, there was no sign of the parcel on the bench. Oleg walked off empty-handed. He'd passed his gun to one of the cyclists.

'Don't let any of those cyclists leave the park!' Max shouted into his radio. But de Vater wasn't answering. His radio was being swamped by his desperate men, confused and clueless as to what to do.

'Who do we follow?' they were asking.

'All of them,' de Vater ordered. Which was hopeless. There were too many of them. The bird had flown.

Max could also see that the painting had gone from the bench. But what about Sophie? He cast his binoculars around the Museumplein, looking for a girl slumped somewhere.

'Where is she?' Max shouted into his radio. 'Will someone fucking answer?' But he knew de Vater and his men had screwed up.

'You bastard,' he said to himself as he pulled his pay-as-you-go phone out of his pocket.

Where the fuck is she? he typed into it and pressed send to Pallesson's office mobile.

Pallesson had enjoyed his 'Thomas Crown' moment in the park, as the cyclists had scattered like partridges. There were similarities, he thought, between the two of them. Both masters of their universe, both capable of getting anything they wanted.

The cyclists had all been wearing the same black anoraks and blue woollen hats. Anonymous and invisible once they left the park. And they'd all thought they were being paid as extras in a film.

Pallesson had watched the whole charade through the pair of Kronos 26 x 70 Soviet naval binoculars that a grateful Russian sailor had given him.

But Pallesson's smug pleasure took a jolt when his phone lit up. Although he didn't recognise the number, the message could only have come from one person. Max. But he was predictable. And stupid enough to reveal he was still alive. It wouldn't take long for Oleg to wipe him out.

Pallesson had no idea what he wanted Sophie for at this

stage, but she was bound to come in useful for something. Assuming she hadn't blown herself up.

Van Ossen had been impatient to get his hands on the painting. But his haste was tempered by the need to ensure that Pallesson wasn't followed. So he'd given him detailed instructions on checking the painting and changing its packaging.

Pallesson was then talked through a route so complicated that anyone following him would have been spotted easily. When Pallesson finally arrived at the agreed rendezvous, he was searched by Piek, who removed his phones and took them for a walk.

Fransen followed Pallesson past the sign saying *Dierenkliniek* into the veterinary surgery, where van Ossen was sitting in the treatment room with his art expert, wearing the same grubby corduroy jacket that he'd worn before.

Pallesson recognized the veterinary surgeon, in spite of his white tunic, face mask and surgical gloves. He was leaning over a large, anesthetized guard dog who'd seen better days. Its intestines were lying in a stainless-steel pan.

The vet merely nodded to his assistant, who immediately left his side and went over to the X-ray machine.

Fransen seemed preoccupied with the dog. He started stroking his head. The vet looked up at him as if to say, I'd rather you kept your filthy, unsterilized hands to yourself. Then their eyes met and the vet, apparently reconsidering the reprimand, returned his attention to the dog.

Van Ossen took the painting from Pallesson and removed it from the light packaging. He took a quick glance at it, and then handed it over to the expert.

Again, the academic figure, glasses balanced on the bridge of his nose, turned it over and examined the back of the picture first. His face gave no indication of his thoughts. Next he laid it on its back and asked for a scalpel. Fransen was too busy watching the vet's every move – as if checking he was doing the job right – so it was left to the veterinary assistant to hand the expert a scalpel.

Once again he proceeded to pick carefully away at the painting. Then he lowered his nose to the canvas and had a good sniff. Giving nothing away, he directed the assistant to place the painting on to the X-ray machine.

Van Ossen remained silent and impassive. Pallesson began to have a pang of doubt. Had Ward stitched him up again? Was this the copy from the embassy? Was that why the pick-up had been so smooth?

'Look, this is the painting that was handed over in the park. I'm not a bloody expert. It's hardly my fault if it's the wrong one—'

'SHUT UP,' van Ossen barked. 'You've had your chance.'

It hadn't occurred to Pallesson that Ward would swap the original for the copy in the embassy. He had the girl, after all. But Ward might have been stupid enough to think he was really going to exchange her.

The X-ray machine clanked and flashed, and the expert disappeared behind a screen to look at the result. He stayed there for thirty seconds, and then reappeared. Even van Ossen couldn't wait any longer.

'Well?'

The expert took off his glasses, folded them and put them back in his top pocket. Van Ossen gave Fransen a rap on his arm to get his attention from the dog, which was now having a large tumour cut out. He took a step towards Pallesson.

'In my opinion,' the expert said, pausing slightly, 'the painting is a little disappointing.' Pallesson thought his heart was going to explode. 'But it is original,' the expert confirmed.

'Wrap it up,' van Ossen said to Fransen. 'And leave that bloody dog alone. Let's get out of here. I hate the smell of this place.'

As van Ossen was about to leave the surgery, he had one final thought.

'The forger. He is dead, I assume?'

'Correct.' Pallesson wasn't about to complicate matters by mentioning Sophie.

Fransen made sure he was the last to leave the room.

'Will he be okay?' he grunted quietly at the vet. The vet shrugged, and then carried on with his work. He was more used to patching up men these days than animals.

'Is Nuttall ready?' van Ossen asked Pallesson as they stepped out on to the street.

'He is. Are you?'

Van Ossen didn't answer questions like that.

'Tell him we're back on track. Same time, same place.'

The thought that the deal had ever not been on track curdled like cold vomit in vinegar in Pallesson's mind. He pictured his mother being pulled out of her wheelchair and thrown across a room.

'I'll tell Nuttall everything is fixed,' he said calmly.

Van Ossen nodded and set off down the street.

'Oh, one thing,' Pallesson called after him. 'Look after the painting for me. It's only collateral.'

Pallesson knew van Ossen didn't like him. He didn't show him enough respect. Not that he cared. He watched van Ossen and his two heavies walk the short distance to the canal, and then board his unmistakable launch.

As it pulled away, Pallesson's suspicious eyes picked up on a nondescript boat with an outboard motor that seemed to appear from nowhere. Instinctively he knew the body language of the solitary, hunched figure driving it was furtive. Someone was following van Ossen.

27

The Hague

Max prayed Data Dave would still be in the embassy, poring over some conundrum, and not out at lunch. He rang Arthur on the front desk and asked to be put through to his extension.

'Dave?'

'That's me.'

'Are you on your own?'

'Well, there're a few people around. But no one can hear me. Problem?'

'Yup. Problem. Any sign of Pallesson?'

'Haven't seen him all morning.'

'Good. Can you hang on there for me?'

'Sure. Miss Sweden will wait.'

'Sorry?'

'Only joking, Max.'

Max was having to gamble that Data Dave hadn't already been got at by Pallesson. Dave looked like he led a fairly steady life. There was every chance that Pallesson wouldn't have been able to compromise him even if he'd wanted to.

Max knew he was being distracted. He should be finding

275

Pallesson and following him to the deal. But right now he couldn't help being unprofessional. He was desperate about Sophie.

Max borrowed a bicycle from outside a smoking coffee shop. They'll never remember where they left it when they come out anyway, he reasoned as he pedalled off.

He needed to approach the front of the embassy at speed and get through the entrance before anyone could shoot him. Pallesson had already had one unsuccessful attempt to take him out. He wouldn't leave it at that. As soon as he was just around the corner, Max phoned Arthur and told him to open the door.

Turning right into the Lange Voorhout by the Hotel Des Indes, he sped past the Danish and Spanish Embassies and the statue of Flaneur. He normally acknowledged the jaunty bronze figure waving his hat in the air, but not today.

He had about a hundred metres of the tree-lined avenue to go before he came to the British Embassy. His tyres crunched the crushed seashells as he drew closer.

On a park bench fifty metres from the shiny green embassy door two people were eating sandwiches. Assassins didn't eat on the job, Max assured himself.

As he got to within fifty metres of the red-brick building with its grand Georgian sash windows, the green door swung open. Max veered off the bike path, across the narrow slip road that passed close to the embassy and over the pavement through the front door. The couple eating their lunch on the park bench looked slightly perplexed and carried on with their sandwiches.

'In a hurry, sir?' Arthur asked.

'Sort of, Arthur. Have you seen Pallesson?'

'Not a sight of him.'

'Good. If he arrives while I'm upstairs, phone up to Data Dave's extension, will you?'

'Don't worry, sir. I won't let the little shit creep up on you.'
Arthur knew better than to ask what it was all about.

'One other thing, Arthur. You don't happen to know where
Pallesson lives, do you?'

'Well, I shouldn't . . .'

'I know, Arthur. But it could be life or death. If by chance
you could find out, I'd be most grateful.'

One look at Max's face persuaded Arthur that he wasn't
exaggerating.

Dave was at his desk playing *Angry Birds* on a company iPad
when Max appeared.

'Got a map?' Max asked, dispensing with any cordial
greeting.

'Of Amsterdam?'

'No, Istanbul. Of course Amsterdam, Dave. For fuck's sake!
And the surrounding area.'

Dave picked up on his sense of urgency. As it happened, he
had a tourist map in his desk. He'd been planning a trip to
Utrecht to look at the steam-engine museum.

'What happened to you?' Dave asked.

'Walked into a door. So to speak. You should see the door.'

'There you go,' Dave said amiably as he spread the map out
on his desk. 'Shoot.'

'I need to pinpoint a location.'

'Right. Any clues?'

'Yup. It's twenty minutes from Castle Vleuylen, by car. And
forty minutes from the Centraal railway station.'

'At what speed?'

'Don't know.'

'Right. Can we estimate?'

Max took Data Dave through both journeys, trying to guess-
timate what roads they'd been on. The journey from the castle
hadn't been smooth. They'd gone around a lot of bends, and

it had been stop-start. The drive to the station, however, when Max had also been blindfolded, had been much smoother and faster. Predominantly on motorways, presumably.

'There's a program I need to download,' Data Dave said as Max came to the end of his description.

'Oh fuck,' Max said as Dave was downloading the software.

'What?'

'Louise.'

Louise was making her way across the office towards Max and Dave.

'Hello, stranger,' Louise said, eyebrows arched. Her mouth was stretched by an expectant smile.

'Hi, Louise,' Max replied, making it quite clear that he was engrossed in what Dave was doing. Dave didn't say anything. She clearly hadn't come to speak to him. In fact, she'd never addressed a word of a personal nature to him, ever. And he desperately fancied her. He could feel himself blushing as he smelt her scent, which was quite strong.

'So . . .'

'Louise, we're snowed under here,' Max snapped, without making eye contact.

'I was just thinking, we could—'

'We're dealing with a fucking emergency here, Louise. Not now.'

Louise's neck went red with fury. No one brushed her off like that. Particularly someone who'd taken advantage of her body when it suited him. She stormed off towards the door without another word.

'Lovely,' Dave said wistfully to his computer screen.

'What?' Max asked, incredulously.

'Nothing,' Dave said guiltily. 'Ready to go,' he added.

Dave spent the next twenty minutes pumping information

278

into his computer. Max got impatient. There was nothing for him to do. And he quickly got fed up hovering over Dave. He picked up the phone on the neighbouring desk and rang down to Arthur.

'Pop outside and have one of your filthy Navy Cut, Arthur, would you? See if anyone's hanging around.'

Arthur didn't need to be asked twice.

'Right,' Dave finally said. 'That's about as good as I'm going to get it with the info we have. Give us that map.'

Data Dave had effectively created a circle around Vleuylen twenty minutes from the castle. It was, he pointed out, a combination of guesswork and summation. He'd then used the same principles to draw a circle around the station. The circles crossed in two places.

'Take an area of about five square miles around those two points, and you'll find your pot of gold,' Data Dave predicted, lightly shadowing the two areas with a pencil. One looked heavily built up. The other was mainly woodland and agricultural land.

'Jesus. That doesn't narrow it down much.'

'No. Not unless you can add another layer of information. What exactly are you looking for?'

'Sorry. I forgot to tell you that. Looking for a large-ish building, I would imagine, with a cellar. Or a vault. Something underground.'

'Anything else?'

'Well . . .' Max instinctively looked around the office, but it was deserted. 'Well, it's connected with our friend Pallesson. But that doesn't help much. And some pretty unsavoury acquaintances of his. Van Ossen's mob.'

'That's a bit more promising. Have we got any surveillance that links the Kalverstraat to either of those areas?'

'God knows. Can you jump off what you're doing, Dave, and

cross-check anything we've got on them that might relate to those areas?'

'How deep do you want me to dig?'

'How do you mean?'

'Well, you mentioned Pallesson. Shall I have a little look through his files to see if anything comes up?'

'How will you do that?'

Data Dave blushed again for the second time in half an hour.

'You can hack into his files? So that's what you do with yourself the whole time. I should have known, you old fox. Yes. Dig away. Have you got a note of those areas? I need to find de Vater and show him this map. Not that he's a lot of help. His unit is about as watertight as a duck's arse.'

'Tight as a duck's arse. Not watertight,' Dave pointed out.

'Whatever.' Max slapped Data Dave on the shoulder, and picked up the map.

'If Pallesson appears, ring me.'

'Wilko.'

'You were right, sir,' Arthur said the instant Max stepped out of the lift. Max had his mind on Louise. He feared she might be loitering with intent to launch a 'who do you think you are?' missile in his direction.

'Sorry, Arthur?'

'Bloke hanging about. Nasty-looking individual. Wearing a red beanie. Spotted him half an hour ago. On the far side of the avenue to start with. But he's moved closer. Just to the right of the exit.'

Max expected as much. But he couldn't stall. He needed to show de Vater Dave's shaded map.

'Just pop out and have another fag, would you? Check exactly how far he is from the door.'

'No problem. Oh, I think this was what you wanted,' Arthur

said, handing Max a folded piece of paper with Pallesson's address on it.

Max phoned de Vater, who couldn't talk – he said he was with someone. Probably one of his infiltrated team. Max agreed to meet him on the terrace of the Smits Koffiehuis outside the Amsterdam Centraal railway station – away from prying eyes and ears – in an hour and a half.

'He's standing on the edge of the pavement, fifty metres to the right. He's on his phone. Six foot two, heavy set and unshaven. Sounded Russian.' Arthur was enjoying his part.

'Russian?'

'Think so. I just picked up a couple of words.'

'Thank you, Arthur. Batten the hatches down. The peace of The Hague is about to have its feathers ruffled. It obviously won't have anything to do with me, though, when they come asking.'

'Of course not, sir.'

Max strolled out through the embassy front door, pretending to be distracted by a conversation he was having on his phone. He clocked Oleg standing exactly where Arthur had said he was. He was wearing wrap-around dark glasses and a different-coloured coat. But Max recognized him immediately.

'So it was you doing Pallesson's dirty work again, in the park,' Max muttered into his phone.

Max set his trajectory to make it look as if he would walk past him. When he was ten metres away, Oleg reached inside his jacket pocket. He was going for the same silenced pistol he'd used on Eduart.

Max didn't make eye contact. The conversation he was having with his phone became very animated.

'I don't give a fuck what he says,' Max shouted into his phone.

Oleg was now five metres in front of him, and about two

metres to his left. He'd become distracted by Max's agitated conversation and hand gestures. He never saw Max's left leg lash out towards him.

Max's boot caught him fully in the chest, square on. Totally unprepared and knocked off balance, Oleg flew backwards. If he hadn't fallen into the road, he would simply have picked himself up and shot Max, before wandering off with a slightly wounded pride having been caught off guard.

But fall into the road he did. Though Max had gambled that something would hit him, he'd have paid long odds on achieving the spectacular result of a scaffolding lorry passing down the narrow slip road at the perfect moment.

Its front left wheel crushed Oleg's head, squirting its contents across the road. The lorry driver slammed on his brakes, juddering to a violent halt, all too late. The driver of the car behind him was fiddling with his radio and piled into the back of the lorry. His air bag went off and his horn blared. Max didn't hang around for the postmortem.

Arthur had been keeping an eye on things from the safety of the embassy. He puffed out his cheeks and went to call the emergency services.

'What's happened?' someone asked, alerted by the mayhem in the street.

'Jaywalker got flattened,' Arthur reported.

Max skirted around the carnage in front of the embassy and made his way down the avenue towards the taxi rank in front of the Hotel Des Indes. It wasn't far to the station, but he didn't have time on his side.

The only taxi on the rank pulled away as he got to it. So he set off on foot; down Schouwburgstraat, past the miserably modern box-like French Embassy, slavishly flying its European flag, right down Prinsessegracht where a bunch of Brits were blocking the pavement loading a bus to the bulb fields – Max wasted another thirty seconds trying to shove his way through them – and finally over the canal, which was smelling rank, into Den Haag Centraal.

It had taken him seven minutes from the taxi rank. Seven minutes he didn't have. He missed the train to Amsterdam by two minutes. He'd have to wait twenty minutes for the next train.

Max paid ten euros for his ticket and sat on the upper tier of the train waiting for it to move. He knew it wouldn't leave a minute early or a second late. But was he going to be too late for Sophie?

28

Sophie was lying motionless on the mattress in the corner of her prison. Her eyes were shut, but she wasn't asleep – just mentally trying to escape. The mattress was wet, and the smell of urine hit her guard as he approached her.

'This is all we've got,' he said, putting some porridge in a bowl on the floor. She opened her eyes and stared blankly at him, but said nothing.

The guard looked at the pathetic, harmless girl slumped on the mattress. What was the point in connecting the bomb to her? She was hardly going to escape. But he had his orders. And he didn't fancy Pallesson coming back and finding that he hadn't obeyed them. He'd wire up the bomb that afternoon before dark.

The girl looked freezing cold. He went to the next-door cell to get her another blanket.

Although van Ossen was being followed when he left the vet's surgery with the painting, Pallesson had no intention of telling him. Van Ossen would undoubtedly blame him. So he'd simply deal with the situation himself, as he had with the other two – Tryon had been taken care of and Oleg was dealing with Max Ward.

But it was now imperative that he learnt the identity of their contact in the Dutch police. Because the figure lurking in the Amsterdam shadows, tracking van Ossen, was almost certainly a member of their force. He'd moved like a policeman.

Pallesson dialled the mobile phone that he'd given Iain Jenkins when they first started 'supporting' each other. After all, he could hardly ring Jenkins at GCHQ. Jenkins answered after three rings.

'Iain,' Pallesson said, trying to sound unflustered. 'Can you talk?'

He could.

'I'm up against it here, Iain, so I'll cut straight to the chase. You know we had that problem with Tryon briefing against me. Well he's popped up in Amsterdam, working with some pretty bad people.'

This surprised Jenkins.

'You thought he'd disappeared,' Pallesson replied with as much surprise as he could muster. 'God, I only wished he had. He's causing us all sorts of problems. About to blow the cover of a couple of agents right on the front line.'

Jenkins muttered away to the effect that they never knew when to quit.

'Look, Iain, if I'm to contain the damage to the Service, I need to know who Tryon is working with at the Dienst Nationale Recherche. Pretty bloody quickly.'

It didn't take Jenkins long to look up the contacts web that he helped to collate on every agent in the field. Some considered it spying on their own; others, such as Jenkins, felt it was for their own safety.

Jenkins could find no record of Tryon having direct contact

with anyone who appeared to be a Dutch policeman; but Tryon had had regular contact with a Pete Carr before he ceased communicating. Jenkins recognized Pete Carr's name. And he knew the sort of work he did for their operatives from time to time.

Pete Carr had just been delivering some bad news to the woman who'd had her kids' schoolbags wired up. Her suspicion that the nanny was up to something had been confirmed – the nanny was up to her husband.

Pete had heavily edited the evidence. It was a bit steamy. He stored the really hot stuff away in his 'rainy day' file.

Pallesson's caller ID came up as Unknown Number. That didn't bother Pete. He took calls like that every day.

'Pete Carr,' he answered.

'I'm hoping you can help me,' said the voice on the other end of the phone. Carr dealt with some pretty fucked-up people, but this bloke sounded creepy by any standards.

'Really?' Pete replied.

'You know a friend of mine. Tryon.'

'I know a lot of people, mate. What's your drift?'

'He's in trouble. He needs my help.'

'Is that right?' Pete didn't like the sound of this bloke one little bit.

'I need some information.'

'Do you? And who do you think I am? The bloody Yellow Pages?'

Pallesson sensed he wasn't getting anywhere. He'd hoped by playing the friend card, the man would sing like a canary. That clearly wasn't going to happen.

'Of course, I'll pay for any information you can give me. Whatever your going rate is.'

Pallesson was now speaking Pete's language. He didn't really care who he worked for. As long as it paid. He had four hundred odd grand's worth of equipment hanging around. That didn't pay for itself.

'So how can I help you?' Pete asked, softening his tone.

Mercenary bastard, Pallesson thought as he considered how to tread.

'Tryon was working on a project with the Dutch police. I'm sure you know that?'

Pete said nothing. If he was fishing, he wasn't going to get a free bite. Pallesson waited for Pete to concur, but all he got was silence.

'To be able to help him, I need to know who Tryon was liaising with in the Dienst Nationale Recherche,' Pallesson continued.

A broad smirk washed across Pete Carr's face. He was longing to quip that it must be Aart de Vater season. But Pete had rules. He could sell this weirdo de Vater's name with a clear conscience. However, it would be wrong to let him know that Max was a couple of furlongs in front of him. That would expose Max's rear.

'I can help you with that,' Pete said succinctly.

'How quickly? If I'm to help Tryon, I need to act fast.'

Pete let the word 'help' run past him uncensored. He wasn't an employee of the Office. Whatever shenanigans they got up to was their own business.

'As soon as you can pay me, mate.'

'How do you want to be paid?'

'Don't mind, mate. But until I have the payment, you don't get the name.'

'What?' Pallesson was wriggling on the other end of the line. He'd assumed his word would have been good enough. 'But a delay could cost Tryon his life.'

'Credit-card details, then. You give me all the details and it should only take a couple of minutes to process the payment.'

'But I'm a member of Her Majesty's Service. This is outrageous. It's . . . it's treason. You're withholding information that could save an operator.'

'Really? Well, I'll tell you what I'll do then,' Pete replied, unfazed. 'I'll ring Vauxhall Cross and tell someone there who Tryon was working with. That way you can get the information for nothing.'

Pallesson knew he'd run out of wriggle room. He was holding no cards in this negotiation.

'That's an absurd suggestion. We don't work like that. How much, for Christ's sake? You're wasting my time.'

'Fifty grand.'

'What?'

'You heard me. Fifty grand.'

Pete had been thinking about the price as the conversation had progressed. His starting point had been ten grand. Not a penny less. But he'd taken against this creep.

Pallesson had assumed he'd have to agree to five grand. He was dealing with a proper money-grasping scumbag. Still, it didn't matter, since he had no intention of paying him anyway. He might even have him taken out for his insolence.

'You're playing a very dangerous game, Mr Carr. We know where you work, we know where you live.'

Pete Carr had flirted with danger all his life. And he'd been beaten up a few times. His most recent kicking had come as a result of being caught bugging the phones in a Russian energy company's London office. He'd even asked the boss's PA for a cup of tea while he was doing the job. The element of danger attached to his work didn't bother him. It made him feel alive. Carr put the phone down without another word and went to put the kettle on. It hadn't boiled by the time Pallesson rang back.

'You're wasting my time, Mr Carr.'

Pete was straight on to the front foot.

'No. You're wasting my time. Now either pay up or piss off.'

It was the winning call in their delicate negotiation. Pallesson gave him his credit-card details, and five minutes later he got Aart de Vater's name.

Barry Nuttall was getting nothing but grief from his missus while he waited for Ashmal to turn up with the readies.

'Why don't you just tell me where you're bloody going? If it's someone else, Barry, I'm off.'

Barry had met Jayne six months before in the club where she'd worked in Chelmsford. She hadn't been wearing much at the time. He'd 'bought' her for the rest of the night – and the night after. And two weeks later she'd moved into Barry's fake-Georgian mansion outside Braintree, secure behind his wrought-iron security gates that kept the Rottweilers in and everyone else out.

Barry's house was his castle, and he was justifiably proud of it. He'd designed the outside himself: the water feature in the fish pond, full of his carp, the coach lights illuminating the drive and the life-size stone lions either side of his front door. All signs that he had taste. That he'd moved on.

'Don't be stupid, love. It's work; and you don't want to know.'

Jayne's life had got a lot more comfortable since she moved in with Barry. She had a midnight-blue soft-top BMW and a whole new wardrobe. But life wasn't perfect.

'He keeps looking at me. Can't you have a word?'

The 'he' Jayne was referring to was Daz, Barry's stroppy sixteen-year-old kid from his first marriage.

'Everyone looks at you, love. You don't exactly hide it, do you?'

Jayne was wearing a skin-tight pair of shorts that left very little to the imagination and a crop top that stuck to her like a barnacle. She'd left the shiny shell suits in Chelmsford with the rest of her life.

'Have you seen what he looks at on that computer in his bedroom? It's disgusting.'

'He's a teenager. They all look at it.'

'What about the dogs? Who's going to look after them while you're away? I don't bloody trust them, neither.'

'Daz will deal with the dogs. They're for your own good.'

'Will he just?'

As if on cue, the dogs erupted from their bored slumber as Ashmal pulled up outside the gates.

Ashmal had a good little number going at his bureau de change in Notting Hill. Dollars and euros came in from 'tourists' and sterling went out. The police kept an eye on him, but they hadn't been able to nail him.

Ashmal was also very useful when it came to collecting the cash from Barry's investors before a job. It kept them one step away from Barry, which suited everyone. And if the Filth did go poking their nose in, Ashmal had a kosher reason why he had so much cash on him.

'Nice place you got here,' Ashmal said as he got out of the car. Barry liked that. He knew his house was a statement – which wasn't bad for business.

'Well, it isn't much – but it's home,' Barry said a trifle too ironically. 'And I don't get any bother here. Know what I mean?'

Ashmal certainly did. He nodded his head appreciatively and went round to the boot of the car.

'Two-hundred-euro notes,' he said as he opened it.

'Pain in the arse about those five-hundred-euro notes being phased out.'

'Yeah. They put a stop to them. Bit of a liberty, really.'

'Two mil?'

'All there. Nice and prompt they were this time.'

'Good boy,' Barry said as he moved the case over to the back of his car. 'I would ask you in, but . . .'

'Got to be on my way.'

'Bit of a rush. You know.'

Ashmal wasn't there to make a social call. And he didn't expect to invade the privacy of Barry's house. There was no need to hang about.

Daz was in the kitchen making as much mess as it takes for a teenager to butter a couple of slices of toast.

'All right, Daz?' Barry asked. Daz grunted and sloped off to the front room and the safety of the television.

'See? He's good as gold,' Barry pointed out to Jayne.

'And I suppose you're going to clear up behind him?'

Barry looked across the kitchen at Jayne. She was a nice piece of kit, no question. But she could be a right cow when she felt like it.

The train's progress was excruciatingly slow. Max couldn't get his mind off Sophie. Were they abusing her? He didn't want to think about it. But every minute the train took was another minute before de Vater's men could spring her. Once de Vater had Data Dave's map, they would find her much quicker.

His heart was telling him to find her and spring her on his own. But his head dictated that he had to check out the address Arthur had given him and stake out Pallesson. Nailing Pallesson had to be the priority. Everything else came second.

Max stared out of the window. There was nothing to look at except green fields, cows and ditches full of water. If there was ever a world shortage of water, he'd come and live in Holland.

The train ground to a halt in Leiden Centraal. The driver seemed in no hurry to get to Amsterdam. Even after the guard's whistle had gone, he hesitated for a minute before getting going. Talking, probably.

The houses on the outskirts of Leiden sunk Max's gloomy mood further. Had Gemma been playing him all along? She'd asked a lot of questions in Monaco. Had she been reporting back to Casper, and hence Pallesson? And then used what they'd told her about Sophie as an excuse to cut him dead?

Dead. Was his dash to see de Vater a waste of time? Would the Dutch police find Sophie?

Max dragged his thoughts back to Pallesson. He had the address in his pocket. It was worth a stab checking it out after he'd seen de Vater.

The train plunged into a black tunnel and came to a halt at Schiphol airport.

The wait at Leiden had felt as if it went on forever. If anything, this stop was worse. The train waited and waited and waited before it finally pulled out.

Max thought about Keate. Where had he got to? It seemed strange that he'd been around to give his aunt *The Peasants in Winter* for safekeeping. And then vanished. He sent him another text message.

Max was going mad by the time the train pulled into Amsterdam Centraal. Fifty minutes after it had left Den Haag, as scheduled. But it felt like fifty hours.

He ducked and dived along the platform, rushed through the passenger tunnel to the exit. The exterior of the station was one giant building site, but Max knew where he was going. He threaded his way along the temporary pavements and was outside Smits Koffiehuis a couple of minutes later. He was ten minutes too late for de Vater.

29

Amsterdam

Aart de Vater was feeling uneasy. It was very unlike Marianne not to answer her mobile. By now she should have picked up Frits from school and been back home. But she wasn't answering the home number either.

De Vater lived fairly close to the Central railway station – where he was meeting the English agent – and although it would make him late for their meeting, Aart decided to drop by the house to check everything was all right. Frits had been struggling with his schoolwork recently – maybe the lack of communication had something to do with that?

It hadn't been very difficult for Pallesson to find out what de Vater's wife was called. And once he knew that, getting his tame Dutch government official to hack into the driving licence register to see where she lived was routine. There was only one Marianne de Vater in Amsterdam, and she lived off Haarlemmerstraat in a small street called Binnen Vissersstraat.

How very unlike the maverick policeman to live somewhere so conservative, so quiet, Pallesson thought, as he planned his next move.

De Vater had to be taken out. He was the only threat to the whole operation – apart from Ward, whom Oleg should have dispatched by now.

But before he killed de Vater, Pallesson needed to make sure the cop was acting alone, as he had so often in the past. And the surest way to get that information was with the help of Marianne and the couple's son, Frits.

Pallesson was walking through a market on the way to the address when he had a brainwave. It got round the problem of how to get Marianne or, even better, Frits, to let him into the house without setting off any panic alarm they might have.

If any of their neighbours had been watching as Pallesson approached, all they would have seen was a jovial Mickey Mouse character, in full costume and mask, standing at the door of the de Vaters' house with a big bunch of balloons.

His gods were smiling on him. It was Frits, not Marianne, who saw Mickey Mouse approaching their front door. He couldn't get it open fast enough. By the time Marianne had put down what she was doing in the kitchen and made it to the hall, the beaming Mickey Mouse had the door closed, a tight hold of the boy and a silenced revolver to his head. Pallesson made Marianne lie down on the floor while he dealt with Frits.

Using the rope and sticking tape he'd brought with him to secure, silence and 'blindfold' the boy and his mother, Pallesson positioned them so that de Vater wouldn't see them and retreat when he came into the hall.

Aart de Vater liked Haarlemmerstraat. There was a baker on the corner who made fresh bread every day in the back of the shop, a juice bar, a vegetable shop and most important of all, as far as Frits was concerned, the best sweet shop in

Amsterdam – De SnoepBoom. Aart would take him there after his meeting with Max Ward.

'Where's Frits?' Aart called out as he let himself in. But his usual homecoming shout was met by silence. Aart was becoming increasingly apprehensive. The lights were on – and they should be home.

The sitting-room door on the right of the hall was open. Pallesson was sitting in an armchair, out of sight of the door, with Frits on the floor in front of him, his shoulders wedged between Pallesson's knees. Marianne, like Frits, had tape across her eyes, her mouth and her ears. She would be a clueless witness, so Pallesson was able to remove his facemask.

There was a certain trepidation about Aart as he walked into the room. He could smell the fear without knowing it.

'Put your hands on your head,' Pallesson said as Aart's horrified eyes alighted on the scene. 'Don't try anything – or the boy will get it.'

Aart involuntarily retched. He was trained for most situations, but not a gunman holding a revolver to his son's head.

'Don't do anything. Please. You can have what you want. Anything.'

Aart immediately recognized the cold, black eyes from the photograph Tryon had given him of Pallesson. It was still pinned up on his office wall.

'I intend to,' Pallesson said coldly. 'Gun?'

'Under my jacket.'

'Take it out. Slowly. Chuck it to me – and don't even think about trying anything. I'll shoot the boy first.'

De Vater did as he was told. He had no option.

'Kneel. Put your hands behind your head.'

Aart could hear his wife sobbing through all the tape she was wrapped up in. He could also see her shoulders shuddering.

'What do you want?' he asked.

'I'll ask the questions. You piss me off, I'll shoot the boy, and then you.'

De Vater kept quiet. He'd been trained to negotiate, not to antagonize. He looked at his son, who was paralysed with fear.

'If you lie to me, I'll start with the boy's knees. Got that?'

'Yes.' De Vater nodded.

'Good. So let's start at the beginning. What are you working on, right now?'

'A load of things,' de Vater answered truthfully.

'You need to do better than that. What are you working on with the British? One more vague answer will be the end of your son's right knee.'

'A drug shipment. Coming in any time,' the Dutchman said quickly.

'Where?'

'No idea. I promise you. We have little information.'

'Who are you working with on the British side?'

'Only one person. He's on his own, I think. Max Ward.'

'Are you working on this alone?'

Aart de Vater wasn't stupid. He knew instinctively that he had to lie at this point. And he had to lie without hesitation.

'No.'

'No,' was not what Pallesson wanted to hear. But was the cop bluffing?

'Who else knows about this operation?'

De Vater knew that question was coming. He was having to make it up as he went along, without burying any particular officer.

'The drug squad. They've been handed details.'

'What details? You said you didn't know where the shipment was coming in.'

'Details on van Ossen's movements.' De Vater's brain was moving like lightning. He had a plan.

'What do they know?'

'We have an informant inside van Ossen's gang,' de Vater lied. 'But they don't know about you.' He had to make Pallesson believe there was an exit from this that didn't involve killing him.

'Who?'

'One of his bodyguards. Fransen. Ex-military. He was a plant,' de Vater lied again, trying to cause confusion in Pallesson's mind.

Pallesson thought about that for a minute. But he sensed, whether true or untrue, that it was a smokescreen.

'So they don't know about me?'

'No. You've never been mentioned,' de Vater said, slightly too quickly.

'Who am I?'

De Vater knew he was cornered.

'Pallesson. Ward told me about you. But the drug squad don't know. I can do a deal.'

'Oh, can you,' Pallesson said with mock surprise. 'And what might that be?'

'Cut me in on the deal. I've done plenty before. I'll keep the drug squad off your back. I don't care what you do to Ward. Just make sure they don't find the body.'

Pallesson thought about his offer for a moment. He might even have gone for it – having a bent cop like de Vater in Amsterdam was very attractive – had it not been for one sentence: *I've done plenty before.* Pallesson knew that was a lie.

'So you expect me to believe that you know that I'm involved, and yet the drug squad don't?'

'Yes.' Aart de Vater nodded. He knew Pallesson hadn't taken the bait.

'Nice of Fransen to leave me out of the frame.'

'They weren't interested in the painting.'

'Of course, you know about the painting, too. Ward has got you well informed.'

'I'm not interested in the painting. Cut me in on the deal and I'll keep them off your back.' De Vater was trying to keep the desperation out of his voice.

Pallesson's whole mood suddenly appeared to lighten.

'Okay. If you tell me where the shipment is coming in, I'll cut you in on the deal,' he said breezily.

'But I can't. We don't know.'

Pallesson was now satisfied that they really didn't know.

'Excellent,' he said, a broad smile spreading across his face. 'In which case, I don't need to cut you in on the deal.'

Then he raised the revolver from Frits's head for the first time, pointed it at Aart de Vater and squeezed the trigger.

Max finished his second cappuccino on the terrace of the Smits Koffiehuis, blind to the majesty of the domes of St Nicolaaskerk opposite him. It was now an hour after de Vater was supposed to meet him. Sure, he'd been ten minutes late, but that was no reason for the Dutch policeman to leave and no reason for him to stop answering his phone. Max tried it again. This time someone answered.

'Who is this?' the voice said urgently. Max could hear all sorts of agitated noises in the background.

'I'm waiting for de Vater to meet me,' Max replied, ignoring the question.

'Who is speaking?' the officious voice said. It sounded like a policeman. And it was. A homicide detective who was now dealing with a horrendous scene.

'Has something happened to de Vater?' Max asked.

'I can't comment. Who is this, please?'

'Who are you?'

'A police officer. Answer my question, or you will become a suspect.'

That was all Max needed to hear. He rang off and gazed at the canal. Someone had taken de Vater out. Max had to get the hell out of there.

30

Amsterdam

Not for the first time, Max felt well and truly marooned. De Vater had been crucial to saving Sophie. Now he'd been taken out, and Max would probably be next.

He was pretty certain that de Vater would have kept the operation close to his chest, so it was unlikely that any of his men would follow up rescuing Sophie. And he had no idea where the drug shipment would land, or where the painting was. All in all, the whole 'sting' was a mess.

He now had two options. He could tell all to Graham Smith, his immediate superior in the Office, and hope that Smith would believe him and not Pallesson. He'd have no evidence to present, other than busting himself for stealing a work of art owned by the Dutch government. With the gambling stain on his record – the Saudi Arabia incident would be there – any allegation that Pallesson made against him could stick. Pallesson, on the other hand, had the track record of a hero. It wasn't a very attractive prospect. Tryon, after all, had warned him that if he was caught switching the painting, he was on his own.

The alternative course of action wasn't much more appealing, but it had to be considered. During his last presentation in the embassy, Pallesson had identified Jorgan Stam as a gang boss running drugs in league with the Taliban and al-Qaeda. It was presumably a smokescreen to divert attention from van Ossen's operations. But the fact Pallesson had selected Stam as the fall guy suggested that he must be a rival whose removal would benefit van Ossen. Assuming the reverse was true, and Jorgan Stam would be happy to see van Ossen taken out, that made him a potential ally so far as Max was concerned.

He recalled the photo of Stam on the whiteboard: weaselly features, thin, sandy swept-back hair and a weak moustache.

There had been no photograph of Stam's number two, whom Pallesson had described in the vaguest terms. Did that mean Pallesson was protecting his source? It wasn't beyond the wit of Pallesson to have informants in both camps, playing one gang off against the other.

As he walked, Max ran through everything else he could remember from Pallesson's briefing on Jorgan Stam. He had mentioned the name 'Wielart'. And the casino that Stam supposedly owned, the Dice, off Oudezijds Achterburgwal in the red-light district. It wasn't much to go on. But with no other option available to him, Max was going to have to step into the lion's den.

It took a couple of false turns before he found the right street. En route he could have beaten a naked dwarf, been cuddled in a set of nappies by an Amazon in a nurse's uniform, or chained up and tickled with a feather by a gay fetish prostitute. Max could only marvel at the thriving market that seemed to exist for these various services.

The doorman at the Dice Club Casino wore the obligatory black leather jacket, open-collared black shirt, faded jeans and a snarl on his pockmarked face.

DRINK ALL YOU LIKE – ONE HOUR – NAKED GIRLS – 50€, the sign

301

next to the door announced. Max didn't suppose there'd be many takers at eleven in the morning.

'What do you want?' the doorman asked. Even he didn't expect someone who was neither drunk nor high to take up such an invitation at that time of the day.

'Are you open?'

'*Ja.*'

'Well, in that case, I'll have a ticket to drink as much as I like with a naked girl.'

The doorman wasn't too worried about trade descriptions – he didn't give money back to unhappy customers, even if there were no naked girls around at this hour – but his instincts told him this smart-arse was trouble. So he said as much to his colleague downstairs using his two-way radio.

As Max made his way down the dark staircase, the smell of cheap perfume, sweat and stale beer hit his nostrils. At the bottom of the stairs was an entrance swaddled in thick, dark curtains and attended by what looked like a waxwork image of the lump of meat outside the front door.

'Morning,' Max said breezily as he walked past him into the club. He didn't even grunt.

The casino was quiet. A barman was moving bottles around. Max sat at the bar and surveyed the scenery. Even in semi-darkness, it looked worse than it smelt. Everything that was soft was stained and worn; everything hard was chipped or dented. The tables were deserted and quiet.

'Can I help you?' the barman asked.

'I'll take a sparkling water,' Max replied. It wasn't an order the barman was used to. Mind you, the only customers he generally got at that time of the day tended to be past their best after drinking through the night. This guy was sober and English, which was unusual.

As Max's eyes adjusted to the dim lighting, he studied the other people in the club. On a table fairly close to him, two dishevelled men were sitting in silence, apparently going through messages on their phones. Two half-drunk bottles of beer stood on the table between them. There was no sign of any naked girls cheering them along.

A few tables away, four men were eating and chatting away amongst themselves. They looked like staff. The door near their table swung open and a waiter brought out a tray of food and banged it down unceremoniously on the table. They were definitely staff.

Max then focused on the table in the corner. The man at the table facing in his direction had a thin face. His hair was swept back. More than that, Max couldn't make out. The papers spread out on the table in front of him gave the impression he was working. He certainly didn't look like a customer.

Two girls were sitting at his table. They weren't naked, but neither were they dressed for the cold. Both of them were listening intently to him. From the tone of his voice, it sounded as though he wasn't happy.

Max's eyes had now completely adjusted to the light. There was no question about it; this was the man whose photograph Pallesson had pinned to the whiteboard: Jorgan Stam.

As soon as the barman bent down behind the bar, Max slipped off his chair and moved swiftly, but not too abruptly, towards the corner table. He had twenty metres' start on the bouncer who'd been keeping an eye on him.

The man with the thin face, the sandy swept-back hair and nondescript moustache looked surprised as Max approached.

'Jorgan Stam?' Max asked, as he arrived at the table.

One of the girls started laughing at him. The weasel-faced man in front of him looked even more surprised. And Max knew from the mocking tone of the girl's laugh and the expression on the weasel's face that he definitely wasn't Jorgan Stam. Max could see the shifty eyes looking past him, presumably towards the cavalry, who were indeed bearing down on Max.

'Do you know where I can find Jorgan Stam? I have some very important information for him,' Max spluttered, trying to cover his initial mistake.

Max felt a vice-like grip on his upper arm. Whoever it was sitting in front of him began to look more self-assured.

'Who are you?' he asked.

'My conversation needs to be with Jorgan Stam. It would be in his interest to talk to me.'

'What's your business?'

'My business is with Jorgan Stam.'

Max was then conscious of a second person arriving behind him. He now had the attention of both bouncers.

'Take him outside. Find out what his story is,' the weasel hissed at his two henchmen.

'This is important,' Max said, as he was ushered away. But whoever had been in Pallesson's photograph had dismissed him and was giving all his attention to the girls.

Once again, Max had been duped. Pallesson had given them a bum steer on Jorgan Stam.

As he was being escorted towards the door where the tray of food had come out of, Max rapidly considered his options. He didn't mind having the shit kicked out of him if it was an entrée to Jorgan Stam, but it seemed highly unlikely that the two bouncers would pick him up after his beating, brush off his jacket and deliver him to Jorgan Stam's office simply because he told them he worked for the British secret service.

Wielart didn't like going to the Dice. Even via the back door. But the sums of money that they laundered through the casino were vast, and there was no way anyone else could be trusted to deal with it.

He would arrive at the casino with a file full of bogus invoices from their own suppliers, and depart, escorted by two of van Ossen's men, with the cash to cover the invoices. He then went straight to the bank and paid the appropriate amounts into the accounts of the suppliers.

Wielart worked in a secluded office down the corridor from the kitchens, close to the back door of the club. In the office was a large safe where the cash was stored. The office had a security door, and the back door of the casino was reinforced as well. Only he and Stam had keys to the safe. Even the weasel-faced manager, who Pallesson had put up as Stam during his briefing in the embassy, didn't have access to the safe. Or that office.

Wielart still had his homburg hat on as he fished for the keys to the office. As he put them in the lock and turned the key, he heard a loud crashing, and a savage scream from the direction of the kitchen. His heart started racing. Something violent was going on, and it was too close for his liking.

A second later, the door at the end of the corridor exploded open and Max came flying through it. He had dispatched one of the bouncers with a saucepan of boiling water, which he'd grabbed and chucked at him, but he was now being pursued by the second bouncer and a chef wielding a cleaver.

Max pushed past Wielart towards the back door – which was locked. Once Max had unsuccessfully tried the door, he turned back towards Wielart, who looked terrified.

In the second that he had to react, Max grabbed Wielart and pulled his arm behind his back.

'I'll break his neck,' Max shouted to the bouncer and the chef, wrapping his forearm around Wielart's throat. Max had no idea if they'd give a fuck. But he had run out of other options.

305

The reaction of his two assailants was extraordinary; better than Max could have hoped for. Both of them raised their hands and backed off, with horrified looks on their faces.

Max took more notice of his hostage, and a hunch hit him.

'Wielart?' he asked, with purpose in the tone of his voice.

'What do you want?' Wielart replied, his voice faltering.

Max had hit the jackpot.

'I need to talk to you. I have some information for you. Information you will want to hear.'

The bouncer and the chef held their ground. The terrified Wielart could feel the pressure of Max's forearm on his throat.

'Let me go,' Wielart said weakly.

'Only if we can talk without them.'

'We can talk,' he agreed. He had no choice. He could feel the power of the man holding him. It was a bad feeling, knowing that someone could snap your windpipe any minute.

Max tried the handle of the heavy security door on his right. It opened smoothly. To his relief, no one was in there. Max pulled Wielart into the room, took the key out of the lock and shut the door behind them.

Once Max had locked the door, he frisked Wielart for weapons and let him go. The man was no physical threat to him. And they would need a tank to break the door down.

'Sorry about that,' Max said apologetically.

Wielart was shaken. He didn't reply.

'Sit down,' Max said, pulling a chair up for him. 'We need to talk.'

For the next few minutes, Max gave Wielart chapter and verse on van Ossen's deal with Nuttall and Pallesson. All of which was of interest to Wielart.

When Max filled him in on what MI6 knew about Stam, and didn't know about him, Wielart saw the opportunity.

'But you knew who I was,' Wielart queried.

'It was a guess, I assure you. You're not on the radar.'

'And Stam is?'

'Very much so.'

Wielart quickly turned things over in his mind.

'So what's in it for you? Or is it suddenly Christmas?'

'I need to bring down Pallesson. Which will do you no harm. And I need to rescue a girl from van Ossen.'

'In which order?' Wielart asked, his brain already weighing everything up. But before Max could answer, the noise levels the other side of the door started rising.

'I need to calm everyone down outside. They'll be assembling an army if I don't stop them.'

'How can I trust you?' Max asked.

'If you want my help, you'll have to. And then we'll get out of here.'

There seemed to be no choice. He had to get out of the club – and it was either going to be with Wielart as his protection, or in pieces.

Max nodded towards the door, and let Wielart open it. The corridor was teeming with testosterone.

'A misunderstanding,' Wielart said firmly to the armed guard. 'You can all relax.'

Two hours later, Francisca Deetman glanced at the shining bronze plaque on the wall and stepped through Wielart's office front door for the first time since her initial visit.

She walked self-assuredly across the black-and-white marble floor towards the desk of his PA, who guarded the door to his office.

Francisca noted with satisfaction that the semi-open-plan design of the office meant that at least four people noticed her. And she had dressed to be remembered, in a very short red leather skirt and a tight white top. She quite obviously wasn't wearing a bra.

'Mr Wielart has asked to see me. Urgently,' Francisca said to the disapproving gatekeeper.

'I'm sorry, but you need to—'

'He'll see me,' Francisca said, walking past her and opening the heavy oak door.

Wielart looked horrified as she walked in.

'What are you doing, coming in the front?' he barked when the door was closed.

'I forgot,' Francisca lied as she sat down in one of the stiff brown leather chairs. 'Anyway, you are the partner of my father. What is wrong with my coming here?'

'I warned you, if you ever mention anything about that, it will be your father, not me, who goes to prison.'

'I haven't,' Francisca said with as much contriteness as she could muster.

'Just don't forget, I saved your family from ruin and humiliation. If you ever fail me, they will pay.'

Wielart looked at the girl sitting in front of him. What a slut she'd become. Hardly recognizable from the innocent girl who had grown up with his daughter. The heavy make-up she wore couldn't disguise the black bags under her eyes. Thank God, Josebe hadn't ended up like her.

'Why do you dress like that, coming in here?' Wielart asked irritably.

'Because van Ossen likes me to,' she replied with contempt. 'Just like he enjoys coming round to my flat. What do you think he does there?' she added with contempt.

Wielart didn't like Francisca's rhetorical question. It reminded him that she wouldn't do whatever she did in her flat with him. And although she was far more useful seducing van Ossen than having sex with him, he would have liked both.

'So, have you heard about any drug deal?'

'Sure.'

'And you didn't tell me before?'

'I didn't know you were into drugs.'

'Don't get cute with me. You're there to tell me everything. So?'

'Tonight. It's tonight. In the docks.'

Wielart was suddenly flustered. He questioned Francisca further, and everything she said seemed to tally with what Max had told him. Nevertheless he was uneasy.

'You do know, don't you, that if any of this information is wrong, or you've betrayed me in any way, your father will pay?'

'I haven't,' Francisca answered truthfully. 'I have my own reasons for wanting you to succeed.'

'And what is that?'

'Van Ossen won't come out of this alive. And then I won't have to be his whore any more.'

Wielart smiled. The conniving little cow. But he was satisfied. She had two reasons to report the truth to him.

Her freedom, however, Wielart mused, would be short-lived. Once Stam had killed van Ossen, and the English agent had killed Stam – which he would have to do if he ever wanted to see his girlfriend alive again – Wielart would be a very powerful man. And he wouldn't want this crazy bint alive to screw things up for him.

31

Orford Ness

Barry Nuttall drove his car right on to the slipway at Orford and parked up. He wasn't dragging the suitcase with the money in it all the way from the car park. Even if the suitcase did have wheels. The way his luck was going, he'd get bloody mugged by some lunatic.

'See you're taking plenty of clothes with you,' Gerry observed.

Gerry had looked after the slipway that serviced Orford Ness for donkey's years. And Barry had always looked after Gerry very generously. Most of the boat owners were either muppets who took their craft out at weekends for a sail on the River Alde, or lunatics who left the estuary and went out fishing in the North Sea. But although Barry purported to go out fishing in his Wally tender, Gerry knew better than to ask. The trouble was, Gerry's cost of living had gone through the roof with the new bird he had.

'Going right out, Gerry. Thought I'd get a few line-caught cod. Won't find any of them inshore. Did you fill her up?'

'To the brim.'

'And the spare tanks?'

'Full. You could go to the Continent and back with that lot.'

Even though Barry knew that Gerry knew, and Gerry knew that Barry knew that he knew, Barry still never said as much in black and white. Careless talk costs lives.

'I'll be back during the night, probably. If the fish bite. Leave the lights on, would you?'

'No problem. Need a hand when you get back?'

'No. Don't worry about it. Key for the gates in the normal place?'

'It will be.'

Barry heaved the case on to the Wally, and unlocked the cabin. He'd slept perfectly comfortably on the tender loads of times. She was 13.6 metres long. Barry had paid three hundred and fifty grand cash for her off the Internet. Delivered. She was the perfect boat for his job. Had a draught of only 0.88 metres, which made her a doddle to manoeuvre through the estuary. And her two 420-horsepower engines did fifty knots. He could pretty well out-run anything.

Barry had checked the tides and made his calculations. If he left himself three hours to cover the 105 nautical miles to Rotterdam, he'd have time to spare. And given the tides and the currents, he'd be back in closer to two and a half hours.

'Got plenty of bait with you?' Gerry asked with a sly smile.

'Enough fucking bait to catch a big fish,' Barry replied, getting close to breaking his own rules.

He stowed the case in the cabin next to the bunk bed and started the engines. Their deep-throated roar sounded like a juggernaut lorry starting up.

Barry left the tender to warm up, parked the car where it wouldn't be particularly noticed, and then reappeared on the slipway burdened down with his grub: eight flasks of coffee, a packet of ProPlus and six boxes of corned-beef sandwiches, made with white bread.

Gerry was still trying to calculate how much money was in

311

the case as he chucked Barry his mooring rope. Of course, Barry had always been good to him. But living wasn't getting any cheaper. And the thought of a big fish had made Gerry think. After all, he could get into trouble if Barry was caught.

By the time Barry was passing Orford Ness lighthouse – which would guide him back in during the early hours – Gerry had made his decision.

Wielart and Max entered the Dice Club by the back entrance.

'Cheaper coming in this way,' Max observed. 'By the way, I'm still owed from last time.'

Wielart ignored him.

Stam was waiting for them in the secure office. He didn't stand up when they entered the room. Max offered him his hand. Stam didn't take it.

'This is Max Ward,' Wielart bumbled. Max could tell Wielart was nervous. Was it as obvious to Stam?

'He's got something for us—'

'Let him tell me,' Stam said, cutting his partner off.

'It's pretty straightforward,' Max said, meeting Stam's visual interrogation with a defiant stare. 'I want you to help me rescue a source of ours. In return, you get van Ossen. He has a major drug deal going down tonight – I've given Wielart details of where and when. One of my colleagues is involved. I want a guarantee that he will be found alive at the scene by the police – once you've departed with the drugs and the money.'

'Why us?'

'Simple, really. The only Dutch policeman who had his head around this has now had it blown off – and I'm never going to get our lot to get their act together in time. That, for better or worse, just leaves you.' Max then shut up and let it sink in.

'What are we talking about here?'

'Well, the buyer will be stepping up to the plate with two

million euros. He'll be coming in from England by boat. Van Ossen and my bent colleague will also arrive by boat with a work of art that's been nicked from the British Embassy as collateral.'

Stam nodded. 'And the drugs?'

'They'll most likely be in the warehouse already. And if they're not there now, they'll be there before tonight.'

'How do you know?'

'A mole,' Max said without hesitation, making it sound as if the mole was his – as opposed to Wielart's.

Jorgan Stam weighed up what he was being told. He didn't look too excited.

'So where do we come in?'

'Through the warehouse gates,' Wielart interjected, a little too enthusiastically.

'Oh, really. And you're going to lead the way, are you? Like you normally do?'

Stam's sarcasm and his reference to Wielart never being anywhere near the action unnerved the accountant.

'And how, pray, do we get through the front gates?' Stam continued.

Max hesitated.

'Good question. There's a load of JCBs sitting in a neighbouring warehouse. Big-wheeled loading shovels. Two-hundred-odd horsepower. They'll go through anything. Your men can sit in the buckets and be better protected than in an armoured troop carrier.'

'You've got it all worked out, haven't you?' Stam said snidely. 'Your source. Where's he?'

'It's a she, actually. And I'm not quite sure.' Max took Data Dave's map out of his pocket and spread it on the desk in front of Stam. 'Any thoughts? I think she's in one of those areas.'

'There.' Stam immediately pointed to the rural shaded area.

'The bastard tortured one of my men there a couple of years ago. It's a remote farmyard with some light industrial units.'

'Underground?'

'You've been there?'

Max nodded.

Stam didn't bother to ask how he got out. The fact that he'd volunteered the information was enough.

'Why should I trust you? We don't even know you.'

Max shrugged.

'Your call. But if you don't, you'd be turning your back on one hell of an opportunity to catch them by surprise.'

'How will we know the exact time?'

'We'll have to get in position and wait. Someone will need to keep watch for the boats arriving.'

Stam was quiet for a moment. Weighing up the options. Then he nodded.

'You'll be with me. If anything goes wrong, you'll be the first to get it. From me.'

Max had been expecting that 'comfort' demand.

'I need to go and rescue the girl. If you send a couple of men with me, they can keep an eye on me.'

'Forget it. You're coming with me. We'll send someone else to get her out.'

Max had been wrestling with where he should be when it went off. He didn't trust Stam's men not to fuck up Sophie's rescue. And he owed it to her to get her out. On the other hand, he didn't trust Stam to take Pallesson alive and make sure he was nailed to the warehouse floor – preferably lying next to *The Peasants in Winter* – when the police rocked up.

He tried to put Sophie out of his mind. The thought of her hanging from the cellar ceiling was messing with his judgement. What had they done to her since then? He felt sick thinking about it. He wanted to be the one that dealt with her captors. But he knew he couldn't be. His duty was to nail Pallesson.

'We need to get her out now. They might have killed her by this evening.'

'What, and risk warning them we're on their case? Forget it.'

Max couldn't argue with that.

'If you send your best man, I'll live with that,' Max agreed, knowing he was in no position to bargain.

'I'll send someone good. What plans do you have for this evening, Mr Wielart? Going to the theatre with your wife?'

Wielart stuttered and scratched his face. This moment was pivotal to his whole plan. But the cards had to fall in his favour without him touching them.

'Since this is your magnificent master plan, why don't you join in for a change? Instead of skulking in the background, counting your money.'

Result. Wielart had been praying that Stam's suspicion would demand as much.

'Why not?' Wielart concurred. 'Suits me.' The only way he could be certain that his partner caught a bullet was to be on site and fire it himself if need be.

After the meeting had broken up, Max detached himself from the others and checked his text messages to see if Keate had responded. But it wasn't a text from Keate that stunned him. The message that he was now looking at was either a trap or a text from the dead. Max took a gamble and punted on the outsider – a text from the dead.

He replied, detailing the rendezvous in full. Timings and location. He also sent Pallesson's address, as requested.

32

Amsterdam

Barry Nuttall had a dream run across the North Sea. He'd never known it so calm – like a millpond. And it gave him blessed relief from Jayne bending his ear on the phone.

Just off the Essex coast, he'd passed through a massive wind farm. The turbines had been motionless – like an army of paralysed giants. 'What a fucking waste of money,' Barry said to himself as he steered between them for the devilment of it. He was prepared to lay odds that some pissed Asian captain would flatten one of them with a tanker before the year was out.

Two and half hours, and three flasks of coffee later, he was approaching the mouth of the Nieuwe Maas, the main channel into Rotterdam port.

Barry's Wally tender, with its coating of matt-black paint, was the maritime equivalent of a stealth bomber. He throttled back and glided to a halt. The only illumination he had to go by was the ambient light from the shore. And he didn't want too much of that.

If Barry was spotted, he only had one option. To make a

run for it. He'd be able to out-run any vessel and, once out at sea, they'd never find him in the dark.

It was time to make Pallesson work for his cut.

Sophie had lost track of time in the permanent semi-darkness. The cellar was damp, silent and cold. She felt weak and exhausted, and drifted in and out of sleep. Her guard had connected the wires to the explosive belt while she'd been asleep and warned her that she would explode if she moved.

Half of her was relieved that he'd done it. At least he wouldn't come near her now. She thought about pulling one of the wires out the next time he brought her some food – and taking him with her. But she felt no animosity towards him. When the Russian thug who'd caused her father to be killed came back, she would end it. And him. If Pallesson was with him, so much the better.

In the meantime, she painted pictures in her head. And wondered if Max was trying to save her.

Wevers van Ossen knew he was distracted. And he knew it was time to quit. This would be his last deal. In fact, he hadn't been himself since he'd started his affair with Francisca. He could think about nothing else but her. Which was dangerous in his line of business.

He'd take her to South America to start with – maybe Buenos Aires? It would be hard to leave Anneka behind, but she'd have to stay with her mother. All that mattered now was what Francisca wanted, and he couldn't expect her to put up with Anneka.

Van Ossen hated the tugboat that they were using that night. But his own boat was not up to the journey from Amsterdam round the Hook of Holland to Rotterdam. It was suited to the shallow canals of Amsterdam, not the open sea. Besides, his elegant little craft would have stood out like a saw thumb in the Rotterdam dock.

The tug stank of burnt oil and van Ossen could barely bring himself to sit down on any of the filthy benches. Still, it would serve its purpose. They'd transfer the money to his own boat near Amsterdam and then coast invisibly back into the canals.

'So, what will you do with the painting?' van Ossen asked Pallesson, who was sitting the other side of the narrow table, next to the heavily wrapped work of art.

'Put it back, I suppose,' Pallesson lied. 'Don't want to chance them finding out.'

Van Ossen didn't believe him. But he didn't care either.

Pallesson had been surprised to see Fransen on board. He'd passed on what de Vater had told him: that Fransen was an informant. So why was he there?

Fransen had no idea why he was there either. Van Ossen had told him and Piek that there was a big deal going down the next day near the airport. So what were they doing, freezing their bollocks off in the Rotterdam docks? Then again, he wasn't paid to know.

Pallesson's mind turned to his cut of the deal. His share would come from Nuttall once the drugs got sold on. Casper Rankin would move the funds out to Montenegro and they'd carry on buying up strategic property. Meanwhile, *The Peasants in Winter* would take her rightful place in his collection. And the next deal with Kroshtov wasn't too far away. Which reminded him: Oleg still hadn't reported in.

Pallesson's phone vibrated. It was the call he'd been expecting from Nuttall.

'You here?' Pallesson asked.

'Oh yes. Get to work.'

'Will do.'

Pallesson turned to van Ossen.

'He's here. You can set your watch by my man. Shall we go?'

'You go. Piek will take you in the dinghy. I'll wait here until you're satisfied.'

Pallesson had expected van Ossen to go ashore with him and watch him test the purity of 'the brown stuff' for Nuttall, but it was no big deal. The warehouse was safe. The right people had been looked after. He picked up the small bag with his testing kit and set off for the quay with Piek.

Jorgan Stam, Wielart, Max and Michael Murphy had parked up half a kilometre from the docks and were making their way on foot across some wasteland to the perimeter fence at the back of the warehouses.

Murphy originated from Ballymakegoge, near Tralee on the west coast of Ireland. He'd managed a cache of weapons there for the IRA that had come in from the USA. And he knew how to use them. But when things had gone quiet on the Republican front, Murphy had moved to Holland and joined Stam's 'outside operations' team. There was no better man to have on your side when the shit hit the fan than Michael Murphy.

The two drivers, who were their advanced guard, had carefully cut the fence and got into the warehouse where the JCBs were awaiting shipment to Africa.

Max said nothing as he advanced with them. He was clearing his head of Sophie and focusing on the job in hand. He could feel the handcuffs, which he might need to pin Pallesson to the scene, rubbing on his belt. Stam had told him to stay near the front. Where he could see him.

Wielart was not a natural athlete. The short march was testing him. And he wasn't straight in his mind how he'd carry out his plan. But whatever happened, he planned to stick close to Stam.

Stam was on edge. He'd always believed that if something seemed too good to be true, then it probably was. He was walking into this operation without anything like his usual amount of reconnaissance.

He knew from the men he'd put on the ground a couple of hours earlier that there'd been traffic into the warehouse after dark. But that didn't mean the whole thing wasn't a set up. This wasn't something that he'd organized. It was someone else's party that he was gatecrashing.

A large white van drove slowly down Van Ostadestraat, checked there were no lights on in the front of Pallesson's house and then turned right at the bottom of the street. A minute later it parked next to Pallesson's blue van in the yard at the rear of his house.

Two athletic-looking men jumped out of the van dressed in blue overalls, and carried a bag of tools to the back door. They cut straight through the locks with a diamond-tipped metal saw.

Three minutes later, one of the men came back out to the van, and was followed into the house by an older, frailer-looking individual.

Once inside, Keate had to make quick decisions. He was taken to a room in the front of the house. Pallesson's five girls were hanging there.

'Well, I never,' he muttered, taking a close look at them. 'How strange to hang them like that.'

Keate was puzzled by the gap above the Vinckboons. But one by one he examined them, and each time he nodded. His assistants were amazed how easily and quickly each painting clipped out of its gilt frame.

'I think we should hang the frames back on the wall, don't you? Shame to leave a mess,' Keate suggested.

Keate was then shown another room at the rear of the house. His task here was altogether more complicated.

There was a Jan van Goyen. Or something that was presented as such according to the plaque on its frame. Keate wasn't so sure. And a Hendrick Avercamp, which Keate recognized from Windsor Castle. Like many others, he fell for the deception.

'We'll take that one,' he said, pointing at the Avercamp. 'The owner may not know it's missing, but I'm sure she'd like it back. As for the van Goyen, I think we'll re-hang that. And while we're at it, let's find a box to take that egg in the front room. It might get rather lonely on its own.'

A couple of minutes later, Keate and his men were on their way.

Pallesson walked through the big metal sliding doors into the warehouse, which was lit by banks of ancient strip lights. Straight in front of him, about a hundred metres away, were the doors that led out to the back of the vast metal structure. They were chained from the inside in case any unwanted visitors happened to drop by.

Down the left-hand side of the building, a couple of hundred wooden crates, bound by tensioned nylon straps, were stacked on top of each other. Three forklift trucks were parked neatly beside them.

On the other side of the warehouse, vast cylindrical bales of paper were stacked on pallets, wrapped in brown cardboard. Now there's an idea, Pallesson thought. If you were hiding something, they'd never open up one of those. All you'd have to do was put a lid about a foot thick on top, glue it down and use the void in the middle to conceal the drugs. He'd suggest that to Kroshtov.

The only movement that Pallesson's distrustful eyes picked

up was van Ossen's two men hovering around a pallet beside the forklift trucks.

The heroin was inside several large tins of pomegranates, which were neatly arrayed on the pallet. Pallesson was already making a quick calculation as he approached the men. They looked uneasy and on edge. Piek nodded consent to them.

Pallesson opened his bag and took out an old spring-loaded weighing device. Then he carefully selected one of the large tins from the centre of the pallet and placed it on top of the others. He removed a lethal looking double-ended hook from another pocket and drove it into the top of the chosen tin. Then he suspended the tin from the scales. It weighed just over 4 kilos. But not by much.

'See, we're paying for the tins,' he said out loud to no one in particular.

Pallesson then took out a small piece of black plastic, two small pots, two pipettes, a magnifying glass, a long metal rod the same dimensions as a drinking straw, some silver foil and two lighters and laid them on top of the tins.

He unscrewed the lid of one of the pots, which contained 0.4 millilitres of water, and carefully pushed the metal straw down through the hole he'd made with the hook. The rod had a solid end, but was hollow through the middle with one side exposed. Pallesson pulled the rod back out, having taken a sample from the centre of the tin.

He placed a small amount of the heroin into the pot, screwed the lid back on and gave it a good shake to dissolve the heroin. He then extracted some of the solution with the pipette and carefully placed one drop of it on to the black plastic.

The other pot contained a solution of 1.0 kilogram sodium carbonate in 5.0 litres of water. Pallesson used the second pipette to suck up some of it, then dripped one drop on to the black plastic. When the drops mixed, an off-white precipitate was instantly formed. He checked the colour of the residue with his magnifying glass and nodded.

Pallesson then tapped the remaining heroin from the metal straw on to the silver foil. He held the flame from one of the lighters under the foil and started to heat the heroin.

As it vaporized, Pallesson took a cautious sniff – just enough to confirm what was burning off – and then he examined the residue. It was about the right amount. Pallesson was now happy that the heroin was 85 per cent pure. He nodded to Piek, who had watched every move like a hawk, fiddling with the semi-automatic machine pistol slung over one shoulder.

Fransen was standing on the stern of the tugboat waiting for something to happen; sooner rather than later as far as he was concerned. He was thinking about the red-light district in Rotterdam, which stretched either side of the main road back to Amsterdam.

Its main function was to serve the workers in the port, so it would be quiet at this time of night. He knew one *privehuizen* that would still be open. It never closed. Fransen was getting himself excited.

Van Ossen climbed the wooden steps towards the stern of the boat, and came up behind Fransen.

'There's something out there,' van Ossen said to him, pointing into the darkness. Fransen tried to focus his eyes as he strained to see what van Ossen was pointing at. As he did so, van Ossen took his pistol, with an Omega silencer attached to its barrel, out of the deep inside pocket of his cashmere overcoat, and shot him in the back of the head. The momentum of the bullet threw Fransen off the back of the boat. Van Ossen fired two more shots into his back before he hit the water.

Van Ossen hadn't actually seen anything in the dark behind

323

his boat, but that wasn't to say there was nothing there to see. Even with night-vision glasses, however, it was unlikely that he'd have spotted the crouched rower in a sleek skull lurking in the shadows.

Tryon was insulated against the cold in his black wetsuit. Under the cover of darkness he'd silently rowed his skull into the dockyard that Max had detailed in his text and holed up behind the hull of a container ship. He could see everyone coming and going, but they couldn't see him.

He'd watched through his infrared binoculars as the lookout on the stern of the boat had the back of his head blown off. And seen that van Ossen was the perpetrator.

As silently and swiftly as a mayfly, Tryon skimmed across the water to the tugboat, and attached his device to its hull. Max had been wrong about the type of boat that van Ossen was using. The tug was much bigger than Tryon had anticipated, but that didn't matter. The magnets holding the explosives were powerful enough to cling to the metal even in the roughest of seas. He'd just wait until they were well out to sea before he detonated it.

Barry Nuttall was turning the sums over in his mind as he drifted off the coast. He'd agreed to buy a hundred kilos of heroin at twenty grand sterling a kilo, in used two-hundred-euro notes, fifty-pound notes and hundred-dollar bills.

By the time it had been passed down the chain, it would have a street value of twenty million quid. Out of that, he'd be trousering a couple of million.

Barry's phone lit up. He answered it and said nothing.

'How's the weather?' Pallesson said.

'How's the weather' was the code that Barry needed to hear. If Pallesson had said anything else, he was out of there.

'Good. See you in a minute,' Barry replied. There was no point talking on the phone for longer than necessary.

He started the Wally up and steered to the right of the shipping channel.

The location couldn't have suited him any better. Nipping into the first dock on the right at the mouth of Rotterdam was a doddle compared to trying to get into Amsterdam.

Once he left the navigation channel and turned right into the first dock, Barry knew he was vulnerable and would remain so until he headed out to open water again, even though he'd been assured that the security guards in that part of the port had been looked after.

He cruised silently past the vast oil terminal on his right, towards the lights on the quay. A subtle blue light was flashing straight in front of him. All he had to do was pull alongside it and tie up.

Everything was nice and quiet. The dock appeared to be deserted. Barry was cool. He was looking forward to the full English he'd have when he got back to the café in Orford.

Stam and his raiding party found the hole in the fence and crawled through it. It was only a couple of hundred metres from there to the warehouse, where they were met by their advance party. Their job had been to make sure they'd be able to get the JCBs started without the keys. Thanks to van Ossen bribing the harbour security team, they hadn't even had to tie up the watchmen – every last one of them had dutifully knocked off early and gone to the red-light district to spend some of their 'earnings'.

They had the cabs of two JCB 456 wheeled loading shovels open. Once they started up the 216-horsepower engines, they would have to move fast. During the day, when Stam's men had run the engines for a while, they'd just sounded like an ordinary port noise. But at night the roar of the engines would set off alarm bells in the warehouse next door.

Stam checked his watch.

'We've got five minutes,' he said as he glanced at Max and Wielart, his eyes searching for deceit.

'What about the raid on the cellar? I want to hear you give the order. Or I'm going nowhere.'

Stam nodded, his face giving away nothing. But he had done as he'd promised. Two good men and a driver were lying in wait a mile down the road from van Ossen's hideout.

Stam dialled his men.

'Get her out of there,' was all he said into his phone. 'Go.'

Max checked his own watch.

'I hope they're as good as you say they are,' he said. But he knew there was nothing he could do about it. He'd rolled the dice. All he could do now was nail Pallesson.

33

Piek and Pallesson walked out of the warehouse and on to the
quay. Van Ossen's tugboat was the first to dock. His skipper
expertly nudged the fenders up against a metal ladder, which
was set into the concrete face of the quay wall. But Piek was
surprised that it was van Ossen and not Fransen who tossed
him the rope.

'Where's Fransen?' he asked as he got to the top of the ladder.

'He's gone for a swim,' said van Ossen. 'Don't worry about
it now.'

Piek looked very perplexed.

Almost instantaneously, Barry Nuttall appeared out of the
darkness. He slipped his engine into neutral and tied four
fenders to the starboard side of his tender. Then he clicked her
back into gear and gently came alongside the quay wall yards
from where the blue light was flickering.

Barry found another metal ladder to pull alongside, and
threw a rope up to Pallesson.

'Everyone present and correct?' Barry asked Pallesson
cheerily.

'Yup. Good trip?'

'Lovely. Might stop and do a bit of fishing on the way home. Like a millpond out there. Weather forecast good, too.'

Pallesson couldn't tell if he was joking or not. He wouldn't have put it past Nuttall.

'Mr Nuttall, I presume?' van Ossen asked as he brushed off his cashmere overcoat.

'None other, Mr van Ossen? All well?'

'Of course.'

'Anyone about?'

'Taken care of.'

'Lovely. Well, shall we get started? Can't be hanging about all night, can we?'

As Barry Nuttall climbed back down into his boat to get the money, van Ossen's skipper checked his knots and then climbed up the ladder to stand watch on the quay.

Barry passed the case to Pallesson and quickly followed it up.

'We might as well put the money straight into my boat. No point in carrying it into the warehouse and then back out again,' van Ossen observed.

'Yeah, right. How about we put the brown stuff in my boat first, and then I give you the money. Call me old-fashioned, mate, but I like to do these things by the book. Let's go.'

'While we're at it, the painting may as well come with us. Be a terrible shame if you forgot to hand it back,' Pallesson said to van Ossen.

Van Ossen was reluctant; but he knew the painting had only been a guarantee that they were good for the money. Now that the money was here, he had no reason to object.

'Fair enough. I thought you might have given it to me as a gesture of good will,' he said grudgingly.

'I think two million euros is sufficient for one day,' Pallesson replied.

Barry pulled the handle of the case out, and then he set off wheeling it towards the warehouse door. He looked, Pallesson thought, like a tourist walking into an airport.

'I am assuming that you've got the fucking gear here, or am I missing something?' Barry said over his shoulder. He didn't like van Ossen's attitude.

'Everything's fine,' Pallesson assured him.

'As you wish, Mr Nuttall. It's all here. Just trying to save you the bother,' van Ossen added, setting off after him.

Sophie's mouth felt like sandpaper. She had barely eaten or drunk anything for two days. She probably couldn't have talked if she'd wanted to, she was now so dehydrated. And she'd become delirious.

Sometimes she heard talking outside the cellar door. She had no idea how many people were out there. She'd only seen one of them; it was always the same nervous face observing her from the doorway. Apart from that, there was silence. And still no sign of Max. She'd given up hope of him coming.

Then suddenly all hell was let loose outside her cellar.

Jorgan Stam's snatch squad had been given very simple instructions. Kill whoever gets in your way as quickly as possible, grab the girl and no one else – then get out of there.

The driver had taken out the lookout with a sniper's rifle. Stam's ex-Chechnyan fighter then burst in and took out another guard, blasting him with his machine gun. He moved quickly to the only closed door he could see and hit it full on with the heel of his boot. It was old and rusty and flew open readily.

His flashlight picked up the girl lying in a corner of the cellar. She looked terrified. He flashed the light around the cellar to see if anyone else was in there.

Delirious and blinded by the light, Sophie thought she was

being attacked. She panicked. And pulled one of the wires out of the explosive belt.

Barry sized up the stack of brown as he walked towards the two men minding it. Like Pallesson, it didn't take him long to figure out how many cans were on the pallet. He picked up one of the catering-size tins and held it. It felt about right.

'Just over four kilos each. I've weighed a few of them,' Pallesson lied.

There were twenty-four tins on the pallet. Even Nuttall could do the maths.

'Tests all right?' Barry asked, even though he'd already had the answer.

'Spot on. Better than all right.'

If Barry and Pallesson hadn't been so preoccupied, they would have registered the noise of engines outside.

Seconds later the JCBs exploded through the metal doors at the back of the warehouse. Van Ossen reacted first, diving behind one of the giant rolls of paper before Stam and his assault team could take in the lie of the land.

Stam and Max were crouched in the bottom of the bucket of the first JCB into the warehouse. The bucket had clinically cut through the doors; the weight of the digger smashed through what had been left.

In the bucket of the second digger, Wielart was being shadowed by Murphy. The Irishman had been told to kill anyone and everyone, if need be, except Stam.

The first person Stam saw when he raised his pump-action shotgun above the protection of the metal bucket was Barry Nuttall, momentarily frozen to the spot. Stam loosed off two rounds at him. The shot ripped into Nuttall's chest, blowing him backwards off his feet.

The two guards returned fire, but their pistol shots

ricocheted off the digger bucket. And they were totally exposed in front of the pallet of heroin.

Max used the cover of Stam's fire to break cover and stick his head above the bucket. The first people he saw were the two guards crouching. He ripped off four shots at them in quick succession. One got it in the neck. It severed the left carotid artery, spraying blood all over the heroin. The other took a bullet in his stomach that disabled him, but didn't kill him outright.

Then a hail of bullets slammed into the JCB. Max hit the deck as they pinged off the bucket. Piek had moved quickly behind one of the forklift trucks and opened fire with a semi-automatic.

His most obvious targets were the windows of the cabs. The glass, which still had protective plastic stuck over the wind-screens, exploded into clouds of shattered glass. The diggers ploughed into each other and came to a standstill.

As soon as Piek emptied and had to reload, Stam and Murphy bounced up again to regain the initiative and attack. They couldn't stay in the buckets or they'd become sitting targets.

Murphy located Piek, who was only partly hidden by the forklift, took aim and fired off six shots in his direction. One of them hit Piek. He went down with an agonized scream.

From his hiding place among the rolls of paper, Van Ossen had a clear view of the diggers. He rested the silencer of his pistol on the paper and took aim. The only shot he fired passed straight through Stam's heart and into his spine.

Max had been about to pop up and open fire when Stam toppled back into the bucket, blood pumping out of his chest.

'Fuck,' Max swore. They were meant to have the tactical advantage. That hadn't panned out too well. He now had no idea how many men they were up against. Worse, they were pinned down. Barely able to hear himself think above the noise of the JCBs, Max felt about as safe as a duck at a funfair shooting gallery.

The digger with Murphy and Wielart in its bucket was meant to have swerved off at an angle, so that Murphy's fire would come from a flank. But after the drivers had been taken out, the JCBs had rammed into each other. Which meant one gunman could cover them both. Max's move would have to be quick and perfectly timed. Which was easier said than done when it came to clambering out of a digger's bucket.

Pallesson had yet to fire a shot from his lightweight pistol. He'd somehow survived the initial blasting that had caught Barry, and made it to the doors leading out to the quay.

Once he'd taken cover, he'd regained his composure pretty quickly. He wasn't paid to fight and he had no intention of doing so. He'd hover at the back, and see how it panned out. If whoever had come crashing into the warehouse got the upper hand, he'd make himself scarce. If, on the other hand, van Ossen's men fought them off, he'd claim either the money or the drugs. One or other was rightfully his. He was, after all, Nuttall's partner. And Nuttall was lying in a pool of blood.

Van Ossen looked across the warehouse. One of the drivers had collapsed on to the throttle of his digger, which was now at full revs, drowning out the sound of anything else. He could see Piek writhing around on the floor. Of the two guards, one looked to be stone dead; and the other might just as well have been for all the use he was. Where Pallesson might have got to, he had no idea. And he didn't have a clue how many men the others had. But it was too many.

When Wevers van Ossen was a younger man, he would have fought to the death for two million euros in cash and a hundred kilos of heroin. He hadn't become the hardest hood in Amsterdam by scarpering like a rat when the going got tough.

But he was no longer a young man. These lunatics who had just blasted their way into the warehouse would keep spraying bullets around until none came back. Van Ossen decided it was time to leave.

Having calculated that he could get to the back door without exposing himself to fire from the JCBs, van Ossen slipped from his hiding place. As he ran, he looked around for Pallesson but there was no sign of him. Not that he gave a shit. He'd go without him.

When he got to the doors he took one last glance around and then set off towards his boat, which was fifty metres away by the quay. There was no sign of his skipper. He'd be at the wheel, ready to go, he assumed.

For the second time that night, van Ossen hadn't seen someone, but they were watching him. Pallesson had observed van Ossen's retreat and was now following him towards the quay. The noise from the warehouse drowned the sound of his footsteps. He knew he had to kill van Ossen – because if he didn't, van Ossen would surely kill him for this fuck-up.

Max steeled himself to make his move. Whatever the risks of being taken out, he was determined to nail Pallesson.

'Stam's down, Murph. Are you okay?' Max shouted. His voice was barely audible above the roar of the diggers.

'I'm grand,' Murphy shouted back.

'What about Wielart?'

'Wielart's focking grand, too. I think he's doing the accounts.'

Murphy looked down at Wielart in the bottom of the digger bucket. He'd been cowering there since they'd approached the warehouse doors. Weirdly, Murphy thought he detected some sort of smile across the little shite's face. It must be fear, he assumed.

'We got to go. On the count of five. One, two . . .'

On the count of five, Max and Murphy leapt out of their buckets and dived for cover behind them. The volley of fire they'd been expecting didn't come. But then they heard a shot. The sound seemed to come from the back of the warehouse. Max and Murphy started to weave their way towards the drugs.

Pallesson got to within ten metres of van Ossen, who was half walking, half running towards his boat. The light pouring out of the huge warehouse doors illuminated the concrete quay. He thought about calling out to him. To make him stop and stand still. But then he thought better of it.

Coming to a standstill, Pallesson spread his legs slightly apart and supported his right wrist with his left hand. Then he aimed at the middle of van Ossen's cashmere overcoat and squeezed the trigger.

Van Ossen stumbled forward, and fell face down. The bullet-proof jacket that he was wearing had done its job. He turned and saw Pallesson's bemused face looking at him. Van Ossen raised his pistol, with which he never missed. But Pallesson got a second round off before the Dutchman could pull the trigger.

Pallesson had been the top marksman in the Eton Corps. He didn't miss from ten metres either. His second shot hit van Ossen exactly where he aimed: right between the eyes.

Max was frantically working his way through the warehouse. Although the noise of the digger engines had made it impossible to pinpoint where the shot had come from, his gut instinct was that Pallesson and van Ossen were making for the boats.

Murphy didn't take any chances as they advanced past the wounded men. He had no intention of getting shot from behind. He finished off both Piek and the guard who was still alive with a shot into the chest. Nuttall and the other guard didn't need one.

As they got to the warehouse door, they heard another shot. Max could see a body lying halfway down the quay.

He knew he'd be totally exposed if he kept going towards it, but he had no option.

'Cover me, Murph,' he shouted to the Irishman.

When Max got to van Ossen's body, he stooped down to check who it was.

That was when he heard the roar of a boat starting up. It had to be Pallesson.

Tryon watched events on the quay unfolding from the dark shadows of the container ship hull. Things, however, weren't panning out satisfactorily.

He'd hoped Pallesson would be lying in a pool of blood in the warehouse. As a back-up plan, he'd set explosives to blow van Ossen and Pallesson out of the water if they tried to make their escape in the tugboat.

But instead of taking the tug, Pallesson had jumped into Nuttall's Wally tender.

In desperation, Tryon detonated the device. But the concrete wall of the dock absorbed most of the blast as the tugboat exploded.

Though Pallesson was blown off his feet and debris crashed on to the deck of the tender, Tryon could see that he wasn't badly injured. Nuttall's boat kept going, heading out to sea.

34

Wielart sat at his desk and methodically went over the situation. Van Ossen was dead and his team were as good as wiped out. Whatever remnants of his gang might have survived couldn't possibly challenge him.

Jorgan Stam was no longer. And he had left no heir apparent to challenge Wielart for his share of the business. Not that they'd be able to find it, anyway. He'd give Stam's wife enough to look after her and the kid; but no more than was necessary.

The police would be ecstatic. The two most powerful gangland bosses in Amsterdam appeared to have taken each other out fighting over something. They would focus their energies on emphasizing the positives to the press, rather than hunting down whatever it was that they'd died over. Part of which was now sitting comfortably on his office floor.

Wielart allowed himself to relax for a moment as he admired Barry Nuttall's suitcase. Two million pounds in used notes. It would take him some time to wash that amount of cash through the businesses. Probably six months.

The drugs he would be careful to keep at arm's length. By

entrusting them to Michael Murphy, he'd created someone who'd watch his back. Setting up a totally new chain of small businesses – and giving a half-share in them, as he'd already promised, to his new lieutenant, would avoid sharing any of Stam's wealth, while at the same time guaranteeing his own safety going forwards.

There remained only one person who could pose a threat to Wielart. Max Ward knew too much. That particular fly in the ointment would have to be got rid of. But it was nothing that cash couldn't solve. And right now, he had a lot of that.

Wielart was deep in his thoughts when he heard someone try the handle of the door leading into his office from the back passage – which he'd locked. The hair stood up on the back of his neck. Who had tracked him here?

'Who is it?' he shouted, fear etched into his words. He pulled his gun out and checked it was loaded.

'It's me – Francisca.'

Wielart breathed a sigh of relief. Visions of the police, or some rogue element coming after the money ebbed away.

'What do you want? I'm busy.'

'Let me in,' she replied.

Wielart could have told her to go away. But he didn't want a scene. If she started playing up, the light of unwelcome attention might shine in his direction.

'Hang on a minute,' Wielart said, as he dragged the money behind the sofa, away from prying eyes. It was the best he could do. There was nowhere else to hide it.

Wielart could smell Francisca had been drinking – and smoking dope. Her eyes were a bit of a giveaway too. It made him a tad more uncomfortable than he already was.

'What is it?' he asked impatiently.

'That's not very friendly, after the help I gave you. I've come round for a drink.'

'It's not a good time.'

'I've come round for a drink. Are you going to pour me one, or shall I help myself?'

Wielart wanted to throw her out. But he didn't dare. A dissatisfied, off-her-head Francisca crashing around town that night might be very dangerous.

'If you ever say anything, you know—'

'Yes, yes, yes,' Francisca interrupted. 'I'm not going to say anything. That's not why I'm here. Get me a drink.' Francisca took her coat off and carried it over to the sofa. She noticed the case behind it. She wasn't as pissed as Wielart thought.

Wielart poured Francisca a very weak whisky and water. He needed to contain this situation. A sober Francisca thinking straight was easy for him to control. Drunk and angry, she was a much tougher proposition. For the moment, the priority was to placate her. Within the next couple of days, though, she was going to get the same treatment as Max. She was a major liability. He should have squared her off that evening.

By the time Wielart had finished fixing her drink, Francisca had kicked her shoes off and was lying back on the chaise longue. Her face was no longer that of the innocent child with whom he'd been so infatuated. But her body was more voluptuous and provocative than ever. Wielart felt himself get an erection as he handed her the whisky and water. She suddenly seemed to be available.

'Cheers,' Francisca said, smiling at Wielart and raising her glass. 'To the new boss.'

Wielart had also poured himself a drink, but suddenly he actually felt like drinking it. Francisca's demeanour seemed calmer. And friendlier. And, as she had pointed out, he was the new boss.

'Successful evening?' Francisca asked.

'Very,' Wielart replied, with a satisfied smile.

'Is a woman allowed to make a mistake and be forgiven?' Francisca asked, looking at Wielart above her glass as she took a large gulp of her whisky.

'How do you mean?'

'I was young and stupid when you first approached me. I didn't know about sex. But I do now. In fact, I know quite a lot now. Can we try again?'

Wielart thought he was going to burst. His head was swimming.

'After all, you are the king now,' Francisca added. Then she smiled at him.

She was right, Wielart thought. And when you're the king, you get more than just money.

When they'd finished, Francisca shut the door carefully, and then made her way down the camera-less alley, pulling the large suitcase along behind her on its wheels.

As she set off down the main street, baseball cap and scarf hiding her face, she looked just like any other student mooching their way around Amsterdam.

Wielart's emotionally constipated PA would be in for a shock when she walked into his office tomorrow morning. Never, in a million years, would she have suspected that he was into erotic asphyxiation.

Wielart would be lying naked on his chaise longue, cold and stiff. His tie twisted around his neck and attached to a standard lamp, which had been moved to stand directly behind the headrest. Wielart's fingerprints would be found on the lamp stand.

Francisca's fingerprints and DNA would also be found in his office. But there would be a perfectly logical reason for that. She'd been seen entering his office the day before for a meeting.

There would be no CCTV footage of anyone entering the

front door of the building; and it would be correctly assumed that Wielart had used the side door to gain access, where there happened to be no security cameras. There was nothing to investigate. Just a rather embarrassing episode to hush up.

All the junior accountancy clerks, however, would now know why their boss always wore a tie.

It took Pallesson about half an hour to drive Nuttall's Wally tender round the Hook to Amsterdam. All the way there he was coldly assessing his options and plotting his next move.

First, he needed to load 'his girls' into their van and take them on holiday for a while. He glided through the canal network until he was about half a mile from his house. Barry Nuttall's fingerprints would be all over the boat when the police found it. He, however, was wearing gloves.

It took Pallesson ten minutes to get to his front door. He retrieved a spare key from a digital safe that acted as a secure delivery box and opened his front door.

As soon as he stepped into his house, he knew something was wrong. The door to his front room was open. He never left it open. Pallesson stepped into the room and turned the lights on.

Staring at him from the wall was the Jan van Goyen forgery. And four empty frames.

When Max woke up, he had a vicious headache, his ears had a deafening ringing noise in them and the side of his face stung like hell. He was lying on his bed with his clothes on. But within a second his mind was racing.

Before his concussed brain could start to compute, he rolled over. And saw the unmistakable back of Sophie's head. She was fast asleep.

Max got out of bed gingerly and walked into the kitchen.

He put the kettle on and then noticed a package on the kitchen table. Unmistakably the same packaging that he'd given to the tramp to hand over. It was *The Peasants in Winter*. Next to the package was a piece of paper with the name Michael Murphy written on it and a telephone number. He rang it.

'You're alive then. That's good. How's the missus?'

'Asleep – but breathing. My head hurts. What happened?'

'Jesus, you were lucky. The focking boat went up. Knocked you clean off your feet.'

'What about Pallesson?'

'The bollocks got away. Couldn't believe it. How the fock he didn't get blown up, I'll never know.'

'How did Sophie get here?'

'The lads dropped her off. She scared the bloody daylights out of them. Had a bomb strapped to her, and she tried to set it off. Good job it wasn't wired up properly.'

Max could hardly take in what he was hearing.

'And the picture. How did that get here?'

'Little present from me. I figured we were getting the drugs. And I'm not a great art collector.'

'That's some present – thank you. And thank the guys who rescued Sophie, will you. I don't suppose we'll be having a reunion.'

'You never know.'

Max said goodbye. As he made the tea, his phone vibrated. He looked at the message. It simply said: See you at the boathouse – Wednesday – usual time.

341

35

England

'Don't speak to any strangers,' Max told Sophie as he got out of the De Lorean in the normal Chiswick back street that he parked up in.

'Don't be long, Max,' Sophie said, sounding like she meant it. She was still feeling frail.

The pavements had been cleared of snow, but it remained bitterly cold. At the bottom of the alley, Max waited his customary one minute and fifteen seconds and then checked no one was tailing him.

The side door to the boathouse was ajar. Max stepped in. He immediately smelt the unmistakable aroma of Tryon's tobacco. A wave of relief broke over him; even though he hadn't doubted that Tryon would be there.

'You're late, Ward,' Tryon's voice barked.

'Well, at least I'm here. Good of you to show up – unlike last time.'

'Very funny. Glad to see you didn't have your sense of humour blown out of you.'

Max felt as if he had.

'What the hell has been going on?' Max said. He was determined to get some answers.

'It got a bit complicated just before our last meeting here,' Tryon said, with the same amount of emotion that he would have used to read out a shopping list. 'I was looking out for you on the security camera – that's what it's for – and I saw an unwelcome visitor creeping along the towpath towards the side door. With a gun, which residents around here tend not to carry when they're walking their dogs.'

'You don't say.'

'I caught him on the back of his head with a broken oar as he came through the door. One blow did it. Russian, working as an energy analyst, according to his ID. Very unimaginative, the Russians these days, with their spies.'

'Working for Pallesson?'

'Well, doing a job for him. Pallesson had texted him. Instructing him to kill me. Nice. So I texted Pallesson back on the Russian's phone saying "job done".'

'What did you do with him?'

'Dragged him down the slipway and pushed him into the river. He floated off quite happily.'

'As did you. Why disappear on me? What did that achieve?'

'Pallesson thought I was dead. It needed to stay that way. If you'd known differently, you could have blown my cover if he'd tortured you.'

'I would never—'

'It was best that you didn't know I was alive.'

'So why did you text me before the deal?'

'I thought you'd find de Vater. But once you'd lost him, you needed my help. And in order to provide help I needed to know where and when the deal was going down.'

Max thought about this explanation.

343

'Jacques and Sophie – was it best for them, too? Why didn't you move them to a safe house?'

'I wish I could have. But Pallesson had to think that he was containing the damage – otherwise he'd have called the whole deal off.'

'So it was just bad luck for Jacques and Sophie?'

'Exactly. That's how our business works, Max.'

'But not for Keate?'

'Keate serves a different purpose. He looks after things for me. There was no downside to moving him away from Eton – out of harm's way. That didn't indicate anything to Pallesson. And a very nice job he made of cleaning out Pallesson's house.'

'Good. So where do we go from here?'

'We find Pallesson. We might have finished him in the British Intelligence system, but we haven't got him.'

'What have we got?'

'Well, we know who his business pals are. And we'll follow the money. I don't suppose he'll be far away from whatever he's squirrelled away. Losing his art collection will have been a bit of a blow though. Maybe we can even use the wife of one of his business pals to track him down . . .'

'Very funny. That, I think, is a cold trail. And, yes, maybe you were right. Any news on her?'

'Mr and Mrs Rankin were last seen boarding a private jet at Northolt. Destination Montenegro.'

Max swung the De Lorean under college arch and pulled up by Keate's gate.

'He's a character,' Max reminded Sophie. 'And he's not that used to dealing with women. He might be a bit shy. But don't be put off.'

'As long as he doesn't bite me, I don't mind. Don't forget my picture.'

Max pushed the gate open. He wondered how long it would be before it squeaked again.

He looked nervously up at the big Georgian study window, but his old tutor wasn't standing there. He hoped Keate would approve of Sophie.

Keate may not have heard them arrive, but he was ready for them. Tea was laid out on a card table next to a sofa that swallowed up anyone who sat into it.

Telling Max to make himself useful pouring the tea, Keate ushered Sophie to a slightly worn armchair.

'I hear you've had a bad do, my dear,' he said gently. 'I'm so sorry about your father.'

'Thank you.'

Sophie hadn't talked to Max about her father's death – or her failed detonation of the bomb strapped to her in the cellar. He wanted to give her time before he went there. But she opened up to Keate about her father more than he'd expected. He let the two of them chat away without interruption.

'So what's that then?' Keate said, drawing a line under the subject when he thought she'd told him as much as she wanted to.

'Sophie has brought you a present,' Max said. 'Shall I unwrap it for you?'

'Please do.'

'Max took the original back to the embassy, Mr Keate. But we weren't sure what to do with the copy. We thought you might like it. It's only a copy – and probably not a very good one at that.'

'How marvellous. Splendid!' Keate said. 'It's magnificent. And all the better for being painted by you, my dear.'

Sophie laughed at the flattery as she approached the painting. But she stopped fairly quickly as soon as she looked at it.

'It's truly a masterpiece, isn't it?' Max remarked to his old tutor.

'It most certainly is. And she will hang very nicely with the others.'

'The others?'

Keate realized his slip of the tongue.

'Well, never mind that,' he said, recovering quickly.

But his slip up had gone totally over Sophie's head. Her attention was on Max. He had some explaining to do. There was no extra bird in the tree.